'First-rate'
Publishers Weekly

'Gruesome and unrelenting'
Stephen King

'Koontz has outdone himself.
A terrifying story'
Philadelphia Daily News

DEAN KOONTZ

PHANTOMS

HEADLINE

The right of Dean Koontz to be identified as the Author of
the Work has been asserted by him in accordance with the
Copyright, Designs and Patents Act 1988.

First published in Great Britain in 1983 by
W H Allen & Co PLC

First published in paperback in 1983 by
Star Books

This edition was published in 2017 by
HEADLINE PUBLISHING GROUP

4

Cataloguing in Publication Data is available from the British Library

ISBN 978 1 4722 4818 3

Typeset in 11.5/14 pt Fournier MT by Jouve (UK), Milton Keynes

Printed and bound in Great Britain by CPI Group (UK) Ltd, Croydon, CR0 4YY

HEADLINE PUBLISHING GROUP
An Hachette UK Company
Carmelite House
50 Victoria Embankment
London EC4Y 0DZ

www.headline.co.uk
www.hachette.co.uk

PART ONE
Victims

Fear came upon me, and trembling

—The Book of Job, 4:14

The civilized human spirit . . . cannot get rid of a feeling of the uncanny.

—Dr Faustus, Thomas Mann

1

THE TOWN JAIL

THE SCREAM was distant and brief. A woman's scream.

Deputy Paul Henderson looked up from his copy of *Time*. He cocked his head, listening.

Motes of dust drifted lazily in a bright shaft of sunlight that pierced one of the mullioned windows. The thin, red second hand of the wall clock swept soundlessly around the dial.

The only noise was the creak of Henderson's office chair as he shifted his weight in it.

Through the large front windows, he could see a portion of Snowfield's main street, Skyline Road, which was perfectly still and peaceful in the golden afternoon sunshine. Only the trees moved, leaves aflutter in a soft wind.

After listening intently for several seconds, Henderson was not sure he had actually heard anything.

Imagination, he told himself. Just wishful thinking.

He almost would have preferred that someone *had* screamed. He was restless.

During the off season, from April through September, he was the only full-time sheriff's deputy assigned to the Snowfield substation, and the duty was dull. In the winter, when the town was host to several thousand skiers, there were drunks to be dealt with, fist fights to be broken up, and room burglaries to be investigated at the inns, lodges, and motels where the skiers stayed. But now, in early

3

September, only the Candleglow Inn, one lodge, and two small motels were open, and the natives were quiet, and Henderson — who was just twenty-four years old and concluding his first year as a deputy — was bored.

He sighed, looked down at the magazine that lay on his desk — and heard another scream. As before, it was distant and brief, but this time it sounded like a man's voice. It wasn't merely a shriek of excitement or even a cry of alarm; it was the sound of terror.

Frowning, Henderson got up and headed towards the door, adjusting the holstered revolver on his right hip. He stepped through the swinging gate in the railing that separated the public area from the bull pen, and he was halfway to the door when he heard movement in the office behind him.

That was impossible. He had been alone in the office all day, and there hadn't been any prisoners in the three holding cells since early last week. The rear door was locked, and that was the only other way into the jail.

When he turned, however, he discovered that he wasn't alone any more. And suddenly he wasn't the least bit bored.

2

COMING HOME

DURING THE twilight hour of that Sunday in early September, the mountains were painted in only two colours: green and blue. The trees – pine, fir, spruce – looked as if they had been fashioned from the same felt that covered billiard tables. Cool, blue shadows lay everywhere, growing larger and deeper and darker by the minute.

Behind the wheel of her Pontiac Trans Am, Jennifer Paige smiled, buoyed by the beauty of the mountains and by a sense of homecoming. This was where she belonged.

She turned the Trans Am off the three-lane state road, onto the county-maintained, two-lane blacktop that twisted and climbed, four miles through the pass to Snowfield.

In the passenger seat, her fourteen-year-old sister, Lisa, said, 'I love it up here.'

'So do I.'

'When will we get some snow?'

'Another month, maybe sooner.'

The trees crowded close to the roadway. The Trans Am moved into a tunnel formed by overhanging boughs, and Jenny switched on the headlights.

'I've never seen snow, except in pictures,' Lisa said.

'By next spring, you'll be sick of it.'

'Never. Not me. I've always dreamed about living in snow country, like you.'

Jenny glanced at the girl. Even for sisters, they looked remarkably alike: the same green eyes, the same auburn hair, the same high cheekbones.

'Will you teach me to ski?' Lisa said.

'Well, honey, once the skiers come to town, there'll be the usual broken bones, sprained ankles, wrenched backs, torn ligaments . . . I'll be pretty busy then.'

'Oh,' Lisa said, unable to conceal her disappointment.

'Besides, why learn from me when you can take lessons from a real pro?'

'A pro?' Lisa asked, brightening somewhat.

'Sure. Hank Sanderson will give you lessons if I ask him.'

'Who's he?'

'He owns Pine Knoll Lodge, and he gives skiing lessons, but only to a handful of favoured students.'

'Is he your boyfriend?'

Jenny smiled, remembering what it was like to be fourteen years old. At that age, most girls were obsessively concerned about boys, boys above all else. 'No, Hank isn't my boyfriend. I've known him for two years, ever since I came to Snowfield, but we're just good friends.'

They passed a green sign with white lettering: SNOWFIELD – 3 MILES.

'I'll bet there'll be lots of really neat guys my age.'

'Snowfield's not a very big town,' Jenny cautioned. 'But I suppose you'll find a couple of guys who're neat enough.'

'Oh, but during the ski season, there'll be dozens!'

'Whoa, kid! You won't be dating out-of-towners – at least not for a few years.'

'Why won't I?'

'Because I said so.'

'But why not?'

'Before you date a boy, you should know where he comes from, what he's like, what his family is like.'

'Oh, I'm a terrific judge of character,' Lisa said. 'My first impressions are completely reliable. You don't have to worry about me. I'm not going to hook up with an axe murderer or a mad rapist.'

'I'm sure you won't,' Jenny said, slowing the Trans Am as the road curved sharply, 'because you're only going to date local boys.'

Lisa sighed and shook her head in a theatrical display of frustration. 'In case you haven't noticed, Jenny, I passed through puberty while you've been gone.'

'Oh, that hasn't escaped my attention.'

They rounded the curve. Another straight stretch lay ahead, and Jenny accelerated again.

Lisa said, 'I've even got boobs now.'

'I've noticed that, too,' Jenny said, refusing to be rattled by the girl's blunt approach.

'I'm not a child any more.'

'But you're not an adult, either. You're an adolescent.'

'I'm a young woman.'

'Young? Yes. Woman? Not yet.'

'Jeez.'

'Listen, I'm your legal guardian. I'm responsible for you. Besides, I'm your sister, and I love you. I'm going to do what I think – what I *know* – is best for you.'

Lisa sighed noisily.

'Because I love you,' Jenny stressed.

Scowling, Lisa said, 'You're going to be just as strict as Mom was.'

Jenny nodded. 'Maybe worse.'

'Jeez.'

Jenny glanced at Lisa. The girl was staring out of the passenger-side window. Her face was only partly visible, but she didn't appear to be angry; she wasn't pouting. In fact, her lips seemed to be gently curved in a vague smile.

Whether they realize it or not, Jenny thought, all kids want to have rules laid down for them. Discipline is an expression of concern and love. The trick is not to be too heavy-handed about it.

Looking at the road again, flexing her hands on the steering wheel, Jenny said, 'I'll tell you what I *will* let you do.'

'What?'

'I'll let you tie your own shoes.'

Lisa blinked. 'Huh?'

'And I'll let you go to the bathroom whenever you want.'

Unable to maintain a pose of injured dignity any longer, Lisa giggled. 'Will you let me eat when I'm hungry?'

'Oh, absolutely.' Jenny grinned. 'I'll even let you make your own bed every morning.'

'Positively permissive!' Lisa said.

At that moment the girl seemed even younger than she was. In tennis shoes, jeans, and a Western-style blouse, unable to stifle her giggles, Lisa looked sweet, tender and terribly vulnerable.

'Friends?' Jenny asked.

'Friends.'

Jenny was surprised and pleased by the ease with which she and Lisa had been relating to each other during the long drive north from Newport Beach. After all, in spite of their blood tie, they were virtually strangers. At thirty-one, Jenny was seventeen years older than Lisa. She had left home before Lisa's second birthday, six months before their father had died. Throughout her years in medical school and during her internship at Columbia Presbyterian Hospital in New York, Jenny had been too overworked and too far from home to see either her mother or Lisa with any regularity. Then, after completing her residency, she returned to California to open an office in Snowfield. For the past two years, she had worked extremely hard to establish a viable medical practice that served Snowfield and a few other small towns in the mountains. Recently, her mother had died, and only then had Jenny begun to miss not having had a closer relationship with Lisa. Perhaps they could begin to make up for all the lost years – now that there were only the two of them left.

The county lane rose steadily, and the twilight temporarily grew brighter as the Trans Am ascended out of the shadowed mountain valley.

'My ears feel like they're stuffed full of cotton,' Lisa said, yawning to equalize the pressure.

They rounded a sharp bend, and Jenny slowed the car. Ahead lay a long, up-sloping straight stretch, and the county lane became Skyline Road, the main street of Snowfield.

Lisa peered intently through the streaked windshield, studying the town with obvious delight. 'It's not at all what I thought it would be!'

'What did you expect?'

'Oh, you know, lots of ugly little motels with neon signs, too many gas stations, that sort of thing. But this place is really, really neat!'

'We have strict building codes,' Jenny said. 'Neon isn't acceptable. Plastic signs aren't allowed. No garish colours, no coffee shops shaped like coffee pots.'

'It's super,' Lisa said, gawking as they drove slowly into town.

Exterior advertising was restricted to rustic wooden signs bearing each store's name and line of business. The architecture was somewhat eclectic – Norwegian, Swiss, Bavarian, Alpine-French, Alpine-Italian – but every building was designed in one mountain-country style or another, making liberal use of stone, slate, bricks, wood, exposed beams and timbers, mullioned windows, stained and leaded glass. The private homes along the upper end of Skyline Road were also graced by flower-filled window boxes, balconies, and front porches with ornate railings.

'Really pretty,' Lisa said as they drove up the long hill towards the ski lifts at the high end of the town. 'But is it always this quiet?'

'Oh, no,' Jenny said. 'During the winter, the place really comes alive and . . .'

She left the sentence unfinished as she realized that the town was not merely quiet. It looked *dead*.

On any other mild Sunday afternoon in September, at least a few residents would have been strolling along the cobblestone pavements and sitting on the porches and balconies that overlooked Skyline Road. Winter was coming, and these last days of good weather were to be treasured. But today, as afternoon faded into evening, the pavements, balconies, and porches were deserted, Even in those shops and houses where there were lights burning, there was no sign of life. Jenny's Trans Am was the only moving car on the long street.

She braked for a stop sign at the first intersection. St Moritz Way crossed Skyline Road, extending three blocks east and four blocks west. She looked in both directions, but she could see no one.

The next block of Skyline Road was deserted, too. So was the block after that.

'Odd,' Jenny said.

'There must be a terrific show on TV,' Lisa said.

'I guess there must be.'

They passed the Mountainview Restaurant at the corner of Vail Lane and Skyline. The lights were on inside and most of the interior was visible through the big corner windows, but there was no one to be seen. Mountainview was a popular gathering place for locals both in the winter and during the off season, and it was unusual for the restaurant to be completely deserted at this time of day. There weren't even any waitresses in there.

Lisa already seemed to have lost interest in the uncanny stillness, even though she had noticed it first. She was again gawking at and delighting in the quaint architecture.

But Jenny couldn't believe that everyone was huddled in front of TV sets, as Lisa had suggested. Frowning, perplexed, she looked at every window as she drove farther up the hill. She didn't see a single indication of life.

Snowfield was six blocks long from top to bottom of its sloping main street, and Jenny's house was in the middle of the uppermost block, on the west side of the street, near the foot of the ski lifts. It was a two-storey, stone and timber chalet with three dormer windows along the street side of the attic. The many-angled, slate roof was a mottled grey-blue-black. The house was set back twenty feet from the cobblestone pavement, behind a waist-high evergreen hedge. By one corner of the porch stood a sign that read JENNIFER PAIGE, MD; it also listed her office hours.

Jenny parked the Trans Am in the short driveway.

'What a nifty house!' Lisa said.

It was the first house Jenny had ever owned; she loved it and was proud of it. The mere sight of the house warmed and relaxed her, and for a moment she forgot about the strange quietude that blanketed Snowfield. 'Well, it's somewhat small, especially since half of the downstairs is given over to my office and waiting room. And the bank owns more of it than I do. But it sure does have character, doesn't it?'

'Tons,' Lisa said.

They got out of the car, and Jenny discovered that the setting sun had given rise to a chilly wind. She was wearing a long-sleeved, green sweater with her jeans, but she shivered anyway. Autumn in the Sierras was a succession of mild days and contrastingly crisp nights.

She stretched, uncramping muscles that had knotted up during the long drive, then pushed the door shut. The sound echoed off the mountain above and through the town below. It was the *only* sound in the twilight stillness.

At the rear of the Trans Am, she paused for a moment, staring down Skyline Road, into the centre of Snowfield. Nothing moved.

'I could stay here forever,' Lisa declared, hugging herself as she happily surveyed the town below.

11

Jenny listened. The echo of the slammed car door faded away – and was replaced by no other sound except the soft soughing of the wind.

There are silences and silences. No one of them is like another. There is the silence of grief in the velvet-draped rooms of a plushly carpeted funeral parlour, which is far different from the bleak and terrible silence of grief in a widower's lonely bedroom. To Jenny, it seemed curiously as if there was cause for grieving in Snowfield's silence; however, she didn't know why she felt that way or even why such a peculiar thought had occurred to her in the first place. She thought of the silence of a gentle summer night, too, which isn't actually a silence at all, but a subtle chorus of moth wings tapping on windows, crickets moving in the grass, and porch swings ever-so-faintly sighing and creaking. Snowfield's soundless slumber was embued with some of that quality, too, a hint of fevered activity – voices, movement, struggle – just beyond the reach of the senses. But it was more than that. There is also the silence of a winter night, deep and cold and heartless, but containing an expectation of the bursting, growing noises of spring. *This* silence was filled with expectation, too, and it made Jenny nervous.

She wanted to call out, ask if anyone was here. But she didn't because her neighbours might come out, startled by her cry, all of them safe and sound and bewildered by her apprehension, and then she would look foolish. A doctor who behaved foolishly in public on Sunday was a doctor without patients on Monday.

'. . . stay here forever and ever and ever,' Lisa was saying, still swooning over the beauty of the mountain village.

'It doesn't make you . . . uneasy?' Jenny asked.

'What?'

'The silence.'

'Oh, I love it. It's so peaceful.'

It *was* peaceful. There was no sign of trouble.

So why am I so damned jumpy? Jenny wondered.

She opened the trunk of the car and lifted out one of Lisa's suit-cases, then another.

Lisa took the second suitcase and reached into the trunk for a book bag.

'Don't overload yourself,' Jenny said. 'We've got to make a couple more trips, anyway.'

They crossed the lawn to a stone walkway and followed that to the front porch, where, in response to the amber-purple sunset, shadows were rising and opening petals as if they were night-blooming flowers.

Jenny opened the front door, and stepped into the dark foyer. 'Hilda, we're home!'

There was no answer.

The only light in the house was at the far end of the hall, beyond the open kitchen door.

Jenny put down the suitcase and switched on the hall light. 'Hilda?'

'Who's Hilda?' Lisa asked, dropping her suitcase and the book bag.

'My housekeeper. She knew what time we expected to arrive. I thought she'd be starting dinner about now.'

'Wow, a housekeeper! You mean, a live-in?'

'She has the apartment above the garage,' Jenny said, putting her purse and car keys on the small foyer table that stood beneath a large, brass-framed mirror.

Lisa was impressed. 'Hey, are you rich or something?'

Jenny laughed. 'Hardly, I can't really afford Hilda – but I can't afford to be without her, either.'

Wondering why the kitchen light was on if Hilda wasn't there, Jenny headed down the hall, with Lisa following close behind.

'What with keeping regular office hours and making emergency house calls to three other towns in these mountains, I'd never eat more than cheese sandwiches and doughnuts if it wasn't for Hilda.'

'Is she a good cook?' Lisa asked.

'Marvellous. *Too* good when it comes to desserts.'

The kitchen was a large, high-ceilinged room. Pots, pans, ladles and other utensils hung from a gleaming, stainless-steel utility rack above a central cooking island with four electric burners, a grill, and a work area. The counter tops were ceramic tile, and the cabinets were dark oak. On the far side of the room were double sinks, double ovens, a microwave oven, and the refrigerator.

Jenny turned left as soon as she stepped through the door, and went to the built-in secretariat where Hilda planned menus and composed shopping lists. It was there she would have left a note. But there was no note, and Jenny was turning away from the small desk when she heard Lisa gasp.

The girl had walked around to the far side of the central cooking island. She was standing by the refrigerator, staring down at something on the floor in front of the sinks. Her face was flour-white, and she was trembling.

Filled with sudden dread, Jenny stepped quickly around the island.

Hilda Beck was lying on the floor, on her back, dead. She stared at the ceiling with sightless eyes, and her discoloured tongue thrust stiffly between swollen lips.

Lisa looked up from the dead woman, stared at Jenny, tried to speak, could not make a sound.

Jenny took her sister by the arm and led her around the island to the other side of the kitchen, where she couldn't see the corpse. She hugged Lisa.

The girl hugged back. Tightly. Fiercely.

'Are you okay, honey?'

Lisa said nothing. She shook uncontrollably.

Just six weeks ago, coming home from an afternoon at the movies, Lisa had found her mother lying on the kitchen floor of the house in Newport Beach, dead of a massive cerebral haemorrhage. The girl had been devastated. Never having known her father, who had died when she was only two years old, Lisa had been especially close to her mother. For a while, that loss had left her deeply shaken, bewildered, depressed. Gradually, she had accepted her mother's death, had discovered how to smile and laugh again. During the past few days, she had seemed like her old self. And now this.

Jenny took the girl to the secretariat, urged her to sit down, then squatted in front of her. She pulled a tissue from the box of Kleenex on the desk and blotted Lisa's damp forehead. The girl's flesh was not only as pale as ice; it was ice-cold as well.

'What can I do for you, Sis?'

'I'll b-be okay,' Lisa said shakily.

They held hands. The girl's grip was almost painfully tight.

Eventually, she said, 'I thought . . . When I first saw her there . . . on the floor like that . . . I thought . . . crazy, but I thought . . . that it was Mom.' Tears shimmered in her eyes, but she held them back. 'I kn-know Mom's gone. And this woman here doesn't even look like her. But it was . . . a surprise . . . such a shock . . . and so confusing.'

They continued to hold hands, and slowly Lisa's grip relaxed.

After a while, Jenny said, 'Feeling better?'

'Yeah. A little.'

'Want to lie down?'

'No.' She let go of Jenny's hand in order to pluck a tissue from the box of Kleenex. She wiped at her nose. She looked at the cooking island, beyond which lay the body. 'Is it Hilda?'

'Yes,' Jenny said.

'I'm sorry.'

Jenny had liked Hilda Beck enormously. She felt sick at heart about the woman's death, but right now she was more concerned about Lisa than about anything else. 'Sis, I think it would be better if we got you out of here. How about waiting in my office while I take a closer look at the body. Then I've got to call the sheriffs office and the county coroner.'

15

'I'll wait here with you.'

'It would be better if—'

'No!' Lisa said, suddenly breaking into shivers again. 'I don't want to be alone.'

'All right,' Jenny said soothingly. 'You can sit right here.'

'Oh, Jeez,' Lisa said miserably. 'The way she looked . . . all swollen . . . all black and b-blue. And the expression on her face –' She wiped at her eyes with the back of one hand. 'Why's she all *dark* and puffed up like that?'

'Well, she's obviously been dead for a few days,' Jenny said. 'But listen, you've got to try not to think about things like—'

'If she's been dead for a few days,' Lisa said quaveringly, 'why doesn't it stink in here? Wouldn't it stink?'

Jenny frowned. Of course, it should stink in here if Hilda Beck had been dead long enough for her flesh to grow dark and for her body tissues to bloat as much as they had. It *should* stink. But it didn't.

'Jenny, what *happened* to her?'

'I don't know yet.'

'I'm scared.'

'Don't be scared. There's no reason to be scared.'

'That expression on her face,' Lisa said. 'It's awful.'

'However she died, it must have been quick. She doesn't seem to have been sick or to have struggled. She couldn't have suffered much pain.'

'But . . . it looks like she died in the middle of a scream.'

3

THE DEAD WOMAN

JENNY PAIGE had never seen a corpse like this one. Nothing in medical school or in her own practice of medicine had prepared her for the peculiar condition of Hilda Beck's body. She crouched beside the corpse and examined it with sadness and distaste – but also with considerable curiosity and with steadily increasing bewilderment.

The dead woman's face was swollen; it was now a round, smooth, and somewhat shiny caricature of the countenance she had worn in life. Her body was bloated, too, and in some place it strained against the seams of her grey and yellow housedress. Where flesh was visible – the neck, lower arms, hands, calves, ankles – it had a soft, overripe look. However, this did not appear to be the gaseous bloating that was a natural consequence of decomposition. For one thing, the stomach should have been grossly distended with gas, far more bloated than any other part of the body, but it was only moderately expanded. Besides, there was no odour of decay.

On close inspection, the dark, mottled skin did not appear to be the result of tissue deterioration. Jenny couldn't locate any certain, visible signs of ongoing decomposition: no lesions, no blistering, no weeping pustules. Because they were composed of comparatively soft tissue, a corpse's eyes usually bore evidence of physical degeneration before most other parts of the body. But Hilda Beck's eyes – wide open, staring – were perfect specimens. The whites of her eyes were clear, neither yellowish nor discoloured by burst blood vessels. The irises were clear as well; there were not even milky, post-mortem cataracts to obscure the warm, blue colour.

In life, there had usually been merriment and kindness in Hilda's eyes. She had been sixty-two, a grey-haired woman with a sweet face and a grandmotherly way about her. She spoke with a slight German accent and had a surprisingly lovely singing voice. She had often sung while cleaning the house or cooking, and she had found joy in the most simple things.

Jenny was stricken by a sharp pang of grief as she realized how very much she would miss Hilda. She closed her eyes for a moment, unable to look at the corpse. She collected herself, suppressed her tears. Finally, when she had re-established her professional detachment, she opened her eyes and went on with the examination.

The longer she looked at the body, the more the skin seemed *bruised*. The colouration was indicative of severe bruising: black, blue, and a deep sour yellow, the colours blending in and out of one another. But this was unlike any contusion Jenny had ever seen. As far as she could tell, it was *universal*; not even one square inch of visible skin was free of it. She carefully took hold of one sleeve of the dead woman's housedress and pulled it up the swollen arm as far as it would easily slide. Under the sleeve, the skin was also dark, and Jenny suspected that the entire body was covered with an incredible series of continuous bruises.

She looked again at Mrs Beck's face. Every last centimetre of skin was contusive. Sometimes, a victim of a serious car accident sustained injuries that left him with bruises over *most* of his face, but such a severe condition was always accompanied by more serious trauma, such as a broken nose, split lips, a broken jaw . . . How could Mrs Beck have acquired bruises as grotesque as these without also suffering other, more serious injuries?

'Jenny?' Lisa said. 'Why're you taking so long?'

'I'll only be a minute. You stay there.'

18

So . . . perhaps the contusions that covered Mrs Beck's body were not the result of externally administered blows. Was it possible that the discolouration of the skin was caused, instead, by internal pressure, by the swelling of subcutaneous tissue? That swelling was, after all, vividly present. But surely, in order to have caused such thorough bruising, the swelling would have had to have taken place suddenly, with incredible violence. Which didn't make sense, dammit. Living tissue couldn't swell that fast. Abrupt swelling was symptomatic of certain allergies, of course; one of the worst was severe allergic reaction to penicillin. But Jenny was not aware of anything that could cause critical swelling with such suddenness that hideously ugly, universal bruising resulted.

And even if the swelling wasn't simply classic postmortem bloat – which she was sure it wasn't – and even if it was the cause of the bruising, what in the name of God had caused the swelling in the first place? She had ruled out allergic reaction.

If a poison was responsible, it was an extremely exotic variety. But where would Hilda have come into contact with an exotic poison? She had no enemies. The very idea of murder was absurd. And whereas a child might be expected to put a strange substance into his mouth to see if it tasted good, Hilda wouldn't do anything so foolish. No, not poison.

Disease?

If it was disease, bacterial or viral, it was not like anything that Jenny had been taught to recognize. And what if it proved to be contagious?

'Jenny?' Lisa called.

Disease.

Relieved that she hadn't touched the body directly, wishing that she hadn't even touched the sleeve of the housedress, Jenny lurched to her feet, swayed, and stepped back from the corpse.

A chill rippled through her.

For the first time, she noticed what lay on the cutting board beside the sink. There were four large potatoes, a head of cabbage, a bag of carrots, a long knife, and a vegetable peeler. Hilda had been preparing a meal when she had dropped dead. Just like that. *Bang*. Apparently, she hadn't been ill, hadn't had any warning. Such a sudden death sure as hell wasn't indicative of disease.

What disease resulted in death without first progressing through ever more debilitating stages of illness, discomfort, and physical deterioration? None. None that was known to modern medicine.

'Jenny, can we get out of here?' Lisa asked.

'Ssssshhh! In a minute. Let me think,' Jenny said, leaning against the island, looking down at the dead woman.

In the back of her mind, a vague and frightening thought had been stirring: *plague*. The plague – bubonic and other forms – was not a stranger to parts of California and the Southwest. In recent years, a couple of dozen cases had been reported; however, it was rare that anyone died of the plague these days, for it could be cured by the administration of streptomycin, chloramphenicol, or any of the tetracyclines. Some strains of the plague were characterised by the appearance of petechiae; these were small, purplish, haemorrhagic spots on the skin. In extreme cases, the petechiae became almost black and spread until large areas of the body were afflicted by them; in the Middle Ages, it had been known, simply, as the Black Death. But could petechiae arise in such abundance that the victim's body would turn as completely dark as Hilda's?

Besides, Hilda had died suddenly, while cooking, without first suffering vomiting, fever, incontinence – which ruled out the plague. And which, in fact, ruled out every other known infectious disease, too.

Yet there were no blatant signs of violence. No bleeding gunshot wounds. No stab wounds. No indications that the housekeeper had been beaten or strangled.

Jenny stepped around the body and went to the counter by the sink. She touched the head of cabbage and was startled to find that it was still chilled. It hadn't been here on the cutting board any longer than an hour or so.

She turned away from the counter and looked down at Hilda again, but with even greater dread than before.

The woman had died within the past hour. The body might even still be warm to the touch.

But what had killed her?

Jenny was no closer to an answer now than she had been before she'd examined the body. And although disease didn't seem to be the culprit here, she couldn't rule it out. The possibility of contagion, though remote, was frightening.

Hiding her concern from Lisa, Jenny said, 'Come on, honey. I can use the phone in my office.'

'I'm feeling better now,' Lisa said, but she got up at once, obviously eager to go.

Jenny put an arm around the girl, and they left the kitchen.

An unearthly quiet filled the house. The silence was so deep that the whisper of their footsteps on the hall carpet was thunderous by contrast.

Despite overhead fluorescent lights, Jenny's office wasn't a stark, impersonal room like those that many physicians preferred these days. Instead, it was an old-fashioned, country doctor's office, rather like a Norman Rockwell painting in the *Saturday Evening Post*. Bookshelves were overflowing with books and medical journals. There were six antique wooden filing cabinets that Jenny had bought for a good price at an auction. The walls were hung with diplomas, anatomy charts, and two large water-colour studies of Snowfield. Beside the locked drug cabinet, there was a scale, and beside the scale, on a small table, was a box of inexpensive toys – little plastic cars, tiny soldiers, miniature dolls – and packs of sugarless chewing gum that were dispensed as rewards – or bribes – to children who didn't cry during examinations.

21

A large, scarred, dark pine desk was the centrepiece of the room, and Jenny guided Lisa into the big leather chair behind it.

'I'm sorry,' the girl said.

'Sorry?' Jenny said, sitting on the edge of the desk and pulling the telephone towards her.

'I'm sorry I flaked out on you. When I saw . . . the body . . . I . . . well . . . I got hysterical.'

'You weren't hysterical at all. Just shocked and frightened, which is understandable.'

'But *you* weren't shocked or frightened.'

'Oh, yes,' Jenny said, 'Not just shocked; *stunned*.'

'But you weren't scared, like I was.'

'I was scared, and I still am.' Jenny hesitated, then decided that, after all, she shouldn't hide the truth from the girl. She told her about the disturbing possibility of contagion. 'I don't think it *is* a disease that we're dealing with here, but I could be wrong. And if I'm wrong . . .'

The girl stared at Jenny with wide-eyed amazement. 'You were scared, like me, but you still spent all that time examining the body. Jeez, I couldn't do that. Not me. Not ever.'

'Well, honey, I'm a *doctor*. I'm trained for it.'

'Still . . .'

'You didn't flake out on me,' Jenny assured her.

Lisa nodded, apparently unconvinced.

Jenny lifted the telephone receiver, intending to call the sheriff's Snowfield substation before contacting the coroner over in Santa Mira, the county seat. There was no dial tone, just a soft hissing sound. She jiggled the disconnect buttons on the phone's cradle, but the line remained dead.

There was something sinister about the phone being out of order when a dead woman lay in the kitchen. Perhaps Mrs Beck *had* been murdered. If someone cut the telephone line and crept into the house, and if he sneaked up on Hilda with care and cunning . . .

22

well . . . he could have stabbed her in the back with a long-bladed knife that had sunk deep enough to pierce her heart, killing her instantly. In that case, the wound would have been where Jenny couldn't have seen it – unless she had turned the corpse completely over, onto its stomach. That didn't explain why there wasn't any blood. And it didn't explain the universal bruising, the swelling. Nevertheless, the wound could be in the housekeeper's back, and since she had died within the past hour, it was also conceivable that the killer – if there *was* a killer – might still be here, in the house.

I'm letting my imagination run away with me, Jenny thought.

But she decided it would be wise for her and Lisa to get out of the house right away.

'We'll have to go next door and ask Vince or Angie Santini to make the calls for us,' Jenny said quietly, getting up from the edge of the desk. 'Our phone is out of order.'

Lisa blinked. 'Does that have anything to do with . . . what happened?'

'I don't know,' Jenny said.

Her heart was pounding as she crossed the office towards the half-closed door. She wondered if someone was waiting on the other side.

Following Jenny, Lisa said, 'But the phone being out of order *now* . . . it's kind of strange, isn't it?'

'A little.'

Jenny half-expected to encounter a huge, grinning stranger with a knife. One of those sociopaths who seemed to be in such abundant supply these days. One of those Jack the Ripper imitators whose bloody handiwork kept the TV reporters supplied with grisly film for the six o'clock news.

She looked into the hall before venturing out there, prepared to jump back and slam the door if she saw anyone. It was deserted.

Glancing at Lisa, Jenny saw the girl had quickly grasped the situation.

23

They hurried towards the front of the house, and as they approached the stairs to the second floor, which lay just this side of the hall, Jenny's nerves were wound tighter than ever. The killer – if there is a killer, she reminded herself exasperatedly – might be on the stairs, listening to them as they moved towards the front door. He might lunge down the steps as they passed him, a knife raised high in his hand . . .

But no one waited on the stairs.

Or in the hall. Or on the front porch.

Outside, the twilight was fading rapidly into night. The remaining light was purplish, and shadows – a zombie army of them – were rising out of tens of thousands of places in which they had hidden from the sunlight. In ten minutes, it would be dark.

4

THE HOUSE NEXT DOOR

THE SANTINIS' stone and redwood house was of more modern design than Jenny's place, all rounded corners and gentle angles. It thrust up from the stony soil, conforming to the contours of the slope, set against a backdrop of massive pines – it almost appeared to be a natural formation. Lights were on in a couple of the downstairs rooms.

The front door was ajar. Classical music was playing inside.

Jenny rang the bell and stepped back a few paces, where Lisa was waiting. She believed that the two of them ought to keep some distance between themselves and the Santinis; it was possible they had been contaminated merely by being in the kitchen with Mrs Beck's corpse.

'Couldn't ask for better neighbours,' she told Lisa, wishing the hard, cold lump in her stomach would melt. 'Nice people.'

No one responded to the doorbell.

Jenny stepped forward, pressed the button again, and returned to Lisa's side. 'They own a ski shop and a gift store in town.'

The music swelled, faded, swelled. Beethoven.

'Maybe no one's home,' Lisa said.

'Must be someone here. The music, the lights . . .'

A sudden, sharp whirlwind churned under the porch roof, blades of air chopping up the strains of Beethoven, briefly transforming that sweet music into irritating, discordant sound.

Jenny pushed the door all the way open. A light was on in the study, to the left of the hall. Milky luminescence spilled out of the open study doors, across the oak-floored hall, to the brink of the dark living room.

'Angie? Vince?' Jenny called.

No answer.

Just Beethoven. The wind abated, and the torn music was knitted together again in the windless calm. The Third Symphony, *Eroica*.

'Hello? Anybody home?'

The symphony reached its stirring conclusion, and when the last note faded, no new music began. Apparently, the stereo had shut itself off.

'Hello?'

Nothing. The night behind Jenny was silent, and the house before her was now silent, too.

'You aren't going in there?' Lisa asked anxiously.

Jenny glanced at the girl. 'What's the matter?'

Lisa bit her lip. 'Something's wrong here. You feel it, too, don't you?'

Jenny hesitated. Reluctantly, she said, 'Yes. I feel it, too.'

'It's as if . . . as if we're alone here . . . just you and me . . . and then again . . . *not* alone.'

Jenny *did* have the strangest feeling that they were being watched. She turned and studied the lawn and the shrubs, which had been almost completely swallowed by the darkness. She looked at each of the blank windows that faced onto the porch. There was light in the study, but the other windows were flat, black, and shiny. Someone could be standing just beyond any of those panes of glass, cloaked in shadow, seeing but unseen.

'Let's go, please,' Lisa said. 'Let's get the police or somebody. Let's go *now*. Please.'

Jenny shook her head. 'We're overwrought. Our imagination is

26

getting the best of us. Anyway, I should take a look in there, just in case someone's hurt – Angie, Vince, maybe one of the kids . . .'

'Don't.' Lisa grabbed Jenny's arm, restraining her.

'I'm a doctor. I'm obliged to help.'

'But if you picked up a germ or something from Mrs Beck, you might infect the Santinis. You said so yourself.'

'Yes, but maybe they're already dying of the same thing that killed Hilda. What then? They might need medical attention.'

'I don't think it's a disease,' Lisa said bleakly, echoing Jenny's own thoughts. 'It's something worse.'

'What could be worse?'

'I don't know. But I . . . I *feel* it. Something worse.'

The wind rose up again and rustled the shrubs along the porch.

'Okay,' Jenny said. 'You wait here while I go have a look at—'

'No,' Lisa said quickly. 'If you're going in there, so am I.'

'Honey, you wouldn't be flaking out on me if you—'

'I'm going,' the girl insisted, letting go of Jenny's arm. 'Let's get it over with.'

They went into the house.

Standing in the hall, Jenny looked through the open door on the left.

'Vince?'

Two lamps cast warm golden light into every corner of Vince Santini's study, but the room was deserted.

'Angie? Vince? Is anyone here?'

No sound disturbed the preternatural silence, although the darkness itself seemed somehow alert, watchful – as if it were an immense, crouching animal.

To Jenny's right, the living room was draped with shadows as thick as densely woven black bunting. At the far end, a few splinters of light gleamed at the edges and at the bottom of a set of doors that closed off the dining room, but that meagre glow did nothing to dispel the gloom on this side.

She found a wall switch that turned on a lamp, revealing the unoccupied living room.

'See,' Lisa said, 'no one's home.'

'Let's have a look in the dining room.'

They crossed the living room, which was furnished with comfortable beige sofas and elegant, emerald-green Queen Anne wing chairs. The stereo record player and tape deck were nestled inconspicuously in a corner wall unit. That's where the music had been coming from; the Santinis had gone out and left it playing.

At the end of the room, Jenny opened the double doors, which squeaked slightly.

No one was in the dining room, either, but the chandelier shed light on a curious scene. The table was set for an early Sunday supper: four placemats; four clean dinner plates; four matching salad plates, three of them shiny-clean, the fourth holding a serving of salad; four sets of stainless-steel cutlery; four glasses – two filled with milk, one with water, and one with an amber liquid that might be apple juice. Ice cubes, only partly melted, floated in both the juice and the water. In the centre of the table were serving dishes: a bowl of salad, a platter of ham, a potato casserole, and a large dish of peas and carrots. Except for the salad, from which one serving had been taken, all of the food was untouched. The ham had grown cold. However, the cheesy crust on top of the potatoes was unbroken, and when Jenny put one hand against the casserole, she found that the dish was still quite warm. The food had been put on the table within the past hour, perhaps only thirty minutes ago.

'Looks like they had to go somewhere in an awful hurry,' Lisa said.

Frowning, Jenny said, 'It almost looks as if they were taken away against their will.'

There were a few unsettling details. Like the overturned chair. It was lying on one side, a few feet from the table. The other chairs were upright, but on the floor beside one of them lay a serving

28

spoon and a two-pronged meat fork. A balled-up napkin lay on the floor, too, in a corner of the room, as if it had not merely been dropped but *flung* aside. On the table itself, a salt shaker was overturned.

Small things. Nothing dramatic. Nothing conclusive.

Nevertheless, Jenny worried.

'Taken away against their will?' Lisa asked, astonished.

'Maybe.' Jenny continued to speak softly, as did her sister. She still had the disquieting feeling that someone was lurking nearby, hiding, watching them – or at least listening.

Paranoia, she warned herself.

'I've never heard of anyone kidnapping an entire family,' Lisa said.

'Well . . . maybe I'm wrong. What probably happened was that one of the kids took ill suddenly, and they had to rush to the hospital over in Santa Mira. Something like that.'

Lisa surveyed the room again, cocked her head to listen to the tomblike silence in the house. 'No. I don't think so.'

'Neither do I,' Jenny admitted.

Walking slowly around the table, studying it as if expecting to discover a secret message left behind by the Santinis, her fear giving way to curiosity, Lisa said, 'It sort of reminds you of something I read about once in a book of strange facts. You know – *The Bermuda Triangle* or a book like that. There was this big sailing ship, the *Mary Celeste* . . . this is back in 1870 or around then . . . Anyway, the *Mary Celeste* was found adrift in the middle of the Atlantic, with the table set for dinner, but the entire crew was missing. The ship hadn't been damaged in a storm, and it wasn't leaking or anything like that. There wasn't any reason for the crew to abandon her. Besides, the lifeboats were all still there. The lamps were lit, and the sails were properly rigged, and the food was on the table like I said; everything was exactly as it should have been, except that every last man aboard had vanished. It's one of the great mysteries of the sea.'

'But I'm sure there's no great mystery about *this*,' Jenny said uneasily. 'I'm sure the Santinis haven't vanished forever.'

Halfway around the table, Lisa stopped, raised her eyes, blinked at Jenny. 'If they *were* taken against their will, does that have something to do with your housekeeper's death?'

'Maybe. We just don't know enough to say for sure.'

Speaking even more quietly than before, Lisa said, 'Do you think we ought to have a gun or something?'

'No, no.' She looked at the untouched food congealing in the serving dishes. The spilled salt. The overturned chair. She turned away from the table. 'Come on, honey.'

'Where now?'

'Let's see if the phone works.'

They went through the door that connected the dining room to the kitchen, and Jenny turned on the light.

The phone was on the wall by the sink. Jenny lifted the receiver, listened, tapped the disconnect buttons, but could get no dial tone.

This time, however, the line wasn't actually dead, as it had been at her own house. It was an open line, filled with the soft hiss of electronic static. The number of the fire department and the sheriff's substation were on a sticker on the base of the phone. In spite of having no dial tone, Jenny punched out the seven digits for the sheriff's office, but she couldn't get a connection.

Then, even as Jenny put her fingers on the disconnect buttons to jiggle them again, she began to suspect that someone was on the line, listening to her.

Into the receiver, she said, 'Hello?'

Far away hissing. Like eggs on a griddle.

'Hello?' she repeated.

Just distant static. What they called 'white noise'.

She told herself there was nothing except the ordinary sounds of an open phone line. But what she *thought* she could hear was someone listening intently to her while she listened to him.

Nonsense.

A chill prickled the back of her neck, and, nonsense or not, she quickly put down the receiver.

'The sheriff's office can't be far in a town this small,' Lisa said.

'A couple of blocks.'

'Why don't we walk there?'

Jenny had intended to search the rest of the house, in case the Santinis were lying sick or injured somewhere. Now she wondered if someone *had* been on the telephone line with her, listening on an extension phone in another part of the house. That possibility changed everything. She didn't take her medical vows lightly; actually, she enjoyed the special responsibilities that came with her job, for she was the kind of person who needed to have her judgment, wits, and stamina put to the test on a regular basis; she thrived on challenge. But right now, her first responsibility was to Lisa and to herself. Perhaps the wisest thing to do was to get the deputy, Paul Henderson, return here with him, and *then* search the rest of the house.

Although she wanted to believe it was only her imagination, she still sensed inquisitive eyes; someone watching . . . waiting.

'Let's go,' she said to Lisa. 'Come on.'

Clearly relieved, the girl hurried ahead, leading the way through the dining room and living room to the front door.

Outside, night had fallen. The air was cooler than it had been at dusk, and soon it would get downright cold – forty-five or forty degrees, maybe even a bit colder – a reminder that autumn's tenancy in the Sierras was always brief and that winter was eager to move in and take up residence.

Along Skyline Road, the streetlamps had come on automatically with the night's descent. In several store windows, after-hours lights also had come on, activated by light-sensing diodes that had responded to the darkening world outside.

On the pavement in front of the Santinis' house, Jenny and Lisa stopped, struck by the sight below them.

Shelving down the mountainside, its peaked and gabled roofs thrusting into the night sky, the town was even more beautiful now than it had been at twilight. A few chimneys issued ghostly plumes of wood smoke. Some windows glowed with light from within, but most, like dark mirrors, cast back the beams of the streetlamps. The mild wind made the trees sway gently, in a lullaby rhythm, and the resultant susurration was like the soft sighs and dreamy murmurs of a thousand peacefully slumbering children.

However, it wasn't just the beauty that was arresting. The perfect stillness, the silence — *that* was what made Jenny pause. On their arrival, she had found it strange. Now she found it ominous.

'The sheriff's substation is on the main street,' she told Lisa. 'Just two and a half blocks from here.'

They hurried into the unbeating heart of town.

5

THREE BULLETS

A SINGLE fluorescent lamp shone in the gloom of the town jail, but its flexible neck bent sharply, focusing the light on the top of a desk, revealing little else of the big main room. An open magazine lay on the desk blotter, directly in the bar of hard, white light. Otherwise, the place was dark except for the pale luminescence that filtered through the mullioned windows from the streetlights.

Jenny opened the door and stepped inside, and Lisa followed close behind her.

'Hello? Paul? Are you here?'

She located a wall switch, snapped on the overhead lights – and physically recoiled when she saw what was on the floor in front of her.

Paul Henderson. Dark, bruised flesh. Swollen. Dead.

'Oh, Jesus!' Lisa whimpered, quickly turning away. She stumbled to the open door, leaned against the jamb, and sucked in great shuddering breaths of the cool night air.

With considerable effort, Jenny quelled the primal fear that began to rise within her, and she went to Lisa. Putting a hand on the girl's slender shoulder, she said, 'Are you okay? Are you going to be sick?'

Lisa seemed to be trying hard not to gag. Finally she shook her head. 'No. I w-won't be sick. I'll be all right. L-let's get out of here.'

'In a minute,' Jenny said. 'First I want to take a look at the body.'

'You can't *want* to look at that.'

'You're right. I don't want to, but maybe I can get some idea what we're up against. You can wait here in the doorway.'

The girl sighed with resignation.

Jenny went to the corpse that was sprawled on the floor, knelt beside it.

Paul Henderson was in the same condition as Hilda Beck. Every visible inch of the deputy's flesh was bruised. The body was swollen: a puffy, distorted face; the neck almost as large as the head; fingers that resembled knotted links of sausage; a distended abdomen. Yet Jenny couldn't detect even the vaguest odour of decomposition.

Unseeing eyes bulged from the mottled, storm-coloured face. Those eyes, together with the gaping and twisted mouth, conveyed an unmistakable emotion: *fear*. Like Hilda, Paul Henderson appeared to have died suddenly – and in the powerful, icy grip of terror.

Jenny hadn't been a close friend of the dead man's. She had known him, of course, because everyone knew everyone else in a town as small as Snowfield. He had seemed pleasant enough, a good law officer. She felt wretched about what had happened to him. As she stared at his contorted face, a rope of nausea tied itself into a knot of dull pain in her stomach, and she had to look away.

The deputy's sidearm wasn't in his holster. It was on the floor, near the body. A .45-calibre revolver.

She stared at the gun, considering the implications. Perhaps it had slipped out of the leather holster as the deputy had fallen to the floor. Perhaps. But she doubted it. The most obvious conclusion was that Henderson had drawn the revolver to defend himself against an attacker.

If that were the case, then he hadn't been felled by a poison or a disease.

Jenny glanced behind her. Lisa was still standing at the open door, leaning against the jamb, staring out at Skyline Road.

Getting off her knees, turning away from the corpse, Jenny crouched over the revolver for long seconds, studying it, trying to

34

decide whether or not to touch it. She was not as worried about contagion as she had been immediately after finding Mrs Beck's body. This was looking less and less like a case of some bizarre plague. Besides, if an exotic disease *was* stalking Snowfield, it was frighteningly virulent, and Jenny almost certainly was contaminated by now. She had nothing to lose by picking up the revolver and studying it more closely. What concerned her most was that she might obliterate incriminating fingerprints or other important evidence.

But even if Henderson *had* been murdered, it wasn't likely that his killer had used the victim's own gun, conveniently leaving fingerprints on it. Furthermore, Paul didn't appear to have been shot; on the contrary, if any shooting had been done, he was probably the one who had pulled the trigger.

She picked up the gun and examined it. The cylinder had a six-round capacity, but three of the chambers were empty. The sharp odour of burnt gunpowder told her that the weapon had been fired recently; sometime today; maybe even within the past hour.

Carrying the .45, scanning the blue tile floor, she rose and walked to one end of the reception area, then to the other. Her eye caught a glint of brass, another, then another: three expended cartridges.

None of the shots had been fired downwards, into the floor. The highly polished blue tiles were unmarked.

Jenny pushed through the swinging gate in the wooden railing, moving into the area that TV cops always called the 'bull pen'. She walked down an aisle between facing pairs of desks, filing cabinets, and work tables. In the centre of the room, she stopped and let her gaze travel slowly over the pale green walls and the white acoustictile ceiling, looking for bullet holes. She couldn't find any.

That surprised her. If the gun hadn't been discharged into the floor, and if it hadn't been aimed at the front windows – which it hadn't; no broken glass – then it had to have been fired with the muzzle pointing into the room, waist-high or higher. So where had the slugs gone? She couldn't see any ruined furniture, no splintered wood or torn sheet-metal or shattered plastic, although she knew that a .45-calibre bullet would do considerable damage at the point of impact.

If the expended rounds weren't in this room, there was only one other place they could be: in the man or men at whom Paul Henderson had taken aim.

But if the deputy had wounded an assailant – or two or three assailants – with three shots from a .45 police revolver, three shots so squarely placed in the assailant's body trunk that the bullets had been stopped and had not passed through, then there would have been blood everywhere. But there wasn't a drop.

Baffled, she turned to the desk where the gooseneck fluorescent lamp cast light on an open issue of *Time*. A brass nameplate read SERGEANT PAUL J. HENDERSON. This was where he had been sitting, passing an apparently dull afternoon, when whatever had happened . . . happened.

Already sure of what she would hear, Jenny lifted the receiver from the telephone that stood on Henderson's desk. No dial tone. Just the electronic, insect-wing hiss of an open line.

As before, when she had attempted to use the telephone in the Santinis' kitchen, she had the feeling that she wasn't the only one on the line.

She put the receiver down – too abruptly, too hard.

Her hands were trembling.

Along the back wall of the room, there were two bulletin boards, a photocopier, a locked gun cabinet, a police radio (a home base set), and a teletype link. Jenny didn't know how to operate the teletype. Anyway, it was silent and appeared to be out of order. She couldn't make the radio come to life. Although the power switch was in the on-position, the indicator lamp didn't light. The microphone remained dead. Whoever had done in the deputy had also done in the teletype and the radio.

Heading back to the reception area at the front of the room, Jenny saw that Lisa was no longer standing in the doorway, and for an instant her heart froze. Then she saw the girl hunkered down beside Paul Henderson's body, peering intently at it.

Lisa looked up as Jenny came through the gate in the railing. Indicating the badly swollen corpse, the girl said, 'I didn't realize skin could stretch as much as this without splitting.' Her pose – scientific inquisitiveness, detachment, studied indifference to the horror of the scene – was as transparent as a window. Her darting eyes betrayed her. Pretending she didn't find it stressful, Lisa looked away from the deputy and stood up.

'Honey, why didn't you stay by the door?'

'I was disgusted with myself for being such a coward.'

'Listen, Sis, I told you—'

'I mean, I'm afraid something's going to happen to us, something bad, right here in Snowfield, tonight, any minute maybe, something really awful. But I'm not ashamed of *that* fear because it's only common sense to be afraid after what we've seen. But I was even afraid of the deputy's body, and that was just plain childish.'

When Lisa paused, Jenny said nothing. The girl had more to say, and she needed to get it off her chest.

'He's dead. He can't hurt me. There's no reason to be so scared of him. It's wrong to give in to irrational fears. It's wrong and weak and stupid. A person should face up to fears like that,' Lisa insisted. 'Facing up to them is the only way to get over them. Right? So I decided to face up to *this*.' With a tilt of her head, she indicated the dead man at her feet.

There's such anguish in her eyes, Jenny thought.

It wasn't merely the situation in Snowfield that was weighing heavily on the girl. It was the memory of finding her mother dead of a stroke on a hot, clear afternoon in July. Suddenly, because of all of *this*, all of *that* was coming back to her, coming back hard.

'I'm okay now,' Lisa said. 'I'm still afraid of what might happen to us, but I'm not afraid of *him*.' She glanced down at the corpse to prove her point, then looked up and met Jenny's eyes. 'See? You can count on me now. I won't flake out on you again.'

For the first time, Jenny realized that she was Lisa's role model. With her eyes and face and voice and hands, Lisa revealed, in countless subtle ways, a respect and an admiration for Jenny that was far greater than Jenny had imagined. Without resorting to words, the girl was saying something that deeply moved Jenny: *I love you, but even more than that, I like you; I'm proud of you; I think you're terrific, and if you're patient with me, I'll make you proud and happy to have me for a kid sister.*

The realisation that she occupied such a lofty position in Lisa's personal pantheon was a surprise to Jenny. Because of the difference in their ages and because Jenny had been away from home almost constantly since Lisa was two, she had thought that she was virtually a stranger to the girl. She was both flattered and humbled by this new insight into their relationship.

'I know I can count on you,' she assured the girl. 'I never thought I couldn't.'

Lisa smiled self-consciously.

Jenny hugged her.

For a moment, Lisa clung to her fiercely, and when they pulled apart, she said, 'So . . . did you find any clue to what happened here?'

'Nothing that makes sense.'

'The phone doesn't work, huh?'

'No.'

'So they're out of order all over town.'

'Probably.'

They walked to the door and stepped outside, onto the cobblestone pavement.

Surveying the hushed street, Lisa said, 'Everybody's dead.'

'We can't be sure.'

'Everyone,' the girl insisted softly, bleakly. 'The whole town. All of them. You can *feel* it.'

'The Santinis were missing, not dead,' Jenny reminded her.

A three-quarter moon had risen above the mountains while she and Lisa had been in the sheriff's substation. In those night-clad places where the streetlamps and shop lights did not reach, the silvery light of the moon lined the edges of shadowed forms. But the moonglow revealed nothing. Instead, it fell like a veil, clinging to some objects more than to others, providing only vague hints of their shapes and, like all veils, somehow managing to make all things beneath it more mysterious and obscure than they would have been in total darkness.

'A graveyard,' Lisa said. 'The whole town's a graveyard. Can't we just get in the car and go for help?'

'You know we can't. If a disease has . . .'

'It's not disease.'

'We can't be absolutely sure.'

'I am. I'm sure. Anyway, you said you'd almost ruled it out, too.'

'But as long as there's the slightest chance, however remote, we've got to consider ourselves quarantined.'

Lisa seemed to notice the gun for the first time. 'Did that belong to the deputy?'

'Yes.'

'Is it loaded?'

'He fired it three times, but that leaves three bullets in the cylinder.'

'Fired at what?'

'I wish I knew.'

'Are you keeping it?' Lisa asked, shivering.

Jenny stared at the revolver in her right hand and nodded. 'I guess maybe I should.'

'Yeah. Then again . . . it didn't save *him*, did it?'

6

NOVELTIES AND NOTIONS

THEY PROCEEDED along Skyline Road, moving alternately through shadows, yellowish sodium-glow from the streetlamps, darkness, and phosphoric moonlight. Regularly spaced trees grew from kerbside planters on the left. On the right, they passed a gift shop, a small café, and the Santinis' ski shop. At each establishment, they paused to peer through the windows, searching for signs of life, finding none.

They also passed townhouses that faced directly onto the pavement. Jenny climbed the steps at each house and rang the bell. No one answered, not even at those houses where light shone beyond the windows. She considered trying a few doors and, if they were unlocked, going inside. But she didn't do it because she suspected, just as Lisa did, that the occupants (if they could be found at all) would be in the same grotesque condition as Hilda Beck and Paul Henderson. She needed to locate living people, survivors, witnesses. She couldn't learn anything more from corpses.

'Is there a nuclear power plant around here?' Lisa asked.

'No. Why?'

'A big military base?'

'No.'

'I thought maybe . . . radiation.'

'Radiation doesn't kill this suddenly.'

'A really *strong* blast of radiation?'

'Wouldn't leave victims who look like these.'

'No?'

'There'd be burns, blisters, lesions.'

They came to the Lovely Lady Salon, where Jenny always had her hair cut. The shop was deserted, as it would have been on any ordinary Sunday. Jenny wondered what had happened to Madge and Dani. She hoped to God they'd been out of town all day, visiting their boyfriends over in Mount Larson.

'Poison?' Lisa asked as they turned away from the beauty shop.

'How could the entire town be poisoned simultaneously?'

'Bad food of some kind.'

'Oh, maybe if everyone had been at the town picnic, eating the same tainted potato salad or infected pork or something like that. But they weren't. There's only one town picnic, and that's on the Fourth of July.'

'Poisoned water supply?'

'Not unless everyone just happened to take a drink at precisely the same moment, so that no one had a chance to warn anyone else.'

'Which is just about impossible.'

'Besides, this doesn't look much like any kind of poison-reaction I've ever heard about.'

Liebermann's Bakery. It was a clean, white building with a blue-and-white-striped awning. During the skiing season, tourists lined up halfway down the block, all day long, seven days a week, just to buy the big flaky cinnamon wheels, the sticky buns, chocolate-chip cookies, almond cupcakes and gooey mandarin-chocolate centres, and other goodies that Jakob and Aida Liebermann produced with tremendous pride and delicious artistry. The Leibermanns enjoyed their work so much that they even chose to live near it, in an apartment above the bakery (no light visible up there now), and although there wasn't nearly as much profit in the April-to-October trade as there was the rest of the year, they remained open Monday through Saturday in the off season. People drove over from all the outlying mountain towns – Mount Larson, Shady Roost, and Pineville – to purchase bags and boxes full of the Leibermanns' treats.

Jenny leaned close to the big window, and Lisa put her forehead against the glass. In the rear of the building, back in the part where the ovens were, light poured brightly through an open door, splashing one end of the sales room and indirectly illuminating the rest of the place. Small café tables stood to the left, each with a pair of chairs. The white enamel display cases with glass fronts were empty.

Jenny prayed that Jakob and Aida had escaped the fate that appeared to have befallen the rest of Snowfield. They were two of the gentlest, kindest people she had ever met. People like the Liebermanns made Snowfield a good place to live, a haven from the rude world where violence and unkindness were disconcertingly common.

Turning away from the bakery window, Lisa said, 'How about toxic waste? A chemical spill. Something that would've sent up a cloud of deadly gas.'

'Not here,' Jenny said. 'There aren't any toxic waste dumps in these mountains. No factories. Nothing like that.'

'Sometimes it happens whenever a train derails and a tank car full of chemicals splits open.'

'Nearest railroad tracks are twenty miles away.'

Her brow creasing with thought, Lisa started walking away from the bakery.

'Wait. I want to take a look in here,' Jenny said, stepping to the front door of the shop.

'Why? No one's there.'

'We can't be sure.' She tried the door but couldn't open it. 'The lights are on in the back room, the kitchen. They could be back there, getting things ready for the morning's baking, unaware of what's happened in the rest of the town. This door's locked. Let's go round the back.'

Behind a solid wood gate, a narrow covered serviceway led between Liebermann's Bakery and the Lovely Lady Salon. The gate was held shut by a single sliding bolt, which yielded to Jenny's fumbling fingers. It shuddered open with a squeal and a rasp of unoiled hinges. The tunnel between the buildings was forbiddingly dark; the only light lay at the far end, a dim grey patch in the shape of an arch, where the passageway ended at the alley.

'I don't like this,' Lisa said.

'It's okay, honey. Just follow me and stay close. If you get disoriented, trail one hand along the wall.'

Although Jenny didn't want to contribute to her sister's fear by revealing her own doubts, the unlighted passage made her nervous, too. With each step, it seemed to grow narrower, crowding her.

A quarter of the way into the tunnel, she was stricken by the uncanny feeling that she and Lisa weren't alone. An instant later, she became aware of something moving in the darkest space, under the roof, eight or ten feet overhead. She couldn't say exactly *how* she became aware of it. She couldn't hear anything other than her own and Lisa's echoing footsteps; she couldn't see much of anything, either. She just suddenly sensed a hostile presence, and as she squinted ahead at the coal-black ceiling of the passageway, she was sure the darkness was . . . *changing*.

Shifting. Moving. Moving up there in the rafters.

She told herself she was imagining things, but by the time she was halfway along the tunnel, her animal instincts were screaming at her to get out, to run. Doctors weren't supposed to panic; equanimity was part of the training. She did pick up her pace a bit, but only a little, not much, not in panic; then after a few steps, she picked up the pace a bit more, and a bit *more*, until she was running in spite of herself.

She burst into the alley. It was gloomy there, too, but not as dark as the tunnel had been.

Lisa came out of the passageway in a stumbling run, slipped on a wet patch of asphalt, and nearly fell.

Jenny grabbed her and prevented her from going down.

They backed up, watching the exit from the lightless, covered passage. Jenny raised the revolver that she'd taken from the sheriff's substation.

'Did you feel it?' Lisa asked breathlessly.

'Something up under the roof. Probably just birds or maybe, at worst, several bats.'

Lisa shook her head. 'No, no. N-not under the roof. It was c-crouched up against the w-wall.'

They kept watching the mouth of the tunnel.

'I saw something in the rafters,' Jenny said.

'No,' the girl insisted, shaking her head vigorously.

'What did *you* see then?'

'It was against the wall. On the left. About halfway through the tunnel. I almost stumbled into it.'

'What was it?'

'I . . . I don't know exactly. I couldn't actually see it.'

'Did you hear anything?'

'No,' Lisa said, eyes riveted on the passageway.

'Smell something?'

'No. But . . . the darkness was . . . Well, at one place there, the darkness was . . . different. I could sense something moving . . . or sort of moving . . . shifting . . .'

'That's like what I thought I saw – but up in the rafters.'

They waited. Nothing came out of the passageway.

Gradually, Jenny's heartbeat slowed from a wild gallop to a fast trot. She lowered the gun.

Their breathing grew quiet. The night silence poured back in like heavy oil.

Doubts surfaced. Jenny began to suspect that she and Lisa simply had succumbed to hysteria. She didn't like that explanation one damn bit, for it didn't fit the image she had of herself. But she was sufficiently honest with herself to face the unpleasant fact that, just this one time, she might have panicked.

'We're just jumpy,' she told Lisa. 'If there were anything or

44

anyone dangerous in there, they'd have come out after us by now –
don't you think?'

'Maybe.'

'Hey, you know what it might have been?'

'What?' Lisa asked.

The cold wind stirred up again and soughed softly through the
alleyway.

'It could have been cats,' Jenny said. 'A few cats. They like to
hang out in those covered passages.'

'I don't think it was cats.'

'Could be. A couple of cats up there in the rafters. And one or
two down on the floor, along the wall, where you saw something.'

'It seemed bigger than a cat. It seemed a *lot* bigger than a cat,'
Lisa said nervously.

'Okay, so maybe it wasn't cats. Most likely, it wasn't anything at
all. We're keyed up. Our nerves are wound tight.' She sighed. 'Let's
go see if the rear door of the bakery is open. That's what we came
back here to check out – remember?'

They headed towards the rear of Liebermann's Bakery, but they
glanced repeatedly behind them, at the mouth of the covered passage.

The service door at the bakery was unlocked, and there was light
and warmth beyond it. Jenny and Lisa stepped into a long, narrow
storage room.

The inner door led from the storage room to the huge kitchen,
which smelled pleasantly of cinnamon, flour, black walnuts, and
orange extract. Jenny inhaled deeply. The appetizing fragrances
that wafted through the kitchen were so homely, so natural, so pun-
gently and soothingly reminiscent of normal times and normal
places that she felt some of her tension fading.

The bakery was well-equipped with double sinks, a walk-in
refrigerator, several ovens, several immense white enamel storage
cabinets, a dough-kneading machine, and a large array of other
appliances. The middle of the room was occupied by a long, wide

counter, the primary work area; one end of it had a shiny stainless-steel top, and the other end had a butcher's-block surface. The stainless-steel portion – which was nearest the storeroom door, where Jenny and Lisa had entered – was stacked high with pots, cupcake and cookie trays, baking racks, bun pans, regular cake pans, and pie tins, all clean and bright. The entire kitchen gleamed.

'Nobody's here,' Lisa said.

'Looks that way,' Jenny said, her spirits rising as she walked farther into the room.

If the Santini family had escaped, and if Jakob and Aida had been spared, perhaps most of the town wasn't dead. Perhaps—

Oh, God.

On the other side of the piled cookware, in the middle of the butcher's-block counter, lay a large mound of pie dough. A wooden rolling pin rested on the dough. Two hands gripped the ends of the rolling pin. Two severed, human hands.

Lisa backed up against a metal cabinet with such force that the stuff inside rattled noisily. 'What the *hell* is going on? What the *hell*?'

Drawn by morbid fascination and by an urgent need to understand what was happening here, Jenny moved closer to the counter and stared down at the disembodied hands, regarding them with equal measures of disgust and disbelief – and with fear as sharp as razor blades. The hands were not bruised or swollen; they were pretty much flesh-coloured, though grey-pale. Blood – the first blood she had seen so far – trailed wetly from the raggedly torn wrists and glistened in streaks and drops, midst a fine film of flour dust. The hands were strong; more precisely – they had once been strong. Blunt fingers. Large knuckles. Unquestionably a man's hands, with white hair curled crisply on the backs of them. Jakob Liebermann's hands.

'Jenny!'

Jenny looked up, startled.

Lisa's arm was raised, extended; she was pointing across the kitchen.

Beyond the butcher's-block counter, set in the long wall on the far side of the room, were three ovens. One of them was huge, with a pair of solid, over-and-under, stainless-steel doors. The other two ovens were smaller than the first, though still larger than the conventional models used in most homes; there was one door in each of these two, and each door had a glass portal in the centre. None of the ovens was turned on at the moment, which was fortunate, for if the smaller ones had been in operation, the kitchen would have been filled with a sickening stench.

Each one contained a severed head.

Jesus.

Ghastly, dead faces gazed out into the room, noses pressed to the inside of the oven glass.

Jakob Liebermann. White hair spattered with blood. One eye half shut, the other glaring. Lips pressed together in a grimace of pain.

Aida Liebermann. Both eyes open. Mouth gaping as if her jaws had come unhinged.

For a moment Jenny couldn't believe the heads were real. Too much. Too shocking. She thought of expensive, lifelike Halloween masks peering out of the cellophane windows in costume boxes, and she thought of the grisly novelties sold in joke shops – those wax heads with nylon hair and glass eyes, those gruesome things that young boys sometimes found wildly amusing (and surely that's what *these* were) – and, crazily, she thought of a line from a TV commercial for cake mixes – *Nothin' says lovin' like somethin' from the oven*!

Her heart thudded.

She was feverish, dizzy.

On the butcher's-block counter, the severed hands were still poised on the rolling pin. She half expected them to skitter suddenly across the counter as if they were two crabs.

Where were the Liebermanns' decapitated bodies? Stuffed in the big oven, behind steel doors that had no windows? Lying stiff and frosted in the walk-in refrigerator?

Bitterness rose in her throat, but she choked it back.

The .45 revolver now seemed an ineffectual defence against this incredibly violent, unknown enemy.

Again, Jenny had the feeling of being watched, and the drumbeat of her heart was no longer snare but timpani.

She turned to Lisa. 'Let's get out of here.'

The girl headed for the storeroom door.

'Not that way!' Jenny said sharply.

Lisa turned, blinking, confused.

'Not the alley,' Jenny said. 'And not that dark passage again.'

'God, no,' Lisa agreed.

They hurried across the kitchen and through the other door, into the sales room. Past the empty pastry cases. Past the café tables and chairs.

Jenny had some trouble with the deadbolt lock on the front door. It was stiff. She thought they might have to leave by way of the alley, after all. Then she realized she was trying to turn the thumb-latch the wrong way. Twisted in the proper direction, the bolt slipped back with a *clack,* and Jenny yanked the door open.

They rushed out into cool, night air.

Lisa crossed the pavement to a tall pine tree. She seemed to need to lean against something.

Jenny joined her sister, glancing back apprehensively at the bakery. She wouldn't have been surprised to see two decapitated bodies shambling towards her with demonic intent. But nothing moved back there except the scalloped edge of the blue-and-white-striped awning, which undulated in the inconstant breeze.

The night remained silent.

The moon had risen somewhat higher in the sky since Jenny and Lisa had entered the covered passageway.

After a while the girl said, 'Radiation, disease, poison, toxic gas – boy, we sure were on the wrong track. Only other people, sick people, do that kind of weird stuff. Right? Some weird psycho did all of this.'

48

Jenny shook her head. 'One man can't have done it all. To overwhelm a town of nearly five hundred people, it would take an *army* of psychopathic killers.'

'Then that's what it was,' Lisa said, shivering.

Jenny looked nervously up and down the deserted street. It seemed imprudent, even reckless, to be standing here, in plain sight, but she couldn't think of anywhere else that would be safer.

She said, 'Psychopaths don't join clubs and plan mass murders as if they were Rotarians planning a charity dance. They almost always act alone.'

Flicking her eyes from shadow to shadow as if she expected one of them to have substance and malevolent intentions, Lisa said, 'What about the Charles Manson commune, back in the sixties, those people who killed the movie star – what was her name?'

'Sharon Tate.'

'Yeah. Couldn't this be a group of nuts like that?'

'At most, there were half a dozen people in the core of the Manson family, and that was a *very* rare deviation from the lone wolf pattern. Anyway, half a dozen couldn't do this to Snowfield. It would take fifty, a hundred, maybe more. That many psychopaths just couldn't act together.'

They were both silent for a while. Then Jenny said, 'There's another thing that doesn't figure. Why wasn't there more blood in the kitchen?'

'There was some.'

'Hardly any. Just a few smears on the counter. There should've been blood all over the place.'

Lisa rubbed her hands briskly up and down her arms, trying to generate some heat. Her face was waxen in the yellowish glow of the nearest streetlamp. She seemed years older than fourteen. Terror had matured her.

The girl said, 'No signs of a struggle, either.'

Jenny frowned. 'That's right; there weren't.'

'I noticed it right away,' Lisa said. 'It seemed so odd. They don't seem to've fought back. Nothing thrown. Nothing broken. The rolling pin would've made a pretty good weapon, wouldn't it? But he didn't use it. Nothing was knocked over, either.'

'It's as if they didn't resist at all. As if they . . . willingly put their heads on the chopping block.'

'But why would they do that?'

Why *would* they do that?

Jenny stared up Skyline Road towards her house, which was less than three blocks away, then looked down towards Ye Olde Towne Tavern, Big Nickle Variety Shop, Patterson's Ice Cream Parlour, and Mario's Pizza.

There are silences and silences. No one of them is quite like another. There is the silence of death, found in tombs and deserted graveyards and in the cold-storage room in a city morgue and in hospital rooms on occasion; it is a flawless silence, not merely a hush but a void. As a physician who had treated her share of terminally ill patients, Jenny was familiar with that special, grim silence.

This was it. This was the silence of death.

She hadn't wanted to admit it. That was why she had not yet shouted 'hello' into the funereal streets. She had been afraid no one would answer.

Now she didn't shout because she was afraid someone *would* answer. Someone or something. Someone or something dangerous.

At last she had no choice but to accept the facts. Snowfield was indisputably dead. It wasn't really a town any more; it was a cemetery, an elaborate collection of stone-timber-shingle-brick-gabled-balconied tombs, a graveyard fashioned in the image of a quaint alpine village.

The wind picked up again, whistling under the eaves of the buildings. It sounded like eternity.

7

THE COUNTY SHERIFF

THE COUNTY authorities, headquartered in Santa Mira, were not yet aware of the Snowfield crisis. They had their own problems.

Lieutenant Talbert Whitman entered the interrogation room just as Sheriff Bryce Hammond switched on the tape recorder and started informing the suspect of his constitutional rights. Tal closed the door without making a sound. Not wanting to interrupt just as the questioning was about to get underway, he didn't take a chair at the table, where the other three men were seated. Instead, he went to the big window, the only window, in the oblong room.

The Santa Mira County Sheriff's Department occupied a Spanish-style structure that had been erected in the late 1930s. The doors were all solid and solid-sounding when you closed them, and the walls were thick enough to provide eighteen-inch-deep windowsills like the one which Tal Whitman settled himself.

Beyond the window lay Santa Mira, the county seat, with a population of eighteen thousand. In the mornings, when the sun at last topped the Sierras and burned away the mountain shadows, Tal sometimes found himself looking around in amazement and delight at the gentle, forested foothills on which Santa Mira rose, for it was an exceptionally neat, clean city that had put down its concrete and iron roots with some respect for the natural beauty in which it had grown. Now night was settled in. Thousands of lights sparkled on

51

the rolling hills below the mountains, and it looked as if the stars had fallen here.

For a child of Harlem, black as a sharp-edged winter shadow, born in poverty and ignorance, Tal Whitman had wound up, at the age of thirty, in a most unexpected place. Unexpected but wonderful.

On *this* side of the window, however, the scene was not so special. The interrogation room resembled countless others in police precinct houses and sheriffs' stations all over the country. A cheap linoleum-tile floor. Battered filing cabinets. A round conference table and five chairs. Institutional-green walls. Bare fluorescent bulbs.

At the conference table in the centre of the room, the current occupant of the suspect's chair was a tall, good-looking, twenty-six-year-old real estate agent named Fletcher Kale. He was working himself into an impressive state of righteous indignation.

'Listen, Sheriff,' Kale said, 'can we just cut this crap? You don't have to read me my rights *again*, for Christ's sake. Haven't we been through this a dozen times in the past three days?'

Bob Robine, Kale's attorney, quickly patted his client's arm to make him be quiet. Robine was pudgy, round-faced, with a sweet smile but with the hard eyes of a casino pit boss.

'Fletch,' Robine said, 'Sheriff Hammond knows he's held you on suspicion just about as long as the law allows, and he knows that *I* know it, too. So what he's going to do – he's going to settle this one way or the other within the next hour.'

Kale blinked, nodded, and changed his tactics. He slumped in his chair as if a great weight of grief lay on his shoulders. When he spoke, there was a faint tremor in his voice. 'I'm sorry if I sort of lost my head there for a minute, Sheriff. I shouldn't have snapped at you like that. But it's so hard . . . so very, very hard for me.' His face appeared to cave in, and the tremor in his voice became more pronounced. 'I mean, for God's sake, I've lost my family. My wife . . . my son . . . both gone.'

Bryce Hammond said, 'I'm sorry if you think I've treated you unfairly, Mr Kale. I only try to do what I think is best. Sometimes, I'm right. Maybe I'm wrong this time.'

Apparently deciding that he wasn't in too much trouble, after all, and that he could afford to be magnanimous now, Fletcher Kale dabbed at the tears on his face, sat up straighter in his chair, and said, 'Yeah ... well, uh ... I guess I can see your position, Sheriff.'

Kale was underestimating Bryce Hammond.

Bob Robine knew the sheriff better than his client did. He frowned, glanced at Tal, then stared hard at Bryce.

In Tal Whitman's experience, most people who dealt with the sheriff underestimated him, just as Fletcher Kale had done. It was an easy thing to do. Bryce didn't look impressive. He was thirty-nine, but he seemed a lot younger than that. His thick sandy hair fell across his forehead, giving him a mussed, boyish appearance. He had a pug nose with a spatter of freckles across the bridge of it and across both cheeks. His blue eyes were clear and sharp, but they were hooded with heavy lids that made him seem bored, sleepy, maybe even a little bit dull-witted. His voice was misleading, too. It was soft, melodic, gentle. Furthermore, he spoke slowly at times, and always with measured deliberation, and some people took this careful speech to mean that he had difficulty forming his thoughts. Nothing could have been further from the truth. Bryce Hammond was acutely aware of how others perceived him and, when it was to his advantage, he reinforced their misconceptions with an ingratiating manner, with an almost witless smile, and with a further softening of speech that made him seem like the classic hayseed cop.

Only one thing kept Tal from fully enjoying this confrontation: he knew the Kale investigation had affected Bryce Hammond on a deep, personal level. Bryce was hurting, sick at heart about the pointless deaths of Joanna and Danny Kale, because in a curious way this case echoed events in his own life. Like Fletcher Kale, the sheriff had lost a wife and a son, although the circumstances of his loss were considerably different from Kale's.

A year ago, Ellen Hammond had died instantly in a car crash. Seven-year-old Timmy, sitting on the front seat beside his mother, had suffered serious head injuries and had been in a coma for the past twelve months. The doctors didn't give Timmy much chance of regaining consciousness.

Bryce had nearly been destroyed by the tragedy. Only recently had Tal Whitman begun to feel that his friend was moving away from the abyss of despair.

The Kale case had opened Bryce Hammond's wounds again, but he hadn't allowed grief to dull his senses; it hadn't caused him to overlook anything. Tal Whitman had known the precise moment, last Thursday evening, when Bryce had begun to suspect that Fletcher Kale was guilty of two premeditated murders, for suddenly something cold and implacable had come into Bryce's heavy-lidded eyes.

Now, doodling on a yellow note pad as if only half his mind was on the interrogation, the sheriff said, 'Mr Kale, rather than ask you a lot of questions that you've already answered a dozen times, why don't I summarize what you've told us? If my summary sounds pretty much right to you, then we can get on with these new items I'd like to ask you about.'

'Sure. Let's get it over with and get out of here,' Kale said.

'Okay, then,' Bryce said. 'Mr Kale, according to your testimony, your wife, Joanna, felt she was trapped by marriage and motherhood, that she was too young to have so much responsibility. She felt she had made a terrible mistake and was going to have to pay for it the rest of her life. She wanted some kicks, a way to escape, so she turned to dope. Would you say that's how you've described her state of mind?'

'Yes,' Kale said. 'Exactly.'

54

'Good,' Bryce said. 'So she started smoking pot. Before long, she was stoned almost continuously. For two and a half years, you lived with a pot-head, all the while hoping you could change her. Then a week ago she went berserk, broke a lot of dishes and threw some food around the kitchen, and you had hell's own time calming her down. That was when you discovered she'd recently begun using PCP – what's sometimes called "angel dust" on the street. You were shocked. You knew that some people became maniacally violent while under the influence of PCP, so you made her show you where she kept her stash, and you destroyed it. Then you told her that if she ever used drugs around little Danny again, you'd beat her within an inch of her life.'

Kale cleared his throat. 'But she just laughed at me. She said I wasn't a woman-beater and I shouldn't pretend to be Mr Macho. She said, "Hell, Fletch, if I kicked you in the balls, you'd thank me for livening up your day."'

'And that was when you broke down and cried?' Bryce asked.

Kale said, 'I just . . . well, I realized I didn't have any influence with her.'

From his window seat, Tal Whitman watched Kale's face twist with grief – or with a reasonable facsimile. The bastard was *good*.

'And when she saw you cry,' Bryce said, 'that sort of brought her to her senses.'

'Right,' Kale said. 'I guess it . . affected her . . . a big ox like me bawling like a baby. She cried too, and she promised not to take any more PCP. We talked about the past, about what we had expected from marriage, said a lot of things maybe we should have said before, and we felt closer than we had in a couple of years. At least *I* felt closer. I thought she did, too. She swore she'd start cutting down on the pot.'

Still doodling, Bryce said, 'Then last Thursday you came home early from work and found your little boy, Danny, dead in the

55

master bedroom. You heard something behind you. It was Joanna, holding a meat cleaver, the one she'd used to kill Danny.'

'She was stoned,' Kale said. 'PCP. I could see it right away. That wildness in her eyes, that animal look.'

'She screamed at you, a lot of irrational stuff about snakes that lived inside people's heads, about people being controlled by evil snakes. You circled away from her, and she followed. You didn't try to take the cleaver away from her—'

'I figured I'd be killed. I tried to talk her down.'

'So you kept circling until you reached the nightstand where you kept a .38 automatic.'

'I warned her to drop the cleaver. I *warned* her.'

'Instead, she rushed at you with the cleaver raised. So you shot her. Once. In the chest.'

Kale was leaning forward now, his face in his hands.

The sheriff put down his pen. He folded his hands on his stomach and laced his fingers. 'Now, Mr Kale, I hope you can bear with me a little longer. Just a few more questions, and then we can all get out of here and get on with our lives.'

Kale lowered his hands from his face. It was clear to Tal Whitman that Kale figured 'getting on with our lives' meant he would be released at last. 'I'm all right, Sheriff. Go ahead.'

Bob Robine didn't say a word.

Slouched in his chair, looking loose and boneless, Bryce Hammond said, 'While we've been holding you on suspicion, Mr Kale, we've come up with a few questions we need to have answered, so we can set our minds at rest about this whole terrible thing. Now, some of these things may seem awful trivial to you, hardly worth my time or yours. They *are* little things, I admit that. The reason I'm putting you through more trouble . . . well, it's because I want to get re-elected next year, Mr Kale. If my opponents catch me out on one technicality, on even one tiny little damned thing, they'll huff and puff and blow it into a scandal; they'll say I'm slipping or

56

lazy or something.' Bryce grinned at Kale – actually *grinned* at him. Tal couldn't believe it.

'I understand, Sheriff,' Kale said.

On his window seat, Talbert Whitman tensed and leaned forward.

And Bryce Hammond said, 'First thing is – I was wondering why you shot your wife *and then did a load of laundry* before calling us to report what had happened.'

8

BARRICADES

SEVERED HANDS. Severed heads.

Jenny couldn't get those gruesome images out of her mind as she hurried along the pavement with Lisa.

Two blocks east of Skyline Road, on Vail Lane, the night was as still and as quietly threatening as it was everywhere else in Snowfield. The trees here were bigger than those on the main street; they blocked out most of the moonlight. The streetlamps were more widely spaced, too, and the small pools of amber light were separated by ominous lakes of darkness.

Jenny stepped between two gateposts, onto a brick walk that led to a one-storey English cottage set on a deep lot. Warm light radiated through leaded glass windows with diamond-shaped panes.

Tom and Karen Oxley lived in the deceptively small-looking cottage, which actually had seven rooms and two baths. Tom was the accountant for most of the lodges and motels in town. Karen ran a charming French café during the season. Both were amateur radio operators, and they owned a shortwave set, which was why Jenny had come here.

'If someone sabotaged the radio at the sheriff's office,' Lisa said, 'what makes you think they didn't get this one, too?'

'Maybe they didn't know about it. It's worth taking a look.'

She rang the bell, and when there was no response, she tried the door. It was locked.

They went around to the rear of the property, where brandy-hued light flowed out through the windows. Jenny looked warily at the rear lawn, which was left moonless by tree shadows. Their footsteps echoed hollowly on the wooden floor of the back porch. She tried the kitchen door and found it was locked, too.

At the nearest window, the curtains were drawn aside. Jenny looked in and saw only an ordinary kitchen: green counters, cream-coloured walls, oak cabinets, gleaming appliances, no signs of violence.

Other casement windows faced onto the porch, and one of these, Jenny knew, was a den window. Lights were on, but the curtains were drawn. Jenny rapped on the glass, but no one responded. She tested the window, found that it was latched. Gripping the revolver by the barrel, she smashed a diamond-shaped pane adjacent to the centre post. The sound of shattering glass was jarringly loud. Although this was an emergency, she felt like a thief. She reached through the broken pane, threw open the latch, pulled the halves of the window apart, and went over the sill, into the house. She fumbled through the curtains, then drew them aside, so that Lisa could enter more easily.

Two bodies were in the small den. Tom and Karen Oxley.

Karen was lying on the floor, on her side, legs drawn up towards her belly, shoulders curled forward, arms crossed over her breasts – a foetal position. She was bruised and swollen. Her bulging eyes stared in terror. Her mouth hung open, frozen forever in a scream.

'Their faces are the worst thing,' Lisa said.

'I can't understand why the facial muscles didn't relax upon death. I don't see how they can remain taut like that.'

'What did they *see*?' Lisa wondered.

Tom Oxley was sitting in front of the shortwave radio. He was slumped over the radio, his head turned to one side. He was sheathed in bruises and swollen hideously, just like Karen. His right hand was clenched around a table-model microphone, as if he had perished while refusing to relinquish it. Evidently, however, he had not managed a call for help. If he had gotten a message out of Snowfield, the police would have arrived by now.

The radio was dead.

Jenny had figured as much as soon as she had seen the bodies.

However, neither the condition of the radio nor the condition of the corpses was as interesting as the barricade. The den door was closed and, presumably, locked. Karen and Tom had dragged a heavy cabinet in front of it. They had pushed a pair of easy chairs hard against the cabinet, then wedged a television set against the chairs.

'They were determined to keep something from getting in here,' Lisa said.

'But it got in anyway.'

'How?'

They both looked at the window through which they'd come.

'It was locked from the inside,' Jenny said.

The room had only one other window.

They went to it and pulled back the curtains.

It was also latched securely on the inside.

Jenny stared out at the night, until she felt that something hidden in the darkness was staring back at her, getting a good look at her as she stood unprotected in the lighted window. She quickly drew the curtains.

'A locked room,' Lisa said.

Jenny turned slowly around and studied the den. There was a small outlet from a heating duct, covered with a metal vent plate full of narrow slots, and there was perhaps a half-inch of air space under the barricaded door. But there was no way anyone could have gained access to the room.

She said, 'As far as I can see, only bacteria or toxic gas or some kind of radiation could've gotten in here to kill them.'

'But none of those things killed the Liebermanns.'

60

Jenny nodded. 'Besides, you wouldn't build a barricade to keep out radiation, gas, or germs.'

How many of Snowfield's people had locked themselves in, thinking they had found defensible havens – only to die as suddenly and mysteriously as those who'd had no time to run? And what was it that could enter locked rooms without opening doors or windows? What had passed through this barricade without disturbing it?

The Oxleys' house was as silent as the surface of the moon.

Finally, Lisa said, 'Now what?'

'I guess maybe we have to risk spreading a contagion. We'll drive out of town only as far as the nearest pay phone, call the sheriff in Santa Mira, tell him the situation, and let him decide how to handle it. Then we'll come back here to wait. We won't have any direct contact with anyone, and they can sterilize the telephone booth if they think that's necessary.'

'I hate the idea of coming back here once we've gotten out,' Lisa said anxiously.

'So do I. But we've got to act responsibly. Let's go,' Jenny said, turning towards the open window through which they had entered.

The phone rang.

Startled, Jenny turned towards the strident sound.

The phone was on the same table as the radio.

It rang again.

She snatched up the receiver. 'Hello?'

The caller didn't respond.

'Hello?'

Icy silence.

Jenny's hand tightened on the receiver.

Someone was listening intently, remaining utterly silent, waiting for her to speak. She was determined not to give him that satisfaction. She just pressed the receiver to her ear and strained to hear something, anything, if even nothing more than the faint sea-like

61

ebb and flow of his breathing. He didn't make the slightest sound, but still she could *feel*, at the other end of the line, the presence that she had felt when she'd picked up the phone in the Santinis' house and in the sheriff's substation.

Standing in the barricaded room, in that silent house where Death had crept in with impossible stealth, Jenny Paige felt an odd transformation overtaking her. She was well-educated, a woman of reason and logic, not even mildly superstitious. Thus far, she had attempted to solve the mystery of Snowfield by applying the tools of logic and reason. But for the first time in her life, they had utterly failed her. Now deep in her mind, something . . . *shifted*, as if an enormously heavy iron cover was being slid off a dark pit in her subconscious. In that pit, within ancient chambers of the mind, there lay a host of primitive sensations and perceptions, a superstitious awe that was new to her. Virtually on the level of racial memory stored in the genes, she sensed what was happening in Snowfield. The knowledge was within her; however, it was so alien, so fundamentally illogical, that she resisted it, fighting hard to suppress the superstitious terror that boiled up within her.

Clutching the telephone receiver, she listened to the silent presence on the line, and she argued with herself:

– It isn't a man; it's a *thing*.

– Nonsense.

– It's not human, but it's aware.

– You're hysterical.

– Unspeakably malevolent; perfectly, purely evil.

– Stop it, stop it, *stop it*!

She wanted to slam down the phone. She couldn't do it. The thing on the other end of the line had her mesmerised.

Lisa stepped close. 'What's wrong? What's happening?'

Shaking, drenched with sweat, feeling tainted merely by listening to the despicable presence, Jenny was about to tear the receiver away from her ear when she heard a hiss, a click – and then a dial tone.

For a moment, stunned, she couldn't react.

Then, with a whimper, she jabbed at the 0 button on the phone.

There was a ringing on the line. It was a wonderful, sweet, reassuring sound.

'Operator.'

'Operator, this is an emergency,' Jenny said. 'I've got to reach the county sheriff's office in Santa Mira.'

9

A CALL FOR HELP

'LAUNDRY?' KALE asked. 'What laundry?'

Bryce could see that Kale was jolted by the question and was only pretending not to understand.

'Sheriff, where is this supposed to lead?' Bob Robine asked.

Bryce's hooded eyes remained hooded, and he kept his voice calm, slow. 'Gee, Bob, I'm just trying to get to the bottom of things, so we can all get out of here. I swear, I don't like working on Sundays, and here this one is almost shot to hell already. I have these questions, and Mr Kale doesn't have to answer any one of them, but I *will* ask, so that I can go home and put my feet up and have a beer.'

Robine sighed. He looked at Kale. 'Don't answer unless I say it's okay.'

Worried now, Kale nodded.

Frowning at Bryce, Robine said, 'Go ahead.'

Bryce said, 'When we arrived at Mr Kale's house last Thursday, after he phoned in to report the deaths, I noticed that one cuff of his slacks and the thick bottom edge of his sweater both looked slightly damp, so as you'd hardly notice. I got the notion he'd laundered everything he was wearing and just hadn't left his clothes in the dryer quite long enough. So I had a look in the laundry room, and I found something interesting. In the cupboard right there beside the washer, where Mrs Kale kept all of her soaps and detergents and fabric softeners, there were two bloody fingerprints on the big box of Cheer. One was smeared, but the other was clear. The lab says it's Mr Kale's print.'

'Whose blood was on the box?' Robine asked sharply.

'Both Mrs Kale and Danny were type O. So is Mr Kale. That makes it a little more difficult for us to—'

'The blood on the box of detergent?' Robine interrupted.

'Type O.'

'Then it could have been my client's own blood! He could have gotten it on the box on a previous occasion, maybe after he cut himself gardening last week.'

Bryce shook his head. 'As you know, Bob, this whole blood-typing business is getting highly sophisticated these days. Why, they can break down a sample into so many enzymes and protein signatures that a person's blood is almost as unique as his fingerprints. So they could tell us unequivocally that the blood on the box of Cheer – the blood on Mr Kale's hand when he made those two prints – was little Danny Kale's blood.'

Fletcher Kale's grey eyes remained flat and unexpressive, but he turned quite pale. 'I can explain,' he said.

'Hold it!' Robine said. 'Explain it to me first – in private.' The attorney led his client to the farthest corner of the room.

Bryce slouched in his chair. He felt grey. Washed out. He'd been that way since Thursday, since seeing Danny Kale's pathetic crumpled body.

He had expected to take considerable pleasure in watching Kale squirm. But there was no pleasure in it.

Robine and Kale returned. 'Sheriff, I'm afraid my client did a stupid thing.'

Kale tried to look properly abashed.

'He did something that could be misinterpreted – just as you *have* misinterpreted it. Mr Kale was frightened, confused, and grief-stricken. He wasn't thinking clearly. I'm sure any jury would sympathize with him. You see, when he found the body of his little boy he picked it up—'

'He told us he never touched it.'

Kale met Bryce's gaze forthrightly, and said, 'When I first saw Danny lying on the floor . . . I couldn't *really* believe that he was . . . dead. I picked him up . . . thinking I should rush to the hospital . . . Later, after I'd shot Joanna, I looked down and saw that I was covered with . . . with Danny's blood. I *had* shot my wife, but suddenly I realized it might look as if I'd killed my own son, too.'

'There was still the meat cleaver in your wife's hand,' Bryce said. 'And Danny's blood was all over *her*, too. And you could've figured the coroner would find PCP in her bloodstream.'

'I realize that now,' Kale said, pulling a handkerchief from his pocket and wiping his eyes. 'But at the time, I was afraid I'd be accused of something I'd never done.'

The word 'psychopath' wasn't exactly right for Fletcher Kale, Bryce decided. He wasn't crazy. Nor was he a sociopath, exactly. There wasn't a word that described him properly. However, a good cop would recognize the type and see the potential for criminal activity and, perhaps, the talent for brute violence, as well. There is a certain kind of man who has a lot of vitality and likes plenty of action, a man who has more than his share of shallow charm, whose clothes are more expensive than he can afford, who owns not a single book (just as Kale did not), who seems to have no well-thought-out opinions about politics or art or economics or any issue of real substance, who is not religious except when misfortune befalls him or when he wishes to impress someone with his piety (as Kale, member of no church, now read the Bible in his cell for at least four hours every day), who has an athletic build but who seems to loathe any pursuit as healthy as physical exercise, who spends his leisure time in bars and cocktail lounges, who cheats on his wife as a matter of habit (as did Kale, by all reports), who is impulsive, who is unreliable and always late for appointments (as was Kale), whose

66

goals are either vague or unrealistic ('Fletcher Kale? He's a dreamer.'), who frequently overdraws his current account and lies about money, who is quick to borrow and slow to pay back, who exaggerates, who *knows* he's going to be rich one day but who has no specific plan for acquiring that wealth, who never doubts or thinks about next year, who worries only about himself and only when it's too late. There was such a man, such a type, and Fletcher Kale was a prime example of the animal in question.

Bryce had seen others like him. Their eyes were always flat; you couldn't see into their eyes at all. Their faces expressed whatever emotion seemed required, although every expression was a shade too *right*. When they expressed concern for anyone but themselves, you could detect a bell-clear ring of insincerity. They were not burdened by remorse, morality, love, or empathy. Often, they led lives of acceptable destruction, ruining and embittering those who loved them, shattering the lives of friends who believed in them and relied on them, betraying trusts, but never quite crossing the line into outright criminal behaviour. Now and then, however, such a man went too far. And because he was the type who never did things by halves, he always went much, *much* too far.

Danny Kale's small, torn, bloody body lying in a heap.

The greyness enveloping Bryce's mind grew thicker, until it seemed like a cold, oily smoke. To Kale, he said, 'You've told us that your wife was a heavy marijuana smoker for two and a half years.'

'That's right.'

'On my instructions, the coroner looked for a few things that wouldn't ordinarily have interested him. Like the condition of Joanna's lungs. She wasn't a smoker at all, let alone a pot-head. Lungs were dean.'

'I said she smoked pot, not tobacco,' Kale said.

'Marijuana smoke and ordinary tobacco smoke both damage the lungs,' Bryce said. 'In Joanna's case, there was no damage whatsoever.'

'But, I—'

'Quiet,' Bob Robine advised his client. He pointed a long, slim finger at Bryce, waggled it, and said, 'The important thing is – was there PCP in her blood or wasn't there?'

'There was,' Bryce said. 'It was in her blood, but she didn't *smoke* it. Joanna took the PCP orally. There was still a lot of it in her stomach.'

Robine blinked in surprise but recovered quickly. 'There you go,' he said. 'She took it. Who cares how?'

'In fact,' Bryce said, 'there was more of it in her stomach than in her bloodstream.'

Kale tried to look curious, concerned, and innocent – all at the same time; even his elastic features were strained by that expression.

Scowling, Bob Robine said, 'So there was more in her stomach than in her bloodstream. So what?'

'Angel dust is highly absorbable. Taken orally, it doesn't remain in the stomach for very long. Now, while Joanna had swallowed enough dope to freak out, there hadn't been time for it to affect her. You see, she took the PCP with ice cream. Which coated her stomach and retarded the absorption of the drug. During the autopsy, the coroner found partially digested chocolate fudge ice cream. So there hadn't been time for the PCP to cause hallucinations or to send her into a berserk rage.' Bryce paused, took a deep breath. 'There was chocolate fudge ice cream in Danny's stomach, too, but no PCP. When Mr Kale told us he came home from work early on Thursday, he didn't mention bringing an afternoon treat for the family. A half-gallon of chocolate fudge ice cream.'

Fletcher Kale's face had gone blank. At last, he seemed to have used up his collection of human expressions.

Bryce said, 'We found a partly empty container of ice cream in Kale's freezer. Chocolate fudge. What I think happened, Mr Kale, is that you dished out some ice cream for everyone. I think you secretly laced your wife's helping with PCP, so you could later claim she was in a drug-induced frenzy. You didn't figure the coroner would catch you out.'

'Wait just one goddamned minute!' Robine shouted.

'Then while you washed your bloody clothes,' Bryce said to Kale, 'you cleaned up the ice cream-smeared dishes and put them away because your story was that you had come home from work to find little Danny already dead and his mother already freaked out on PCP.'

Robine said, 'That's only supposition. Have you forgotten motive? Why in God's name would my client do such a hideous thing?'

Watching Kale's eyes, Bryce said, 'High Country Investments.'

Kale's face remained impassive, but his eyes flickered.

'High Country Investments?' Robine asked. 'What's that?'

Bryce stared at Kale. 'Did you buy ice cream before you went home last Thursday?'

'No,' Kale said flatly.

'The manager of the 7-Eleven store over on Calder Street says you did.'

The muscles in Kale's jaws bulged as he clenched his teeth in anger.

'What about High Country Investments?' Robine asked.

Bryce fired another question at Kale. 'Do you know a man named Gene Terr?'

Kale only stared.

'People sometimes just call him "Jeeter".'

Robine said, 'Who is he?'

'Leader of the Demon Chrome,' Bryce said, watching Kale. 'It's a motorcycle gang. Jeeter deals drugs. Actually, we've never been able to catch him at it; we've only been able to jail some of his people. We leaned on Jeeter about this, and he steered us to someone who admitted supplying Mr Kale with grass on a regular basis. Not Mrs Kale. She never bought.'

69

'Who says?' Robine demanded. 'This motorcycle creep? This social reject? This drug pusher? He's not a reliable witness!'

'According to our source, Mr Kale didn't just buy grass last Tuesday. Mr Kale bought angel dust, too. The man who sold the drugs will testify in return for immunity.'

With animal cunning and suddenness, Kale bolted up, seized the empty chair beside him, threw it across the table at Bryce Hammond, and ran for the door of the interrogation room.

By the time the chair had left Kale's hands and was in the air, Bryce was already up and moving, and it sailed harmlessly past his head. He was around the table when the chair crashed to the floor behind him.

Kale pulled open the door and plunged into the corridor.

Bryce was four steps behind him.

Tal Whitman had come off the window ledge as if he'd been blown off by an explosive charge, and he was one step behind Bryce, shouting.

Reaching the corridor, Bryce saw Fletcher Kale heading for a yellow exit door about twenty feet away. He went after the son of a bitch.

Kale hit the crashbar and flung the metal door open.

Bryce reached him a fraction of a second later, as Kale was setting foot onto the macadamed parking lot.

Sensing Bryce close behind him. Kale turned with catlike fluidity and swung one huge fist.

Bryce ducked the blow, threw a punch of his own, connecting with Kale's hard, flat belly. Then he swung again, hitting him in the neck.

Kale stumbled back, putting his hands to his throat, gagging and choking.

Bryce moved in.

But Kale wasn't as badly stunned as he pretended to be. He leapt forward as Bryce approached and grabbed him in a bear hug.

'Bastard,' Kale said, spraying spittle.

His grey eyes were wide. His lips were skinned back from his teeth in a fierce snarl. He looked lupine.

Bryce's arms were pinned, and although he was a strong man himself, he couldn't break Kale's iron hold on him. They staggered a few steps backwards, stumbled, and went down, with Kale on top. Bryce's head thumped hard against the pavement, and he thought he was going to black out.

Kale punched him once, ineffectively, then rolled off him and crawled away fast.

Warding off the darkness that rose behind his eyes, surprised that Kale had surrendered the advantage, Bryce pushed up onto his hands and knees. He shook his head – and then saw what the other man had gone after.

A revolver.

It lay on the macadam, a few yards away, gleaming darkly in the glow of the yellowish sodium-vapour lights.

Bryce felt his holster. Empty. The revolver on the ground was his own. Apparently, it had slipped out of his holster and had spun across the pavement when he'd fallen.

The killer's hand closed on the weapon.

Tal Whitman stepped in and swung a nightstick, striking Kale across the back of the neck. The big man collapsed on top of the gun, unconscious.

Crouching, Tal rolled Kale over and checked his pulse.

Holding the back of his own throbbing skull, Bryce hobbled over to them. 'Is he all right, Tal?'

'Yeah. He'll be coming around in a few minutes.' He picked up Bryce's gun and got to his feet.

Accepting the revolver, Bryce said, 'I owe you one.'

'Not at all. How's your head?'

'I should be so lucky to own an aspirin company.'

'I didn't expect him to run.'

'Neither did I,' Bryce said. 'When things get worse and worse for a man like that, he usually just gets calmer, cooler, more careful.'

'Well, I guess this one saw the walls closing in.'

Bob Robine was standing in the open doorway, staring out at them, shaking his head in consternation.

A few minutes later, as Bryce Hammond sat at his desk, filling out the forms charging Fletcher Kale with two homicides, Bob Robine rapped on the open door.

Bryce looked up. 'Well, counsellor, how's your client?'

'He's okay. But he's not my client any more.'

'Oh? His decision or yours?'

'Mine. I can't handle a client who lies to me about *everything*. I don't *like* being made a fool of.'

'So does he want to call another attorney tonight?'

'No. When he's arraigned, he's going to ask the judge for a public defender.'

'That'll be the first thing in the morning.'

'Not wasting any time, huh?'

'Not with this one,' Bryce said.

Robine nodded. 'Good. He's a *very* bad apple, Bryce. You know, I've been a lapsed Catholic for fifteen years,' Robine said softly. 'I made up my mind long ago that there weren't such things as angels, demons, miracles. I thought I was too well educated to believe that Evil – with a capital E – stalks the world on cloven hooves. But back there in the cell, Kale suddenly whirled on me and said, "They won't get me. They won't destroy me. Nobody can. I'll walk away from this." When I warned him against excessive optimism, he said, "I'm not afraid of your kind. Besides, I didn't commit murder; I just disposed of some garbage that was stinking up my life."'

'Jesus,' Bryce said.

They were both silent. Then Robine sighed. 'What about High Country Investments? How's it provide a motive?'

Before Bryce could explain, Tal Whitman rushed in from the hall. 'Bryce, could I have a word with you?' He glanced at Robine. 'Uh, this better be in private.'

'Sure,' Robine said.

Tal closed the door behind the lawyer. 'Bryce, do you know Dr Jennifer Paige?'

'She set up practice in Snowfield sometime back.'

'Yeah. What kind of person would you say she is?'

'I've never met her. I heard she's a fine doctor, though. And folks up in those little mountain towns are glad they don't have to drive all the way in to Santa Mira for a doctor any more.'

'I've never met her either. I was just wondering if maybe you'd heard anything about . . . about whether she drinks. I mean . . . booze.'

'No, I haven't heard any such thing. Why? What's going on?'

'She called a couple of minutes ago. She says there's been a disaster up in Snowfield.'

'Disaster? What's she mean?'

'Well, she says she doesn't know.'

Bryce blinked. 'Did she sound hysterical?'

'Frightened, yeah. But not hysterical. She doesn't want to say much of anything to anyone but you. She's on line three right now.'

Bryce reached for the phone.

'One more thing,' Tal said, worry lines creasing his forehead.

Bryce paused, hand on the receiver.

Tal said: 'She did tell me one thing, but it doesn't make sense. She said . . .'

'Yes?'

'She said that everyone's dead up there. Everyone in Snowfield. She said she and her sister are the only ones alive.'

73

10

SISTERS AND COPS

JENNY AND Lisa left the Oxley house the same way they had entered: through the window.

The night was growing colder. The wind had risen once more.

They walked back to Jenny's house at the top of Skyline Road and got jackets to ward off the chill.

Then they went downhill again to the sheriff's substation. A wooden bench was bolted to the cobblestones by the kerb in front of the town jail, and they sat waiting for help from Santa Mira.

'How long will it take them to get here?' Lisa asked.

'Well, Santa Mira is more than thirty miles away, over some pretty twisty roads. And they've got to take some unusual precautions.' Jenny looked at her wristwatch. 'I guess they'll be here in another forty-five minutes. An hour at most.'

'Jeez.'

'It's not so long, honey.'

The girl turned up the collar of her fleece-lined, denim jacket. 'Jenny, when the phone rang at the Oxley place and you picked it up . . .'

'Yes?'

'Who was calling?'

'No one.'

'What did you hear?'

'Nothing,' Jenny lied.

'From the look on your face, I thought someone was threatening you or something.'

'Well, I was upset, of course. When it rang, I thought the phones were working again, but when I picked it up and it was only another dead line, I felt . . . crushed. That was all.'

'Then you got a dial tone?'

'Yes.'

She probably doesn't believe me, Jenny thought. She thinks I'm trying to protect her from something. And, of course, I am. How can I explain the feeling that something evil was on that phone with me? I can't even begin to understand it myself. Who or what *was* on that telephone? Why did he – or *it* – finally let me have a dial tone?

A scrap of paper blew along the street. Nothing else moved.

A thin rag of cloud passed over one corner of the moon.

After a while, Lisa said, 'Jenny, in case something happens to me tonight—'

'Nothing's going to happen to you, honey.'

'But in case something *does* happen to me tonight,' Lisa insisted, 'I want you to know that I . . . well . . . I really am . . . proud of you.'

Jenny put an arm around her sister's shoulders, and they moved even closer together. 'Sis, I'm sorry that we never had much time together over the years.'

'You got home as often as you could,' Lisa said. 'I know it wasn't easy. I must've read a couple of dozen books about what a person has to go through to become a doctor. I always knew there was a lot on your shoulders, a lot you had to worry about.'

Surprised, Jenny said, 'Well, I still could've got home more often.'

She had stayed away from home on some occasions because she had not been able to cope with the accusation in her mother's sad eyes, an accusation which was even more powerful and affecting

75

because it was never bluntly put into words: *You killed your father, Jenny; you broke his heart, and that killed him.*

Lisa said, 'And Mom was always so proud of you, too.'

That statement not only surprised Jenny, it rocked her.

'Mom was always telling people about her daughter the doctor.' Lisa smiled, remembering. 'I think there were times her friends were ready to throw her out of her bridge club if she said just one more word about your scholarships or your good grades.'

Jenny blinked. 'Are you serious?'

'Of course, I'm serious.'

'But didn't Mom . . .'

'Didn't she what?' Lisa asked.

'Well . . . didn't she ever say anything about . . . about Dad? He died twelve years ago.'

'Jeez, I know that. He died when I was two and a half.' Lisa frowned. 'But what're you talking about?'

'You mean you never heard Mom blame me?'

'Blame you for what?'

Before Jenny could respond, Snowfield's graveyard tranquillity was snuffed out. All the lights went off.

Three patrol cars set out from Santa Mira, headed into the night-enshrouded hills, towards the high, moon-bathed slopes of the Sierras, towards Snowfield, their red emergency lights flashing.

Tal Whitman drove the car at the head of the speeding procession, and Sheriff Hammond sat beside him. Gordy Brogan was in the back seat with another deputy, Jake Johnson.

Gordy was scared.

He knew his fear wasn't visible, and he was thankful for that. In fact, he looked as if he didn't know *how* to be afraid. He was tall, large-boned, slab-muscled. His hands were strong and as large as the hands of a professional basketball player; he looked capable of slam-dunking anyone who gave him trouble. He knew that his face was handsome enough; women had told him so. But it was also a rather rough-looking face, dark. His lips were thin, giving his mouth a cruel aspect. Jake Johnson had said it best: *Gordy, when you frown, you look like a man who eats live chickens for breakfast.*

But in spite of his fierce appearance, Gordy Brogan was scared. It wasn't the prospect of disease or poison that occasioned fear in Gordy. The sheriff had said there were indications that the people in Snowfield had been killed not by germs or by toxic substances but *by other people.* Gordy was afraid that he would have to use his gun for the first time since he had become a deputy, eighteen months ago; he was afraid he would be forced to shoot someone – either to save his own life, the life of another deputy, or that of a victim.

He didn't think he could do it.

Five months ago, he had discovered a dangerous weakness in himself when he had answered an emergency call from Donner's Sports Shop. A disgruntled former employee, a burly man named Leo Sipes, had returned to the store two weeks after being fired, had beaten up the manager, and had broken the arm of the clerk who had been hired to replace him. By the time Gordy arrived on the scene, Leo Sipes – big and dumb and drunk – was using a wood-man's hatchet to smash and splinter all of the merchandise. Gordy was unable to talk him into surrendering. When Sipes started after him, brandishing the hatchet, Gordy had pulled his revolver. And then found he couldn't use it. His trigger finger became as brittle and inflexible as ice. He'd had to put the gun away and risk a physical confrontation with Sipes. Somehow, he'd wrested the hatchet away from him.

Now, five months later, as he sat in the rear of the patrol car and listened to Jake Johnson talking to Sheriff Hammond, Gordy's stomach clenched and turned sour at the thought of what a .45-calibre hollow-nose bullet would do to a man. It would *literally* take off his head. It would smash a man's shoulder into rags of flesh and broken needles of bone. It would rip open a man's chest, shattering the heart and everything else in its path. It would blow off a leg if it struck a kneecap, would turn a face to bloody slush. And Gordy Brogan, God help him, was just not capable of doing such a thing to anyone.

That was his terrible weakness. He knew there were people who would say that his inability to shoot another being was not a weakness but a sign of moral superiority. However, he knew that was not always true. There were times when shooting was a moral act. An officer of the law was sworn to protect the public. For a cop, the inability to shoot (when shooting was clearly justified) was not only weakness but madness, perhaps even sinful.

During the past five months, following the unnerving episode at Donner's Sports Shop, Gordy had been lucky. He'd drawn only a few calls involving violent suspects. And fortunately, he had been able to bring his adversaries to heel by using his fists or his nightstick or threats – or by firing warning shots into the air. Once, when it had seemed that shooting someone was unavoidable, the other officer, Frank Autry, had fired first, winging the gunman, before Gordy had been confronted with the impossible task of pulling the trigger.

But now something unimaginably violent had transpired up in Snowfield. And Gordy knew all too well that violence frequently had to be met with violence.

The gun on his hip seemed to weigh a thousand pounds.

He wondered if the time was approaching when his weakness would be revealed. He wondered if he would die tonight – or if he would cause, by his weakness, the unnecessary death of another.

He ardently prayed that he could beat this thing. Surely, it was possible for a man to be peaceful by nature and still possess the nerve to save himself, his friends, his kind.

Red emergency beacons flashing on their roofs, the three white and green squad cars followed the winding highway into the night-cloaked mountains, up towards the peaks where the moonlight created the illusion that the first snow of the season had already fallen.

Gordy Brogan was scared.

The streetlamps and all other lights went out, casting the town into darkness.

Jenny and Lisa bolted up from the wooden bench.

'What happened?'

'Ssshh!' Jenny said. '*Listen!*'

But there was only continued silence.

The wind had stopped blowing, as if startled by the town's abrupt blackout. The trees waited, boughs hanging as still as old clothes in a closet.

Thank God for the moon, Jenny thought.

Heart thudding, Jenny turned and studied the buildings behind them. The town jail. A small café. The shops. The townhouses.

All the doorways were so clotted with shadows that it was difficult to tell if the doors were open or closed – or if, just now, they were slowly, slowly coming open to release the hideous, swollen, demonically reanimated dead into the night streets.

Stop it! Jenny thought. The dead don't come back to life.

Her eyes came to rest on the gate in front of the covered serviceway between the sheriff's substation and the gift shop next door. It was exactly like the cramped, gloomy passageway beside Liebermann's Bakery.

Was something hiding in this tunnel, too? And, with the lights out, was it creeping inexorably towards the far side of the gate, eager to come out onto the dark pavement?

That primitive fear again.

That sense of evil.

That superstitious terror.

'Come on,' she said to Lisa.

'Where?'

'In the street. Nothing can get us out there—'

'—without our seeing it coming,' Lisa finished, understanding.

They went into the middle of the moonlit roadway.

'How long until the sheriff gets here?' Lisa asked.

'At least fifteen or twenty minutes yet.'

The town's lights all came on at once. A brilliant shower of electric radiance stung their eyes with surprise – then darkness again.

Jenny raised the revolver, not knowing where to point it.

Her throat was fear-parched, her mouth dry.

A blast of sound – an ungodly wail – slammed through Snowfield.

Jenny and Lisa both cried out in shock and turned, bumping against each other, squinting at the moon-tinted darkness.

Then silence.

Then another shriek.

Silence.

'What?' Lisa asked.

'The firehouse!'

It came again: a short burst of the piercing siren from the east side of St Moritz Way, from the Snowfield Volunteer Fire Company stationhouse.

Bong!

Jenny jumped again, twisted around.

Bong! Bong!

'A church bell,' Lisa said.

'The Catholic Church, west on Vail.'

The bell tolled once more – a loud, deep, mournful sound that reverberated in the blank windows along the dark length of Skyline Road and in other, unseen windows throughout the dead town.

'Someone has to pull a rope to ring a bell,' Lisa said. 'Or push a button to set off a siren. So there *must* be someone else here besides us.'

Jenny said nothing.

The siren sounded again, whooped and then died, whooped and

died, and the church bell began to toll again, and the bell and the siren cried out at the same time, again and again, as if announcing the advent of someone of tremendous importance.

In the mountains, a mile from the turnoff to Snowfield, the night landscape was rendered solely in black and moon-silver. The looming trees were not green at all; they were sombre shapes, mostly shadows, with albescent fringes of vaguely defined needles and leaves.

In contrast, the shoulders of the highway were blood-coloured by the light that splashed from the revolving beacons atop the three Ford sedans which all bore the insignia of the Santa Mira County Sheriff's Department on their front doors.

Deputy Frank Autry was driving the second car, and Deputy Stu Wargle was slouched down on the passenger's seat.

Frank Autry was lean, sinewy, with neatly trimmed salt-and-pepper hair. His features were sharp and economical, as if God hadn't been in the mood to waste anything the day that He had edited Frank's genetic file: hazel eyes under a finely chiselled brow; a narrow, patrician nose; a mouth that was neither too parsimonious nor too generous; small, nearly lobeless ears tucked flat against the head. His moustache was most carefully groomed.

He wore his uniform precisely the way that the service manual said he should: black boots polished to a mirrored shine, brown slacks with a knife-edge crease, leather belt and holster kept bright and supple with lanolin, brown shirt crisp and fresh.

'It isn't fucking fair,' Stu Wargle said.

'Commanding officers don't always have to be fair – just right,' Frank said.

'What commanding officer?' Wargle asked querulously.

'Sheriff Hammond. Isn't that who you mean?'

'I don't think of him as no commanding officer.'

'Well, that's what he is,' Frank said.

'He'd like to break my ass,' Wargle said. 'The bastard.'

Frank said nothing.

Before signing up with the county constabulary, Frank Autry had been a career military officer. He had retired from the United States Army at the age of forty-four, after twenty-five years of distinguished service, and had moved back to Santa Mira, the town in which he'd been born and raised. He had intended to open a small business of some kind in order to supplement his pension and to keep himself occupied, but he hadn't been able to find anything that looked interesting. Gradually, he had come to realize that, for him at least, a job without a uniform and without a chain of command and without an element of physical risk and without a sense of public service was just not a job worth having. Three years ago, at the age of forty-six, he had signed up with the sheriff's department, and in spite of the demotion from major, which was the rank he'd held in the service, he had been happy ever since.

That is, he had been happy except for those occasions, usually one week a month, when he'd been partnered with Stu Wargle. Wargle was insufferable. Frank tolerated the man only as a test of his own self-discipline.

Wargle was a slob. His hair often needed washing. He always missed a patch of bristles when he shaved. His uniform was wrinkled, and his boots were never shined. He was too big in the gut, too big in the hips, too big in the butt.

Wargle was a bore. He had absolutely no sense of humour. He read nothing, knew nothing – yet he had strong opinions about every current social and political issue.

Wargle was a creep. He was forty-five years old, and he still picked his nose in public. He belched and farted with aplomb.

Still slumped against the passenger-side door, Wargle said, 'I'm supposed to go off duty at ten o'clock. Ten goddamned *o'clock*! It's not fair for Hammond to pull me for this Snowfield crap. And me with a hot number all lined up.'

Frank didn't take the bait. He didn't ask who Wargle had a date with. He just drove the car and kept his eyes on the road and hoped that Wargle wouldn't tell him who this 'hot number' was.

'She's a waitress over at Spanky's Diner,' Wargle said. 'Maybe you've seen her. Blonde broad. Name's Beatrice; they call her Bea.'

'I seldom stop at Spanky's,' Frank said.

'Oh. Well, she don't have a half-bad face, see. One hell of a set of knockers. She's got a few extra pounds on her, not much, but she thinks she looks worse than she does. Insecurity, see? So if you play her right, if you kind of work on her doubts about herself, see, and then if you say you want her, anyway, in spite of the fact that she's let herself get a little pudgy – why, hell, she'll do any damned thing you want. *Anything.*'

The slob laughed as if he had said something unbearably funny.

Frank wanted to punch him in the face. Didn't.

Wargle was a woman-hater. He spoke of women as if they were members of another, lesser species. The idea of a man happily sharing his life and innermost thoughts with a woman, the idea that a woman could be loved, cherished, admired, respected, valued for her wisdom and insight and humour – that was an utterly alien concept to Stu Wargle.

Frank Autry, on the other hand, had been married to his lovely Ruth for twenty-six years. He adored her. Although he knew it was a selfish thought, he sometimes prayed that he would be the first to die, so that he wouldn't have to handle life without Ruth.

'That fuckin' Hammond wants my ass nailed to a wall. He's always needling me.'

'About what?'

'Everything. He don't like the way I keep my uniform. He don't like the way I write up my reports. He told me I should try to improve my attitude. Christ, my *attitude*! He wants my ass, but he won't get it. I'll hang in five more years, see, so I can get my thirty-year pension. That bastard won't squeeze me out of my pension.'

Almost two years ago, voters in the city of Santa Mira approved a ballot initiative that dissolved the metropolitan police, putting law enforcement for the city into the hands of the county sheriff's department. It was a vote of confidence in Bryce Hammond, who had built the county department, but one provision of the initiative required that no city officers lose their jobs or pensions because of the transfer of power. Thus, Bryce Hammond was stuck with Stewart Wargle.

They reached the Snowfield turnoff.

Frank glanced in the rearview mirror and saw the third patrol car pull out of the three-car train. As planned, it swung across the entrance to Snowfield road, setting up a blockade.

Sheriff Hammond's car continued on towards Snowfield, and Frank followed it.

'Why the hell did we have to bring water?' Wargle asked.

Three five-gallon bottles of water stood on the floor in the back of the car.

Frank said, 'The water in Snowfield might be contaminated.'

'And all that food we loaded into the trunk?'

'We can't trust the food up there, either.'

'I don't believe they're all dead.'

'The Sheriff couldn't raise Paul Henderson at the substation.'

'So what? Henderson's a jerk-off.'

'The doctor up there said Henderson's dead, along with—'

'Christ, the doctor's off her nut or drunk. Who the hell would go to a woman doctor, anyway? She probably screwed her way through medical school.'

'*What?*'

'No broad has what it takes to *earn* a degree like that!'

'Wargle, you never cease to amaze me.'

'What's eating you?' Wargle asked.

'Nothing. Forget it.'

Wargle belched. 'Well, I don't believe they're all dead.'

Another problem with Stu Wargle was that he didn't have any imagination.

'What a lot of crap. And me lined up with a hot number.'

Frank Autry, on the other hand, had a very good imagination. Perhaps too good. As he drove higher into the mountains, as he passed a sign that read SNOWFIELD – 2 MILES, his imagination was humming like a well-lubricated machine. He had the disturbing feeling – premonition? hunch? – that they were driving straight into Hell.

The firehouse siren screamed.

The church bell tolled faster, faster.

A deafening cacophony clattered through the town.

'Jenny!' Lisa shouted.

'Keep your eyes open! Look for movement!'

The street was a patchwork of ten thousand shadows; there were too many dark places to watch.

The siren wailed, and the bell rang, and now the lights began to flash again – house lights, shop lights, streetlights – on and off, on and off so rapidly that they created a strobe-like effect. Skyline Road flicked; the buildings seemed to jump towards the street, then fall back, then jump forward; the shadows danced jerkily.

Jenny turned in a complete circle, the revolver thrust out in front of her.

If something was approaching under cover of the stroboscopic light show, she couldn't see it.

She thought: What if, when the sheriff arrives, he finds two severed heads in the middle of the street? Mine and Lisa's.

The church bell was louder than ever, and it banged away continuously, madly.

The siren swelled into a teeth-jarring, bone-piercing screech. It seemed a miracle that windows didn't shatter.

Lisa had her hands over her ears.

85

Jenny's gun hand was shaking. She couldn't keep it steady.

Then as abruptly as the pandemonium had begun, it ceased. The siren died. The church bell stopped. The lights stayed on.

Jenny scanned the street, waiting for something more to happen, something worse.

But nothing happened.

Again, the town was as tranquil as a graveyard.

A wind sprang out of nowhere and caused the trees to sway, as if responding to ethereal music beyond the range of human hearing.

Lisa shook herself out of a daze and said, 'It was almost as if . . . as if they were *trying* to scare us . . . teasing us.'

'Teasing,' Jenny said. 'Yes, that's exactly what it was like.'

'Playing with us.'

'Like a cat with mice,' Jenny said softly.

They stood in the middle of the silent street, afraid to go back to the bench in front of the town jail, lest their movement should start the siren and the bell again.

Suddenly, they heard a low grumbling. For an instant, Jenny's stomach tightened. She raised the gun once more, although she could see nothing at which to shoot. Then she recognized the sound: automobile engines labouring up the steep mountain road.

She turned and looked down the street. The grumble of engines grew louder. A car appeared around the curve, at the bottom of town.

Flashing red roof lights. A police car. Two police cars.

'Thank God,' Lisa said.

Jenny quickly led her sister to the cobblestone pavement in front of the substation.

The two white and green patrol cars came slowly up the deserted street and angled to the kerb in front of the wooden bench. The two engines were cut off simultaneously. Snowfield's deathlike hush took possession of the night once more.

A rather handsome black man in a deputy's uniform got out of the first car, letting his door stand open. He looked at Jenny and Lisa but didn't immediately speak. His attention was captured by the preternaturally silent, unpeopled street.

A second man got out of the front seat of the same vehicle. He had unruly, sandy hair. His eyelids were so heavy that he looked as if he was about to fall asleep. He was dressed in civilian clothing – grey slacks, a pale blue shirt, a dark blue nylon jacket – but there was a badge pinned to the jacket.

Four other men got out of the cruisers. All six newcomers stood there for a long moment without speaking, eyes moving over the quiet stores and houses.

In that strange, suspended bubble of time, Jenny had an icy premonition that she didn't want to believe. She was certain – she sensed; she *knew* – that not all of them would leave this place alive.

11

EXPLORING

BRYCE KNELT on one knee beside the body of Paul Henderson.

The other seven – his own men, Dr Paige, and Lisa – crowded into the reception area, outside the wooden railing, in the Snowfield substation. They were quiet in the presence of Death.

Paul Henderson had been a good man with decent instincts. His death was a terrible waste.

Bryce said, 'Dr Paige?'

She crouched down at the other side of the corpse. 'Yes?'

'You didn't move the body?'

'I didn't even touch it, Sheriff.'

'There was no blood?'

'Just as you see it now. No blood.'

The wound might be in his back,' Bryce said.

'Even if it was, there'd still be some blood on the floor.'

'Maybe.' He stared into her striking eyes – green flecked with gold. 'Ordinarily, I wouldn't disturb a body until the coroner had seen it. But this is an extraordinary situation. I'll have to turn this man over.'

'I don't know if it's safe to touch him.'

'Someone has to do it,' Bryce said.

Dr Paige stood up, and everyone moved back a couple of steps.

Bryce put a hand to Henderson's purple-black, distorted face. The skin is still slightly warm,' he said in surprise.

Dr Paige said, 'I don't think they've been dead very long.'

'But a body doesn't discolour and bloat in just a couple of hours,' Tal Whitman said.

'*These* bodies did,' the doctor said.

Bryce rolled the corpse over, exposing the back. No wound.

Hoping to find an unnatural depression in the skull, Bryce thrust his fingers into the dead man's thick hair, testing the bone. If the deputy had been struck hard on the back of the head . . . But that wasn't the case, either. The skull was intact.

Bryce got to his feet. 'Doctor, these two decapitations you mentioned . . . I guess we'd better have a look at those.'

'Do you think one of your men could stay here with my sister?'

'I understand your feelings,' Bryce said. 'But I don't really think it would be wise for me to split up my men. Maybe there isn't any safety in numbers; then on the other hand, maybe there *is*.'

'It's okay,' Lisa assured Jenny. 'I don't want to be left behind, anyway.'

She was a spunky kid. Both she and her older sister intrigued Bryce Hammond. They were pale, and their eyes were alive with dervish shadows of shock and horror – but they were coping a great deal better than most people would have in this bizarre, waking nightmare.

The Paiges led the entire group out of the substation and down the street to the bakery.

Bryce found it difficult to believe that Snowfield had been a normal, bustling village only a short while ago. The town felt as dry and burnt-out and dead as an ancient lost city in a far desert, off in a corner of the world where even the wind often forgot to go. The hush that cloaked the town seemed a silence of countless years, of decades, of centuries, a silence of unimaginably long epochs piled on epochs.

Shortly after arriving in Snowfield, Bryce had used an electric bullhorn to call for a response from the silent houses. Now it seemed foolish ever to have expected an answer.

They entered Liebermann's Bakery through the front door and went into the kitchen at the rear of the building.

On the butcher's-block table, two severed hands gripped the handles of a rolling pin.

Two severed heads peered through two oven doors.

'Oh, my God,' Tal said quietly.

Bryce shuddered.

Clearly in need of support, Jake Johnson leaned against a tall white cabinet.

Wargle said, 'Christ, they were butchered like a couple of god-damned cows,' and then everyone was talking at once.

'—why the hell anyone would—'

'—sick, twisted—'

'—so where are the bodies?'

'Yes,' Bryce said, raising his voice to override the babble, 'where are the *bodies*? Let's find them.'

For a couple of seconds, no one moved, frozen by the thought of what they might find.

'Dr Paige, Lisa – there's no need for you to help us,' Bryce said. 'Just stand aside.'

The doctor nodded. The girl smiled in gratitude.

With trepidation, they searched all the cupboards, opened all the drawers and doors. Gordy Brogan looked inside the big oven that wasn't equipped with a porthole, and Frank Autry went into the walk-in refrigerator. Bryce inspected the small, spotless lavatory off one end of the kitchen. But they couldn't find the bodies – or any other pieces of bodies – of the two elderly people.

'Why would the killers cart away the bodies?' Frank asked.

'Maybe we're dealing with some sort of cultists,' Jake Johnson said. 'Maybe they wanted the bodies for some weird ritual.'

'If there was any ritual,' Frank said, 'it looks to me like it was conducted right here.'

Gordy Brogan bolted for the lavatory, stumbling and weaving, a big gangling kid who seemed to be composed solely of long legs and long arms and elbows and knees. Retching sounds came through the door that he had slammed behind himself.

Stu Wargle laughed and said, 'Jesus, what a ninny.'

Bryce turned on him and scowled. 'What in God's name do you find so funny, Wargle? People are dead here. Seems to me that Gordy's reaction is a lot more natural than any of ours.'

Wargle's pig-eyed, heavy-jowled face clouded with anger. He didn't have the wit to be embarrassed.

God, I despise that man, Bryce thought.

When Gordy came back from the bathroom, he looked sheepish. 'Sorry, Sheriff.'

'No reason to be, Gordy.'

They trooped through the kitchen, across the sales room, out onto the pavement.

Bryce went immediately to the wooden gate between the bakery and the shop next door. He stared over the top of the gate, into the lightless, covered passageway. Dr Paige moved to his side, and he said, 'Is this where you thought something was in the rafters?'

'Well, Lisa thought it was crouched along the wall.'

'But it was *this* serviceway?'

'Yes.'

The tunnel was utterly black.

He took Tal's long-handled flashlight, opened the creaking gate, drew his revolver, and stepped into the passage. A vague, dank odour clung to the place. The squeal of the rusty gate hinges and then the sound of his own footsteps echoed down the tunnel ahead of him.

The beam of the flash was powerful; it carried over half the length of the passageway. However, he focused it close at hand, swept it back and forth over the immediate area, studying the concrete walls, then looking up at the ceiling, which was eight or ten feet overhead. In this part of the serviceway, at least, the rafters were deserted.

With each step, Bryce grew increasingly certain that drawing his revolver had been unnecessary – until he was almost halfway through the tunnel. Then he suddenly felt . . . something odd . . . a tingle, a cold augural quiver along the spine. He sensed that he wasn't alone any longer.

He was a man who trusted his hunches, and he didn't discount this one. He stopped advancing, brought the revolver up, listened more closely than before to the silence, moved the flashlight rapidly over the walls and ceiling, squinted with special care at the rafters, looked ahead into the gloom almost as far as the mouth of the alleyway, and even glanced back to see if something had crept magically around behind him. Nothing waited in the darkness. Yet he continued to feel that he was being watched by unfriendly eyes.

He started forward again, and his light caught something. Covered by a metal grille, a foot-square drain opening was set in the floor of the serviceway. Inside the drain, something indefinable glistened, reflecting the flashlight beam; it *moved*.

Cautiously, Bryce stepped closer and directed the light straight down into the drain. Whatever had glistened was gone now.

He squatted beside the drain and peered between the ribs of the grille. The light revealed only the walls of a pipe. It was a storm drain, about eighteen inches in diameter, and it was dry, which meant he had not merely seen water.

A rat? Snowfield was a resort that catered to a relatively affluent crowd; therefore, the town took unusually stringent measures to keep itself free of all manner of pests. Of course, in spite of Snowfield's diligence in such matters, the existence of a rat or two certainly wasn't impossible. It *could* have been a rat. But Bryce didn't believe that it *had* been.

He walked all the way to the alley, then retraced his steps to the gate where Tal and the others waited.

'See anything?' Tal asked.

'Not much,' Bryce said, stepping onto the pavement and closing the gate behind him. He told them about his feeling of being watched and about the movement in the drain.

'The Liebermanns were killed by people,' Frank Autry said. 'Not by something small enough to crawl through a drain.'

'That certainly would seem to be the case,' Bryce agreed.

'But you did *feel* it in there?' Lisa asked anxiously.

'I felt something,' Bryce told the girl. 'It apparently didn't affect me as strongly as you said it did you. But it was definitely . . . strange.'

'Good,' Lisa said. 'I'm glad you don't think we're just hysterical women.'

'Considering what you've been through, you two are about as *un*hysterical as you could get.'

'Well,' the girl said, 'Jenny's a doctor, and I think maybe I'd like to be a doctor some day, and doctors simply can't afford to get hysterical.'

She was a cute kid – although Bryce couldn't help noticing that her older sister was even better looking. Both the girl and the doctor had the same lovely shade of auburn hair; it was the dark red-brown of well-polished cherry wood, thick and lustrous. Both of them had the same golden skin, too. But because Dr Paige's features were more mature than Lisa's, they were also more interesting and appealing to Bryce. Her eyes were a shade greener than her sister's, too.

Bryce said, 'Dr Paige, I'd like to see that house where the bodies were barricaded in the den.'

'Yeah,' Tal said. 'The locked room murders.'

'That's the Oxley place over on Vail.' She led them down the street towards the corner of Vail Lane and Skyline Road.

The dry shuffle of their footsteps was the only sound, and it made Bryce think of desert places again, of scarabs swarming busily across stacks of ancient brittle papyrus scrolls in desert tombs.

Rounding the corner onto Vail Lane, Dr Paige halted and said, 'Tom and Karen Oxley live . . . uh *lived* two blocks further along here.'

Bryce studied the street. He said, 'Instead of walking straight to the Oxleys', let's have a look in all the houses and shops between here and there – at least on this side of the street. I think it's safe to split up into two squads, four to a group. We won't be going off entirely in different directions. We'll be close enough to help each other if there's trouble. Dr Paige, Lisa – you stay with Tal and me. Frank, you're in charge of the second team.'

Frank nodded.

The four of you stick together,' Bryce warned them. 'And I mean *together*. Each of you remain within sight of the other three at all times. Understood?'

'Yes, Sheriff,' Frank Autry said.

'Okay, you four have a look in the first building past the restaurant here, and we'll take the place next door to that. We'll hopscotch our way along the street and compare notes at the end of the block. If you come across something really interesting, something more than just additional bodies, come get me. If you need help, fire two or three rounds. We'll hear the gunshots even if we're inside another building. And you listen for gunfire from us.'

'May I make a suggestion?' Dr Paige asked.

'Sure,' Bryce said.

To Frank Autry, she said, 'If you come across any bodies that show signs of haemorrhaging from the eyes, ears, nose or mouth, let me know at once. Or any indications of vomiting or diarrhoea.'

'Because those things might indicate disease?' Bryce asked.

'Yes,' she said. 'Or poisoning.'

'But we've ruled that out, haven't we?' Gordy Brogan asked.

Jake Johnson, looking older than his fifty-seven years, said, 'It wasn't a disease that cut off those people's heads.'

'I've been thinking about that,' Dr Paige said. 'What if this is a disease or a chemical toxin that we've never encountered before – a mutant strain of rabies, say – that kills some people but merely drives others stark raving mad? What if the mutilations were done by those who were driven into a savage madness?'

'Is such a thing likely?' Tal Whitman asked.

'No. But then again, maybe not impossible. Besides, who's to say what's likely or unlikely any more? Is it *likely* that this would have happened to Snowfield in the first place?'

Frank Autry tugged at his moustache and said, 'But if there are packs of rabid maniacs roaming around out there . . . where *are* they?'

Everyone looked at the quiet street. At the deepest pools of shadow spilling over lawns and pavements and parked cars. At unlit attic windows. At dark basement windows.

'Hiding,' Wargle said.

'Waiting,' Gordy Brogan said.

'No, that doesn't make sense,' Bryce said. 'Rabid maniacs just wouldn't hide and wait and *plan*. They'd charge us.'

'Anyway,' Lisa said quietly, 'it isn't rabid people. It's something a lot stranger.'

'She's probably right,' Dr Paige said.

'Which somehow doesn't make me feel any better,' Tal said.

'Well, if we find any indications of vomiting, diarrhoea, or haemorrhaging,' Bryce said, 'then we'll know. And if we don't . . .'

'I'll have to come up with a new hypothesis,' Dr Paige said.

They were silent, not eager to begin the search because they didn't know what they might find – or what might find them.

Time seemed to have stopped.

Dawn, Bryce Hammond thought, will never come unless we move.

'Let's go,' he said.

The first building was narrow and deep, with a combination art gallery and crafts shop on the first floor. Frank Autry broke a pane of glass in the front door, reached inside, and released the lock. He entered and switched on the lights.

Motioning the others to follow, he said, 'Spread out. Don't stay too close together. We don't want to offer an easy target.'

As Frank spoke, he was reminded of the two tours of duty he had served in Vietnam almost twenty years ago. This operation had the nerve-twisting quality of a search-and-destroy mission in guerilla territory.

They prowled cautiously through the gallery's display but found no one. Likewise, there was no one in the small office at the rear of the showroom. However, a door in that office opened onto stairs that led to the second floor.

They took the stairs in military fashion. Frank climbed to the top alone, gun drawn, while the others waited. He located the light switch at the head of the stairs, snapped it on, and saw that he was in one corner of the living room of the gallery owner's apartment. When he was certain the room was deserted, he motioned for his men to come up. As the others climbed the stairs, Frank moved into the living room, staying close to the wall, watchful.

They searched the rest of the apartment, treating every doorway as a potential point of ambush. The den and dining room were both deserted. No one was hiding in the closets.

On the kitchen floor, however, they found a dead man. He was wearing only blue pyjamas, propping the refrigerator door open with his bruised and swollen body. There were no visible wounds. There was no look of horror on his face. Apparently, he had died too suddenly to have got a glimpse of his assailant – and without the slightest warning that death was near. The makings of a sandwich were scattered on the floor around him: a broken jar of mustard, a package of salami, a partially squashed tomato, a package of Swiss cheese.

'It sure wasn't no illness killed him,' Jake Johnson said emphatically. 'How sick could he have been if he was gonna eat salami?'

'And it happened real fast,' Gordy said. 'His hands were full of the stuff he got out of the refrigerator, and as he turned around . . . it just happened. *Bang*: just like that.'

In the bedroom they discovered another corpse. She was in bed, naked. She was no younger than about twenty, no older than forty; it was difficult to guess her age because of the universal bruising and swelling. Her face was contorted in terror, precisely as Paul Henderson's had been. She had died in the middle of a scream.

Jake Johnson took a pen from his shirt pocket and slipped it through the trigger guard of a .22 automatic that was lying on the rumpled sheets beside the body.

'I don't think we have to be careful with that,' Frank said. 'She wasn't shot. There aren't any wounds, no blood. If anybody used the gun, it was her. Let me see it.'

He took the automatic from Jake and ejected the clip. It was empty. He worked the slide, pointed the muzzle at the bedside lamp, and squinted into the barrel; there was no bullet in the chamber. He put the muzzle to his nose, sniffed, smelled gun powder.

'Fired recently?' Jake asked.

'Very recently. Assuming the clip was full when she used it, that means she fired off ten rounds.'

'Look here,' Wargle said.

Frank turned and saw Wargle pointing to a bullet hole in the wall opposite the foot of the bed. It was at about the seven-foot level.

'And here,' Gordy Brogan said, drawing their attention to another bullet lodged in the splintered wood on the dark pine tallboy.

They found all ten of the brass shell casings in or around the bed, but they couldn't find where the other eight bullets were lodged.

'You don't think she scored eight hits?' Gordy asked Frank.

'Christ, she can't have!' Wargle said, hitching his gun belt up on his fat hips. 'If she'd hit somebody eight times, she wouldn't be the only damned corpse in the room.'

'Right,' Frank said, though he disliked having to agree with Stu

Wargle about anything. 'Besides, there's no blood. Eight hits would mean a lot of blood.'

Wargle went to the foot of the bed and stared at the dead woman. She was propped up by a couple of plump pillows, and her legs were spread in a grotesque parody of desire. 'The guy in the kitchen must've been in here, screwing this broad,' Wargle said. 'When he was finished with her, he went into the kitchen to get them somethin' to eat. While they was separated, someone came in and killed her.'

'They killed the man in the kitchen first,' Frank said. 'He couldn't have been taken by surprise if he'd been attacked *after* she fired ten shots.'

Wargle said, 'Man, I sure wish *I'd* spent all day in the sack with a broad like that.'

Frank gaped at him. 'Wargle, you're disgusting. Are you even turned on by a bloated corpse – just because it's naked?'

Wargle's face reddened, and he looked away from the corpse. 'What the hell's the matter with you, Frank? What d'ya think I *am* – some kind of pervert? Huh? Hell, *no*. I seen that picture over on the nightstand.' He pointed to a silver-framed photograph beside the lamp. 'See, she's wearin' a bikini. You can see she was a hell of a nice lookin' broad. Big jugs on her. Great legs, too. *That's* what turned me on, pal.'

Frank shook his head. 'I'm just amazed that anything could turn you on in the midst of *this*, in the midst of so much death.'

Wargle thought it was a compliment. He winked.

If I get out of this business alive, Frank thought, I won't ever let Bryce Hammond partner me with Wargle. I'll quit first.

Gordy Brogan said, 'How could she have made eight hits and not have stopped something? How come there's not one drop of blood?'

Jake Johnson pushed a hand through his white hair again. 'I don't know, Gordy. But one thing I *do* know – I sure wish Bryce'd never picked me to come up here.'

Next to the art gallery, the sign on the front of the quaint two-storey building read:

Brookhart's

BEER * WINE * LIQUOR * TOBACCO
MAGAZINES * NEWSPAPERS * BOOKS

The lights were on, and the door was unlocked. Brook-hart's stayed open until nine even on Sunday evenings during the off season.

Bryce went in first, followed by Jennifer and Lisa Paige. Tal entered last. When choosing a man to protect his back in a dangerous situation, Bryce always preferred Tal Whitman. He trusted no one else as much as he trusted Tal, not even Frank Autry.

Brookhart's was a cluttered place, but curiously warm and pleasing. There were tall glass-doored coolers filled with cans and bottles of beer, shelves and racks and bins laden with bottles of wine and liquor, and other racks brimming with paperbacks, magazines, and newspapers. Cigars and cigarettes were stacked in boxes and cartons, and tins of pipe tobacco were displayed in haphazard mounds on several counter tops. A variety of goodies were tucked in wherever there was space: candy bars, Lifesavers, chewing gum, peanuts, popcorn, pretzels, potato chips, corn twisties, tortilla chips.

Bryce led the way through the deserted store, looking for bodies in the aisles. But there were none.

There was, however, an enormous puddle of water, about an inch deep, that covered half the floor. They stepped gingerly around it.

'Where'd all this water come from?' Lisa wondered.

'Must be a leak in the condensation pan under one of the beer coolers,' Tal Whitman said.

They came around the end of a wine bin and took a good look at all of the coolers. There was no water anywhere near those softly humming appliances.

'Maybe there's a leak in the plumbing,' Jennifer Paige suggested.

They continued their exploration, descending into the cellar, which was used for the storage of wine and booze in cardboard cases, then going up to the top floor, above the store, where there was an office. They found nothing out of the ordinary.

In the store again, heading towards the front door, Bryce stopped and squatted down for a closer look at the puddle on the floor. He moistened one fingertip in the stuff; it *felt* like water, and it was odourless.

'What's wrong?' Tal asked.

Standing again, Bryce said, 'It's odd – all this water here.'

Tal said, 'Most likely, it's what Dr Paige said – only a leak in the plumbing.'

Bryce nodded. However, although he couldn't say why, the big puddle seemed significant to him.

Tayton's Pharmacy was a small place that served Snowfield and all of the outlying mountain towns. An apartment occupied two floors above the pharmacy; it was decorated in shades of cream and peach, with emerald-green accent pieces, and with a number of fine antiques.

Frank Autry led his men through the entire building, and they found nothing remarkable – except for the sodden carpet in the living room. It was literally soaking wet; it squished beneath their shoes.

The Candleglow Inn positively radiated charm and gentility: the deep eaves and elaborately carved cornices, the mullioned windows flanked by carved white shutters. Two carriage lamps were fixed atop stone pilasters, bracketing the short stone walkway. Three small spotlights spread dramatic fans of light across the face of the inn.

Jenny, Lisa, the sheriff, and Lieutenant Whitman paused on the pavement in front of the Candleglow, and Hammond said, 'Are they open this time of year?'

'Yes,' Jenny said. 'they manage to stay about half full during the off season. But then they have a marvellous reputation with discriminating travellers – and they only have sixteen rooms.'

'Well . . . let's have a look.'

The front doors opened onto a small, comfortably appointed lobby: an oak floor, a dark oriental carpet, light beige sofas, a pair of Queen Anne chairs unholstered in a rose-coloured fabric, cherry wood end tables, brass lamps.

The registration desk was off to the right. A bell rested on the wooden counter, and Jenny struck it several times, rapidly, expecting no response and getting none.

'Dan and Sylvia keep an apartment behind this office area,' she said, indicating the cramped business quarters beyond the counter.

'They own the place?' the sheriff asked.

'Yes. Dan and Sylvia Kanarsky.'

The sheriff stared at her for a moment. 'Friends?'

'Yes. Close friends.'

Then maybe we'd better not look in their apartment,' he said.

Warm sympathy and understanding shone in his heavy-lidded blue eyes. Jenny was surprised by a sudden awareness of the kindness and intelligence that informed his face. During the past hour, watching him operate, she had gradually realized that he was considerably more alert and efficient than he had at first appeared to be. Now, looking into his sensitive compassionate eyes, she realized he was perceptive, interesting, formidable.

'We can't just walk away,' she said. 'This place has to be searched sooner or later. The whole town has to be searched. We might as well get this part of it out of the way.'

She lifted a hinged section of the wooden counter top and started to push through a gate into the office space beyond.

'Please, Doctor,' the sheriff said, 'always let me or Lieutenant Whitman go first.'

She backed out obediently, and he preceded her into Dan's and Sylvia's apartment, but they didn't find anyone. No dead bodies.

Thank God.

Back at the registration desk, Lieutenant Whitman paged through the guest book. 'Only six rooms are being rented right now, and they're all on the second floor.'

The sheriff located a pass key on a pegboard beside the mailboxes.

With almost monotonous caution, they went upstairs and searched the six rooms. In the first five, they found luggage and cameras and half-written postcards and other indications that there actually had been guests at the inn, but they didn't find the guests themselves.

In the sixth room, when Lieutenant Whitman tried the door to the adjoining bath, he found it locked. He hammered on it and shouted, 'Police! Is anyone there?'

No one answered.

Whitman looked at the doorknob, then at the sheriff. 'No lock button on this side, so someone must be in there. Break it down?'

'Looks like a solid-core door,' Hammond said. 'No use dislocating your shoulder. Shoot the lock.'

Jenny took Lisa's arm and drew the girl aside, out of the path of any debris that might blow back.

Lieutenant Whitman called a warning to anyone who might be in the bathroom, then fired one shot. He kicked the door open and went inside fast. 'Nobody's here.'

'Maybe they climbed out of a window,' the sheriff said.

'There aren't any windows in here,' Whitman said, frowning.

'You're sure the door was locked?'

'Positive. And it could only be done from the inside.'

'But how – if no one was in there?'

Whitman shrugged. 'Besides that, there's something you ought to have a look at.'

They all had a look at it, in fact, for the bathroom was large enough to accommodate four people. On the mirror above the sink, a message had been hastily printed in bold, greasy, black letters:

TIMOTHY
FLYTE
THE ANCIENT
ENEMY

In another apartment above another shop, Frank Autry and his men found another water-soaked carpet that squished under their feet. In the living room, dining room, and bedrooms, the carpet was dry, but in the hallway leading to the kitchen, it was saturated. And in the kitchen itself, three-quarters of the vinyl-tile floor was covered with water up to a depth of one inch in places.

Standing in the hallway, staring into the kitchen, Jake Johnson said, 'Must be a plumbing leak.'

'That's what you said at the other place,' Frank reminded him. 'Seems coincidental, don't you think?'

Gordy Brogan said, 'It *is* just water. I don't see what it could have to do with . . . all the murders.'

'Shit,' Stu Wargle said, 'we're wastin' time. There's nothin' here. Let's go.'

Ignoring them, Frank stepped into the kitchen, treading carefully through one end of the small lake, heading for a dry area by a row of cupboards. He opened several cupboard doors before he found a small plastic tub used for storing leftovers. It was clean and dry, and it had a snap-on lid that made an airtight seal. In a drawer he found a measuring spoon, and he used it to scoop water into the plastic container.

'What're you doing?' Jake asked from the doorway.

'Collecting a sample.'

'Sample? Why? It's only water.'

'Yeah,' Frank said, 'but there's something funny about it.'

The bathroom. The mirror. The bold, greasy, black letters.

Jenny stared at the five printed words.

Lisa said, 'Who's Timothy Flyte?'

'Could be the guy who wrote this,' Lieutenant Whitman said.

'Is the room rented to Flyte?' the sheriff asked.

'I'm sure I didn't see that name on the registry,' the lieutenant said. 'We can check it out when we go downstairs, but I'm really sure.'

'Maybe Timothy Flyte is one of the killers,' Lisa said. 'Maybe the guy renting this room recognized him and left this message.'

The sheriff shook his head. 'No. If Flyte's got something to do with what's happened to this town, he wouldn't leave his name on the mirror like that. He would've wiped it off.'

'Unless he didn't know it was there,' Jenny said.

The lieutenant said, 'Or maybe he knew it was there, but he's one of the rabid maniacs you talked about, so he doesn't care whether we catch him or not.'

Bryce Hammond looked at Jenny. 'Anyone in town named Flyte?'

'Never heard of him.'

'Do you know everyone in Snowfield?'

'Yeah.'

'All five hundred?'

'Nearly everyone,' she said.

'*Nearly* everyone, huh? Then there *could* be a Timothy Flyte here?'

'Even if I'd never met him, I'd still have heard someone mention him. It's a *small* town, Sheriff, at least during the off season.'

'Could be someone from over in Mount Larson, Shady Roost, or Pineville,' the lieutenant suggested.

She wished they could go somewhere else to discuss the message on the mirror. Outside. In the open. Where nothing could creep close to them without revealing itself. She had the uncanny, unsupported, but undeniable feeling that something – something damned strange – was moving about in another part of the inn right this minute, stealthily carrying out some dreadful task of which she and the sheriff and Lisa and the deputy were dangerously unaware.

'What about the second part of it?' Lisa asked, indicating THE ANCIENT ENEMY.

Jenny finally said, 'Well, we're back to what Lisa first said. It looks as if the man who wrote this was telling us that Timothy Flyte was his enemy. Our enemy, too, I guess.'

'Maybe,' Bryce Hammond said dubiously. 'But it seems like an unusual way to put it – "the ancient enemy". Kind of awkward. Almost archaic. If he locked himself in the bathroom to escape Flyte and then wrote a hasty warning, why wouldn't he say, "Timothy Flyte, my old enemy", or something straightforward?'

Lieutenant Whitman agreed. 'In fact, if he wanted to leave a message accusing Flyte, he'd have written, "Timothy Flyte did it", or maybe "Flyte killed them all". The *last* thing he'd want is to be obscure.'

The sheriff began sorting through the articles on the deep shelf that was above the sink, just under the mirror: a bottle of Mennen's Skin Conditioner, lime-scented aftershave, a man's electric razor, a pair of toothbrushes, toothpaste, combs, hairbrushes, a woman's makeup kit. 'From the looks of it, there were two people in this room. So maybe they both locked themselves in the bath – which means *two* of them vanished into thin air. But what did they write on the mirror with?'

'It looks as if it must've been an eyebrow pencil,' Lisa said.

Jenny nodded. 'I think so, too.'

They searched the bathroom for a black eyebrow pencil. They couldn't find it.

'Terrific,' the sheriff said exasperatedly. 'So the eyebrow pencil disappeared along with maybe two people who locked themselves in here. Two people kidnapped out of a locked room.'

They went downstairs to the front desk. According to the guest register, the room in which the message had been found was occupied by a Mr and Mrs Harold Ordnay of San Francisco.

'None of the other guests was named Timothy Flyte,' Sheriff Hammond said, closing the register.

'Well,' Lieutenant Whitman said, 'I guess that's about all we can do here right now.'

Jenny was relieved to hear him say that.

'Okay,' Bryce Hammond said. 'Let's catch up with Frank and the others. Maybe they've found something we haven't.'

They started across the lobby. After a couple of steps, Lisa stopped them with a scream.

They all saw it a second after it caught the girl's attention. It was on an end table, directly in the fall of light from a rose-shaded lamp, so prettily lit that it seemed almost like a piece of artwork on display. A man's hand. A severed hand.

Lisa turned away from the macabre sight.

Jenny held her sister, looking over Lisa's shoulder with ghastly fascination. The hand. The damned, mocking, impossible hand.

It was holding an eyebrow pencil firmly between its thumb and first two fingers. *The* eyebrow pencil. The same one. It *had* to be.

Jenny's horror was as great as Lisa's, but she bit her lip and suppressed a scream. It wasn't merely the sight of the hand that repelled and terrified her. The thing that made the breath catch and burn in her chest was the fact that this hand hadn't been on this end table a short while ago. Someone had placed it here while they were upstairs, knowing that they would find it; someone was mocking them, someone with an extremely twisted sense of humour.

Bryce Hammond's hooded eyes were open further than Jenny had yet seen them. 'Dammit, this thing wasn't here before – was it?'

'No,' Jenny said.

The sheriff and deputy had been carrying their revolvers with the muzzles pointed at the floor. Now they raised their weapons as if they thought the severed hand might drop the eyebrow pencil, launch itself off the table towards someone's face, and gouge out someone's eyes.

They were speechless.

The spiral patterns in the oriental carpet seemed to have become refrigeration coils, casting off waves of icy air.

Overhead, in a distant room, a floorboard or an unoiled door creaked, groaned, creaked.

Bryce Hammond looked up at the ceiling of the lobby.

Creeeeeaaak.

It could have been only a natural settling noise. Or it could have been something else.

'There's no doubt, now,' the sheriff said.

'No doubt about what?' Lieutenant Whitman asked, looking not at the sheriff but at other entrances to the lobby.

The sheriff turned to Jenny. 'When you heard the siren and the church bell just before we arrived, you said you realized that whatever had happened to Snowfield might still *be* happening.'

'Yes.'

'And now we know you're right.'

12

BATTLEGROUND

JAKE JOHNSON waited with Frank, Gordy, and Stu Wargle at the end of the block, on a brightly lit stretch of pavement in front of Gilmartin's Market, a grocery store.

He watched Bryce Hammond coming out of the Candleglow Inn, and wished to God the sheriff would move faster. He didn't like standing here in all this light. Hell, it was like being on stage. Jake felt vulnerable.

Of course, a few minutes ago, while conducting a search of some of the buildings along the street, they'd had to pass through dark areas where the shadows had seemed to pulse and move like living creatures, and Jake had looked with fierce longing towards this very same stretch of brightly lit pavement. He had feared the darkness as much as he now feared the light.

He nervously combed one hand through his thick white hair. He kept his other hand on the butt of his holstered revolver.

Jake Johnson not only believed in caution, he worshipped it – caution was his god. *Better safe than sorry; a bird in the hand is worth two in the bush; fools rush in where angels fear to tread* . . . He had a million maxims. They were, to him, lightposts marking the one safe route, and beyond those lights lay only a cold void of risk, chance and chaos.

Jake had never married. Marriage meant taking on a lot of new responsibilities. It meant risking your emotions and your money and your entire future.

Where finances were concerned, he had also lived a cautious, frugal existence. He had put away a rather substantial nest egg, spreading his funds over a wide variety of investments.

Jake, now fifty-eight, had worked for the Santa Mira County Sheriff's Department for over thirty-seven years. He could have retired and claimed a pension a long time ago. But he had worried about inflation, so he had stayed on, building his pension, putting away more and more money.

Becoming an officer of the law was perhaps the only incautious thing that Jake Johnson had ever done. He hadn't *wanted* to be a cop. God, no! But his father, Big Ralph Johnson, had been county sheriff in the 1940s and 50s, and he had expected his son to follow in his footsteps. Big Ralph never took no for an answer. Jake had been pretty sure that Big Ralph would disinherit him if he didn't go into police work. Not that there was a vast fortune in the family; there wasn't. But there had been a nice house and respectable bank accounts. And behind the family garage, buried three feet below the lawn, there had been several big mason jars filled with tightly rolled wads of twenty- and fifty- and hundred-dollar bills, money that Big Ralph had taken in bribes and had set aside against bad times. So Jake had become a cop like his daddy, who had finally died at the age of eighty-two, when Jake was fifty-one. By then Jake was stuck with being a cop for the rest of his working life because it was the only thing he knew.

He was a *cautious* cop. For instance, he avoided taking domestic disturbance calls because policemen sometimes got killed by step-ping between hot-tempered husbands and wives; passions ran too high in confrontations of that sort. Just look at this real estate agent, Fletcher Kale. A year ago, Jake had bought a piece of mountain property through Kale, and the man had seemed as normal as any-one. Now he had killed his wife and son. If a cop had stepped into that scene, Kale would have killed him, too. And when a dispatcher alerted Jake to a robbery-in-progress, he usually lied about his location, putting himself so far from the scene of the crime that other officers would be closer to it; then he showed up later, when the action was over.

He wasn't a coward. There had been times when he'd found himself in the line of fire, and on those occasions he'd been a tiger, a lion, a raging bear. He was just cautious.

There was some police work he actually enjoyed. The traffic detail was okay. And he positively delighted in paperwork. The only pleasure he took in making an arrest was the subsequent filling out of numerous forms that kept him safely tied up at headquarters for a couple of hours.

Unfortunately, this time, the trick of dawdling over paperwork had backfired on him. He'd been at the office, filling out forms, when Dr Paige's call had come in. If he'd been out on the street, driving patrol, he could have avoided the assignment.

But now here he was. Standing in bright light making a perfect target of himself. Damn.

To make matters worse, it was obvious that something extremely violent had transpired inside Gilmartin's Market. Two of the five large panes of glass along the front of the market had been broken from inside; glass lay all over the pavement. Cases of canned dog food and six-packs of Dr Pepper had crashed through the windows and now lay scattered across the pavement. Jake was afraid the sheriff was going to make them go into the market to see what had happened, and he was afraid that someone dangerous was still in there, waiting.

The sheriff, Tal Whitman, and the two women finally reached the market, and Frank Autry showed them the plastic container that held the sample of water. The sheriff said he'd found another enormous puddle back at Brookhart's, and they agreed it might mean something. Tal Whitman told them about the message on the mirror – and about the severed hand; sweet Jesus! – at the Candleglow Inn, and no one knew what to make of that, either.

110

Sheriff Hammond turned towards the shattered front of the market and said what Jake was afraid he would say: 'Let's have a look.'

Jake didn't want to be one of the first through the doors. Or one of the last either. He slipped into the middle of the procession.

The grocery store was a mess. Around the three cash registers, black metal display stands had been toppled. Chewing gum, candy, razor blades, paperback books, and other small items spilled over the floor.

They walked across the front of the store, looking into each aisle as they passed it. Goods had been pulled off the shelves and thrown to the floor. Boxes of cereal were smashed, torn open, the bright cardboard poking up through drifts of cornflakes and crispies. Smashed bottles of vinegar produced a pungent stench. Jars of jam, pickles, mustard, mayonnaise and relish were tumbled in a jagged, glutinous heap.

At the head of the last aisle, Bryce Hammond turned to Dr Paige. 'Would the store have been open this evening?'

'No,' the doctor said, 'but I think sometimes they stock the shelves on Sunday evenings. Not often, but sometimes.'

'Let's have a look in the back,' the sheriff said. 'Might find something interesting.'

That's what I'm afraid of, Jake thought.

They followed Bryce Hammond down the last aisle, stepping over and around five-pound bags of sugar and flour, a few of which had split open.

Waist-high coolers for meat, cheese, eggs, and milk were lined up along the rear of the store. Beyond the coolers lay the sparkling-clean work area where the meat was cut, weighed, and wrapped for sale.

Jake's eyes nervously flicked over the porcelain and butcher's-block tables. He sighed with relief when he saw that nothing lay on any of them. He wouldn't have been surprised to see the store manager's body neatly chopped into steaks, roasts, and cutlets.

111

Bryce Hammond said, 'Let's have a look in the storeroom.'

Let's not, Jake thought.

Hammond said, 'Maybe we—'

The lights went out.

The only windows were at the front of the store, but even up there it was dark; the streetlights had gone out, too. Here, the darkness was complete, blinding.

Several voices spoke at once:

'Flashlights!'

'Jenny!'

'Flashlights!'

Then a lot happened very fast.

Tal Whitman switched on a flashlight, and the bladelike beam stabbed down at the floor. In the same instant, something struck him from behind, something unseen that had approached with incredible speed and stealth under the cover of darkness. Whitman was flung forward. He crashed into Stu Wargle.

Autry was pulling the other long-handled flashlight from the utility loop on his gun belt. Before he could switch it on, however, both Wargle and Tal Whitman fell against him, and all three went down.

As Tal fell, the flashlight flew out of his hand.

Bryce Hammond, briefly illuminated by the airborne light, grabbed for it; missed.

The flashlight struck the floor and spun away, casting wild and leaping shadows with each revolution, illuminating nothing.

And something cold touched the back of Jake's neck. Cold and slightly moist – yet something that was *alive*.

He flinched at the touch, tried to pull away and turn.

Something encircled his throat with the suddenness of a whip.

Jake gasped for breath.

Even before he could raise his hands to grapple with his assailant, his arms were seized and pinned.

He was being lifted off his feet as if he were a child.

He tried to scream, but a frigid hand clamped over his mouth. At least he *thought* it was a hand. But it felt like the flesh of an eel, cold and damp.

It stank, too. Not much. It didn't send out clouds of stink. But the odour was so different from anything Jake had ever smelled before, so bitter and sharp and unclassifiable that even in small whiffs it was nearly intolerable.

Waves of revulsion and terror broke and foamed within him, and he sensed he was in the presence of something unimaginably strange and unquestionably evil.

The flashlight was still spinning across the floor. Only a couple of seconds had passed since Tal had dropped it, although to Jake it seemed much longer than that. Now it spun one last time and clanged against the base of the milk cooler; the lens burst into countless pieces, and they were denied even that meagre, erratic light. Although it had illuminated nothing, it had been better than total darkness. Without it, hope was extinguished, too.

Jake strained, twisted, flexed, jerked, and writhed in an epileptic dance of panic, a spasmodic fandango of escape. But he couldn't free even one hand. His unseen adversary merely tightened its grip.

Jake heard the others calling to one another, they sounded far away.

13

SUDDENLY

JAKE JOHNSON had disappeared.

Before Tal could locate the unbroken flashlight, the one that Frank Autry had dropped, the market's lights flickered and then came on bright and steady. The darkness had lasted no longer than fifteen or twenty seconds.

But Jake was gone.

They searched for him. He wasn't in the aisles, the meat locker, the storeroom, the office, or the employees' bathroom.

They left the market – only seven of them now – following Bryce, moving with extreme caution, hoping to find Jake outside, in the street, But he wasn't there, either.

Snowfield's silence was a mute, mocking shout of ridicule.

Tal Whitman thought the night seemed infinitely darker now than it had been a few minutes ago. It was an enormous maw into which they had stepped, unaware. This deep and watchful night was hungry.

'Where could he have gone?' Gordy asked, looking a little savage, as he always did when he frowned, even though, right now, he was actually just scared.

'He didn't go anywhere,' Stu Wargle said. 'He was *taken*.'

'He didn't call for help.'

'Never had a chance.'

'You think he's alive . . . or dead?' the young Paige girl asked.

'Little doll,' Wargle said, rubbing the beard stubble on his chin,

'I wouldn't get my hopes up if I was you. I'll bet my last buck we'll find Jake somewhere, stiff as a board, all swelled up and purple like the rest of 'em.'

The girl winced and sidled closer to her sister.

Bryce Hammond said, 'Hey, let's not write Jake off that quickly.'

'I agree,' Tal said. 'There *are* a lot of dead people in this town. But it seems to me that most of them *aren't* dead. Just missing.'

'They're all deader than napalmed babies. Isn't that right, Frank?' Wargle said, never missing a chance to needle Autry about his service in Vietnam. 'We just haven't found 'em yet.'

Frank didn't rise to the bait. He was too smart and too self-controlled for that. Instead, he said 'What I don't understand is why it didn't take all of us when it had the chance? Why did it just knock Tal down?'

'I was switching on the flashlight,' Tal said. 'It didn't want me to do that.'

'Yes,' Frank said, 'but why was Jake the only one of us it grabbed, and why did it do a fast fade right after?'

'It's teasing us,' Dr Paige said. The streetlamp made her eyes flash with green fire. 'It's like I said about the church bell and the fire siren. It's like a cat playing with mice.'

'But *why*?' Gordy asked exasperatedly. 'What's it get out of all this? What's it want?'

'Hold on a minute,' Bryce said. 'How come everyone's all of a sudden saying "it"? Last time I took an informal survey, seems to me the general consensus was that only a pack of psychopathic killers could've done this. Maniacs. *People.*'

They regarded one another with unease. No one was eager to say what was on his or her mind. Unthinkable things were now thinkable. They were things that reasonable people could not easily put into words.

The wind gusted out of the darkness, and the obeisant trees bent reverently.

The streetlamps flickered.

Everyone jumped, startled by the lights' inconsistency. Tal put his hand on the butt of his holstered revolver. But the lights did not go out.

They listened to the cemeterial town. The only sound was the whisper of the wind-stirred trees, like the last long exhalation of breath before the grave, an extended dying sigh.

Jake *is* dead, Tal thought. Wargle is right for once. Jake is dead and maybe the rest of us are, too, only we don't know it yet.

To Frank Autry, Bryce said, 'Frank, why'd you say "it" instead of "they" or something else?'

Frank glanced at Tal, seeking support, but Tal wasn't sure why he, himself, had said 'it'. Frank cleared his throat. He shifted his weight from one foot to the other and looked at Bryce. He shrugged. 'Well, sir, I guess I said "it" because . . . well . . . a soldier, a *human* adversary, would have blown us away right there in the market when he had the opportunity, all of us at once, in the darkness.'

'So you think – what? – that this adversary isn't human?'

'Maybe it could be some kind of . . . animal.'

'Animal? Is that really what you think?'

Frank looked exceedingly uncomfortable. 'No, sir.'

'What *do* you think?' Bryce asked.

'Hell, I don't *know* what to think,' Frank said in frustration. 'I'm military-trained, as you know. A military man doesn't like to plunge blindly into any situation. He likes to plan his strategy carefully. But good, sound strategic planning depends on a reliable body of experience. What happened in comparable battles in other wars? What have other men done in similar circumstances? Did they succeed or fail? But this time there just *aren't* any comparable battles; there's no experience to draw upon. This is so strange. I'm going to go right on thinking of the enemy as a faceless, neutral "it".'

Turning to Dr Paige, Bryce said, 'What about you? Why did you use the word "it"?'

'I'm not sure. Maybe because Officer Autry used it.'

'But you were the one who advanced the theory about a mutant strain of rabies that could create a pack of homicidal maniacs. Are you ruling that out now?'

She frowned. 'No. We can't rule out anything at this point. But, Sheriff, I never meant that that was the only possible theory.'

'Do you have any others?'

'No.'

Bryce looked at Tal. 'What about you?'

Tal felt every bit as uncomfortable as Frank had looked. 'Well, I guess I used "it" because I can't accept the homicidal maniac theory any more.'

Bryce's heavy eyelids lifted higher than usual. 'Oh? Why not?'

'Because of what happened at the Candleglow Inn,' Tal said. 'When we came downstairs and found that hand on the table in the lobby, holding the eyebrow pencil we'd been looking for . . . well . . . that just didn't seem like something a homicidal nutcase would *do*. We've all been cops long enough to've dealt with our share of unbalanced people. Have any of you ever encountered one of those types who had a sense of humour? Even an ugly, twisted sense of humour? They're humourless people. They've lost the ability to laugh at *anything*, which is probably part of the reason they're crazy. So when I saw that hand on the lobby table it just didn't seem to fit. I agree with Frank; for now I'm going to think of our enemy as a faceless "it".'

'Why won't any of you admit what you're feeling?' Lisa Paige said softly. She was fourteen, an adolescent, on her way to being a lovely young lady, but she gazed at each of them with the unselfconscious directness of a child. 'Somehow, deep down inside where it really counts, we all *know* it wasn't people who did these things. It's something really awful – Jeez, just *feel* it out there – something strange and disgusting. Whatever it is, we all *feel* it. We're all scared of it. So we're all trying hard not to admit it's there.'

Only Bryce returned the girl's stare; he studied her thoughtfully. The others looked away from Lisa. They didn't want to meet one another's eyes, either.

We don't want to look inside ourselves, Tal thought, and that's exactly what the girl's telling us to do. We don't want to look inward and find primitive superstition. We're all civilized, reasonably well-educated *adults*, and adults aren't supposed to believe in the bogeyman.

'Lisa's right,' Bryce said. 'The only way we're going to solve this one – maybe the only way we're going to avoid becoming victims ourselves – is to keep our minds open and let our imaginations have free rein.'

'I agree,' Dr Paige said.

Gordy Brogan shook his head. 'But what are we supposed to think, then? *Anything*? I mean, aren't there any limits? Are we supposed to start worrying about ghosts and ghouls and werewolves and . . . and vampires? There's got to be *some* things we can rule out.'

'Of course,' Bryce said patiently. 'Gordy, no one's saying we're dealing with ghosts and werewolves. But we've got to realize that we're dealing with the unknown. That's all. *The unknown*.'

'I don't buy it,' Stu Wargle said sullenly. 'The unknown, my ass. When it's all said and done, what we'll find is that it's the work of some pervert, some stinkin' scumbag pretty much like all the stinkin' scumbags we've dealt with before.'

Frank said, 'Wargle, your kind of thinking is exactly what'll cause us to overlook important evidence. And it's also the kind of thinking that'll get us killed.'

'You just wait,' Wargle told them. 'You'll find out I'm right.' He spat on the pavement, hooked his thumbs in his gun belt, and tried to give the impression that he was the only level-headed man in the group.

Tal Whitman saw through the macho posturing; he saw terror in

Wargle, too. Though he was one of the most insensitive men Tal had ever known, Stu was not unaware of the primitive response of which Lisa Paige had spoken. Whether he admitted it or not, he clearly felt the same bone-deep chill that shivered through all of them.

Frank Autry also saw that Wargle's imperturbability was a pose. In a tone of exaggerated, insincere admiration, Frank said, 'Stu, by your fine example, you fortify us. You inspire us. What would we do without you?'

'Without me,' Wargle said sourly, 'you'd go right down the old toilet, Frank.'

With mock dismay, Frank looked around at Tal, Gordy, and Bryce. 'Does that sound like a swelled head?'

'Sure does. But don't blame Stu. In his case,' Tal said, 'a swelled head is just a result of Nature's frenzied efforts to fill a vacuum.'

It was a small joke, but the laugh it elicited was large. Although Stu enjoyed wielding the needle, he despised being on the pricking end of it; yet even he managed to dredge up a smile.

Tal knew they were not laughing at the joke as much as they were laughing at Death, laughing in its skeletal face.

But when the laughter faded, the night was still dark.

The town was still unnaturally silent.

Jake Johnson was still missing.

And *it* was still out there.

Dr Paige turned to Bryce Hammond and said, 'Are you ready to take a look at the Oxley house?'

Bryce shook his head. 'Not right now. I don't think it's wise for us to do any more exploring until we get some reinforcements. I'm not going to lose another man. Not if I can help it.'

Tal saw anguish pass through Bryce's eyes at the mention of Jake.

He thought: Bryce, my friend, you always take too much of the responsibility when something goes wrong, just like you're always too quick to share the credit for successes that have been entirely yours.

'Let's go back to the substation,' Bryce said. 'We've got to plan our moves carefully, and I've got calls to make.'

They returned along the route by which they had come. Stu Wargle, still determined to prove his fearlessness, insisted on being the rear guard this time, and he swaggered along behind them.

As they reached Skyline Road, a church bell tolled, startling them. It tolled again, slowly, again, slowly, again . . .

Tal felt the metallic sound reverberating in his teeth.

They all stopped at the corner, listening to the bell and staring west, towards the other end of Vail Lane. Only a little more than one block away, a brick church tower rose above the other buildings; there was one small light at each corner of the peaked, slate belfry roof.

'The Catholic church,' Dr Paige informed them, raising her voice to compete with the bell. 'It serves all the towns around here. Our Lady of the Mountains.'

The pealing of a church bell could be a joyous music. But there was nothing joyous about this one, Tal decided.

'Who's ringing it?' Gordy wondered aloud.

'Maybe nobody's ringing it,' Frank said. 'Maybe it's hooked up to a mechanical device of some kind; maybe it's on a timer.'

In the lighted belfry, the bell swung, casting off a glint of brass along with its one clear note.

'Does it usually ring this time on a Sunday night?' Bryce asked Dr Paige.

'No.'

'Then it's not on a timer.'

A block away, high above the ground, the bell wink-flashed and rang again.

'So who's pulling the rope?' Gordy Brogan asked.

A macabre image crept into Tal Whitman's mind: Jake Johnson, bruised and bloated and stone-cold dead, standing in the bell-ringer's chamber at the bottom of the church tower, the rope gripped in his bloodless hands, dead but demonically animated, dead but nevertheless pulling on the rope, pulling and pulling, dead face turned up, grinning the wide mirthless grin of a corpse, protuberant eyes staring at the bell that swung and clanged under the peaked roof.

Tal shuddered.

'Maybe we should go over to the church and see who's there,' Frank said.

'No,' Bryce said instantly. 'That's what it wants us to do. It wants us to come have a look. It wants us to go inside the church, and then it'll turn out the lights again . . .'

Tal noticed that Bryce, too, was now using the pronoun 'it'.

'Yeah,' Lisa Paige said. 'It's over there right this minute, waiting for us.'

Even Stu Wargle wasn't prepared to encourage them to visit the church tonight.

In the open belfry, the visible bell swung, splintering off another shard of brassy light, swung, gleamed, swung, winked, as if flashing out a semaphoric message of hypnotic power at the same time that it issued its monotonous clang: *You are growing drowsy, even drowsier, sleepy, sleepy . . . you are deep asleep, in a trance . . . you are under my power . . . you will come to the church . . . you will come now, come, come, come to the church and see the wonderful surprise that awaits you here . . . come . . . come . . .*

Bryce shook himself as if casting off a dream. He said, 'If it wants us to come to the church, that's a good reason not to go. No more exploring until daylight.'

They all turned away from Vail Lane and went north on Skyline Road, past the Mountainview Restaurant, towards the substation.

They had gone perhaps twenty feet when the church bell stopped tolling.

121

Once more, the uncanny silence poured like viscous fluid through the town, coating everything.

When they reached the substation, they discovered that Paul Henderson's corpse was gone. It seemed us if the dead deputy had simply got up and walked away. Like Lazarus.

14

CONTAINMENT

BRYCE WAS sitting at the desk that had belonged to Paul Henderson. He had pushed aside the open issue of *Time* that Paul apparently had been reading when Snowfield had been wiped out. A yellow sheet of notepaper lay on the blotter, filled with Bryce's economical handwriting.

Around him, the six others were busily carrying out tasks that he had assigned to them. A wartime atmosphere prevailed in the stationhouse. Their grim determination to survive had caused a fragile but steadily strengthening camaraderie to spring up among them. There was even guarded optimism, perhaps based on the observation that they were still alive while so many others were dead.

Bryce quickly scanned the list he had made, trying to determine if he had overlooked anything. Finally, he pulled the telephone to him. He got a dial tone immediately, and he was grateful for it, considering Jennifer Paige's difficulties in that field.

He hesitated before placing the first call. A sense of the immense importance of the moment weighed heavily on him. The savage obliteration of Snowfield's entire population was like nothing that had ever happened before. Within hours, journalists would be coming to Santa Mira County by the scores, by the hundreds, from all over the world. By morning, the Snowfield story would have pushed all other news off the front pages. CBS, ABC and NBS would all be interrupting regularly scheduled broadcasts for updates and bulletins throughout the duration of the crisis. The media coverage would be intense. Until the world knew whether or not some mutated germ had a role in the events here, hundreds of millions of people would wait breathlessly, wondering if their own death notices had been issued in Snowfield. Even if disease were ruled out, the world's attention wouldn't be diverted from Snowfield until the mystery had been explained. The pressure to find a solution was going to be unbearable.

On a personal level, Bryce's own life would be forever changed. He was in charge of the police contingent; therefore, he would be featured in all the news stories. That prospect appalled him. He wasn't the kind of sheriff who liked to grandstand. He preferred to keep a low profile.

But he couldn't just walk away from Snowfield now.

He dialled the emergency number at his own offices in Santa Mira, bypassing the switchboard operator. The desk sergeant on duty was Charlie Mercer, a good man who could be counted on to do precisely what he was told to do.

Charlie answered the phone halfway through the second ring. 'Sheriff's Department.' He had a flat, nasal voice.

'Charlie, this is Bryce Hammond.'

'Yes, sir. We've been wondering what's happening up there.'

Bryce succinctly outlined the situation in Snowfield.

'Good God!' Charlie said. 'Jake's dead, too?'

'We don't know for sure that he's dead. We can hope not. Now listen, Charlie, there are a lot of things we've got to do in the next couple of hours, and it would be easier for all of us if we could maintain secrecy until we've established our base here and secured the perimeters. *Containment*, Charlie. That's the key word. Snowfield has to be sealed off tight, and that'll be a lot easier to accomplish if we can do it before the newsmen start tramping through the mountains. I know I can count on you to keep your mouth shut, but there are a few of the men . . .'

'Don't worry,' Charlie said. 'We can hold it close to the vest for a couple of hours.'

'All right. First thing I want is twelve more men. Two more on the roadblock at the Snowfield turnoff. Ten here with me. Wherever you can, select single men without families.'

'It really looks that bad?'

'It really does. And better select men who don't have relatives in Snowfield. Another thing: they'll have to bring a couple of days' worth of drinking water and food. I don't want them consuming anything in Snowfield until we know for sure that the stuff is safe here.'

'Right.'

'Every man should bring his sidearm, a riot gun, and tear gas.'

'Got it.'

'This'll leave you short-handed, and it'll get worse when the media people start pouring in. You'll have to call in some of the auxiliary deputies for directing traffic and crowd control. Now, Charlie, you know this part of the country pretty well – don't you?'

'I was born and raised in Pineville.'

'That's what I thought. I've been looking at the county map, and so far as I can see, there are only two passable routes into Snowfield. First, there's the highway, which we've already blockaded.'

He swivelled on his chair and stared at the huge, framed map on the wall.

'Then there's an old fire trail that leads about two-thirds of the way up the other side of the mountain. Where the fire trail leaves off, an established wilderness trail seems to pick up. It's just a footpath from that point, but from the way it looks on the map, it comes out smack-dab at the top of the longest ski-run on this side of the mountain, up here above Snowfield.'

'Yeah,' Charlie said. 'I've backpacked through that neck of the woods. It's officially the Old Mount Greentree Wilderness Trail. Or as we locals used to call it – the Muscle Lineament Highway.'

'We'll have to station a couple of men at the bottom of the fire trail and turn back anyone who tries to come in that way.'

'It would take one hell of a determined reporter to try it.'

'We can't take chances. Are you aware of any other route that isn't on the map?'

'Nope,' Charlie said. 'Otherwise, you'd have to come into Snowfield straight overland, making your own trail every damned step of the way. That *is* wilderness out there; it's not just a playground for weekend campers, by God. No experienced backpacker would try to come overland. That'd be plain stupid.'

'All right. Something else I need is a phone number from the files. Remember that law enforcement seminar I went to in Chicago . . . oh . . . about sixteen months ago. One of the speakers was an army man. Copperfield, I think. General Copperfield.'

'Sure,' Charlie said. 'The Army Medical Corps' CBW Division.'

'That's it.'

'I think they call Copperfield's office the Civilian Defence Unit. Hold on.' Charlie was off the line less than a minute. He came back with the number, read it to Bryce. 'That's out in Dugway, Utah. Jesus, do you think this could be something that'd bring those boys running? That's scary.'

'Real scary,' Bryce agreed. 'A couple of other things. I want you to put a name on the teletype. Timothy Flyte.' Bryce spelled it. 'No description. No known address. Find out if he's wanted anywhere. Check with the FBI, too. Then find out all you can about a Mr and Mrs Harold Ordnay of San Francisco.' He gave Charlie the address that had been in the Candleglow Inn's guest register. 'One more thing. When those new men come up here, have them bring some plastic body bags from the county morgue.'

'How many?'

'To start with . . . two hundred.'

'Uh . . . two . . . *hundred?*'

'We might need a great many more than that before we're

through. We might have to borrow from other counties. Better check that out. A lot of people seem just to've disappeared, but their bodies may still turn up. There were about five hundred people living here. We could possibly need that many body bags.'

And maybe even more than five hundred, Bryce thought. Because we might need a few bags for ourselves, too.

Although Charlie had listened attentively when Bryce told him that the entire town had been wiped out, and although there was no doubt that he believed Bryce, he obviously hadn't fully, *emotionally* comprehended the awful dimensions of the disaster until he'd heard the request for two hundred body bags. An image of all those corpses, sealed in opaque plastic, stacked atop one another in Snowfield's streets – that was what had finally pierced him.

'Holy Mother of God . . .' Charlie Mercer whispered.

While Bryce Hammond was on the telephone to Charlie Mercer, Frank and Stu started to dismantle the hulking, policeband radio that stood against the back wall of the room. Bryce had told them to find out what was wrong with the set, for there weren't any visible signs of damage.

The front plate was fastened down by ten tightly turned screws. Frank worked them loose one at a time.

As usual, Stu wasn't much help. He kept glancing around at Dr Paige, who was at the other end of the room, working with Tal Whitman on another project.

'She's sure a sweet piece of meat,' Stu said, casting a covetous look at the doctor and picking his nose at the same time.

Frank said nothing.

Stu looked at what he'd pried out of his nose, inspecting it as if it were a pearl found in an oyster. He glanced back at the doctor again. 'Look at the way she fills out them jeans. Christ, I'd love to dip my wick in that.'

Frank stared at the three screws he'd removed from the radio and counted to ten, resisting the urge to drive one of the screws straight into Stu's thick skull. 'You aren't stupid enough to make a pass at her, I hope.'

'Why not? That's a hot number if ever I did see one.'

'You try it, and the sheriff'll kick your ass.'

'He don't spook me.'

'You amaze me, Stu. How can you be thinking about sex right now? Hasn't it occurred to you that we all might die here, tonight, maybe even in the next minute or two?'

'All the more reason to make a play for her if I get a chance,' Wargle said. 'I mean, shit, if we're livin' on borrowed time, who cares? Who wants to die limp? Right? Even the other one's nice.'

'The other what?'

'The girl, the kid,' Stu said.

'She's only fourteen.'

'Sweet stuff.'

'She's a *child*, Wargle.'

'She plenty old enough.'

'That's sick.'

'Wouldn't you like to have her firm little legs wrapped around you, Frank?'

The screwdriver slipped out of the notch on the head of the screw and skidded across the metal cover plate with a stuttering screech.

In a voice which was nearly inaudible but which nevertheless froze Wargle's grin, Frank said, 'If I ever hear of you laying one filthy finger on that girl or on any other young girl, anywhere, any-time, I won't just help press charges against you; *I'll come after you*. I know how to go after a man, Wargle. I wasn't just a desk jockey in Nam. I was in the field. And I still know how to handle myself. I know how to handle *you*. You hear me? You believe me?'

For a moment Wargle was unable to speak. He just stared into Frank's eyes.

Conversations drifted over from other parts of the big room, but none of the words were clear. Still, it was obvious that no one realized what was happening by the radio.

Wargle finally blinked and licked his lips and looked down at his shoes and then looked up and put on an aw-shucks grin. 'Hey, gee, Frank, don't get sore. Don't get so riled up. I didn't *mean* it.'

'You believe me?' Frank insisted.

'Sure, sure. But I tell you I didn't mean nothin'. I was just shootin' off at the mouth. Locker room talk. You know how it is. You know I didn't mean it. Am I some kind of pervert, for God's sake? Hey, come on, Frank, lighten up. Okay?'

Frank stared at him a moment longer, then said, 'Let's get this radio dismantled.'

Tal Whitman opened the tall metal gun locker.

Jenny Paige said, 'Good heavens, it's a regular arsenal.'

He passed the weapons to her, and she lined them up on a nearby work table.

The locker seemed to contain an excessive amount of firepower for a town like Snowfield. Two high-powered rifles with sniper scopes. Two semi-automatic shotguns. Two non-lethal riot guns, which were specially modified shotguns that fired only soft plastic pellets. Two flare guns. Two rifles that fired tear gas grenades. Three handguns: a pair of .38s and a big Smith & Wesson .357 Magnum.

As the lieutenant piled boxes of ammunition on the table, Jenny gave the Magnum a close inspection. 'This is a real monster, isn't it?'

'Yeah. You could stop a Brahman bull with that one.'

'Looks as if Paul kept everything in first-rate condition.'

'You handle guns like you know all about them,' the lieutenant said, putting more ammunition on the table.

'Always hated guns. Never thought I'd own one,' she said. 'But after I'd been living up here three months, we started having trouble

129

with a motorcycle gang that decided to set up a sort of summer retreat on some land out along the Mount Larson Road.'

'The Demon Chrome.'

'That's them,' Jenny said. 'Rough-looking crowd.'

'That's putting it kindly.'

'A couple of times, when I was making a house call at night, over to Mount Larson or Pineville, I got an unwanted motorcycle escort. They rode on each side of the car, too close for safety, grinning in the side windows at me, shouting at me, waving, being foolish. They didn't actually try anything, but it sure was . . .'

'Threatening.'

'You said it. So I bought a gun, learned how to shoot it, and got a permit to carry.'

The lieutenant began to open the boxes of ammunition. 'Ever have occasion to use it?'

'Well,' she said, 'I never had to shoot anyone, thank God. But I did have to show it once. It was just after dark. I was on my way to Mount Larson, and the Demons gave me another escort, but this time it was different. Four of them boxed me in, and they all started slowing down, forcing me to slow down, too. Finally, they brought me to a complete stop in the middle of the road.'

'That must've given your heart a good workout.'

'Did it ever! One of the Demons got off his bike. He was big, maybe six feet three or four, with long curly hair and a beard. He wore a bandanna around his head. And one gold earring. He looked like a pirate.'

'Did he have a red and yellow eye tattooed on the palm of each hand?'

'Yes! Well, at least on the palm he put against the car window when he was looking in at me.'

The lieutenant leaned against the table on which they had placed the guns. 'His name's Gene Terr. He's the leader of the Demon Chrome. They don't come much meaner. He's been in the slammer two or three times but never for anything serious and never for long. Whenever it looks as if Jeeter's going to have to do hard time, one of his people takes the blame for all the charges. He has an incredible hold on his followers. They'll do anything he wants; it's almost as if they worship him. Even after they're in jail, Jeeter takes care of them, smuggling money and drugs in to them, and they stay faithful to him. He knows we can't touch him, so he's always infuriatingly polite and helpful to us, pretending to be an upstanding citizen; it's a big joke to him. Anyway, Jeeter came over to your car and looked in at you?'

'Yes. He wanted me to get out, and I wouldn't. He said I should at least roll down the window, so we wouldn't have to shout to hear each other. I said I didn't mind shouting a little. He threatened to smash the window if I didn't roll it down. I knew if I did, he'd reach right inside and unlock the door, so I figured it was better to get out of the car willingly. I told him I'd come out if he'd back off a little. He stepped away from the door, and I snatched the gun from under the seat. As soon as I opened the door and got out, he tried to move in on me. I jammed the muzzle into his belly. The hammer was pulled back, fully cocked; he saw that right away.'

'God, I wish I'd seen the look on his face!' Lieutenant Whitman said, grinning.

'I was scared to death,' Jenny said, remembering. 'I mean, I was scared of him, of course, but I was also scared I might have to pull the trigger. I wasn't even sure I *could* pull the trigger. But I knew I couldn't let Jeeter see I had any doubts.'

'If he'd seen, he'd have eaten you alive.'

'That's what I thought. So I was very cold, very firm. I told him that I was a doctor, that I was on my way to see a very sick patient, and that I didn't intend to be detained. I kept my voice low. The other three men were still on their bikes, and from where they were, they couldn't see the gun or hear exactly what I was saying. This Jeeter looked like the type who'd rather die than let anyone see him take any orders from a woman, so I didn't want to embarrass him and maybe make him do something foolish.'

The lieutenant shook his head. 'You sure had him pegged right.'

'I also reminded him that *he* might need a doctor some day. What if he took a spill off that bike of his and was lying on the road, critically injured, and *I* was the doctor who showed up – after he'd hurt me and given me good reason to hurt him in return? I told him there are things a doctor can do to complicate injuries, to make sure the patient has a long and painful recovery. I asked him to think about that.'

Whitman gaped at her.

She said, 'I don't know if that unsettled him or whether it was simply the gun, but he hesitated, then made a big scene for the benefit of his three buddies. He told them I was a friend of a friend. He said he'd met me once, years ago, but hadn't recognized me at first. I was to be given every courtesy the Demon Chrome could extend. No one would ever bother me, he said. Then he climbed back on his Harley and rode away, and the other three followed him.'

'And you just went on to Mount Larson?'

'What else? I still had a patient to see.'

'Incredible.'

'I will admit, though, I had the sweats and the shakes all the way to Mount Larson.'

'And no biker has ever bothered you since?'

'In fact, when they pass me on the roads around here, they all smile and wave.'

Whitman laughed.

Jenny said, 'So there's the answer to your question. Yes, I know how to use a gun, but I hope I never have to shoot anyone.'

She looked at the .357 Magnum in her hand, scowled, opened a box of ammunition, and began to load the revolver.

The lieutenant took a couple of shells from another carton and loaded a shotgun.

132

They were silent for a moment, and then he said, 'Would you have done what you told Gene Terr?'

'What? Shot him?'

'No. I mean, if he'd hurt you, maybe raped you, and then if you'd later had a chance to treat him as a patient . . . would you have . . . ?'

Jenny finished loading the Magnum, clicked the cylinder into place, and put the gun down. 'Well, I'd be tempted. But on the other hand, I have enormous respect for the Hippocratic Oath. So . . . well . . . I suppose this means I'm just a wimp at heart – but I'd give Jeeter the best medical care I could.'

'I knew you'd say that.'

'I talk tough, but I'm just a marshmallow inside.'

'Like hell, he said. The way you stood up to him took about as much toughness as *anybody* has. But if he'd hurt you, and if you'd later abused your trust as a doctor just to get even with him . . . well, that would be different.'

Jenny looked up from the .38 that she'd just taken from the array of weapons on the table, and she met the black man's eyes. They were clear, probing eyes.

'Dr Paige, you have what we call "the right stuff". If you want, you can call me Tal. Most people do. It's short for Talbert.'

'All right, Tal. And you can call me Jenny.'

'Well, I don't know about that.'

'Oh? Why not?'

'You're a doctor and all. My Aunt Becky – she's the one who raised me – always had great respect for doctors. It just seems funny to be calling a doctor by his . . . by *her* first name.'

'Doctors are people too, you know. And considering that we're all in sort of a pressure cooker here—'

'Just the same,' he said, shaking his head.

'If it bothers you, then call me what most of my patients call me.'

'What's that?'

'Just plain Doc.'

'Doc?' He thought about it, and a slow smile spread over his face. 'Doc. It makes you think of one of those grizzled, cantankerous old coots that Barry Fitzgerald used to play in the movies, way back in the thirties and forties.'

'Sorry I'm not grizzled.'

'That's okay. You're not an old coot, either.'

She laughed softly.

'I like the irony of it,' Whitman said. 'Doc. Yeah, and when I think of you jamming that revolver in Gene Terr's belly, it fits.'

They loaded two more guns.

'Tal, why all these weapons for a little substation in a town like Snowfield?'

'If you want to get state and federal matching funds for the county law enforcement budget, you've got to meet their requirements for all sorts of ridiculous things. One of the specifications is for minimal arsenals in substations like this. Now ... well ... maybe we should be glad we've got all this hardware.'

'Except so far we haven't seen anything to shoot at.'

'I suspect we will,' Tal said. 'And I'll tell you something.'

'What's that?'

His broad, dark, handsome face looked unsettlingly dour. 'I don't think you'll have to worry about having to shoot other people. Somehow, I don't believe it's *people* we have to worry about.'

Bryce dialled the private, unlisted number at the governor's residence in Sacramento. He talked to a maid who insisted the governor couldn't come to the phone, not even to take a life-and-death call from an old friend. She wanted Bryce to leave a message. Then he talked to the chief of the household staff, who also wanted him to leave a message. Then, after being put on hold, he talked to Gary Poe, Governor Jack Retlock's chief political aide and advisor.

'Bryce,' Gary said, 'Jack just can't come to the phone right now.

There's an important dinner underway here. The Japanese trade minister and the counsel general from San Francisco.'

'Gary—'

'We're trying damned hard to get that new Japanese-American electronics plant for California, and we're afraid it's going to go to Texas or Arizona or maybe even New York. Jesus, New York!'

'Gary—'

'Why would they even consider New York, with all the labour problems and the tax rates what they are back there? Sometimes I think—'

'Gary, shut up.'

'Huh?'

Bryce never snapped at anyone. Even Gary Poe – who could talk faster and louder than a carnival barker – was shocked into silence.

'Gary, this is an emergency. Get Jack for me.'

Sounding hurt, Poe said, 'Bryce, I'm authorized to—'

'I've got a hell of a lot to do in the next hour or two, Gary. If I live long enough to do it, that is. I can't spend fifteen minutes laying this whole thing out for you and then another fifteen laying it out again for Jack. Listen, I'm in Snowfield. It appears as if everyone who lived here is dead, Gary.'

'What?'

'Five hundred people.'

'Bryce, if this is some sort of joke or—'

'Five hundred dead. And that's the least of it. Now will you for Christ's sake get Jack?'

'But Bryce, five hundred—'

'*Get Jack, dammit!*'

Poe hesitated, then said, 'Old buddy, this better be the straight shit.' He dropped the phone and went for the governor.

Bryce had known Jack Retlock for seventeen years. When he joined the Los Angeles police, he had been assigned to Jack for his rookie year. At that time, Jack was a seven-year veteran of the force, a seasoned hand. Indeed, Jack had seemed so savvy and streetwise that Bryce had despaired of ever being even half as good at the job. In a year, however, he was better. They voted to stay together, partners. But eighteen months later, fed up with a legal system that regularly turned loose the punks he worked so hard to imprison, Jack quit police work and went into politics. As a cop, he'd collected a fistful of citations for bravery. He parlayed his hero image into a seat on the LA city council, then ran for mayor, winning in a landslide. From there, he'd jumped into the governor's chair. It was a far more impressive career than Bryce's own halting progress to the sheriff's post in Santa Mira, but Jack always was the more aggressive of the two.

'Doody? Is that you?' Jack asked, picking up the phone in Sacramento.

Doody was his nickname for Bryce. He'd always said that Bryce's sandy hair, freckles, wholesome face, and marionette eyes made him look like Howdy Doody.

'It's me, Jack.'

'Gary's raving some lunatic nonsense—'

'It's true,' Bryce said.

He told Jack all about Snowfield.

After listening to the entire story, Jack took a deep breath and said, 'I wish you were a drinking man, Doody.'

'This isn't booze talking, Jack. Listen, the first thing I want is—'

'National Guard?'

'No!' Bryce said. 'That's exactly what I want to avoid as long as we have any choice.'

'If I don't use the Guard and every agency at my disposal, and then if it later turns out I should've sent them in first thing, my ass will be grass, and there'll be a herd of hungry cows all around me.'

'Jack, I'm counting on you to make the right decisions, not just the right *political* decisions. Until we know more about the situation, we don't want hordes of Guardsmen tramping around up here. They're great for helping out in a flood, a postal strike, that sort of thing. But they're not full-time military men. They're shoe salesmen and attorneys and carpenters and school teachers. This calls for a tightly controlled, efficient little police action, and that sort of thing can be conducted only by real cops, full-time cops.'

'And if your men can't handle it?'

'Then I'll be the first to yell for the Guard.'

Finally Retlock said, 'Okay. No Guardsmen. For now.'

Bryce sighed. 'And I want to keep the State Health Department out of here, too.'

'Doody, be reasonable. How can I do that? If there's any chance that a contagious disease has wiped out Snowfield – or some kind of environmental poisoning—'

'Listen, Jack, Health does a fine job when it comes to tracking down and controlling vectors for outbreaks of plague or mass food poisoning or water contamination. But essentially, they're bureaucrats; they move slowly. We can't *afford* to move slowly on this. I have the gut feeling that we're living strictly on borrowed time. All hell could break loose at any moment; in fact, I'll be surprised if it doesn't. Besides, the Health Department doesn't have the equipment to handle it, and they don't have a contingency plan to cover the death of an entire town. But there's someone who does, Jack. The Army Medical Corps' CBW Division has a relatively new programme they call the Civilian Defence Unit.'

'CBW Division?' Retlock asked. There was a new tension in his voice. 'You don't mean the chemical and biological warfare boys?'

'Yes.'

'Christ, you don't think it has anything to do with nerve gas or germ war—'

'Probably not,' Bryce said, thinking of the Liebermanns' severed heads, of the creepy feeling that had overcome him inside the covered passageway, of the incredible suddenness with which Jake

137

Johnson had vanished. 'But I don't know enough about it to rule out CBW or anything else.'

A hard edge of anger had crystallised in the governor's voice. 'If the damned army has been careless with one of its fucking dooms-day viruses, I'm going to have their heads!'

'Easy, Jack. Maybe it's not an accident. Maybe it's the work of terrorists who got their hands on a sample of some CBW agent. Or maybe it's the Russians running a little test of our CBW analysis and defence system. It was to handle those kinds of situations that the Army Medical Corps instructed its CBW Division to create General Copperfield's office.'

'Who's Copperfield?'

'General Galen Copperfield. He's the commanding officer of the Civilian Defence Unit of the CBW Division. This is precisely the kind of situation they want to be notified about. Within hours, Copperfield can put a team of well-trained scientists into Snowfield. First-rate biologists, virologists, bacteriologists, pathologists with training in the very latest forensic medicine, at least one immunolo-gist and biochemist, a neurologist – and even a neuropsychologist. Copperfield's department has designed elaborate mobile field labo-ratories. They've got them garaged at depots all over the country, so there must be one relatively close to us. Hold off the State Health gang, Jack. They don't have people of the calibre that Copperfield can provide, and they don't have state-of-the-art diagnostic equip-ment as mobile as Copperfield's. I want to call the general; I *am* going to call him, in fact, but I'd prefer to have your agreement and your guarantee that state bureaucrats won't be tramping around here, interfering.'

After a brief hesitation, Jack Retlock said, 'Doody, what kind of world have we let it become when things like Copperfield's depart-ment are even necessary?'

'You'll hold off Health?'

'Yes. What else do you need?'

Bryce glanced down at the list in front of him. 'You could approach the telephone company about pulling the Snowfield circuits off automatic switching. When the world finds out what's happened up here, every phone in town will be ringing off the hook, and we won't be able to maintain essential communications. If they could route all calls to and from Snowfield through a few special operators and weed out the crank stuff and—'

'I'll handle it,' Jack said.

'Of course, we could lose the phones at any time. Dr Paige had trouble getting a call out when she first tried, so I'll need a short-wave set. The one here at the substation seems to've been sabotaged.'

'I can get you a mobile shortwave unit, a van that has its own gasoline generator. The Office of Earthquake Preparedness has a couple. Anything else?'

'Speaking of generators, it'd be nice if we didn't have to depend on the public power supply. Evidently, our enemy here can tamper with it at will. Could you get two big generators for us?'

'Can do. Anything else?'

'If I think of anything, I won't hesitate to ask.'

'Let me tell you, Bryce, as a friend, I hate like hell to see you in the middle of this one. But as a governor, I'm damned glad it fell in your jurisdiction, whatever the hell it is. There are some prize assholes out there who'd already have screwed it up if it'd fallen in *their* laps. By now, if it was a disease, they'd have spread it to half the state. We sure can use you up there.'

'Thanks, Jack.'

They were both silent for a moment.

Then Retlock said, 'Doody?'

'Yeah, Jack.'

'Watch out for yourself.'

'I will, Jack,' Bryce said. 'Well, I've got to get on to Copperfield. I'll call you later.'

The governor said, 'Please do that, Bryce. Call me later. Don't *you* vanish, old buddy.'

Bryce put down the phone and looked around the substation. Stu Wargle and Frank were removing the front access plate from the radio. Tal and Dr Paige were loading guns. Gordy Brogan and young Lisa Paige, the biggest and the smallest of the group, were making coffee and putting food on one of the work tables.

Even in the midst of disaster, Bryce thought, even here in the Twilight Zone, we have to have our coffee and supper. Life goes on.

He picked up the receiver to call Copperfield's number out at Dugway, Utah.

There was no dial tone.

He jiggled the disconnect button.

'Hello,' he said.

Nothing.

Bryce sensed someone or something listening. He could feel the presence, just as Dr Paige had described it.

'Who is this?' he asked.

He didn't really expect an answer, but he got one. It wasn't a voice. It was a peculiar yet familiar sound; the cry of birds, perhaps gulls; yes, seagulls shrieking high above a windswept shoreline.

It changed. It became a clattering sound. A rattle. Like beans in a hollow gourd. The warning sound of a rattlesnake. Yes, no doubt about it. The very distinct sound of a rattlesnake.

And then it changed again. Electronic buzzing. No, not electronic. Bees. Bees buzzing, swarming.

And now the cry of gulls once more.

And the call of another bird, a trilling musical voice.

And panting. Like a tired dog.

And snarling. Not a dog. Something larger.

And the hissing and spitting of fighting cats.

Although there was nothing especially menacing about the

sounds themselves — except, perhaps, for the rattlesnake and the snarling — Bryce was chilled by them.

The animal noises ceased.

Bryce waited, listened, said, 'Who is this?'

No answer.

'What do you want?'

Another sound came over the wire, and it pierced Bryce as if it were a dagger of ice. Screams. Men and women and children. More than a few of them. Dozens, scores. Not stage screams; not make-believe terror. They were the stark, shocking cries of the damned: screams of agony, fear, and soul-searing despair.

Bryce felt sick.

His heart raced.

It seemed to him that he had an open line to the bowels of Hell.

Were these the cries of Snowfield's dead, captured on a record-ing tape? By whom? Why? Is it live or is it Memorex?

One final scream. A child. A little girl. She cried out in terror, then in pain, then in unimaginable suffering, as if she were being torn apart. Her voice rose, spiralled up and up—

Silence.

The silence was even worse than the screaming because the unnamable presence was still on the line, and Bryce could feel it more strongly now. He was stricken by an awareness of pure, unre-lenting evil.

It was there.

He quickly put down the phone.

He was shaking. He had not been in any danger — yet he was shaking.

He looked around the bull pen. The others were still busy with the tasks he had assigned to them. Apparently, no one had noticed that his most recent session on the phone had been far different from those that had gone before it.

Sweat trickled down the back of his neck.

Eventually, he would have to tell the others what had happened. But not right now. Because right now he couldn't trust his voice. They would surely hear the nervous flutter, and they would know that this strange experience had badly shaken him.

Until reinforcements arrived, until their foothold in Snowfield was more firmly established, until they all felt less afraid, it wasn't wise to let the others see him shaking with dread. They looked to him for leadership, after all; he didn't intend to disappoint them.

He took a deep, cleansing breath.

He picked up the receiver and immediately got a dial tone.

Immensely relieved, he called the CBW Civilian Defence Unit in Dugway, Utah.

Lisa liked Gordy Brogan.

At first he had seemed menacing and sullen. He was such a big man, and his hands were so enormous they made you think of the Frankenstein monster. His face was rather handsome, actually, but when he frowned, even if he wasn't angry, even if he was just worrying about something or thinking especially hard, his brows knitted together in a fierce way, and his black-black eyes grew even blacker than usual, and he looked like doom itself.

A smile transformed him. It was the most astonishing thing. When Gordy smiled, you knew right away that you were seeing the *real* Gordy Brogan. You knew that the other Gordy – the one you *thought* you saw when he frowned or when his face was in repose – was purely a figment of your imagination. His warm, wide smile drew your attention to the kindness shining in his eyes, the gentleness in his broad brow.

When you got to know him, he was like a big puppy, eager to be liked. He was one of those rare adults who could talk to a kid without being self-conscious or condescending or patronising. He was even better in that regard than Jenny. And even under the current circumstances, he could laugh.

As they put the food on the table – luncheon meat, bread, cheese, fresh fruit, doughnuts – and brewed the coffee, Lisa said, 'You just don t seem like a cop to me.'

'Oh?' Gordy said. 'What's a cop supposed to seem like?'

'Whoops. Did I say the wrong thing? Is "cop" an offensive word?'

'In some quarters, it is. Like in prisons, for instance.'

She was amazed that she still could laugh after everything that had happened this evening. She said 'Seriously. What do officers of the law prefer to be called? Policemen?'

'It doesn't matter. I'm a deputy, policeman, cop – whatever you like. Except you think I don't really look the part.'

'Oh, you look the part all right,' Lisa said. 'Especially when you scowl. But you don't *seem* like a cop.'

'What do I seem like to you?'

'Let me think.' She took an immediate interest in this game, for it diverted her mind from the nightmare around her. 'Maybe you seem like . . . a young minister.'

'*Me*?'

'Well, in the pulpit, you'd be just fantastic delivering a fire-and-brimstone sermon. And I can see you sitting in a parsonage, an encouraging smile on your face, listening to people's problems.'

'Me, a minister,' he said, clearly astonished. 'With that imagination of yours, you should be a writer when you grow up.'

'I think I should be a doctor like Jenny. A doctor can do so much good.' She paused. 'You know why you don't seem like a cop? It's because I can't picture you using *that*.' She pointed at his revolver. 'I can't picture you shooting someone. Not even if he deserved it.'

She was startled by the expression that came over Gordy Brogan's face. He was visibly shocked.

Before she could ask what was wrong, the lights flickered.

She looked up.

The lights flickered again. And again.

She glanced at the front windows. Outside, the streetlights were blinking, too.

No, she thought. No, please, God, not again. Don't throw us into darkness again; please, *please*!

The lights went out.

15

THE THING AT THE WINDOW

BRYCE HAMMOND had spoken to the night-duty officer manning the emergency line at the CBW Civilian Defence Unit at Dugway, Utah. He hadn't needed to say much before he'd been patched through to General Galen Copperfield's home number. Copperfield had listened, but he hadn't said much. Bryce wanted to know whether it seemed at all likely that a chemical or biological agent had caused Snowfield's agony and obliteration. Copperfield said, 'Yes.' But that was all he *would* say. He warned Bryce that they were speaking on an unsecured telephone line, and he made vague but stern references to classified information and security clearances. When he'd heard all of the essentials but only a few details, he cut Bryce off rather curtly and suggested they discuss the rest of it when they met face to face. 'I've heard enough to be convinced that my organization should be involved.' He promised to send a field lab and a team of investigators into Snowfield by dawn or shortly thereafter.

Bryce was putting down the receiver when the lights flickered, dimmed, flickered, wavered – and went out.

He fumbled for the flashlight on the desk in front of him, found it, and switched it on.

Upon returning to the substation a while ago, they had located two additional, long-handled, police flashlights. Gordy had taken one; Dr Paige had taken the other. Now, both of those lights flicked on simultaneously, carving long bright wounds in the darkness.

They had discussed a plan of action, a routine to follow if the lights went off again. Now, as planned, everyone moved to the centre of the room, away from the doors and windows, and clustered together in a circle, facing outward, their backs turned to one another, reducing their vulnerability.

No one said anything. They were all listening intently.

Lisa Paige stood to the left of Bryce, her slender shoulders hunched, her head tucked down.

Tal Whitman stood at Bryce's right. His teeth were bared in a silent snarl as he studied the darkness beyond the sweeping scythe of the flashlight beam.

Tal and Bryce were holding revolvers.

The three of them faced the rear half of the room, while the other four – Dr Paige, Gordy, Frank, and Stu – faced the front.

Bryce played the beam of his flashlight over everything, for even the shadowy outlines of the most mundane objects suddenly appeared threatening. But nothing hid or moved among the familiar pieces of furniture and equipment.

Silence.

Set in the back wall, towards the right-hand corner of the room, were two doors. One led to the corridor that served the three holding cells. They had searched that part of the building earlier; the cells, the interrogation room, and the two bathrooms that occupied that half of the ground floor were all deserted. The other door led to stairs that went up to the deputy's apartment; those rooms, too, were unoccupied. Nevertheless, Bryce repeatedly brought the beam of light back to the half-open doors; he was uneasy about them.

In the darkness, something thumped softly.

'What was that?' Wargle asked.

'It came from over this way,' Gordy said.

'No, from over this way,' Lisa Paige said.

'Quiet!' Bryce said sharply.

Thump . . . thump-thump.

It was the sound of a padded blow. Like a dropped pillow striking the floor.

Bryce swept his light rapidly back and forth.

Tal tracked the beam with his revolver.

Bryce thought: What do we do if the lights are out for the rest of the night? What do we do when the flashlight batteries finally go dead? What happens *then*?

He had not been afraid of darkness since he'd been a small child. Now he remembered what it was like.

Thump-thump . . . thump . . . thump-thump.

Louder. But not closer.

Thump!

'The windows!' Frank said.

Bryce swung around, probing with his flashlight.

Three bright beams found the front windows at the same time, transforming the mullioned squares of glass into mirrors that hid whatever lay beyond them.

'Turn your lights towards the floor or ceiling,' Bryce said.

One beam swung up, two down.

The backsplash of light revealed the windows, but it didn't turn them into reflective silver surfaces.

Thump!

Something struck a window, rattled a loose pane, and rebounded into the night. Bryce had an impression of wings.

'What was it?'

'—bird—'

'—not a bird of any kind I ever—'

'—something—'

'—awful—'

It returned, battering itself against the glass with greater determination than before: *Thump-thump-thump-thump-thump!*

Lisa screamed.

147

Frank Autry gasped, and Stu Wargle said, 'Holy shit!'

Gordy made a strangled, wordless sound.

Staring at the window, Bryce felt as if he had lurched through the curtain of reality, into a place of nightmare and illusion.

With the streetlamps extinguished, Skyline Road was dark except for the luminous moonfall; however, the thing at the window was vaguely illuminated.

Even vague illumination of that fluttering monstrosity was too much. What Bryce saw on the other side of the glass – what he *thought* he saw in the kaleidoscopic multiplicity of light, shadow, and shimmering moonlight – was something out of a fever dream. It had a three- or four-foot wingspan. An insectoid head. Short, quivering antennae. Small, pointed, and ceaselessly working mandibles. A segmented body. The body was suspended between the pale grey wings and was approximately the size and shape of two footballs placed end to end; it, too, was grey, the same shade as the wings – a mouldy, sickly grey – and fuzzy and moist-looking. Bryce glimpsed eyes, as well: huge, ink-black, multi-faceted, protuberant lenses that caught the light, refracting and reflecting it, gleaming darkly and hungrily.

If he was seeing what he thought he was seeing, the thing at the window was a moth as large as an eagle. Which was madness.

It bashed itself against the windows with new fury, in a frenzy now, its pale wings beating so fast that it became a blur. It moved along the dark panes, repeatedly rebounding into the night, then returning, trying feverishly to crash through the window. *Thumpthumpthumpthump.* But it didn't have the strength to smash its way inside. Furthermore, it didn't have a carapace; its body was entirely soft, and in spite of its incredible size and formidable appearance, it was incapable of cracking the glass.

Thumpthumpthump.

Then it was gone.

The lights came on.

It's like a damned stage play, Bryce thought.

When they realized that the thing at the window wasn't going to return, they all moved, by unspoken consent, to the front of the room. They went through the gate in the railing, into the public area, to the windows, gazing out in stunned silence.

Skyline Road was unchanged.

The night was empty.

Nothing moved.

Bryce sat down in the creaking chair at Paul Henderson's desk. The others gathered around.

'So,' Bryce said.

'So,' Tal said.

They looked at one another. They fidgeted.

'Any ideas?' Bryce asked.

No one said anything.

'Any theories about what it might have been?'

'Gross,' Lisa said, and shuddered.

'It was that, all right,' Dr Paige said, putting a comforting hand on her younger sister's shoulder.

Bryce was impressed with the doctor's emotional strength and resilience. She seemed to be taking every shock that Snowfield threw at her. Indeed, she seemed to be holding up better than his own men. Hers were the only eyes that didn't slide away when he met them; she returned his stare forthrightly.

This, he thought, is a special woman.

'Impossible,' Frank Autry said. 'That's what it was. Just plain impossible.'

'Hell, what's the matter with you people?' Wargle asked. He screwed up his meaty face. 'It was only a bird. That's all it was out there. Just a goddamned bird.'

'Like hell it was,' Frank said.

'Just a lousy bird,' Wargle insisted. When the others disagreed, he said, 'The bad light and all them shadows out there sort of give you a false impression. You didn't see what you all think you seen.'

'And what do *you* think we saw?' Tal asked him.

Wargle's face became flushed.

'Did we see the same thing you saw, the thing you don't want to believe?' Tal pressed. 'A moth? Did you see one goddamned big, ugly impossible moth?'

Wargle looked down at his shoes. 'I seen a bird. Just a bird.'

Bryce realized that Wargle was so utterly lacking in imagination that the man couldn't encompass the possibility of the impossible, not even when he had witnessed it with his own eyes.

'Where did it come from?' Bryce asked.

No one had any ideas.

'What did it want?' he asked.

'It wanted *us*,' Lisa said.

Everyone seemed to agree with that assessment.

'But the thing at the window wasn't what got Jake,' Frank said. 'It was weak, lightweight. It couldn't carry off a grown man.'

'Then what got Jake?' Gordy asked.

'Something bigger,' Frank said. 'Something a whole lot stronger and meaner.'

Bryce decided that, after all, the time had come to tell them about the things he had heard – and sensed – on the telephone, between his calls to Governor Retlock and General Copperfield: the silent presence; the forlorn cries of seagulls; the warning sound of a rattlesnake; worst of all, the agonizing and despairing screams of men, women, and children. He hadn't intended to mention any of that until morning, until the arrival of daylight and reinforcements. But they might spot something important that he had missed, some scrap, some due that would be of help. Besides, now that they had all seen the thing at the window, the phone incident was, by comparison, no longer very shocking.

The others listened to Bryce, and this new information had a negative effect on their demeanour.

'What kind of degenerate would tape-record the screams of his victims?' Gordy asked.

Tal Whitman shook his head. 'It could be something else. It could be that . . .'

'Yes?'

'Well, maybe none of you wants to hear this right now.'

'Since you've started it, finish it,' Bryce insisted.

'Well,' Tal said, 'what if it wasn't a recording you heard? I mean, we know people have disappeared from Snowfield. In fact as far as we've seen, more have vanished than died. So . . . what if the missing are being held somewhere? As hostages? Maybe the screams were coming from people who were still alive, who were being tortured and maybe killed right *then*, right then while you were on the phone, listening.'

Remembering those terrible screams, Bryce felt his marrow slowly freezing.

'Whether it was tape-recorded or not,' Frank Autry said, 'it's probably a mistake to think in terms of hostages.'

'Yes,' Dr Paige said. 'If Mr Autry means that we've got to be careful not to narrow our thinking to conventional situations, then I wholeheartedly agree. This just doesn't feel like a hostage drama. Something damned peculiar is happening here, something that no one's ever encountered before, so let's not start backsliding just because we'd be more comfortable with cosy, familiar explanations. Besides, if we're dealing with terrorists, how does that fit with the thing we saw at the window? It doesn't.'

Bryce nodded. 'You're right. But I don't believe Tal meant that people were being held for conventional motives.'

'No, no,' Tal said. 'It doesn't have to be terrorists or kidnappers. Even if people are being held hostage, that doesn't necessarily mean *other people* are holding them. I'm even willing to consider that they're being held by something that isn't human. How's *that* for remaining open-minded? Maybe *it* is holding them, the *it* that none of us can define. Maybe it's holding them just to prolong the pleasure it takes from snuffing the life out of them. Maybe it's holding them just to tease us with their screams, the way it teased Bryce on the phone. Hell, if we're dealing with something truly extraordinary, truly unhuman, its reasons for holding hostages – if it *is* holding any – are bound to be incomprehensible.'

'Christ, you're talking like lunatics,' Wargle said.

Everyone ignored him.

They had stepped through the looking glass. The impossible was possible. The enemy was the unknown.

Lisa Paige cleared her throat. Her face was pasty. In a barely audible voice, she said, 'Maybe it spun a web somewhere, down in a dark place, in a cellar or a cave, and maybe it tied all the missing people into its web, sealed them up in cocoons, alive. Maybe it's just saving them until it gets hungry again.'

If absolutely nothing lay beyond the realm of possibility, if even the most outrageous theories could be true, then perhaps the girl was right, Bryce thought. Perhaps there *was* an enormous web vibrating softly in some dark place, hung with a hundred or two hundred or even more man- and woman- and child-size titbits, wrapped in individual packages for freshness and convenience. Somewhere in Snowfield, were there living human beings who had been reduced to the awful equivalent of foil-wrapped Pop Tarts, waiting only to provide nourishment for some brutal, unimaginably evil, darkly intelligent, other-dimensional horror?

No. Ridiculous.

On the other hand: maybe.

Jesus.

Bryce crouched in front of the shortwave radio and squinted at its mangled guts. Circuit boards had been snapped. Several parts appeared to have been crushed in a vice or hammered flat.

Frank said, 'They had to take off the cover plate to get at all this stuff, just the way we did.'

'So after they smashed the crap out of it,' Wargle said, 'why'd they bother to put the plate back on?'

'And why go to all that trouble to begin with?' Frank wondered. 'They could've put the radio out of commission just by ripping the cord loose.'

Lisa and Gordy appeared as Bryce was turning away from the radio. The girl said, 'Food and coffee's ready if anyone wants anything.'

'I'm starved,' Wargle said, licking his lips.

'We should all eat something, even if we don't feel like it,' Bryce said.

'Sheriff,' Gordy said, 'Lisa and I have been wondering about the animals, the pets. What made us think about it was when you said you heard dog and cat sounds over the phone. Sir, what's happened to all the pets?'

'Nobody's seen a dog or cat,' Lisa said. 'Or heard barking.'

Thinking of the silent streets, Bryce frowned and said, 'You're right. It's strange.'

'Jenny says there were some pretty big dogs in town. A few German shepherds. One Doberman that she knows of. Even a Great Dane. Wouldn't you think they'd have fought back? Wouldn't you think some of the dogs would've got away?' the girl asked.

'Okay,' Gordy said quickly, anticipating Bryce's response, 'so maybe *it* was big enough to overwhelm an ordinary, angry dog. Okay, so we also know that bullets didn't stop it, which says that maybe nothing can. It's apparently big, and it's strong. But, sir, big and strong don't necessarily count for much with a *cat*. Cats are greased lightning. It'd take something real damned sneaky to slip up on every cat in town.'

'Real sneaky and real *fast*,' Lisa said.

'Yeah,' Bryce said uneasily. '*Real* fast.'

*

153

Jenny had just begun eating a sandwich when Sheriff Hammond sat down in a chair beside the desk, balancing his plate on his lap. 'Mind some company?'

'Not at all.'

'Tal Whitman's been telling me you're the scourge of our local motorcycle gang.'

She smiled. 'Tal's exaggerating.'

'That man doesn't know how to exaggerate,' the sheriff said. 'Let me tell you something about him. Sixteen months ago, I was away for three days at a law enforcement conference in Chicago, and when I got back, Tal was the first person I saw. I asked him if anything special had happened while I'd been gone, and he said it was just the usual business with drunk drivers, bar fights, a couple of burglaries, various CITs—'

'What's a CIT?' Jenny asked.

'Oh, it's just a cat-in-tree report.'

'Policemen don't really rescue cats, do they?'

'Do you think we're heartless?' he asked, feigning shock.

'CITs? Come on now.'

He grinned. He had a marvellous grin. 'Once every couple of months, we *do* have to get a cat out of a tree. But a CIT doesn't mean *just* cats in trees. It's our shorthand for any kind of nuisance call that takes us away from more important work.'

'Ah.'

'So anyway, when I came back from Chicago that time, Tal told me it'd been a pretty ordinary three days. And then, almost as an afterthought, he said there'd been an attempted robbery at a 7-Eleven. Tal had been a customer, out of uniform, when it went down. But when off duty, a cop's required to carry his gun, and Tal had a revolver in an ankle holster. He told me one of the punks had been armed; he said he'd been forced to kill him, and he said I wasn't to worry about whether it was a justified shooting or not. He said it was as justified as they come. When I got concerned about *him*, he

154

said, "Bryce. It was really just a cakewalk." Later, I found out the two punks had intended to shoot everyone. Instead, Tal shot the gunman – although not before he was shot himself. The punk put a bullet through Tal's left arm, and just about a split second after that, Tal killed him. Tal's wound wasn't serious, but it bled like hell, and it must've hurt something awful. Of course, I hadn't seen the bandage because it was under the shirt sleeve, and Tal hadn't bothered to mention it. So anyway, there's Tal in the 7-Eleven, bleeding all over the place, and he discovers he's out of ammo. The second punk, who grabbed the gun the first one dropped, is also out of ammo, and he decides to run. Tal goes after him, and they have themselves a knock-down-drag-out fight from one end of that little grocery store to the other. The guy was two inches taller and twenty pounds heavier than Tal, and *he* wasn't wounded. But you know what the back-up officer told me they found when they arrived? They said Tal was sitting up on the counter by the cash register, his shirt off, sipping a complimentary cup of coffee, while the clerk tried to staunch the flow of blood. One suspect was dead. The other one was unconscious, sprawled in a sticky mess of Hostess Twinkies and Fudge Fantasies and coconut cupcakes. Seems they'd knocked over a rack of lunchbox cakes right in the middle of the fight. About a hundred packages of snack stuff spilled onto the floor, and Tal and this other guy stepped all over them while they were grappling. Most of the packages broke open. There was icing and crumbled cookies and smashed Twinkies all over one aisle. Staggered footprints were pressed right into the garbage, so that you could follow the progress of the battle just by looking at the sticky trail.'

The sheriff finished his story and looked at Jenny expectantly.

'Oh! Yes, he told you it'd been an easy arrest – just a cakewalk.'

'Yeah. A cakewalk.' The sheriff laughed.

Jenny glanced at Tal Whitman, who was across the room, eating a sandwich, talking to Officer Brogan and to Lisa.

'So you see,' the sheriff said, 'when Tal tells me you're the scourge of the Demon Chrome, I know he's not exaggerating. Exaggeration just isn't his style.'

Jenny shook her head, impressed. 'When I told Tal about my little encounter with this man he calls Gene Terr, he acted as if he thought it was one of the bravest things anyone had ever done. Compared to that "cakewalk" of his, my story must've seemed like a dispute in a kindergarten playground.'

'No, no,' Hammond said. 'Tal wasn't just humouring you. He really does think you did a damned brave thing. So do I. Jeeter's a snake, Dr Paige. Poisonous variety.'

'You can call me Jenny if you like.'

'Well, Jenny-if-you-like, you can call me Bryce.'

He had the bluest eyes she had ever seen. His smile was defined as much by those luminous eyes as it was by the curve of his mouth.

As they ate, they talked about inconsequential things, as if this were an ordinary evening. He possessed an impressive ability to put people at ease regardless of the circumstances. He brought with him an aura of tranquillity. She was grateful for the calm interlude.

When they finished eating, however, he guided the conversation back to the crisis at hand. 'You know Snowfield better than I do. We've got to find a suitable headquarters for this operation. This place is too small. Soon, I'll have ten more men here. And Copperfield's team in the morning.'

'How many is he bringing?'

'At least a dozen people. Maybe as many as twenty. I need an HQ from which every aspect of the operation can be coordinated. We might be here for days, so there'll have to be room where off-duty people can sleep, and we'll need a cafeteria arrangement to feed everyone.'

'One of the inns might be just the place,' Jenny said.

'Maybe. But I don't want people sleeping two by two in a lot of different rooms. They'd be too vulnerable. We've got to set up a single dormitory.'

'Then the Hilltop Inn is your best bet. It's about a block from here, on the other side of the street.'

'Oh, yeah, of course. Biggest hotel in town, isn't it?'

'Yeah. The Hilltop has a large lobby because it doubles as a hotel bar.'

'I've had a drink there once or twice. If we change the lobby furniture, it could be set up as a work area to accommodate everyone.'

'There's also a large restaurant divided into two rooms. One part could be a cafeteria, and we could carry mattresses down from the rooms and use the other half of the restaurant as a dorm.'

Bryce said, 'Let's have a look at it.'

He put his empty paper plate on the desk and got to his feet.

Jenny glanced at the front windows. She thought of the strange creature that had flown into the glass, and in her mind she heard the soft yet frenzied *thumpthumpthumpthumpthump*.

She said, 'You mean . . . have a look at it now?'

'Why not?'

'Wouldn't it be wise to wait for the reinforcements?' she asked.

'They probably won't arrive for a while yet. There's no point in just sitting around, twiddling our thumbs. We'll all feel better if we're doing something constructive; it'll take our minds off . . . the worst things we've seen.'

Jenny couldn't free herself from the memory of those black insect eyes, so malevolent, so hungry. She stared at the windows, at the night beyond. The town no longer seemed familiar. It was utterly alien now, a hostile place in which she was an unwelcome stranger.

'We're not one bit safer in here than we would be out there,' Bryce said gently.

Jenny nodded, remembering the Oxleys in their barricaded room. As she got up from the desk, she said, 'There's no safety anywhere.'

16

OUT OF THE DARK

BRYCE HAMMOND led the way out of the stationhouse. They crossed the moonlight-mottled cobblestones, stepped through a fall of amber light from a streetlamp, and headed into Skyline Road. Bryce carried a shotgun, as did Tal Whitman.

The town was breathless. The trees stood unrespiring, and the buildings were like vapour-thin mirages hanging on walls of air.

Bryce moved out of the light, walked on moon-dappled pavement, crossing the street, finding shadows scattered in the middle of it. Always shadows.

The others came silently behind him.

Something crunched under Bryce's foot, startling him. It was a withered leaf.

He could see the Hilltop Inn further up Skyline Road. It was a four-storey, grey stone building almost a block away, and it was very dark. A few of the fourth-floor windows reflected the nearly full moon, but within the hotel not a single light burned.

They had all reached or passed the middle of the street when something came out of the dark. Bryce was aware, first, of a moon shadow that fluttered across the pavement, like a ripple passing through a pool of water. Instinctively, he ducked. He heard wings. He felt something brush lightly over his head.

Stu Wargle screamed.

Bryce shot up from his crouch and whirled around.

The moth.

It was fixed firmly to Wargle's face, holding on by some means not visible to Bryce. Wargle's entire head was hidden by the thing.

Wargle wasn't the only one screaming. The others cried out and fell back in surprise. The moth was squealing, too, making a high-pitched, keening sound.

In the moon's silvery beams, the impossible insect's huge pale velvety wings flapped and folded and spread with horrible grace and beauty, buffeting Wargle's head and shoulders.

Wargle staggered away, veering downhill, moving blindly, clawing at the outrageous thing that clung to his face. His screams quickly grew muffled; within a couple of seconds, they were silenced altogether.

Bryce, like the others, was paralyzed by disgust and disbelief.

Wargle began to run, but he only went a few yards before coming to an abrupt halt. His hands dropped away from the thing on his face. His knees were buckling.

Snapping out of his brief trance, Bryce dropped his useless shotgun and ran towards Stu.

Wargle didn't crumple to the ground, after all. Instead, his shaky knees locked, and he snapped erect. His shoulders jerked back. His body twitched and shuddered as if an electric current had flashed through him.

Bryce tried to grab the moth and tear it away from Wargle. But the deputy began to weave and thrash in a St Vitus dance of pain and suffocation, and Bryce's hands closed on empty air. Wargle moved erratically across the street, jerked this way and that, heaved and writhed and spun, as if he were attached to strings that were being manipulated by a drunken puppeteer. His hands hung slackly at his sides, which made his frantic and spasmodic capering seem especially eerie. His hands flopped and fluttered weakly, but they did not rise to tear at his assailant. It was almost as if, now, he were in the grip of ecstasy rather than the clutch of pain. Bryce followed him, tried to move in on him, but couldn't get close.

Then Wargle collapsed.

In that same instant, the moth rose and turned, suspended in the air, hovering on rapidly beating wings, eyes night-black and hateful. It swooped at Bryce.

He stumbled backwards and threw his arms across his face. He fell.

The moth sailed over his head.

Bryce twisted around, looked up.

The kite-size insect glided soundlessly across the street, towards the buildings on the other side.

Tal Whitman raised his shotgun. The blast was like cannonfire in the silent town.

The moth pitched sideways in mid-air. It tumbled in a loop, dropped almost to the ground, then it swooped up again and flew on, disappearing over a rooftop.

Stu Wargle was sprawled on the pavement, flat on his back. Unmoving.

Bryce scrambled to his feet and went to Wargle. The deputy lay in the middle of the street, where there was just enough light to see that his face was gone. Jesus. *Gone.* As if it had been torn off. His hair and ragged ribbons of his scalp bristled over the white bone of his forehead. A skull peered up at Bryce.

17

THE HOUR BEFORE MIDNIGHT

TAL, GORDY, Frank, and Lisa sat in red leatherette armchairs in a corner of the lobby of the Hilltop Inn. The inn had been dosed since the end of the past skiing season, and they had removed the dusty white dustcovers from the chairs before collapsing into them, numb with shock. The oval coffee table was still covered by a dustcover; they stared at that shrouded object, unable to look at one another.

At the far end of the room, Bryce and Jenny were standing over the body of Stu Wargle, which lay on a long, low sideboard against the wall. No one in the armchairs could bring himself to look over that way.

Staring at the covered coffee table, Tal said, 'I shot the damned thing. I hjt it I know I did.'

'We all saw it take the buckshot,' Frank agreed.

'So why wasn't it blown apart?' Tal demanded. 'Hit dead-on by a blast from a .20-gauge. It should've been torn to pieces, dammit.'

'Guns aren't going to save us,' Lisa said.

In a distant, haunted voice, Gordy said, 'It could've been any of us. That thing could've gotten me. I was right behind Stu. If he had ducked or jumped out of the way . . .'

'No,' Lisa said. 'No. It wanted Officer Wargle. Nobody else. Just Officer Wargle.'

Tal stared at the girl. 'What do you mean?'

Her flesh had taken paleness from her bones. 'Officer Wargle refused to admit he'd seen it when it was battering against the window. He insisted it was just a bird.'

'So?'

'So it wanted him. Him especially,' she said. 'To teach him a lesson. But mostly to teach *us* a lesson.'

'It couldn't have heard what Stu said.'

'It did. It heard.'

'But it couldn't have understood.'

'It did.'

'I think you're crediting it with too much intelligence,' Tal said. 'It was big, yes, and like nothing any of us has ever seen before. But it was still only an insect. A moth. Right?'

The girl said nothing.

'It's not omniscient,' Tal said, trying to convince himself more than anyone else. 'It's not all-seeing, all-hearing, all-knowing.'

The girl stared silently at the covered coffee table.

Suppressing nausea, Jenny examined Wargle's hideous wound. The lobby lights were not quite bright enough, so she used a flashlight to inspect the edges of the injury and to peer into the skull. The centre of the dead man's demolished face was eaten away clear to the bone; all the skin, flesh, and cartilage were gone. Even the bone itself appeared to be partially dissolved in place, pitted, as if it had been splashed with acid. The eyes were gone. There was, however, normal flesh on all sides of the wound; smooth untouched flesh lay along both sides of the face, from the outer points of the jawbones to the cheekbones, and there was unmarked skin from the midpoint of the chin on down, and from the midpoint of the forehead on up. It was as if some torture artist had designed a frame of healthy skin to set off the gruesome exhibition of bone on display in the centre of the face.

Having seen enough, Jenny switched off the flashlight. Earlier, they had covered the body with a dustcover from one of the chairs. Now Jenny drew the sheet over the dead man's face, relieved to be covering that skeletal grin.

'Well?' Bryce asked.

'No teeth marks,' she said.

'Would a thing like that have teeth?'

'I know it had a mouth, a small chitinous beak. I saw its mandibles working when it bashed itself against the substation windows.'

'Yeah. I saw them, too.'

'A mouth like that would mark the flesh. There'd be slashes. Bite marks. Indications of chewing and tearing.'

'But there were none?'

'No. The flesh doesn't look as if it was ripped off. It seems to've been . . . dissolved. Along the edges of the wound, the remaining flesh is even sort of cauterized, as if it has been seared by something.'

'You think that . . . that insect . . . secreted an acid?'

She nodded.

'And dissolved Stu Wargle's face?'

'And sucked up the liquefied flesh,' she said.

'Oh, Jesus.'

'Yes.'

Bryce was as pale as an untinted deathmask, and his freckles seemed, by contrast, to burn and shimmer on his face. 'That explains how it could've done so much damage in only a few seconds.'

Jenny tried not to think of the bony face peering out of the flesh — like a monstrous visage that had removed a mask of normality.

'I think the blood is gone,' she said. 'All of it.'

'What?'

'Was the body lying in a pool of blood?'

'No.'

'There's no blood on the uniform, either.'

'I noticed that.'

'There should be blood. He should've spouted like a fountain. The eye sockets should be pooled with it. But there's not a drop.'

Bryce wiped one hand across his face. He wiped so hard, in fact, that some colour rose in his cheeks.

'Take a look at his neck,' she said. 'The jugular.'

He didn't move towards the corpse.

She said, 'And look at the insides of his arms and the backs of his hands. There's no blueness of veins anywhere, no trace.'

'Collapsed blood vessels?'

'Yeah. I think all the blood is drained out of him.'

Bryce took a deep breath. He said, 'I killed him. I'm responsible. We should have waited for reinforcements before leaving the substation – just like you said.'

'No, no. You were right. It was no safer there than in the street.'

'But he died in the street.'

'Reinforcements wouldn't have made a bit of difference. The way that damned thing dropped out of the sky . . . hell, not even an army could've stopped it. Too quick. Too surprising.'

Bleakness had taken up tenancy in his eyes. He felt his responsibility far too keenly. He was going to insist on blaming himself for his officer's death.

Reluctantly, she said, 'There's worse.'

'Couldn't be.'

'His brain . . .'

Bryce waited. Then he said, 'What? What about his brain?'

'Gone.'

'Gone?'

'His cranium is empty. Utterly empty.'

'How can you possibly know that without opening—'

She held out the flashlight, interrupting him: 'Take this and shine it into the eye sockets.'

164

He made no move to act upon her suggestion. His eyes were not hooded now. They were wide, startled.

She noticed that she couldn't hold the flashlight steady. Her hand was shaking violently.

He noticed, too. He took the flash away from her and put it down on the sideboard, next to the shrouded corpse. He took both of her hands and held them in his own large, leathery, cupped hands; he warmed them.

She said, 'There's nothing beyond the eye sockets, nothing at all, nothing, nothing whatsoever, except the back of his skull.'

Bryce rubbed her hands soothingly.

'Just a damp, reamed-out cavity,' she said. As she spoke, her voice rose and cracked: 'It ate through his face, right through his eyes, probably about as fast as he could blink, for God's sake, ate into his mouth and took his tongue out by the roots, stripped the gums away from his teeth, then ate up through the roof of his mouth, Jesus, just consumed his brain, consumed all of the blood in his body, too, probably just sucked it up and out of him and—'

'Easy, easy,' Bryce said.

But the words rattle-clanked out of her as if they were links in a chain that bound her to an albatross: '—consumed all of that in no more than ten or twelve seconds, which is impossible, dammit to hell, plain impossible! It devoured – do you understand? – *devoured* pounds and pounds and pounds of tissue – the brain alone weighs six or seven pounds – devoured all of that in ten or twelve *seconds*!'

She stood gasping, hands trapped in his.

He led her to a sofa that lay under a dusty white cover. They sat side by side.

Across the room, none of the others were looking their way.

Jenny was glad of that. She didn't want Lisa to see her in this condition.

Bryce put a hand on her shoulder. He spoke to her in a low, reassuring voice.

She gradually grew calmer. Not less disturbed. Not less afraid. Just calmer.

'Better?' Bryce asked.

'As my sister says – I guess I flaked out on you, huh?'

'Not at all. Are you kidding or what? I couldn't even take the flashlight from you and look in those eyes like you wanted me to. *You're* the one who had the nerve to examine him.'

'Well, thanks for getting me back together. You sure know how to knit up ravelled nerves.'

'Me? I didn't do anything.'

'You sure have a comforting way of doing nothing.'

They sat in silence, thinking of things they didn't want to think about.

Then he said, 'That moth . . .'

She waited.

He said, 'Where'd it *come* from?'

'Hell?'

'Any other suggestions?'

Jenny shrugged. 'The Mesozoic era?' she said half-jokingly.

'When was that?'

'The age of dinosaurs.'

His blue eyes flickered with interest. 'Did moths like that exist back then?'

'I don't know,' she admitted.

'I *can* sort of picture it soaring through prehistoric swamps.'

'Yeah. Preying on small animals, bothering a tyrannosaurus rex about the same way our own tiny summer moths bother us.'

'But if it's from the Mesozoic, where's it been hiding for the last hundred million years?' he asked.

More seconds, ticking.

'Could it be . . . something from a genetic engineering lab?' she wondered. 'An experiment in recombinant DNA?'

'Have they gone that far? Can they produce whole new species?

166

I only know what I read in the papers, but I thought they were years away from that sort of thing. They're still working with bacteria.'

'You're probably right,' she said. 'But still . . .'

'Yeah. Nothing's impossible because the moth is *here*.'

After another silence, she said, 'And what else is crawling or flying around out there?'

'You're thinking about what happened to Jake Johnson?'

'Yeah. What took him? Not the moth. Even as deadly as it is, it couldn't kill him silently, and it couldn't carry him away.' She sighed. 'You know, at first I wouldn't try to leave town because I was afraid we'd spread an epidemic. Now I wouldn't try to leave because I know we wouldn't make it out alive. We'd be stopped.'

'No, no. I'm sure we could get you out,' Bryce said. 'If we can prove there's no disease-related aspect to this, if General Copperfield's people can rule that out, then, of course, you and Lisa will be taken to safety right away.'

She shook her head. 'No. There's something out there, Bryce, something more cunning and a whole lot more formidable than the moth, and it doesn't want us to leave. It wants to play with us before it kills us. It won't let any of us go, so we'd damned well better find it and figure out how to deal with it before it gets tired of the game.'

In both rooms of the Hilltop Inn's large restaurant, chairs were stacked upside-down atop the tables, all covered with green plastic cloths. In the first room, Bryce and the others removed the plastic sheeting, took the chairs off the tables, and began to prepare the place to serve as a cafeteria.

In the second room, the furniture had to be moved out to make way for the mattresses that would later be brought down from upstairs. They had only just begun emptying that part of the restaurant when they heard the faint but unmistakable sound of automobile engines.

Bryce went to the french windows. He looked left, down the hill, towards the foot of Skyline Road. Three county squad cars were coming up the street, red beacons flashing.

'They're here,' Bryce told the others.

He had been thinking of the reinforcements as a reassuringly formidable replenishment of their own decimated contingent. Now he realized that ten more men were hardly better than one more.

Jenny Paige had been right when she'd said that Stu Wargle's life probably wouldn't have been saved by waiting for reinforcements before leaving the substation.

All the lights in the Hilltop Inn and all the lights along the main street flickered. Dimmed. Went out. But they came back on after only a second of darkness.

It was 11:15, Sunday night, counting down towards the witching hour.

18

LONDON, ENGLAND

WHEN MIDNIGHT came to California, it was eight o'clock Monday morning in London.

The day was dreary. Grey clouds melted across the city. A steady, dismal drizzle had been falling since before dawn. The drowned trees hung limply, and the streets glistened darkly, and everyone on the pavements seemed to have black umbrellas.

At the Churchill Hotel in Portman Square, rain beat against the windows and streamed down the glass, distorting the view from the dining room. Occasionally, brilliant flashes of lightning, passing through the water-beaded window panes, briefly cast shadowy images of raindrops onto the clean white tablecloths.

Burt Sandler, in London on business from New York, sat at one of the window tables, wondering how in God's name he was going to justify the size of this breakfast bill on his expense account. His guest had begun by ordering a bottle of good champagne: Mumm's Extra Dry, which didn't come cheap. With the champagne, his guest wanted caviar – champagne and caviar for breakfast! – and two kinds of fresh fruit. And the old fellow clearly had not finished ordering.

Across the table, Dr Timothy Flyte, the object of Sandler's amazement, studied the menu with childlike delight. To the waiter, he said, 'And I should like an order of your croissants.'

'Yes, sir,' the waiter said.

'Are they very flaky?'

'Yes, sir. Very.'

'Oh, good. And eggs,' Flyte said. 'Two lovely eggs, of course, rather soft, with buttered toast.'

'Toast?' the waiter asked. 'Is that in addition to the two croissants, sir?'

'Yes, yes,' Flyte said, fingering the slightly frayed collar of his white shirt. 'And a rasher of bacon with the eggs.'

The waiter blinked. 'Yes, sir.'

At last Flyte looked up at Burt Sandler. 'What's breakfast without bacon? Am I right?'

'I'm an eggs and bacon man myself,' Burt Sandler agreed, forcing a smile.

'Wise of you,' Flyte said sagely. His wire-rimmed spectacles had slipped down his nose and were now perched on its round, red tip. With a long, thin finger, he pushed them back into place.

Sandler noticed that the bridge of the eyeglasses had been broken and soldered. The repair job was so distinctly amateurish that he suspected Flyte had soldered the frames himself, to save money.

'Do you have good pork sausages?' Flyte asked the waiter. 'Be truthful with me. I'll send them back straight away if they aren't of the highest quality.'

'We've quite good sausages,' the waiter assured him. 'I'm partial to them myself.'

'Sausages, then.'

'Is that in place of the bacon, sir?'

'No, no, no. In addition,' Flyte said, as if the waiter's question was not only curious but a sign of thick-headedness.

Flyte was fifty-eight but looked at least a decade older. His bristly white hair curled thinly across the top of his head and thrust out around his large ears as if crackling with static electricity. His neck was scrawny and wrinkled; his shoulders were slight; his body favoured bone and cartilage over flesh. There was some legitimate doubt whether he could actually eat all that he ordered.

'Potatoes,' Flyte added.

'Very well, sir,' the waiter said, scribbling it down on his order pad, on which he had very nearly run out of room to write.

'Do you have suitable pastries?' Flyte inquired.

The waiter, a model of deportment under the circumstances, having made not the slightest allusion to Flyte's amazing gluttony, looked at Burt Sandler as if to say: *Is your grandfather hopelessly senile, sir, or is he, at his age, a marathon runner who needs the calories?*

Sandler merely smiled.

To Flyte, the waiter said, 'Yes, sir, we have several pastries. There's a delicious—'

'Bring an assortment,' Flyte said. 'At the end of the meal, of course.'

'Leave it to me, sir.'

'Good. Very good. Excellent!' Flyte said, beaming. Finally, with a trace of reluctance, he relinquished his menu.

Sandler almost sighed with relief. He asked for orange juice, eggs, bacon, and toast, while Professor Flyte adjusted the day-old carnation pinned to the lapel of his somewhat shiny blue suit.

As Sandler finished ordering, Flyte leaned towards him conspiratorially. 'Will you be having some of the champagne, Mr Sandler?'

'I believe I might have a glass or two,' Sandler said, hoping the bubbly would liberate his mind and help him formulate a believable explanation for this extravagance, a likely tale that would convince even the parsimonious clerks in accounting who would be poring over this bill with an electron miscroscope.

Flyte looked at the waiter. 'Then perhaps you'd better bring *two* bottles.'

Sandler, who was sipping ice-water, nearly choked.

The waiter left, and Flyte looked out through the rain-streaked window beside their table. 'Nasty weather. Is it like this in New York in autumn?'

'We have our share of rainy days. But autumn can be beautiful in New York.'

'Here, too,' Flyte said. 'Though I rather imagine we have more days like this than you. London's reputation for soggy weather isn't entirely undeserved.'

The professor insisted on small talk until the champagne and caviar were served, as if he feared that, once business had been discussed, Sandler would quickly cancel the rest of the breakfast order.

He's a character out of Dickens, Sandler thought.

As soon as they had proposed a toast, wishing each other good fortune, and had sipped the Mumm's, Flyte said, 'So you've come all the way from New York to see me, have you?' His eyes were merry.

'To see a number of writers, actually,' Sandler said. 'I make the trip once a year. I scout out books in progress. British authors are popular in the States, especially thriller writers.'

'MacLean, Follet, Forsyth, Bagley, that crowd?'

'Yes, very popular, some of them.'

The caviar was superb. At the professor's urging, Sandler tried some of it with chopped onions. Flyte piled gobs on small wedges of dry toast and ate it without benefit of condiments.

'But I'm not only scouting for thrillers,' Sandler said. 'I'm after a variety of books. Unknown authors, too. And I suggest projects on occasion, when I have a subject for a particular author.'

'Apparently, you have something in mind for me.'

'First, let me say I read *The Ancient Enemy* when it was first published, and I found it fascinating.'

'A number of people found it fascinating,' Flyte said. 'But most found it infuriating.'

'I hear the book created problems for you.'

'Virtually nothing *but* problems.'

'Such as?'

'I lost my university position fifteen years ago, at the age of forty-three, when most academics are achieving job security.'

'You lost your position because of *The Ancient Enemy*?'

'They didn't put it quite that bluntly,' Flyte said, popping a morsel of caviar into his mouth. 'That would have made them seem too close-minded. The administrators of my college, the head of my department, and most of my distinguished colleagues chose to attack indirectly. My dear Mr Sandler, the competition among power-mad politicians and the Machiavellian backstabbing of junior executives in a major corporation are as nothing, in terms of ruthlessness and spite, when compared to the behaviour of academic types who suddenly see an opportunity to climb the university ladder at the expense of one of their own. They spread rumours without foundation, scandalous tripe about my sexual preferences, suggestions of intimate fraternization with my female students. And with my male students, for that matter. None of those slanders was openly discussed in a forum where I could refute them. Just rumours. Whispered behind the back. Poisonous. More openly, they made polite suggestions of incompetence, overwork, mental fatigue. I was eased out, you see; that's how they thought of it, though there was nothing easy about it from my point of view. Eighteen months after the publication of *The Ancient Enemy,* I was gone. And no other university would have me, ostensibly because of my unsavoury reputation. The true reason, of course, was that my theories were too bizarre for academic tastes. I stood accused of attempting to make a fortune by pandering to the common man's taste for pseudo-science and sensationalism, of selling my credibility.'

Flyte paused to take some champagne, savouring it.

Sandler was genuinely appalled by what Flyte had told him. 'But that's outrageous! Your book was a scholarly treatise. It was never aimed at the best seller lists. The common man would've had enormous difficulty wading through *The Ancient Enemy*. Making a fortune from that kind of work is virtually impossible.'

'A fact to which my royalty statements can attest,' Flyte said. He finished the last of the caviar.

'You were a respected archaeologist,' Sandler said.

'Oh, well, never really all *that* respected,' Flyte said self-deprecatingly. 'Though I was certainly never an embarrassment to my profession, as was so often suggested later on. If my colleagues' conduct seems incredible to you, Mr Sandler, that's because you don't understand the nature of the animal. I mean, the scientist animal. Scientists are educated to believe that all new knowledge comes in tiny increments, grains of sand piled one on another. Indeed, that *is* how most knowledge is gained. Therefore, they are never prepared for those visionaries who arrive at new insights which, overnight, utterly transform an entire field of inquiry. Copernicus was ridiculed by his contemporaries for believing that the planets revolved around the sun. Of course, Copernicus was proved right. There are countless examples in the history of science.' Flyte blushed and drank some more champagne. 'Not that I compare myself to Copernicus or any of those other great men. I'm simply trying to explain why my colleagues were conditioned to turn against me. I should have seen it coming.'

The waiter came to take away the caviar dish. He also served Sandler's orange juice and Flyte's fresh fruit.

When he was alone with Flyte again, Sandler' said, 'Do you still believe your theory has validity?'

'Absolutely!' Flyte said. 'I *am* right; or at least there's an awfully good chance I am. History is filled with mysterious mass disappearances for which historians and archaeologists can provide no viable explanation.'

The professor's rheumy eyes became sharp and probing beneath his bushy white eyebrows. He leaned over the table, fixing Burt Sandler with a hypnotic stare.

'On 10 December 1939,' Flyte said, 'outside the hills of Nanking, an army of three thousand Chinese soldiers, on its way to the front lines to fight the Japanese, simply vanished without a trace before it got anywhere near the battle. Not a single body was ever found.

Not one grave. Not one witness. The Japanese military historians have never found any record of having dealt with that particular Chinese force. In the countryside through which the missing soldiers passed, no peasants heard gunfire or other indications of conflict. An *army* evaporated into thin air. And in 1711, during the Spanish War of Succession, four thousand troops set out on an expedition into the Pyrenees. Every last man disappeared on familiar and friendly ground, before the first night's camp was established!'

Flyte was still as gripped by his subject as he had been when he had written his book, seventeen years ago. His fruit and champagne were forgotten. He stared at Sandler as if daring him to challenge the infamous Flyte theories.

'On a grander scale,' the professor continued, 'consider the great Mayan cities of Copán, Piedras Négras, Palenque, Menché, Seibal, and several others which were abandoned overnight. Tens of thousands, *hundreds* of thousands of Mayans left their homes, approximately in AD 610, perhaps within a single week, even within one *day*. Some appear to have fled northward, to establish new cities, but there is evidence that countless thousands just disappeared. All within a shockingly brief span of time. They didn't bother to take many of their pots, tools, cooking utensils . . . My learned colleagues say the land around those Mayan cities became infertile, thus making it essential that the people move north, where the land would be more productive. But if this great exodus was planned, why were belongings left behind? Why was precious seed corn left behind? Why didn't a single survivor ever return to loot those cities of their abandoned treasures?' Flyte softly struck the table with one fist. 'It's irrational! Emigrants don't set out on long, arduous journeys without preparation, without taking every tool that might assist them. Besides, in some of the homes in Piedras Négras and Seibal, there is evidence that families departed after preparing elaborate dinners – *but before eating them*. This would surely seem to indicate that their leaving was sudden. No current theories adequately answer these questions – except mine, bizarre as it is, odd as it is, *impossible* as it is.'

'Frightening as it is,' Sandler added.

'Exactly,' Flyte said.

The professor sank back in his chair, breathless. He noticed his champagne glass, seized it, emptied it, and licked his lips.

The waiter appeared and refilled their glasses.

Flyte quickly consumed his fruit, as if afraid the waiter might spirit it away while the hothouse strawberries remained untouched.

Sandler felt sorry for the old bird. Evidently, it had been quite some time since the professor had been treated to an expensive meal served in an elegant atmosphere.

'I was accused of trying to explain *every* mysterious disappearance from the Mayans to Judge Crater and Amelia Earhart, all with a single theory. That was most unfair. I never mentioned the judge or the luckless aviatrix. I am interested only in unexplained *mass* disappearances of both humankind and animals, of which there have been literally hundreds throughout history.'

The waiter brought croissants.

Outside, lightning stepped quickly down the sombre sky and put its spiked foot to the earth in another part of the city; its blazing descent was accompanied by a terrible crash and roar that echoed across the entire firmament.

Sandler said, 'If, subsequent to the publication of your book, there had been a new, startling mass disappearance, it would have lent considerable credibility to—'

'Ah,' Flyte interrupted, tapping the table emphatically with one stiff finger, 'but there *have* been such disappearances!'

'But surely they would have been splashed all over the front page—'

'I am aware of two instances. There may be others,' Flyte

insisted. 'One of them involved the disappearance of masses of lower life forms – specifically, *fish*. It was remarked on in the press, but not with any great interest. Politics, murder, sex, and two-headed goats are the only things newspapers care to report. You have to read scientific journals to know what's really happening. That's how I know that, eight years ago, marine biologists noted a dramatic decrease in fish populations in one region of the Pacific. Indeed, the numbers of some species had been cut in half. Within certain scientific circles, there was panic at first, some fear that ocean temperatures might be undergoing a sudden change that would depopulate the seas of all but the hardiest species. But that proved not to be the case. Gradually, sea life in that area – which covered hundreds of square miles – replenished itself. In the end no one could explain what had happened to the millions upon millions of creatures that had vanished.'

'Pollution,' Sandler suggested, between alternating sips of orange juice and champagne.

Dabbing marmalade on a piece of croissant, Flyte said, 'No, no, no. No, sir. It would have required the most massive case of water pollution in history to cause such a devastating depopulation over that wide an area. An accident on that scale could not go unnoticed. But there were no accidents, no oil spills – nothing. Indeed, a mere oil spill could not have accounted for it; the affected region and the volume of water was too vast for that. And dead fish did *not* wash up on the beaches. They merely vanished without a trace.'

Burt Sandler was excited. He could smell money. He had hunches about some books, and none of his hunches had ever been wrong. (Well, except for that diet book by the movie star who, a week before publication day, died of malnutrition after subsisting for six months on little more than grapefruit, papaya, raisin toast, and carrots.) There was a surefire best seller in this: two or three hundred thousand copies in hardcover, perhaps even more; two million in paperback. If he could persuade Flyte to popularize and update the dry academic material in *The Ancient Enemy*, the professor would be able to afford his own champagne for many years to come.

'You said you were aware of *two* mass disappearances since the publication of your book,' Sandler said, encouraging him to continue.

'The other was in Africa in 1980. Between three and four thousand primitive tribesmen – men, women, and children – vanished from a relatively remote area of central Africa. Their villages were found empty; they had abandoned all their possessions, including large stores of food. They seemed to have just run off into the bush. The only signs of violence were a few broken pieces of pottery. Of course, mass disappearances in that part of the world are dismayingly more frequent than they once were, primarily due to political violence. Cuban mercenaries, operating with Soviet weaponry, have been assisting in the liquidation of whole tribes that are unwilling to put their ethnic identities second to the revolutionary purpose. But when entire villages are slaughtered for political purposes, they are always looted, then burned, and the bodies are always interred in mass graves. There was no looting in this instance, no burning, no bodies to be found. Some weeks later, game wardens in that district reported an inexplicable decrease in the wildlife population. No one connected it to the missing villagers; it was reported as a separate phenomenon.'

'But you know differently.'

'Well, I *suspect* differently,' Flyte said, putting strawberry jam on a last bit of croissant.

'Most of these disappearances seem to occur in remote areas,' Sandler said. 'Which makes verification difficult.'

'Yes. That was thrown in my face as well. Actually, most incidents probably occur at sea, for the sea covers the largest part of the earth. The sea can be as remote as the moon, and much of what takes place beneath the waves is beyond our notice. Yet don't forget the two armies I mentioned – the Chinese and Spanish. *Those* disappearances took place within the context of modern civilisation. And if tens of thousands of Mayans fell victim to the ancient enemy whose existence I've theorized, then that was a case in which entire cities, hearts of civilisation, were attacked with frightening boldness.'

'You think it could happen now, today—'

'No question about it!'

'— in a place like New York or even here in London?'

'Certainly! It could happen virtually anywhere that has the geological underpinnings I outlined in my book.'

They both sipped champagne, thinking.

The rain hammered on the windows with greater fury than before.

Sandler was not certain that he believed in the theories Flyte had propounded in *The Ancient Enemy*. He knew they could form the basis for a wildly successful book written in a popular vein, but that didn't mean he had to believe in them. He didn't really *want* to believe. Believing was like opening the door to Hell.

He looked at Flyte, who was straightening his wilted carnation again, and he said, 'It gives me the chills.'

'It should,' Flyte said, nodding. 'It should.'

The waiter came with the eggs, bacon, sausages and toast.

19

THE DEAD OF NIGHT

THE INN was a fortress.

Bryce was satisfied with the preparations that had been made.

At last, after two hours of arduous labour, he sat down at a table in the cafeteria, sipping decaffeinated coffee from a white ceramic mug on which was emblazoned the blue crest of the hotel.

By one-thirty in the morning, with the help of the ten deputies who had arrived from Santa Mira, much had been accomplished. One of the two rooms had been converted into a dormitory; twenty mattresses were lined up on the floor, enough to accommodate any single shift of the investigative team, even after General Copperfield's people arrived. In the other half of the restaurant, a couple of buffet tables had been set up at one end, where a cafeteria line could be formed at mealtimes. The kitchen had been cleaned and put in order. The large lobby had been converted into an enormous operations centre, with desks, makeshift desks, typewriters, filing cabinets, bulletin boards, and a big map of Snowfield.

Furthermore, the inn had been given a thorough security inspection, and steps had been taken to prevent a break-in by the enemy. The two rear entrances – one through the kitchen, one through the lobby – were locked, and additionally secured with slanted two-by-fours, which were wedged under the crashbars and nailed to the frames. Bryce had ordered that extra precaution to avoid wasting guards at those entrances. The door to the emergency stairs was similarly sealed off; nothing could enter the higher floors of the hotel and come down upon them by surprise. Now, only a pair of small elevators connected the lobby level to the three upper floors, and two guards were stationed there. Another guard stood at the front entrance. A detail of four men had ascertained that all upstairs rooms were empty. Another detail had determined that all of the ground-floor windows were locked; most of them were painted shut, as well. Nevertheless, the windows were points of weakness in their fortifications.

At least, Bryce thought, if anything tries to get inside through a window, we'll have the sound of breaking glass to warn us.

A host of other details had been attended to. Wargle's mutilated corpse had been temporarily stored in a utility room that adjoined the lobby. Bryce had drawn up a duty roster, and had structured twelve-hour work shifts for the next three days, should the crisis last that long. Finally, he couldn't think of anything more that could be done until first light.

Now he sat alone at one of the round tables in the dining room, sipping Sanka, trying to make sense of the night's events. His mind kept circling back to one unwanted thought:

His brain was gone. His blood was sucked out of him – every damned drop.

He shook off the sickening image of Wargle's ruined face, got up, went for more coffee, then returned to the table.

The inn was very quiet.

At another table, three of the night shift men – Miguel Hernandez, Sam Potter, and Henry Wong – were playing cards, but they weren't talking much. When they did speak, it was almost in whispers.

The inn was very quiet.

The inn was a fortress.

The inn *was* a fortress, dammit.

But was it safe?

Lisa chose a mattress in a corner of the dormitory, where her back would be up against a blank wall.

Jenny unfolded one of the two blankets stacked at the foot of the mattress, and draped it over the girl.

'Want the other one?'

'No,' Lisa said. 'This'll be enough. It feels funny, though, going to bed with all my clothes on.'

'Things'll get back to normal pretty soon,' Jenny said, but even as she spoke she realized how inane that statement was.

'Are you going to sleep now?'

'Not quite yet.'

'I wish you would,' Lisa said. 'I wish you'd lay down right there on the next mattress.'

'You're not alone, honey.' Jenny smoothed the girl's hair.

A few deputies – including Tal Whitman, Gordy Brogan, and Frank Autry – had bedded down on other mattresses. There were also three heavily armed guards who would watch over everyone through the night.

'Will they turn the lights down any further?' Lisa asked.

'No. We can't risk darkness.'

'Good. They're dim enough. Will you stay with me until I fall asleep?' Lisa asked, seeming much younger than fourteen.

'Sure.'

'And talk to me.'

'Sure. But we'll have to talk softly, so we don't disturb anyone.'

Jenny lay down beside her sister, her head propped up on one hand. 'What do you want to talk about?'

'I don't care. Anything. Anything except . . . tonight.'

'Well, there is something I want to ask you,' Jenny said. 'It's not about tonight, but it's about something you said tonight. Remember when we were sitting on the bench in front of the jail, waiting for the sheriff? Remember how we were talking about Mom, and you said Mom used to . . . used to brag about me?'

Lisa smiled. 'Her daughter, the doctor. Oh, she was *so* proud of you, Jenny.'

As it had done before, that statement unsettled Jenny.

'And Mom never blamed me for Dad's stroke?' she asked.

Lisa frowned. 'Why would she blame you?'

'Well . . . because I guess I caused him some heartache there for a while. Heartache and a lot of worry.'

'*You?*' Lisa asked, astonished.

'And when Dad's doctor couldn't control his high blood pressure and then he had a stroke—'

'According to Mom, the only thing you ever did bad in your entire life was when you decided to give the calico cat a black dye job for Halloween and you got Clairol all over the sun porch furniture.'

Jenny laughed with surprise. 'I'd forgotten that. I was only eight years old.'

They smiled at each other, and in that moment they felt more than ever like sisters.

Then Lisa said, 'Why'd you think Mom blamed you for Daddy's dying? It was natural causes, wasn't it? A stroke. How could it possibly have been your fault?'

Jenny hesitated, thinking back thirteen years to the start of it all. That her mother had never blamed her for her father's death was a profoundly liberating realisation. She felt free for the first time since she'd been nineteen.

'Jenny?'

'Mmmm?'

'Are you crying?'

'No, I'm okay,' she said, fighting back tears. 'If Mom didn't hold it against me, I guess I've been wrong to hold it against myself. I'm just happy, honey. Happy about what you've told me.'

'But what was it you thought you did? If we're going to be good sisters, we shouldn't keep secrets. Tell me, Jenny.'

'It's a long story, Sis. I'll tell you about it eventually, but not now. Now I want to hear all about you.'

They talked about trivialities for a few minutes, and Lisa's eyes grew steadily heavier.

Jenny was reminded of Bryce Hammond's gentle, hooded eyes.

And of Jakob and Aida Leibermann's eyes, glaring out of their severed heads.

And Deputy Wargle's eyes. Gone. Those burnt-out, empty sockets in that hollow skull.

She tried to force her thoughts away from that gruesomeness, from that too-well-remembered, grim reaper's gaze. But her mind kept circling back to that image of monstrous violence and death.

She wished there was someone to talk her to sleep just as she was doing for Lisa. It was going to be a restless night.

In the utility room that adjoined the lobby and backed up against the elevator shaft, the light was off. There were no windows.

A faint odour of cleaning fluids clung to the place. Pinesol. Lysol. Furniture polish. Floor wax. Janitorial supplies were stored on shelves along one wall.

In the right-hand corner, furthest from the door, was a large metal sink. Water dripped from a leaky tap – one drop every ten or twelve seconds. Each pellet of water struck the metal basin with a soft, hollow *ping*.

In the centre of the room, as shrouded in utter blackness as was everything else, the faceless body of Stu Wargle lay on a table, covered by a dustcover.

All was still.

Except for the monotonous *ping* of the dripping water.

A breathless anticipation hung in the air.

Frank Autry huddled under the blanket, his eyes closed, and he thought about Ruth. Tall, willowy, sweet-faced Ruthie. Ruthie with the quiet yet crisp voice, Ruthie with the throaty laugh that most people found infectious, his wife of twenty-six years. She was the only woman he had ever loved; he still loved her.

He had spoken with her by telephone for a few minutes, just before turning in for the night. He had not been able to tell her much about what was happening – just that there was a siege situation underway in Snowfield, that it was being kept quiet as long as possible, and that by the look of it he wouldn't be home tonight. Ruthie hadn't pressed him for details. She had been a good army wife through all his years in the service. She still was.

Thinking of Ruth was his primary psychological defence mechanism. In times of stress, in times of fear and pain and depression, he simply thought of Ruth, concentrated solely on her, and the strife-filled world faded. For a man who had spent so much of his life engaged in dangerous work – for a man whose occupations had seldom allowed him to forget that death was an intimate part of life – a woman like Ruth was indispensable medicine, an inoculation against despair.

Gordy Brogan was afraid to close his eyes again. Each time that he *had* closed them, he had been plagued by bloody visions that had rolled up out of his own private darkness. Now he lay under his blanket, eyes open, staring at Frank Autry's back.

In his mind, he composed his letter of resignation to Bryce Hammond. He wouldn't be able to type and submit that letter until after this Snowfield business was settled. He didn't want to leave his buddies in the middle of a battle; that didn't seem right. He might actually be of some help to them, considering that it didn't appear as if he would be required to shoot at *people*. However, as soon as this thing was settled, as soon as they were back in Santa Mira, he would write the letter and hand-deliver it to the sheriff.

He had no doubt about it now: police work was not – and never had been – for him.

185

He was still a young man; there was time to change careers. He had become a cop partly as an act of rebellion against his parents, for it had been the last thing they had wanted. They'd noted his uncanny way with animals, his ability to win the trust and friendship of any creature on four legs within about half a minute flat, and they had hoped he would become a vet. Gordy had always felt smothered by his mother's and father's unflagging affection, and when they had nudged him towards a career in veterinary medicine, he had rejected the possibility. Now he saw that they were right and that they only wanted what was best for him. Indeed, deep down, he had always known they were right. He was a healer, not a peace-keeper.

He had also been drawn to the uniform and the badge because being a cop had seemed a good way of proving his masculinity. In spite of his muscle and formidable size, in spite of his acute interest in women, he had always believed that others thought of him as androgynous. As a boy, he had never been interested in sports, which had obsessed all of his male contemporaries. And endless talk about hot-rods had simply bored him. His interests lay elsewhere and, to some, seemed effete. Although his talent was only average, he enjoyed painting. He played the French horn. Nature fascinated him, and he was an avid bird-watcher. His abhorrence of violence had not been acquired as an adult; even as a child, he had avoided confrontations. His pacifism, when considered with his reticence in the company of girls, had made him appear, at least to himself, somewhat less than manly. But now, at long last, he saw that he did not need to prove anything.

He would go to school, become a vet. He would be content. His folks would be happy, too. His life would be on the right track again.

He closed his eyes, sighing, seeking sleep. But out of darkness came nightmarish images of the severed heads of cats and dogs, flesh-crawling images of dismembered and tortured animals.

He snapped his eyes open, gasping.

What *had* happened to all the pets in Snowfield?

The utility room off the lobby.

Windowless, lightless.

The monotonous *ping* of water dropping into the metal sink had stopped.

But there wasn't silence now. Something moved in the darkness. It made a soft, wet, stealthy sound as it crept around the pitch-black room.

Not yet ready to sleep, Jenny went into the cafeteria, poured a cup of coffee, and joined the sheriff at a corner table.

'Lisa sleeping?' he asked.

'Like a rock.'

'How're you holding up? This must be hard on you. All your neighbours, friends . . .'

'It's hard to grieve properly,' she said. 'I'm just sort of numb. If I let myself react to every death that's had an effect on me, I'd be a blubbering mess. So I've just let my emotions go numb.'

'It's a normal, healthy response. That's how we're all dealing with it.'

They drank some coffee, chatted a bit. Then:

'Married?' he asked.

'No. You?'

'I was.'

'Divorced?'

'She died.'

'Oh, Christ, of course. I read about it. I'm sorry. A year ago, wasn't it? A traffic accident?'

'A runaway truck.'

She was looking into his eyes, and she thought they clouded and became less blue than they had been. 'How's your son doing?'

'He's still in a coma. I don't think he'll ever come out of it.'

'I'm sorry, Bryce. I really am.'

He folded his hands around his mug and stared down at the coffee. 'With Timmy like he is, it'll be a blessing, really, when he just finally lets go. I was numb about it for a while. I couldn't feel anything, not just emotionally but physically, as well. At one point I cut my finger while I was slicing an orange, and I bled all over the damned kitchen and even ate a few bloody sections of the orange before I noticed that something was wrong. Even then I never felt any pain. Lately, I've been coming around to an understanding, to an acceptance.' He looked up and met Jenny's eyes. 'Strangely enough, since I've been here in Snowfield, the greyness has gone away.'

'Greyness?'

'For a long time, the colour has been leeched out of everything. It's all been grey. But tonight – just the opposite. Tonight, there's been so much excitement, so much tension, so much *fear*, that everything has seemed extraordinarily vivid.'

Then Jenny spoke of her mother's death, of the surprisingly powerful effect it had had on her, despite the twelve years of partial estrangement that should have softened the blow.

Again, Jenny was impressed by Bryce Hammond's ability to make her feel at ease. They seemed to have known each other for years.

She even found herself telling him about the mistakes she had made in her eighteenth and nineteenth years, about her naive and stubbornly wrong-headed behaviour that had grievously hurt her parents. Towards the end of her first year in college, she had met a man who had captivated her. He was a graduate student – Campbell Hudson; she called him Cam – five years her senior. His attentiveness, charm and passionate pursuit of her had swept her away. Until then, she had led a sheltered life; she had never tied herself down to one steady boy-friend, had never really dated heavily at all. She was an easy target. Having fallen for Cam Hudson, she then became not only his lover but his rapt student and disciple and, very nearly, his devoted slave.

'I can't see you subjugating yourself to anyone,' Bryce said.

'I was young.'

'Always an acceptable excuse.'

She had moved in with Cam, taking insufficient measures to conceal her sinning from her mother and father; and *sinning* was how they saw it. Later, she decided – rather, she allowed Cam to decide for her – that she would drop out of college and work as a waitress, help pay his bills until he was finished with his master's and doctoral work.

Once trapped in Cam Hudson's self-serving scenario, she gradually found him less attractive and less charming than he had once been. She learned he had a violent temper. Then her father died while she was still with Cam, and at the funeral she sensed that her mother blamed her for his untimely passing. Within a month of the day that her father was consigned to the grave, she learned she was pregnant. She had been pregnant when he'd died. Cam was furious and insisted on a quick abortion. She asked for a day to consider, but he became enraged at even a twenty-four-hour delay. He beat her so severely that she had a miscarriage. It was over then. The foolishness was over. She grew up suddenly – although her abrupt coming of age was too late to please her father.

'Since then,' she told Bryce, 'I've spent my life working hard – maybe too hard – to prove to my mother that I was sorry and that I was, after all, worthy of her love. I've worked weekends, turned down countless party invitations, skipped most vacations for the past twelve years, all in the name of bettering myself. I didn't go home as often as I should have done. I couldn't face my mother. I could see the accusation in her eyes. And then tonight, from Lisa, I learned the most amazing thing.'

'Your mother never blamed you,' Bryce said, displaying that uncanny sensitivity and perception that she had seen in him before.

'Yes!' Jenny said. 'She never held anything against me.'

'She was probably even proud of you.'

'Yes, again! She never blamed me for Dad's death. It was *me* doing all the blaming. The accusation I thought I saw in her eyes was only a reflection of my own guilty feelings.' Jenny laughed softly and sourly, shaking her head. 'It'd be funny if it wasn't so damned sad.'

In Bryce Hammond's eyes, she saw the sympathy and understanding for which she had been searching ever since her father's funeral.

He said, 'We're a lot alike in some ways, you and I. I think we both have martyr complexes.'

'No more,' she said. 'Life's too short. That's something that's been brought home to me tonight. From now on I'm going to live, really live – if Snowfield will let me.'

'We'll get through this,' he said.

'I wish I could feel sure of that.'

Bryce said, 'You know, having something to look forward to will help us make it. So how about giving *me* something to look forward to?'

'Huh?'

'A date.' He leaned forward. His thick, sandy hair fell into his eyes. 'Gervasio's Ristorante in Santa Mira. Minestrone. Scampi in garlic butter. Some good veal or maybe a steak. A side dish of pasta. They make a wonderful vermicelli al pesto. Good wine.'

She grinned. 'I'd love it.'

'I forgot to mention the garlic bread.'

'Oh, I love garlic bread.'

'Zabaglione for dessert.'

'They'll have to carry us out,' she said.

'We'll arrange for wheelbarrows.'

They chatted for a couple of minutes, relieving tension, and then both of them were finally ready to sleep.

Ping.

In the dark utility room where Stu Wargle's body lay on a table, water had begun to drop into the metal sink again.

190

Ping.

Something continued to move stealthily in the darkness, around and around the table. It make a slick, wet, slithering-through-the-mud noise.

That wasn't the only sound in the room; there were many other noises, all soft and low. The panting of a weary dog. The hiss of an angry cat. Quiet, silvery, haunting laughter; the laughter of a small child. Then a woman's pained whimpering. A moan. A sigh. The chirruping of a swallow, rendered clearly but softly, so as not to draw the attention of any of the guards posted out in the lobby. The warning of a rattlesnake. The humming of bumblebees. The higher-pitched, sinister buzzing of wasps. A dog growling.

The noises ceased as abruptly as they had begun.

Silence returned.

Ping.

The quiet lasted, unbroken except for the regularly spaced notes of the falling water, for perhaps a minute.

Ping.

There was a rustle of cloth in the lightless room. The shroud over Wargle's corpse. The shroud had slipped off the dead man and had fallen to the floor.

Slithering again.

And a dry-wood splintering sound. A brittle, muffled but violent sound. A hard, sharp bonecrack.

Silence again.

Ping.

Silence.

Ping. Ping. Ping.

While Tal Whitman waited for sleep, he thought about fear. That was the key word; it was the foundry emotion that had forged him. Fear. His life was one long vigorous denial of fear, a refutation of its very existence. He refused to be affected by – humbled by, driven by – fear. He would not admit that anything could scare him. Early in his life, hard experience had taught him that even acknowledgement of fear could expose him to its voracious appetite.

He had been born and raised in Harlem, where fear was everywhere: fear of street gangs, fear of junkies, fear of random violence, fear of economic privation, fear of being excluded from the mainstream of life. In those tenements, along those grey streets, fear waited to gobble you up the instant you gave it the slightest nod of recognition.

In childhood, he had not been safe even in the apartment that he had shared with his mother, one brother, and three sisters. Tal's father had been a sociopath, a wife-beater, who had shown up once or twice a month merely for the pleasure of slapping his woman senseless and terrorizing his children. Of course, Mama had been no better than the old man. She drank too much wine, tooted too much dope, and was nearly as ruthless with her children as their father was.

When Tal was nine, on one of the rare nights when his father was home, a fire swept the tenement house. Tal was his family's sole survivor. Mama and the old man had died in bed, overcome by smoke in their sleep. Tal's brother Oliver, and his sisters – Heddy, Louisa, and baby Francesca – were lost, and now all these years later it was sometimes difficult to believe that they had ever really existed.

After the fire, he was taken in by his mother's sister, Aunt Rebecca. She lived in Harlem, too. Becky didn't drink. She didn't use dope. She had no children of her own, but she did have a job, and she went to night school, and she believed in self-sufficiency, and she had high hopes. She often told Tal that there was nothing to fear but Fear Itself and that Fear Itself was like the bogeyman, just a shadow, not worth fearing at all. 'God made you healthy, Talbert, and He gave you a good brain. Now if you mess up, it's nobody's fault but your own.' With Aunt Becky's love, discipline, and guidance, young Talbert had eventually come to think of himself as virtually invincible. He was not scared of anything in life; he was not scared of dying, either.

That was why, years later, after surviving the shootout in the 7-Eleven store over in Santa Mira, he was able to tell Bryce Hammond that it had been a mere cakewalk.

Now, for the first time in a long, long string of years, he had come across a knot of fear.

Tal thought of Stu Wargle, and the knot of fear pulled tighter, squeezing his guts.

The eyes were eaten right out of his skull.

Fear Itself.

But this bogeyman was real.

Half a year from his thirty-first birthday, Tal Whitman was discovering that he could still be afraid, regardless of how strenuously he denied it. His fearlessness had brought him a long way in life. But, in opposition to all that he had believed before, he realized that there were also times when being afraid was merely being smart.

Shortly before dawn, Lisa woke from a nightmare she couldn't recall.

She looked at Jenny and the others who were sleeping, then turned towards the windows. Outside, Skyline Road was deceptively peaceful as the end of night drew near.

Lisa had to pee. She got up and walked quietly between two rows of mattresses. At the archway, she smiled at the guard, and he winked.

One man was in the dining room. He was leafing through a magazine.

In the lobby, two guards were stationed by the elevator doors. The two polished oak front doors of the inn, each with an oval of bevelled glass in the centre, were locked, but a third guard was positioned by that entrance. He was holding a shotgun and staring out through one of the ovals, watching the main approach to the building.

A fourth man was in the lobby. Lisa had met him earlier – a bald, florid-face deputy named Fred Turpner. He was sitting at the largest desk, monitoring the telephone. It must have rung frequently during the night, for a couple of legal-size sheets of paper were filled with messages. As Lisa passed by, the phone rang again. Fred raised one hand in greeting, then snatched up the receiver.

Lisa went directly to the toilets, which were tucked into one corner of the lobby:

SNOW BUNNIES   SNOW BUCKS

That cuteness was out of synch with the rest of the Hilltop Inn.

She pushed through the door marked SNOW BUNNIES. The toilets had been judged safe territory because they had no windows and could be entered only through the lobby, where there were always guards. The women's room was large and clean, with four stalls and sinks. The floors and walls were covered with white ceramic tile bordered by dark blue tile around the edge of the floor and around the top of the walls.

Lisa used the first stall and then the nearest sink. As she finished washing her hands and looked up at the mirror above the sink, she saw him. *Him*. The dead deputy. Wargle.

He was standing behind her, eight or ten feet away, in the middle of the room. Grinning.

She swung around, sure that somehow it was a flaw in the mirror, a trick of the looking glass. Surely he wasn't really there.

But he *was* there. Naked. Grinning obscenely.

His face had been restored: the heavy jowls, the thick-lipped and greasy-looking mouth, the piggish nose, the little quick eyes. The flesh was magically whole again.

Impossible.

Before Lisa could react, Wargle stepped between her and the door. His bare feet made a flat, slapping sound against the tile floor.

Someone was pounding on the door.

Wargle seemed not to hear it.

Pounding and pounding and pounding . . .

Why didn't they just open the door and come in?

Wargle extended his arms and made come-to-me motions with his hands. Grinning.

From the moment Lisa had met him, she hadn't liked Wargle. She had caught him looking at her when he thought her attention was elsewhere, and the expression in his eyes had been unsettling.

'Come here, sweet stuff,' he said.

She looked at the door and realized no one was pounding on it. She was only hearing the frantic thump of her own heart.

Wargle licked his lips.

Lisa suddenly gasped, surprising herself. She had been so totally paralyzed by the man's return from the dead that she had forgotten to breathe.

'Come here, you little bitch.'

She tried to scream. Couldn't.

Wargle touched himself obscenely.

'Bet you'd like a taste of this, huh?' he said, grinning, his lips moist from his hungrily licking tongue.

Again, she tried to scream. Again, she couldn't. She could barely wrench each badly needed breath into her burning lungs.

He's not real, she told herself.

If she closed her eyes for a few seconds, squeezed them tightly shut and counted to ten, he wouldn't be there when she looked again.

'Little bitch.'

He was an illusion. Maybe even part of a dream. Maybe her coming to the bathroom was really just another part of her nightmare.

But she didn't test her theory. She didn't close her eyes and count to ten. She didn't *dare*.

Wargle took a step towards her, still fondling himself.

He isn't real. He's an illusion.

Another step.

He isn't real, he's an illusion.

'Come on, sweet stuff, let me nibble on them titties of yours.'

He isn't real he's an illusion he isn't real he's—

'You're gonna love it, sweet stuff.'

She backed away from him.

'Cute little body you got, sweet stuff. Real cute.'

He continued to advance.

The light was behind him now. His shadow fell on her.

Ghosts didn't throw shadows.

In spite of his laugh and in spite of his fixed grin, his voice became steadily harsher, nastier. 'You stupid little slut. I'm gonna use you real good. Real damned good. Better than any of them high school boys ever used you. You ain't gonna be able to walk right for a week when I'm through with you, sweet stuff.'

His shadow had completely engulfed her.

Her heart slamming so hard that it seemed about to tear loose, Lisa backed up further, further – but soon collided with the wall. She was in a corner.

She looked around for a weapon, something she could at least throw at him. There was nothing.

Each breath was harder to draw than the one before it. She was dizzy and weak.

He isn't real. He's an illusion.

But she couldn't delude herself any longer; she couldn't believe in the dream any more.

Wargle stopped just an arm's length from her. He glared at her. He swayed from side to side, and he rocked back and forth on the balls of his bare feet, as if some mad dark private music swelled and ebbed and swelled within him.

He closed his hateful eyes, swaying dreamily.

A second passed.

What's he doing?

Two seconds, three, six, ten.

Still, his eyes remained closed.

She felt herself carried away in a whirlpool of hysteria.

Could she slip past him? While his eyes were closed? Jesus. No. He was too close. To get away, she would have to brush against him. Jesus. Brush against him? No. God, that would snap him out of his trance or whatever this was, and he would seize her, and his hands would be cold, dead-cold. She could not bring herself to touch him. No.

Then she noticed something odd happening behind his eyes. Wriggling movement. The lids themselves no longer conformed to the curvature of his eyeballs.

He opened his eyes.

They were gone.

Beneath the lids lay only empty black sockets.

She finally screamed, but the cry she brought forth was beyond human hearing. Breath passed out of her in an express-train rush, and she felt her throat working convulsively, but there was absolutely no sound that would bring help.

His eyes.

His empty eyes.

She was certain that those hollow sockets could still see her. They sucked at her with their emptiness.

His grin had not faded.

'Little pussy,' he said.

She screamed her silent scream.

'Little pussy. Kiss me, little pussy.'

Somehow, dark as midnight, those bone-rimmed sockets still held a glimmer of malevolent awareness.

'Kiss me.'

No!

Let me die, she prayed. God, please, let me die first.

197

'I want to suck on your juicy tongue,' Wargle said urgently, bursting into a giggle.

He reached for her.

She pressed hard against the unyielding wall.

Wargle touched her cheek.

She flinched and tried to pull away.

His fingertips trailed lightly down her cheek.

His hand was icy and slick.

She heard a thin, dry, eerie groan – '*Uh-uh-uh-uh-uhhhhhhh*' – and realized that she was listening to herself.

She smelled something strange, acrid. His breath? The stale breath of a dead man, expelled from rotting lungs? Did the walking dead breathe? The stench was faint but unbearable. She gagged.

He lowered his face towards hers.

She stared into his eaten-away eyes, into the swarming blackness beyond, and it was like peering through two peepholes into the deepest chambers of Hell.

His hand tightened on her throat.

He said, 'Give us—'

She heaved in a hot breath.

'—a little kiss.'

She heaved out another scream.

This time the scream wasn't silent. This time she pealed forth a sound that seemed loud enough to shatter the mirrors and to crack the ceramic tile.

As Wargle's dead, eyeless face slowly, slowly descended towards her, as she heard her scream echoing off the walls, the whirlpool of hysteria in which she'd been spinning became, now, a whirlpool of darkness, and she was drawn down into oblivion.

20

BODYSNATCHERS

In the lobby of the Hilltop Inn, on a rust-coloured sofa, against that wall which was furthest from the toilets, Jennifer Paige sat beside her sister, holding the girl.

Bryce squatted in front of the sofa, holding Lisa's hand, which he couldn't seem to make warm again no matter how firmly he pressed and rubbed it.

Except for the guards on duty, everyone had gathered behind Bryce, in a semi-circle around the front of the sofa.

Lisa looked terrible. Her eyes were sunken, guarded, haunted. Her face was as white as the tile floor in the ladies' room, where they had found her unconscious.

'Stu Wargle is dead,' Bryce assured her yet again.

'He wanted me t-t-to . . . kiss him,' the girl repeated, clinging resolutely to her bizarre story.

'There was no one in there but you,' Bryce said. 'Just you, Lisa.'

'He was *there*,' the girl insisted.

'We came running as soon as you screamed. We found you alone—'

'He was there.'

'—on the floor, in the corner, out cold.'

'He was there.'

'His body is in the utility room,' Bryce said, gently squeezing her hand. 'We put it there earlier. You remember, don't you?'

'Is it *still* there?' the girl asked. 'Maybe you'd better look.'

Bryce met Jenny's eyes. She nodded. Remembering that *anything* was possible tonight, Bryce got to his feet, letting go of the girl's hand. He turned towards the utility room.

'Tal?'

'Yeah?'

'Come with me.'

Tal drew his revolver.

Pulling his own sidearm from his holster, Bryce said, 'The rest of you stay back.'

With Tal at his side, Bryce crossed the lobby to the utility room door and paused in front of it.

'I don't think she's the kind of kid who makes up wild stories,' Tal said.

'I know she's not.'

Bryce thought about how Paul Henderson's corpse had vanished from the substation. Dammit, though, that had been very different from this. Paul's body had been accessible, unguarded. But no one could have reached Wargle's corpse – and it couldn't have got up and walked away of its own accord – without being seen by one of the three deputies posted in the lobby. Yet no one and nothing *had* been seen.

Bryce moved to the left of the door and motioned Tal over to its right.

They listened for several seconds. The inn was silent. There was no sound from within the utility room.

Keeping his body out of the doorway, Bryce leaned forward and reached across the door, took hold of the knob, turned it slowly and silently until it had gone as far as it would go. He hesitated. He glanced over at Tal, who indicated his own readiness. Bryce took a deep breath, threw the door inwards, and jumped back, out of the way.

Nothing rushed from the unlit room.

Tal inched to the edge of the jamb, reached around with one arm, fumbled for the light switch and found it.

Bryce was crouched down, waiting. The instant the light came on, he launched himself through the doorway, his revolver poked out in front of him.

Stark fluorescent light spilled down from the twin ceiling panels and glinted off the edges of the metal sink and off the bottles and cans of cleaning materials.

The shroud, in which they had wrapped the body, lay in a pile on the floor, beside the table.

Wargle's corpse was missing.

Deke Coover had been the guard stationed at the front doors of the inn. He wasn't much help to Bryce. He had spent a lot of time looking out at Skyline Road, with his back to the lobby. Someone could have carted Wargle's body away without Coover being the wiser.

'You told me to watch the front approach, Sheriff,' Deke said. 'As long as he didn't accompany himself with a song, Wargle could've come out of there all by his lonesome, doing an old soft-shoe routine and waving a flag in each hand, and he mightn't have attracted my notice.'

The two men stationed by the elevators, near the utility room, were Kelly MacHeath and Donny Jessup. They were two of Bryce's younger men, in their mid-twenties, but they were both able, trustworthy, and reasonably experienced.

MacHeath, a blond and beefy fellow with a bull's neck and heavy shoulders, shook his head and said, 'Nobody went in or out of the utility room all night.'

'Nobody,' Jessup agreed. He was a wiry, curly-haired man with eyes the colour of tea. 'We would've seen them.'

'The door's right *there*,' MacHeath observed.

'And we were here all night.'

'You know us, Sheriff,' MacHeath said.

'You know we aren't slackers,' Jessup said.

'When we're supposed to be on duty—'

'—we *are* on duty,' Jessup finished.

'Dammit,' Bryce said, 'Wargle's body is *gone*. It didn't just climb off that table and walk through a wall!'

'It didn't just climb off that table and walk through that door, either,' MacHeath insisted.

'Sir,' Jessup said, 'Wargle was dead. I didn't see the body myself, but from what I hear, he was *very* dead. Dead men stay where you put them.'

'Not necessarily,' Bryce said. 'Not in this town. Not tonight.'

In the utility room with Tal, Bryce said. 'There's just not another way out of here but the door.'

They walked slowly around the room, studying it.

The leaky tap drooled out a drop of water that struck the pan of the metal sink with a soft *ping*.

'The heating vent,' Tal said, pointing to a grille in one wall, directly under the ceiling. 'What about that?'

'Are you serious?'

'Better have a look.'

'It's not big enough for a man to pass through.'

'Remember the burglary at Krybinsky's Jewellery Store?'

'How could I forget? It's still unsolved, as Alex Krybinsky so pointedly reminds me every time we meet.'

'That guy entered Krybinsky's basement through an unlocked window almost as small as that grille.'

Bryce knew, as did any cop who handled burglaries, that a man of ordinary build required a surprisingly small opening to gain entrance to a building. Any hole large enough to accept a man's head was also large enough to provide an entrance for his entire body. The shoulders were wider than the head, of course, but they could be collapsed forward or otherwise contorted enough to be squeezed through; likewise, the breadth of the hips was nearly always sufficiently alterable to follow where the shoulders had gone. But Stu Wargle hadn't been a man of ordinary build.

'Stu's belly would've stuck in there like a cork in a bottle,' Bryce said.

Nevertheless, he pulled up a stepstool that had been standing in one corner, climbed onto it, and took a closer look at the vent.

'The grille's not held in place by screws,' he told Tal. 'It's a spring-clip model, so it could conceivably have been snapped into place from inside the duct, once Wargle went through, so long as he wriggled in feet-first.'

He pulled the grille off the wall.

Tal handed him a flashlight.

Bryce directed the beam into the dark heating duct and frowned. The narrow, metal passageway ran only a short distance before taking a ninety-degree upward turn.

Switching off the flashlight and passing it down to Tal, Bryce said, 'Impossible. To get through there, Wargle would have had to've been no bigger than Sammy Davis Jr and as flexible as the rubber man in a carnival sideshow.'

Frank Autry approached Bryce Hammond at the central operations desk in the middle of the lobby, where the sheriff was seated, reading over the messages that had come in during the night.

'Sir, there's something you ought to know about Wargle.'

Bryce looked up. 'What's that?'

'Well . . . I don't like to have to speak ill of the dead . . .'

'None of us cared much for him,' Bryce said flatly. 'Any attempt to honour his memory would be hypocritical. So if you know something that'll help me, spill it, Frank.'

Frank smiled. 'You'd have done real well for yourself in the army.' He sat on the edge of the desk. 'Last night, when Wargle and

I were dismantling the radio over at the substation, he made several disgusting remarks about Dr Paige and Lisa.'

'Sex stuff?'

'Yeah.'

Frank recounted the conversation that he'd had with Wargle.

'Christ,' Bryce said, shaking his head.

Frank said, 'The thing about the girl was what bothered me most. Wargle was half serious when he talked about maybe making a move on her if the opportunity arose. I don't think he'd have gone as far as rape, but he was capable of making a *very* heavy pass and using his authority, his badge, to coerce her. I don't think that kid could be coerced; she's too spunky. But I think Wargle might've tried it.'

The sheriff tapped a pencil on the desk, staring thoughtfully into the air.

'But Lisa couldn't have known,' Frank said.

'She couldn't have overheard any of your conversation?'

'Not a word.'

'She might have suspected what kind of man Wargle was from the way he looked at her.'

'But she couldn't have *known*,' Frank said. 'Do you see what I'm driving at?'

'Yes.'

'Most kids,' Frank said, 'if they were going to make up a tall tale, they would be satisfied just to say they'd been chased by a dead man. They wouldn't ordinarily embellish it by saying the dead man wanted to molest them.'

Bryce tended to agree. 'Kids' minds aren't that baroque. Their lies are usually simple, not elaborate.'

'Exactly,' Frank said. 'The fact that she said Wargle was naked and wanted to molest her . . . well . . . to me, that seems to add credibility to her story. Now, we'd all like to believe that someone sneaked into the utility room and stole Wargle's body. And we'd like to believe they put the body in the ladies' room, that Lisa saw it, that she panicked, and that she imagined all the rest. And we'd like to believe that after she fainted, someone got the corpse out of there by some incredibly clever means. But that explanation is full of holes. What happened was a lot stranger than that.'

Bryce dropped his pencil and leaned back in his chair. 'Shit. You believe in ghosts, Frank? The living dead?'

'No. There's a real explanation for this,' Frank said. 'Not a bunch of superstitious mumbo-jumbo. A *real* explanation.'

'I agree,' Bryce said. 'But Wargle's face was . . .'

'I know. I saw it.'

'How could his face have been put back together?'

'I don't know.'

'And Lisa said his eyes . . .'

'Yeah. I heard what she said.'

Bryce sighed. 'You ever worked Rubik's Cube?'

Frank blinked. 'No. I never did.'

'Well, I did,' the sheriff said. 'The damned thing almost drove me crazy, but I stuck with it, and eventually I solved it. Everybody thinks that's a hard puzzle, but compared to this case, Rubik's Cube is a kindergarten game.'

'There's another difference,' Frank said.

'What's that?'

'If you fail to solve Rubik's Cube, the punishment isn't death.'

In Santa Mira, in his cell in the county jail, Fletcher Kale, slayer of wife and son, woke before dawn. He lay motionless on the thin foam mattress and stared at the window which presented a rectangular slab of pre-dawn sky for his inspection.

He would not spend his life in prison. Would *not*.

He had a magnificent destiny. That was the thing no one understood. They saw the Fletcher Kale who existed *now*, without being able to see what he would become. He was destined to have it all: money beyond counting, power beyond imagining, fame, respect.

Kale knew he was different from the ruck of mankind, and it was this knowledge that kept him going in the face of all adversity. The seeds of greatness within him were already sprouting. In time, he would make them all see how wrong they had been about him.

Perception, he thought as he stared up at the barred window, perception is my greatest gift. I'm extraordinarily perceptive.

He saw that, without exception, human beings were driven by self-interest. Nothing wrong with that. It was the nature of the species. That was how humankind was *meant* to be. But most people could not bear to face the truth. They dreamed up so-called inspiring concepts like love, friendship, honour, truthfulness, faith, trust, and individual dignity. They claimed to believe in all those things and more; however, at heart, they knew it was all bullshit. They just couldn't admit it. And so, they stupidly hobbled themselves with a smarmy, self-congratulatory code of conduct, with noble but hollow sentiments, thus frustrating their true desires, dooming themselves to failure and unhappiness.

Fools. God, he despised them.

From his unique perspective, Kale saw that mankind was, in reality, the most ruthless, dangerous, unforgiving species on earth. And he *revelled* in that knowledge. He was proud to be a member of such a race.

I'm ahead of my own time, Kale thought as he sat up on the edge of his bunk and put his bare feet on the cold floor of his cell. I am the next step of evolution. I've evolved beyond the need to believe in morality. That's why they look at me with such loathing. Not because I killed Joanna and Danny. They hate me because I'm better than they are, more completely in touch with my true human nature.

He'd had no choice but to kill Joanna. She had refused to give him the money, after all. She had been prepared to humiliate him professionally, ruin him financially, and wreck his entire future.

He'd *had* to kill her. She was in his way.

It was too bad about Danny. Kale sort of regretted that part. Not always. Just now and then. Too bad. Necessary, but too bad.

Anyway, Danny had always been a regular mama's boy. In fact, he was actually downright distant towards his father. That was Joanna's handiwork. She had probably been brainwashing the kid, turning him against his old man. In the end, Danny really hadn't been Kale's son at all. He'd become a stranger.

Kale got down on the floor of his cell and began to do push-ups.

One-two, one-two, one-two.

He intended to keep himself in shape for that moment when an opportunity for escape presented itself. He knew exactly where he would go when he escaped. Not west, not out of the county, not over towards Sacramento. That's what they would expect him to do.

One-two, one-two.

He knew of a perfect hideout. It was right here in the county. They wouldn't be looking for him under their noses. When they couldn't find him in a day or so, they'd decide he had already split, and they'd stop actively looking in this neighbourhood. When several more weeks passed, when they weren't thinking about him any longer, *then* he would leave the hideout, double back through town, and head west.

One-two.

But first, he would go up into the mountains. That's where the hideout was. The mountains offered him the best chance of eluding the cops once he'd escaped. He had a hunch about it. The mountains. Yeah. He felt *drawn* to the mountains.

Dawn came to the mountains, spreading like a bright stain across the sky, soaking into the darkness and discolouring it.

The forest above Snowfield was quiet. Very quiet.

In the underbrush, the leaves were beaded with morning dew.

207

The pleasant odour of rich humus rose up from the spongy forest floor.

The air was chilly, as if the last exhalation of the night still lay upon the land.

The fox stood motionless on a limestone formation that thrust up from an open slope, just below the treeline. The wind gently ruffled his grey fur.

His breath made a small phosphoric plume in the crisp air.

The fox was not a night hunter, yet he had been on the prowl since an hour before dawn. He had not eaten in almost two days.

He had been unable to find game. The woods had been unnaturally silent and devoid of the scent of prey.

In all his seasons as a hunter, the fox had never encountered such barren quietude as this. The most bitter days of mid-winter were filled with more promise than this. Even in the wind-whipped snows of January, there was always the blood scent, the game scent.

Not now.

Now there was nothing.

Death seemed to have claimed all the creatures in this part of the forest – except for one small, hungry fox. Yet there was not even the scent of death, not even the ripe stench of a carcass mouldering in the underbrush.

But at last, as he had scampered across the low limestone formation, being careful not to set foot in one of the crevices or flute holes that dropped down into the caves beneath, the fox had seen something move on the slope ahead of him, something that had not merely been stirred by the wind. He had frozen on the low rocks, staring uphill at the shadowy perimeter of this new arm of the forest.

A squirrel. Two squirrels. No, there were even more of them than that – five, ten, twenty. They were lined up side by side in the dimness along the treeline.

At first there had been no game whatsoever. Now there was an equally strange abundance of it.

The fox sniffed.

Although the squirrels were only five or six yards away, he could not get their scent.

The squirrels were looking directly at him, but they didn't seem frightened.

The fox cocked his head, suspicion tempering his hunger.

The squirrels moved to their left, all at once, in a tight little group, and then came out of the shadows of the trees, away from the protection of the forest, onto open ground, straight towards the fox. They rolled over and under and around one another, a frantic confusion of brown pelts, a blur of motion in the brown grass. When they came to an abrupt halt, all at the same instant, they were only three or four yards from the fox. And they were no longer squirrels.

The fox twitched and made a hissing sound.

The twenty small squirrels were now four large racoons.

The fox growled softly.

Ignoring him, one of the racoons stood on its hind feet and began washing its paws.

The fur along the fox's back bristled.

He sniffed the air.

No scent.

He put his head low and watched the racoons closely. His sleek muscles grew even more tense than they had been, not because he intended to spring, but because he intended to flee.

Something was very wrong.

All four racoons were sitting up now, forepaws tucked against their chests, tender bellies exposed.

They were watching the fox.

The racoon was not usually prey for the fox. It was too aggressive, too sharp of tooth, too quick with its claws. But though it was safe from foxes, the racoon never enjoyed confrontation, it never flaunted itself as these four were doing.

The fox licked the cold air with his tongue.

He sniffed again and finally *did* pick up a scent.

His ears snapped back flat against his skull, and he snarled.

It wasn't the scent of racoons. It wasn't the scent of any denizen of the forest that he had ever encountered before. It was an unfamiliar, sharp, unpleasant odour. Faint. But repellent.

This vile odour wasn't coming from any of the four racoons that posed in front of the fox. He wasn't quite able to make out where it *was* coming from.

Sensing grave danger, the fox whipped around on the limestone, turning away from the racoons, although he was reluctant to put his back to them.

His paws scraped and his claws clicked on the hard surface as he launched himself down the slope, across the flat weather-worn rock, his tail streaming out behind him. He leapt over a foot-wide crevice in the stone – and in mid-leap he was snatched from the air by something dark and cold and pulsing.

The thing burst up out of the crevice with brutal, shocking force and speed.

The agonized squeal of the fox was sharp and brief.

As quickly as the fox was seized, it was drawn down into the crevice. Five feet below, at the bottom of the miniature chasm, there was a small hole that led into the caves beneath the limestone outcropping. The hole was too small to admit the fox, but the struggling creature was dragged through anyway, its bones snapping as it went.

Gone.

All in the blink of an eye. Half a blink.

Indeed, the fox had been *sucked* into the earth before the echo of its dying cry had even pealed back from a distant hillside.

The racoons were gone.

Now, a flood of field mice poured onto the smooth slabs of limestone. Scores of them. At least a hundred.

They went to the edge of the crevice.

They stared down into it.

One by one, the mice slipped over the edge, dropped to the bottom, and then went through the small natural opening into the cavern below.

Soon, all the mice were gone, too.

Once again, the forest above Snowfield was quiet.

PART TWO
Phantoms

Evil is not an abstract concept. It lives. It has a form. It stalks. It is too real.

—Dr Tom Dooley

Phantoms! Whenever I think I fully understand mankind's purpose on earth, just when I foolishly imagine that I have seized upon the meaning of life . . . suddenly I see phantoms dancing in the shadows, mysterious phantoms performing a gavotte that says, as pointedly as words, 'What you know is nothing, little man; what you have to learn, immense.'

—Charles Dickens

21

THE BIG STORY

SANTA MIRA.

Monday – 1:02 am.

'Hello?'

'Is this the *Santa Mira Daily News*?'

'Yeah.'

'The newspaper?'

'Lady, the paper's closed. It's after one in the morning.'

'Closed? I didn't know a newspaper ever dosed.'

'This isn't the *New York Times*.'

'But aren't you printing tomorrow's edition now?'

'The printing's not done here. These are the business and editorial offices. Did you want the printer or what?'

'Well . . . I have a story.'

'If it's an obituary or a church bake sale or something, what you do is you call back in the morning, after nine o'clock, and you—'

'No, no. This is a *big* story.'

'Oh, a garage sale, huh?'

'What?'

'Never mind. You'll just have to call back in the morning.'

'Wait, listen, I work for the phone company.'

'That's not such a big story.'

'No, see, it's because I work for the phone company that I found out about this thing. Are you an editor?'

'No. I'm in charge of selling ad space.'

'Well . . . maybe you can still help me.'

'Lady, I'm sitting here on a Sunday night – no, a Monday morning now – all alone in a dreary little office, trying to figure out how the devil to drum up enough business to keep this paper afloat. I am tired. I am irritable—'

'How awful.'

'—and I am afraid you'll have to call back in the morning.'

'But something terrible has happened in Snowfield. I don't know exactly what, but I know people are dead. There might even be a *lot* of people dead or at least in danger of dying.'

'Christ, I must be tireder than I thought. I'm getting interested in spite of myself. Tell me.'

'We've rerouted Snowfield's phone service, pulled it off the automatic dialling system, and restricted all ingoing calls. You can only reach two numbers up there now, and both of them are being answered by the sheriff's men. The reason they've set it up that way is to seal the place off before the reporters find out something's up.'

'Lady, what've you been drinking?'

'I don't drink.'

'Then what've you been smoking?'

'Listen, I know a little bit more. They're getting calls from the Santa Mira sheriff's office all the time, and from the governor's office, and from some military base out in Utah, and they—'

San Francisco.

Monday – 1:40 am.

'This is Sid Sandowicz. Can I help you?'

'I keep tellin' them I want to talk to a *San Francisco Chronicle* reporter, man.'

'That's me.'

'Man, you guys have hung up on me three times! What the fuck's the matter with you guys?'

216

'Watch your language.'

'Shit.'

'Listen, do you have any idea how many kids like you call up newspapers, wasting our time with silly-ass gags and hot tip hoaxes?'

'Huh? How'd you even know I was a kid?'

''Cause you sound twelve.'

'I'm fifteen!'

'Congratulations.'

'Shit!'

'Listen, son, I've got a boy your age, which is why I'm bothering to listen to you when the other guys wouldn't. So if you've really got something of interest, spill it.'

'Well, my old man's a professor at Stanford. He's a virologist and an epidemiologist. You know what that means, man?'

'He studies viruses, disease, something like that.'

'Yeah. And he's let himself be corrupted.'

'How's that?'

'He accepted a grant from the fuckin' military. Man, he's involved with some biological warfare outfit. It's supposed to be a peaceful application of his research, but you know that's a lot of horseshit. He sold his soul, and now they're finally claimin' it. The shit's hit the fan.'

'The fact that your father sold out – if he *did* sell out – might be big news in your family, son, but I'm afraid it wouldn't be of much interest to our readers.'

'Hey, man, I didn't call up just to jerk you off. I've got a real *story*. Tonight they came for him. There's a crisis of some kind. I'm supposed to think he had to fly back East on business. I snuck upstairs and listened at their bedroom door while he was layin' it all out for the old lady. There's been some kind of contamination in Snowfield. A big emergency. Everyone's tryin' to keep it secret.'

'Snowfield, California?'

'Yeah, yeah. What I figure, man, is that they were secretly runnin' a test of some germ weapon *on our own people* and it got out of hand. Or maybe it was an accidental spill. Somethin' real heavy's goin' down, for sure.'

'What's your name, son?'

'Ricky Bettenby. My old man's name is Wilson Bettenby.'

'Stanford, you said?'

'Yeah. You gonna follow up on this, man?'

'Maybe there's something to it. But before I start calling people at Stanford, I need to ask you a lot more questions.'

'Fire away. I'll tell you whatever I can. I want to blast this wide open, man. I want him to *pay* for sellin' out.'

Throughout the night, the leaks sprung one by one. At Dugway, Utah, an army officer, who should have known better, used a pay phone off the base to call New York and spill the story to a much-loved younger brother who was a cub reporter for the *Times*. In bed, after sex, an aide to the governor told his lover, a woman reporter. Those and other holes in the dam caused the flow of information to grow from a trickle to a flood.

By three o'clock in the morning, the switchboard at the Santa Mira County Sheriff's Office was overloaded. By dawn, the newspaper, television, and radio reporters were swarming into Santa Mira. Within a few hours of first light, the street in front of the sheriff's offices was crowded with press cars, camera vans bearing the logos of TV stations in Sacramento and San Francisco, reporters, and curiosity seekers of all ages.

The deputies gave up trying to keep people from congregating in the middle of the street, for there were too many of them to be herded onto the pavement. They sealed off the block with sawhorses and turned it into a big open-air press compound. A couple of enterprising kids from a nearby apartment building starting selling Tang, cookies and – with the aid of the longest series of extension cords anyone could remember seeing – hot coffee. Their refreshment stand became the rumour centre, where reporters gathered to share theories and hearsay while they waited for the latest official information handouts.

Other newsmen spread out through Santa Mira, seeking people who had friends or relatives living up in Snowfield, or who were in some way related to the deputies now stationed there. Out at the junction of the state route and Snowfield Road, still other reporters were camping at the police roadblock.

In spite of all this hurly-burly, fully half of the press had not yet arrived. Many representatives of the Eastern media and the foreign press were still in transit. For the authorities who were trying hard to deal with the mess, the worst was yet to come. By Monday afternoon, it would be a circus.

22

MORNING IN SNOWFIELD

NOT LONG after dawn, the shortwave radio and the two gasoline-powered electric generators arrived at the roadblock that marked the perimeter of the quarantine zone. The two small vans, which bore them, were driven by California Highway Patrolmen. They were permitted to pass through the blockade, to a point midway along the four-mile Snowfield Road, where they were parked and abandoned.

When the CHIP officers returned to the roadblock, county deputies radioed a situation report to headquarters in Santa Mira. In turn, headquarters put through a go-ahead call to Bryce Hammond at the Hilltop Inn.

Tal Whitman, Frank Autry, and two other men took a squad car to the midpoint of the Snowfield Road and picked up the abandoned vans. Containment of any possible disease vectors was thus maintained.

The shortwave was set up in one corner of the Hilltop lobby. A message sent to headquarters in Santa Mira was received and answered. Now, if something happened to the telephones, they wouldn't be entirely isolated.

Within an hour, one of the generators had been wired into the circuitry of the streetlamps on the west side of Skyline Road. The other was spliced into the hotel's electrical system. Tonight, if the main power supply was mysteriously cut off, the generators would kick in automatically. Darkness would last only one or two seconds.

Bryce was confident that not even their unknown enemy could snatch away a victim *that* fast.

Jenny Paige began the morning with an unsatisfactory sponge bath, followed by a completely satisfactory breakfast of eggs, sliced ham, toast and coffee.

Then, accompanied by four heavily armed men, she went up the street to her house, where she got some fresh clothes for herself and for Lisa. She also stopped in her office, where she gathered up a stethoscope, a sphygmomanometer, tongue depressors, cotton pads, gauze, splints, bandages, tourniquets, antiseptics, disposable hypodermic syringes, pain-killers, antibiotics, and other instruments and supplies that she would need in order to establish an emergency infirmary in one corner of the Hilltop Inn's lobby.

The house was quiet.

The deputies kept looking around nervously, entering each new room as if they suspected a guillotine was rigged above the door.

As Jenny was finishing packing up supplies in her office, the telephone rang. They all stared at it.

They knew only two phones in town were working, and both were at the Hilltop Inn.

The phone rang again.

Jenny lifted the receiver. She didn't say hello.

Silence.

She waited.

After a second, she heard the distant cries of seagulls. The buzzing of bees. The mewling of a kitten. A weeping child. Another child: laughing. A panting dog. The *chicka-chicka-chicka-chicka* sound of a rattlesnake.

Bryce had heard similar things on the phone last night, in the substation, just before the moth had come tapping at the windows.

He had said that the sounds had been perfectly ordinary, familiar animal noises. They had, nonetheless, unsettled him. He hadn't been able to explain why.

Now Jenny knew exactly what he meant.

Birds singing.

Frogs croaking.

A cat purring.

The purr became a hiss. The hiss became a cat-shriek of anger. The shriek became a brief but terrible squeal of pain.

Then a voice: 'I'm gonna shove my big prick into your succulent little sister.'

Jenny recognized the voice. Wargle. The dead man.

'You hear me, Doc?'

She said nothing.

'And I don't give a rat's ass which end of her I stick it in.' He giggled.

She slammed the phone down.

The deputies looked at her expectantly.

'Uh . . . no one on the line,' she said, deciding not to tell them what she had heard. They were already too jumpy.

From Jenny's office, they went to Tayton's Pharmacy on Vail Lane, where she stocked up with more drugs: additional pain-killers, a wide spectrum of antibiotics, coagulants, anti-coagulants, and anything else she might conceivably need.

As they were finishing in the pharmacy, the phone rang.

Jenny was closest to it. She didn't want to answer, but she couldn't resist.

And *it* was there again.

Jenny waited a moment, then said, 'Hello?'

Wargle said, 'I'm gonna use your little sister so hard she won't be able to walk for a week.'

Jenny hung up.

'Dead line,' she told the deputies.

She didn't think they believed her. They stared at her trembling hands.

Bryce sat at the central operations desk, talking by telephone to headquarters in Santa Mira.

The APB on Timothy Flyte had turned up nothing whatsoever. Flyte wasn't wanted by any police agency in the United States or Canada. The FBI had never heard of him. The name on the bathroom mirror at the Candleglow Inn was still a mystery.

The San Francisco police had been able to supply background on the missing Harold Ordnay and wife, in whose room Timothy Flyte's name had been found. The Ordnays owned two bookstores in San Francisco. One was an ordinary retail outlet. The other was an antiquarian and rare book dealership; apparently, it was by far the most profitable of the two. The Ordnays were well known and respected in collecting circles. According to their family, Harold and Blanche had gone to Snowfield for a four-day weekend to celebrate their thirty-first anniversary. The family had never heard of Timothy Flyte. When police were granted permission to look through the Ordnay's personal address book, they found no listing for anyone named Flyte.

The police had not yet been able to locate any of the bookstores' employees; however, they expected to do so as soon as both shops opened at ten o'clock this morning. It was hoped that Flyte was a business acquaintance of the Ordnays and would be familiar to the employees.

'Keep me posted,' Bryce told the morning desk man in Santa Mira. 'How're things there?'

'Pandemonium.'

'It'll get worse.'

As Bryce was putting down the receiver, Jenny Paige returned from her safari in search of drugs and medical equipment. 'Where's Lisa?'

'With the kitchen detail,' Bryce said.

223

'She's all right?'

'Sure. There are three big, strong, well-armed men with her. Remember? Is something wrong?'

'Tell you later.'

Bryce assigned Jenny's three armed guards to new duties, then helped her establish an infirmary in one corner of the lobby.

'This is probably wasted effort,' she said.

'Why?'

'So far no one's been injured. Just killed.'

'Well, that could change.'

'I think *it* only strikes when it intends to kill. It doesn't take half-way measures.'

'Maybe. But with all these men toting guns, and with everyone so damned jumpy, I wouldn't be half surprised if someone accidentally winged someone else or even shot himself in the foot.'

Arranging bottles in a desk drawer, Jenny said, 'The telephone rang at my place and again over at the pharmacy. It was Wargle.' She told him about both calls.

'You're sure it was really him?'

'I remember his voice clearly. An unpleasant voice.'

'But, Jenny, he was—'

'I know, I know. His face was eaten away, and his brain was gone, and all the blood was sucked out of him. I know. And it's driving me crazy trying to figure it out.'

'Someone doing an impersonation?'

'If it was, then there's someone out there who makes Rich Little look like an amateur.'

'Did he sound as if he—'

Bryce broke off in mid-sentence, and both he and Jenny turned as Lisa ran through the archway.

The girl motioned to them. 'Come on! Quick! Something weird is happening in the kitchen.'

Before Bryce could stop her, she ran back the way she had come.

Several men started after her, drawing their guns as they went, and Bryce ordered them to halt. 'Stay here. Stay on the job.'

Jenny had already sprinted after the girl.

Bryce hurried into the dining room, caught up with Jenny, moved ahead of her, drew his revolver, and followed Lisa through the swinging doors into the hotel kitchen.

The three men assigned to this shift of kitchen duty – Gordy Brogan, Henry Wong, and Max Dunbar – had put down their can openers and cooking utensils in favour of their service revolvers, but they didn't know what to aim at. They glanced up at Bryce, looking disconcerted and baffled.

> *'Here we go 'round the mulberry bush,*
> *the mulberry bush, the mulberry bush.'*

The air was filled with a child's singing. A little boy. His voice was clear and fragile and sweet.

> *'Here we go 'round the mulberry bush,*
> *so early in the moooorrrminnnggg!'*

The sink,' Lisa said, pointing.

Puzzled, Bryce went to the nearest of three double sinks. Jenny came close behind him.

The song had changed. The voice was the same:

> *'This old man, he plays one;*
> *he plays nick-nack on my drum,*
> *With a nick-nack, paddywack,*
> *give a dog a bone—'*

The child's voice was coming out of the drain in the sink, as if he were trapped far down in the pipes.

225

'—this old man goes rolling home.'

For metronomic seconds, Bryce listened with spellbound intensity. He was speechless.

He glanced at Jenny. She gave him the same astonished stare that he had seen on his men's faces when he had first pushed through the swinging doors.

'It just started all of a sudden,' Lisa said, raising her voice above the singing.

'When?' Bryce asked.

'A couple of minutes ago,' Gordy Brogan said.

'I was standing at the sink,' Max Dunbar said. He was a burly, hairy, rough-looking man with warm, shy brown eyes. 'When the singing started up . . . Jesus . . . I must've jumped two feet!'

The song changed again. The sweetness was replaced by a cloying, almost mocking piety:

> *'Jesus loves me; this I know,*
> *for the Bible tells me so.'*

'I don't like this,' Henry Wong said. 'How can it be?'

> *'Little ones to Him are drawn,*
> *They are weak, but He is strong.'*

Nothing about the singing was overtly threatening; yet, like the noises Bryce and Jenny had heard on the telephone, the child's tender voice, issuing from such an unlikely source, was unnerving. Creepy.

> *'Yes, Jesus loves me.*
> *Yes, Jesus loves me.*
> *Yes, Jesus—'*

226

The singing abruptly ceased.

'Thank God!' Max Dunbar said with a shudder of relief, as if the child's melodic crooning had been unbearably harsh, grating, off-key. 'That voice was drilling right through to the roots of my teeth!'

After several seconds had passed in silence, Bryce began to lean towards the drain, to peer into it—

—and Jenny said maybe he shouldn't—

—and something exploded out of that dark, round hole.

Everyone cried out, and Lisa screamed, and Bryce staggered back in fear and surprise, cursing himself for not being more careful, jerking his revolver up, bringing the muzzle to bear on the thing that came out of the drain.

But it was only water.

A long, high-pressure stream of exceptionally filthy, greasy water shot almost to the ceiling and rained down over everything. It was a short burst, only a second or two, spraying in every direction.

Some of the foul droplets struck Bryce's face. Dark blotches appeared on the front of his shirt. The stuff stank.

It was exactly what you would expect to gush out of a blocked-up drain: dirty brown water, threads of gummy sludge, bits of this morning's breakfast scraps which had been run through the garbage disposal.

Gordy got a roll of paper towels, and they all scrubbed at their faces and blotted at the stains on their clothes.

They were still wiping at themselves, still waiting to see if the singing would begin again, when Tal Whitman pushed open one of the swinging doors. 'Bryce, we just got a call. General Copperfield and his team reached the roadblock and were passed through a couple of minutes ago.'

23

THE CRISIS TEAM

SNOWFIELD LOOKED freshly scrubbed and tranquil in the crystalline light of morning. A breeze stirred the trees. The sky was cloudless.

Coming out of the inn, with Bryce and Frank and Doc Paige and a few of the others behind him, Tal glanced up at the sun, the sight of which unlocked a memory of his childhood in Harlem. He used to buy penny candy at Boaz's News-stand, which was at the opposite end of the block from his Aunt Becky's apartment. He favoured the lemondrops. They were the prettiest shade of yellow he had ever seen. And now this morning, he saw that the sun was precisely *that* shade of yellow, hanging up there like an enormous lemondrop. It brought back the sights and sounds and smells of Boaz's with surprising force.

Lisa moved up beside Tal, and they all stopped on the pavement, facing downhill, waiting for the arrival of the CBW Defence Unit.

Nothing moved at the bottom of the hill. The mountainside was silent. Evidently, Copperfield's team was some distance away.

Waiting in the lemon sunshine Tal wondered if Boaz's News-stand was still doing business at its old location. Most likely, it was now just another empty store, filthy and vandalised. Or maybe it was selling magazines, tobacco, and candy only as a front for pushing dope.

As he grew older, he became ever more acutely aware of a tendency towards degeneration in all things. Nice neighbourhoods somehow became shabby neighbourhoods; shabby neighbour-hoods became seedy neighbourhoods; seedy neighbourhoods became slums. Order giving way to chaos. You saw it everywhere these days. More homicides this year than last. Greater and greater abuse of drugs. Spiralling rates of assault, rape, burglary. What saved Tal from being a pessimist about mankind's future was his fervent conviction that good people – people like Bryce, Frank and Doc Paige, people like his Aunt Becky – could stem the tide of devolution and maybe even turn it back now and then.

But his faith in the power of good people and responsible actions was facing a severe test here in Snowfield. This evil seemed unbeatable.

'Listen!' Gordy Borgan said. 'I hear engines.'

Tal looked at Bryce. 'I thought they weren't expected until around noon. They're three hours early.'

'Noon was the latest possible arrival time,' Bryce said. 'Copper-field wanted to make it sooner if he could. Judging from the conversation I had with him, he's a tough taskmaster, the kind of guy who usually gets exactly what he wants out of his people.'

'Just like you, huh?' Tal asked.

Bryce regarded him from under sleepy, drooping eyelids. 'Me? Tough? Why, I'm a pussycat.'

Tal grinned. 'So's a panther.'

'Here they come!'

At the bottom of Skyline Road, a large vehicle hove into view, and the sound of its labouring engine grew louder.

There were three large vehicles in the CBW Civilian Defence Unit. Jenny watched them as they crawled slowly up the long, sloped street towards the Hilltop Inn.

Leading the procession was a gleaming, white mobile home, a lumbering thirty-six-foot behemoth that had been somewhat modi-fied. It had no doors or windows along its flank. The only entrance

229

evidently was at the back. The curved, wraparound windshield of the cab was tinted very dark, so you couldn't see inside, and it appeared to be made of much thicker glass than that used in ordinary mobile homes. There was no identification on the vehicle, no project name, no indication that it was army property. The licence plate was standard California issue. Anonymity during transport was clearly part of Copperfield's programme.

Behind the first mobile home came a second. Bringing up the rear was an unmarked truck pulling a thirty-foot, plain grey trailer. Even the truck's windows were tinted, armour-thick glass.

Not certain that the driver of the lead vehicle had seen their group standing in front of the Hilltop, Bryce stepped into the street and waved his arms over his head.

The payloads in the mobile homes and in the truck were obviously quite heavy. Their engines strained hard, and they ground their way up the street, moving slower than ten miles an hour, then slower than five, inching, groaning, grinding. When at last they reached the Hilltop, they kept on going, made a right-hand turn at the corner, and swung into the cross street that flanked the inn.

Jenny, Bryce and the others went around to the side of the inn as the motorcade pulled up to the kerb and parked. All of the east–west streets in Snowfield ran across the broad face of the mountain, so that most of them were level. It was much easier to park and secure the three vehicles there than on the steeply sloped Skyline Road.

Jenny stood on the pavement, watching the rear door of the first mobile home, waiting for someone to come out.

The three overheated engines were switched off, one after the other, and silence fell in with a weight of its own.

Jenny's spirits were higher than they had been since she'd driven into Snowfield last night. The specialists had arrived. Like most Americans, she had enormous faith in specialists, in technology, and in science. In fact, she probably had more faith than most, for she was a specialist herself, a woman of science. Soon, they would

230

understand what had killed Hilda Beck and the Liebermanns and all the others. The specialists had arrived. The cavalry had ridden in at last.

The back door of the truck opened first, and men jumped down. They were dressed for operations in a biologically contaminated atmosphere. They were wearing the white, airtight vinyl suits of the type developed for NASA, with large helmets that had over-size, plexiglass faceplates. Each man carried his own air supply tank on his back, as well as a briefcase-size waste purification and recla-mation system.

Curiously, Jenny did not, at first, think of the men as resembling astronauts. They seemed like followers of some strange religion, resplendent in their priestly raiments.

Half a dozen agile men had scrambled out of the truck. More were still coming when Jenny realized that they were heavily armed. They spread out around both sides of their caravan and took up positions between their transport and the people on the pave-ment, facing away from the vehicles. These men weren't scientists. They were support troops. Their names were stencilled on their helmets, just above their faceplates: SGT HARKER, PVT FODOR, PVT PASCALLI, LT UNDERHILL. They brought up their guns and aimed outward, securing a perimeter in a determined fashion that brooked no interference.

To her shock and confusion, Jenny found herself staring into the muzzle of a submachine gun.

Taking a step towards the troops, Bryce said, 'What the hell is the meaning of this?'

Sergeant Harker, nearest to Bryce, swung his gun towards the sky and fired a short burst of warning shots.

Bryce stopped abruptly.

Tal and Frank reached automatically for their own sidearms.

'No!' Bryce shouted. 'No shooting, for Christ's sake! We're on the same side.'

231

One of the soldiers spoke. Lieutenant Underhill. His voice issued tinnily from a small radio amplifier in a six-inch-square box on his chest. 'Please stay back from the vehicles. Our first duty is to guard the integrity of the labs, and we will do so at all costs.'

'Dammit,' Bryce said, 'we're not going to cause any trouble. I'm the one who called for you in the first place.'

'Stay back,' Underhill insisted.

The rear door of the first mobile home finally opened. The four individuals who came out were also dressed in airtight suits, but they were not soldiers. They moved unhurriedly. They were unarmed. One of them was a woman; Jenny caught a glimpse of a strikingly lovely, female oriental face. The names on their helmets weren't preceded by designation of rank: BETTENBY, VALDEZ, NIVEN, YAMAGUCHI. These were the civilian physicians and scientists who, in an extreme chemical-biological warfare emergency, walked away from their private lives in Los Angeles, San Francisco, Seattle and other Western cities, putting themselves at Copperfield's disposal. According to Bryce, there was one such team in the West, one in the East, and one in the Southern-Gulf states.

Six men came out of the second mobile home. GOLDSTEIN, ROBERTS, COPPERFIELD, HOUK. The last two were in unmarked suits, no names above their faceplates. They moved up the line, staying behind the armed soldiers, and joined up with Bettenby, Niven, Valdez and Yamaguchi.

Those ten conducted a brief conversation among themselves, by way of inter-suit radio. Jenny could see their lips moving behind their plexiglass visors, but the squawk-boxes on their chests did not transmit a word, which meant they had the capacity to conduct both public and strictly private discussions. For the time being, they were opting for privacy.

But why? Jenny wondered. They don't have anything to hide from us. Do they?

General Copperfield, the tallest of the twenty, turned away from the group at the rear of the first mobile home, stepped onto the pavement and approached Bryce.

Before Copperfield took the initiative, Bryce stepped up to him. 'General, I demand to know why we're being held at gunpoint.'

'Sorry,' Copperfield said. He turned to the stone-faced troopers and said, 'Okay, men. It's a no-sweat situation. Parade rest.'

Because of the air tanks they were carrying, the soldiers couldn't comfortably assume a classic parade rest position. But moving with the fluid harmony of a precision drill team, they immediately slung their submachine guns from their shoulders, spread their feet precisely twelve inches apart, put their arms straight down at their sides, and stood motionless, facing forward.

Bryce had been correct when he'd told Tal that Copperfield sounded like a tough taskmaster. It was obvious to Jenny that there was no discipline problem in the general's unit.

Turning to Bryce again, smiling through his faceplate, Copperfield said, 'That better?'

'Better,' Bryce said. 'But I still want an explanation.'

'Just SOP,' Copperfield said. 'Standard Operating Procedure. It's part of the normal drill. We don't have anything against you or your people, Sheriff. You *are* Sheriff Hammond, aren't you? I remember you from the conference in Chicago last year.'

'Yes, sir, I'm Hammond. But you *still* haven't given me a suitable explanation. SOP just isn't good enough.'

'No need to raise your voice, Sheriff.' With one gloved hand, Copperfield tapped the squawk-box on his chest. 'This thing's not just a speaker. It's also equipped with an extremely sensitive microphone. You see, going into a place where there might be serious biological or chemical contamination, we've got to consider the possibility that we might be overwhelmed by a lot of sick and dying people. Now, we simply aren't equipped to administer cures or even amelioratives. We're a *research* team. Strictly pathology, not treatment. It's our job to find out all we can about the nature of the contaminant, so that properly equipped medical teams can come in right behind us and deal with the survivors. But dying and desperate people might not understand that we can't treat them. They might attack the mobile labs out of anger and frustration.'

'And fear,' Tal Whitman said.

'Exactly,' the general said, missing the irony. 'Our psychological stress simulations indicate that it's a very real possibility.'

'And if sick and dying people *did* try to disrupt your work,' Jenny said, 'would you kill them?'

Copperfield turned to her. The sun flashed off his faceplate, transforming it into a mirror, and for a moment she could not see him. Then he shifted slightly, and his face emerged into view again, but not enough of it for her to see what he really looked like. It was a face out of context, framed in the transparent portion of his helmet.

He said, 'Dr Paige, I presume?'

'Yes.'

'Well, Doctor, if terrorists or agents of a foreign government committed an act of biological warfare against an American community, it would be up to me and my people to isolate the microbe, identify it, and suggest measures to contain it. That is a sobering responsibility. If we allowed anyone, even the suffering victims, to deter us, the danger of the plague spreading would increase dramatically.'

'So,' Jenny said, still pressing him, 'if sick and dying people *did* try to disrupt your work, you'd kill them.'

'Yes,' he said flatly. 'Even decent people must occasionally chose between the lesser of two evils.'

Jenny looked around at Snowfield, which was as much of a graveyard in the morning sun as it had been in the gloom of night. General Copperfield was right. *Anything* he might have to do to protect his team would only be a little evil. The big evil was what had been done – what was still being done – to this town.

She wasn't quite sure why she had been so testy with him.

Maybe it was because she had thought of him and his people as the cavalry, riding in to save the day. She had wanted all the problems to be solved, all the ambiguities cleared up instantly upon Copperfield's arrival. When she'd realized that it wasn't going to work out that way, when they had actually pulled guns on *her*, the dream had faded fast. Irrationally, she blamed the general.

That wasn't like her. Her nerves must be more badly frayed than she had thought.

Bryce began to introduce his men to the general, but Copperfield interrupted. 'I don't mean to be rude, Sheriff, but we don't have time for introductions. Later. Right now, I want to *move*. I want to see all those things you told me about on the phone last night, and then I want to get an autopsy started.'

He wants to skip introductions because it doesn't make sense to be chummy with people who may be doomed, Jenny thought. If we develop disease symptoms in the next few hours, if it turns out to be a brain disease, and if we go berserk and try to rush the mobile labs, it'll be easier for him to have us shot if he doesn't know us very well.

Stop it! she told herself angrily.

She looked at Lisa and thought: Good heavens, kid, if I'm this frazzled, what a state *you* must be in. Yet you've kept as stiff an upper lip as anyone. What a damned fine kid to have for a sister.

'Before we show you around,' Bryce told Copperfield, 'you ought to know about the thing we saw last night and what happened to—'

'No, no,' Copperfield said impatiently. 'I want to go through it step by step. Just the way you found things. There'll be plenty of time to tell me what happened last night. Let's get moving.'

'But, you see, it's beginning to look as if it can't possibly be a disease that's wiped out this town,' Bryce protested.

The general said, 'My people have come here to investigate possible CBW connections. We'll do that first. *Then* we can consider other possibilities. SOP, Sheriff.'

Bryce sent most of his men back into the Hilltop Inn, keeping only Tal and Frank with him.

Jenny took Lisa's hand, and they, too, headed back to the inn.

Copperfield called out to her. 'Doctor! Wait a moment. I want you with us. You were the first physician on the scene. If the condition of the corpses has changed, you're the one most likely to notice.'

Jenny looked at Lisa. 'Want to come along?'

'Back to the bakery? No thanks.' The girl shuddered.

Thinking of the eerily sweet, childlike voice that had come from the sink drain, Jenny said, 'Don't go in the kitchen. And if you have to go to the bathroom, ask someone to go along with you.'

'Jenny, they're all guys!'

'I don't care. Ask Gordy. He can stand outside the stall with his back turned.'

'Jeez, that'd be embarrassing.'

'You want to go into that bathroom by yourself again?'

The colour drained out of the girl's face. 'No way.'

'Good. Keep close to the others. And I mean *close*. Not just in the same room. Stay in the same *part* of the room. 'Promise?'

'Promise.'

Jenny thought about the telephone calls from Wargle this morning. She thought of the gross threats he'd made. Although they had been the threats of a dead man and should have been meaningless, Jenny was frightened.

'You be careful, too,' Lisa said.

She kissed the girl on the cheek. 'Now hurry and catch up with Gordy before he turns the corner.'

Lisa ran, calling ahead: 'Gordy! Wait up!'

The tall young deputy stopped at the corner and looked back.

Watching Lisa sprint along the cobblestone pavement, Jenny felt her heart tightening.

She thought: What if, when I come back, she's gone? What if I never see her alive again?

236

24

COLD TERROR

Bryce, Tal, Frank and Jenny entered the kitchen. General Copperfield and the nine scientists on his team followed closely, and four soldiers, toting submachine guns, brought up the rear.

The kitchen was crowded. Bryce felt uncomfortable. What if they were attacked while they were all jammed together? What if they had to get out in a hurry?

The two heads were exactly where they had been last night: in the ovens, peering through the glass. On the work table the severed hands still clutched the rolling pin.

Niven, one of the general's people, took several photographs of the kitchen from various angles, then about a dozen close-ups of the heads and hands.

The others kept edging around the room to get out of Niven's way. The photographic record had to be completed before the forensic work could begin, which was not unlike the routine policemen followed at the scene of a crime.

As the spacesuited scientists moved, their rubberized clothing squeaked. Their heavy boots scraped noisily on the tile floor.

'You still think it looks like a simple incident of CBW?' Bryce asked Copperfield.

'Could be.'

'Really?'

Copperfield said, 'Phil, you're the resident nerve gas specialist. Are you thinking what I'm thinking?'

The question was answered by the man whose helmet bore the name HOUK. 'It's much too early to tell anything for certain, but it seems as if we could be dealing with a neuroleptic toxin. And there are some things about this – most notably, the extreme psychopathic violence – that lead me to wonder if we've got a case of T-139.'

'Definitely a possibility,' Copperfield said. 'Just what I thought when we walked in.'

Niven continued to snap photographs, and Bryce said, 'So what's this T-139?'

'One of the primary nerve gases in the Russian arsenal,' the general said. The full moniker is Timoshenko-139. It's named after Ilya Timoshenko, the scientist who developed it.'

'What a lovely monument,' Tal said sarcastically.

'Most nerve gases cause death within thirty seconds to five minutes after skin contact,' Houk said. 'But T-139 isn't that merciful.'

'Merciful!' Frank Autry said, appalled.

'T-139 isn't just a killer,' Houk said. That *would* be merciful by comparison. T-139 is what military strategists call a demoralizer.'

Copperfield said, 'It passes through the skin and enters the bloodstream in ten seconds or less, then migrates to the brain and almost instantly causes irreparable damage to cerebral tissues.'

Houk said, 'For a period of about four to six hours, the victim retains full use of his limbs and a hundred per cent of his normal strength. At first, it's only his mind that suffers.'

'Dementia paranoides,' Copperfield said. 'Intellectual confusion, fear, rage, loss of emotional control, and a very strongly held feeling that everyone is plotting against him. This is combined with a fierce compulsion to commit violent acts. In essence, Sheriff, T-139 turns people into mindless killing machines for four to six hours. They prey on one another and on unaffected people outside the area of the gas attack. You can see what an extremely demoralizing effect it would have on an enemy.'

'Extremely,' Bryce said. 'And Dr Paige theorized just such a disease last night, a mutant rabies that would kill some people while turning others into demented murderers.'

'T-139 isn't a disease,' Houk said quickly. 'It's a nerve gas. And if I had my choice, I'd rather this *was* a nerve gas attack. Once gas has dissipated, the threat is over. A biological threat is considerably harder to contain.'

'If it was gas,' Copperfield said, 'it'll have dissipated long ago, but there'll be traces of it on almost everything. Condensative residue. We'll be able to identify it in no time at all.'

They backed against a wall to make way for Niven and his camera.

Jenny said, 'Dr Houk, in regards to this T-139, you mentioned that the ambulatory stage lasts four to six hours. Then what?'

'Well,' Houk said, 'the second stage is the terminal stage, too. It lasts anywhere from six to twelve hours. It begins with the deterioration of the efferent nerves and escalates to paralysis of the cardiac, vasomotor, and respiratory reflex centres in the brain.'

'Good God,' Jenny said.

Frank said, 'Once more for us laymen.'

Jenny said, 'It means that during the second stage of the illness, over a period of six to twelve hours, T-139 gradually reduces the brain's ability to regulate the automatic functions of the body – such as breathing, heartbeat, blood vessel dilation, organ function . . . The victim starts experiencing an irregular heartbeat, extreme difficulty in breathing, and the gradual collapse of every gland and organ. Twelve hours might not seen gradual to you, but it would seem like an eternity to the victim. There would be vomiting, diarrhoea, uncontrollable urination, continuous and violent muscle spasms . . . And if only the efferent nerves were damaged, if the rest of the nervous system remained intact, there would be excruciating, unrelenting pain.'

'Six to twelve hours of hell,' Copperfield confirmed.

'Until the heart stops,' Houk said, 'or until the victim simply stops breathing and suffocates.'

For long seconds, as Niven clicked the last of his photographs, no one spoke.

Finally, Jenny said, 'I still don't think a nerve gas could've played any part in this, not even something like T-139 that would explain these beheadings. For one thing, none of the victims we found showed any signs of vomiting or incontinence.'

'Well,' Copperfield said, 'we could be dealing with a derivative of T-139 that doesn't produce those symptoms. Or some other gas.'

'No gas can explain the moth,' Tal Whitman said.

'Or what happened to Stu Wargle,' Frank said.

Copperfield said, 'Moth?'

'You didn't want to hear about that until you'd seen these other things,' Bryce reminded Copperfield. 'But now I think it's time you—'

Niven said, 'Finished.'

'All right,' Copperfield said. 'Sheriff, Dr Paige, deputies, if you will please maintain silence until we've completed the rest of our tasks here, your cooperation will be much appreciated.'

The others immediately set to work. Yamaguchi and Bettenby transferred the severed heads into a pair of porcelain-lined specimen buckets with locking, airtight lids. Valdez carefully pried the hands away from the rolling pin and put them in a third specimen bucket. Houk scraped some flour off the table and into a small plastic jar, evidently because dry flour would have absorbed – and would still contain – traces of the nerve gas – if, in fact, there had *been* any nerve gas. Houk also took a sample of the pie crust dough that lay under the rolling pin. Goldstein and Roberts inspected the two ovens from which the heads had been removed, and then Goldstein used a small, battery-powered vacuum cleaner to sweep out the first oven. When that was done, Roberts took the bag of sweepings, sealed it, and labelled it, while Goldstein used the vacuum to collect minute and even microscopic evidence from the second oven.

All of the scientists were busy except for the two men who were wearing the suits that had no names on the helmets. They stood to one side, merely watching.

Bryce watched the watchers, wondering who they were and what function they performed.

As the others worked, they described what they were doing and made comments about what they found, always speaking in a jargon that Bryce couldn't follow. No two of them spoke at once; that fact – when coupled with Copperfield's request for silence from those who were not team members – made it seem as if they were speaking for the record.

Among the items that hung from the utility belt around Copperfield's waist there was a tape recorder wired directly into the communications system of the general's suit. Bryce saw that the reels of tape were moving.

When the scientists had got everything they wanted from the bakery kitchen, Copperfield said, 'All right, Sheriff. Where now?'

Bryce indicated the tape recorder. 'Aren't you going to switch that off until we get there?'

'Nope. We started recording from the moment we were allowed past the roadblock, and we'll keep recording until we've found out what's happened to this town. That way, if something goes wrong, if we all die before we find the solution, the new team will know every step we took. They won't have to start from scratch, and they might even have a detailed record of the fatal mistake that got *us* killed.'

The second stop was the arts and crafts gallery into which Frank Autry had led the three other men last night. Again, he led the way through the showroom, into the rear office, and up the stairs to the second-floor apartment.

It seemed to Frank that there was almost something comic about the scene; all these spacemen lumbering up the narrow stairs, their faces theatrically grim behind plexiglass faceplates, the sound of their breathing amplified by the closed spaces of their helmets and projected out of the speakers on their chests at an exaggerated volume, an ominous sound. It was like one of those 1950s science fiction movies – *Attack of the Alien Astronauts* or something equally corny – and Frank couldn't help smiling.

But his vague smile vanished when he entered the apartment kitchen and saw the dead man again. The corpse was where it had been last night, lying at the foot of the refrigerator, wearing only blue pyjama bottoms. Still swollen, bruised, staring wide-eyed at nothing.

Frank moved out of the way of Copperfield's people and joined Bryce beside the counter where the toaster oven stood.

As Copperfield once again requested silence from the uninitiated, the scientists stepped carefully around the sandwich fixings that were scattered across the floor. They crowded around the corpse.

In a few minutes they were finished with a preliminary examination of the body.

Copperfield turned to Bryce and said, 'We're going to take this one for an autopsy.'

'You still think it looks as if we're dealing with just a simple incident of CBW?' Bryce asked, as he had asked before.

'It's entirely possible, yes,' the general said.

'But the bruising and swelling,' Tal said.

'Could be allergic reactions to a nerve gas,' Houk said.

'If you'll slide up the leg of the pyjamas,' Jenny said, 'I believe you'll find that the reaction extends even to unexposed skin.'

'Yes, it does,' Copperfield said. 'We've already looked.'

'But how could the skin react even where no nerve gas came into contact with it?'

'Such gases usually have a high penetration factor,' Houk said. 'They'll pass right through most clothes. In fact, about the only thing that'll stop many of them is vinyl or rubber garments.'

Just what you're wearing, Frank thought, and just what we're not.

'There's another body here,' Bryce told the general. 'Do you want to have a look at that one, too?'

'Absolutely.'

'It's this way, sir.' Frank said.

He led them out of the kitchen and down the hall, his gun drawn.

Frank dreaded entering the bedroom where the dead woman lay naked in the rumpled sheets. He remembered the crude things that Stu Wargle had said about her, and he had the terrible feeling that Stu was going to be there now, coupled with the blonde, their dead bodies locked in cold and timeless passion.

But only the woman was there. Sprawled on the bed. Legs still spread wide. Mouth open in an eternal scream.

When Copperfield and his people had finished a preliminary examination of the corpse and were ready to go, Frank made sure they had seen the .22 automatic which she had apparently emptied at her killer. 'Do you think she would have shot at just a cloud of nerve gas, General?'

'Of course not,' Copperfield said. 'But perhaps she was already affected by the gas, already brain damaged. She could have been shooting at hallucinations, at phantoms.'

'Phantoms,' Frank said. 'Yes, sir, that's just about what they would've had to've been. Because, see, she fired all ten shots in the clip, yet we found only two expended slugs – one in that tallboy over there, one in the wall where you see the hole. That means she mostly hit whatever she was shooting at.'

'I knew these people,' Doc Paige said, stepping forward. 'Gary and Sandy Wechlas. She was something of a markswoman. Always target shooting. She won several competitions at the county fair last year.'

'So she had the skill to make eight hits out of ten,' Frank said. 'And even eight hits didn't stop the thing she was trying to stop. Eight hits didn't even make it bleed. Of course, phantoms don't bleed. But, sir, would a phantom be able to walk out of here *and take those eight slugs with it?*'

Copperfield stared at him, frowning.

All the scientists were frowning, too.

The soldiers weren't only frowning; they were looking around uneasily.

Frank could see that the condition of the two bodies – especially the woman's nightmarish expression – had had an effect on the general and his people. The fear in everyone's eyes was sharper now. Although they didn't want to admit it, they had encountered something beyond their experience. They were still clinging to explanations that made sense to them – nerve gas, virus, poison – but they were beginning to have doubts.

Copperfield's people had brought a zippered plastic body bag with them. In the kitchen, they slipped the pyjama-clad corpse into the bag, then carried it out of the building and left it on the sidewalk, intending to pick it up again on the way back to the mobile labs.

Bryce led them to Gilmartin's Market. Inside, back by the milk coolers where it had happened, he told them about Jake Johnson's disappearance. 'No screams. No sound at all. Just a few seconds of darkness. *A few seconds*. But when the lights came on again, Jake was gone.'

Copperfield said, 'You looked—'

'Everywhere.'

'He could have run away,' Roberts said.

'Yes,' Dr Yamaguchi said, 'Maybe he deserted. Considering the things he'd seen . . .'

'My God,' Goldstein said, 'what if he left Snowfield? He might be beyond the quarantine line, carrying the infection—'

'No, no, no. Jake wouldn't desert,' Bryce said. 'He wasn't exactly the most aggressive officer on the force, but he wouldn't run out on me. He wasn't irresponsible.'

'Definitely not,' Tal agreed. 'Besides, Jake's old man was once county sheriff, so there's a lot of family pride involved.'

'And Jake was a cautious man,' Frank said. 'He didn't do anything on impulse.'

Bryce nodded. 'Anyway, even if he was spooked enough to run, he'd have taken a squad car. He sure wouldn't have *walked* out of town.'

'Look,' Copperfield said, 'he'd have known they wouldn't let him past the roadblock, so he'd have avoided the highway altogether. He might have gone off through the woods.'

Jenny shook her head. 'No, General. The land is *wild* out there. Deputy Johnson would've known he'd get lost and die.'

'And,' Bryce said, 'would a frightened man plunge pell-mell into a strange forest at night? I don't think so, General. But I *do* think it's time you heard about what happened to my other deputy.'

Leaning against a cooler full of cheese and luncheon meat, Bryce told them about the moth, about the attack on Wargle and the blood-curdling condition of the corpse. He told them about Lisa's encounter with a resurrected Wargle and about the subsequent discovery that the body was missing.

Copperfield and his people expressed astonishment at first, then confusion, then fear. But during most of Bryce's tale, they stared at him in wary silence and glanced at one another knowingly.

He finished by telling them about the child's voice that had come from the kitchen drain just moments before their arrival. Then, for the third time, he said, 'Well, General, do you *still* think it looks like a simple incident of CBW?'

Copperfield hesitated, looked around at the littered market, finally met Bryce's eyes, and said, 'Sheriff, I want Dr Roberts and Dr Goldstein to give complete physical examinations to you and to everyone who saw this . . . uh . . . moth.'

'You don't believe me.'

'Oh, I believe that you genuinely, sincerely *think* you saw all of those things.'

'Damn,' Tal said.

Copperfield said, 'Surely, you can understand that, to us, it sounds as if you've all been contaminated, as if you're suffering from hallucinations.'

Bryce was weary of their disbelief and frustrated by their intellectual rigidity. As scientists, they were supposed to be receptive to new ideas and unexpected possibilities. Instead, they appeared determined to *force* the evidence to conform to their preconceived notions of what they would find in Snowfield.

'You think we all could've had the *same* hallucination?' Bryce asked.

'Mass hallucinations aren't unknown,' Copperfield said.

'General,' Jenny said, 'there was absolutely nothing hallucinatory about what we saw. It had the gritty texture of reality.'

'Doctor Paige, I would ordinarily accord considerable weight to any observation you cared to make. But as one of those who claim to have *seen* the moth, your medical judgement in the matter simply isn't objective.'

Scowling at Copperfield, Frank Autry said, 'But, sir, if it was all just something we hallucinated – then where is Stu Wargle?'

'Maybe both he *and* this Jake Johnson ran out on you,' Roberts said. 'And maybe you've merely incorporated their disappearances into your delusions.'

From long experience, Bryce knew that a debate was always lost the moment you became emotional. He forced himself to remain in a relaxed position, leaning against the cooler. Keeping his voice soft and slow, he said, 'General, from the things you and your people have said, someone could get the idea that the Santa Mira County Sheriff's Department is staffed exclusively by cowards, fools, and goldbrickers.'

Copperfield made placating gestures with his rubber-sheathed hands, 'No, no, no. We're not saying anything of the kind. Please, Sheriff, try to understand. We're only being straightforward with you. We're telling you how the situation looks to us – how it would look to *anyone* with any specialized knowledge of chemical and biological warfare. Hallucination is one of the things we expect to find in survivors. It's one of the things we *have* to look for. Now, if you could offer us a logical explanation for the existence of this eagle-size moth . . . well, maybe then we could come to believe in it ourselves. But you can't. Which leaves our suggestion – that you merely hallucinated it – as the only explanation that makes sense.'

Bryce noticed the four soldiers staring at him in a much different way now that he was thought to be a victim of nerve gas. After all, a man suffering from bizarre hallucinations was obviously unstable, dangerous, perhaps even violent enough to cut off people's heads and pop them into bakery ovens. The soldiers raised their submachine guns an inch or two, although they didn't actually aim at Bryce. They regarded him – and Jenny and Tal and Frank – with a new and unmistakable air of suspicion:

Before Bryce could respond to Copperfield, he was startled by a loud noise at the back of the market, beyond the butcher's-block tables. He stepped away from the cooler, turned towards the source of the commotion, and put his right hand on his holstered revolver.

Out of the corner of his eye, he saw two soldiers reacting to him rather than the noise. When he had put his hand on his revolver, they had instantly raised their submachine guns.

It was a hammering sound that had drawn his attention. And a voice. Both were coming from within the walk-in meat locker, on the other side of the butcher's work area, no more than fifteen feet away, almost directly opposite the point at which Bryce and the others were gathered. The thick, insulated door of the locker muffled the blows that were being rained on it, but they were still loud.

247

The voice was muffled, too, the words unclear, but Bryce thought he could hear someone shouting for help.

'Somebody's trapped in there,' Copperfield said.

'Can't be,' Bryce said.

Frank said, 'Can't be locked in because the door opens from both sides.'

The hammering and shouting ceased abruptly.

A clatter.

A rattle of metal on metal.

The handle on the large, burnished-steel door moved up, down, up, down, up . . .

The latch clicked. The door swung open. But only a couple of inches. Then it stopped.

The refrigerated air inside the locker rushed out, mixing with the warmer air in the market. Tendrils of frosty vapour rose along the length of the open door.

Although the light was on in the room beyond the door, Bryce couldn't see anything through the narrow gap. Nevertheless, he knew what the refrigerated meat locker looked like. During last night's search for Jake Johnson, Bryce had been in there, poking around. It was a frigid, windowless, claustrophobic place, about twelve by fifteen feet. There was one other door – equipped with two deadbolt locks – that opened onto the alley for the easy transfer of meat deliveries. A painted concrete floor. Sealed concrete walls. Fluorescent lights. Vents in three of the walls circulated cold air around the sides of beef, veal, and slabs of pork that hung from the ceiling racks.

Bryce could hear nothing except the amplified breathing of the scientists and soldiers in the decontamination suits, and even that was subdued; some of them seemed to be holding their breath.

Then from within the locker came a groan of pain. A pitifully weak voice cried out for help. Rebounding from the cold concrete walls, carried on the spiralling thermals of air that escaped through the narrowly opened door, the voice was shaky – echo-distorted, yet recognizable.

'Bryce . . . Tal . . . ? Who's out there? Frank? Gordy? Is somebody out there? Can . . . somebody . . . help me?'

It was Jake Johnson.

Bryce, Jenny, Tal and Frank stood very still, listening.

Copperfield said, 'Whoever it is, he needs help badly.'

'Bryce . . . please . . . somebody . . .'

'You know him?' Copperfield asked. 'He's calling your name – isn't he, Sheriff?'

Without waiting for an answer, the general ordered two of his man – Sergeant Hacker and Private Pascalli – to look in the meat locker.

'Wait!' Bryce said. 'Nobody goes back there. We're keeping these coolers between us and that locker until we know more.'

'Sheriff, while I fully intend to cooperate with you as far as possible, you have no authority over my men or me.'

'Bryce . . . it's me . . . Jake . . . For God's sake, help me. I broke my damned leg.'

'Jake?' Copperfield asked, squinting curiously at Bryce. 'You mean that man in there is the same one you said was snatched away from here last night?'

'Somebody . . . help Jesus, it's c-cold . . . so c-c-cold.'

'It sounds like him,' Bryce admitted.

'Well, there you are!' Copperfield said. 'Nothing mysterious about it, after all. He's been right here all this time.'

Bryce glared at the general. 'I told you we searched everywhere last night. Even in the goddamned meat locker. He wasn't there.'

'Well, he is now,' the general said.

'Hey, out there! I'm c-cold. Can't m-m-move this . . . damned leg!'

Jenny touched Bryce's arm. 'It's wrong. It's all wrong.'

Copperfield said, 'Sheriff, we can't just stand here and allow an injured man to suffer.'

'If Jake had really been in there all night,' Frank Autry said, 'he would've froze to death by now.'

'Well, if it's a meat locker,' Copperfield said, 'then the air inside isn't freezing. It's just cold. If the man was warmly dressed, he might easily have survived this long.'

'But how'd he get in there in the first place?' Frank asked. 'What the devil's he been *doing* in there?'

'And he wasn't in there last night,' Tal said impatiently.

Jake Johnson called for help again.

'There's danger here,' Bryce told Copperfield. 'I sense it. My men sense it. Dr Paige senses it.'

'I don't,' Copperfield said.

'General, you just haven't been in Snowfield long enough to understand that you've got to expect the utterly unexpected.'

'Like moths the size of eagles?'

Biting back his anger, Bryce said, 'You haven't been here long enough to understand that . . . well . . . nothing's quite what it seems.'

Copperfield studied him sceptically. 'Don't get mystical on me, Sheriff.'

In the meat cooler, Jake Johnson began to cry. His whimpering pleas were awful to hear. He sounded like a pain-wracked, terrified old man. He didn't sound the least bit dangerous.

'We've got to help that man *now*,' Copperfield said.

'I'm not risking my men,' Bryce said. 'Not yet.'

Copperfield again ordered Sergeant Harker and Private Pascalli to look in the meat locker. Although it was obvious from his demeanour that he didn't think there was much danger for men armed with submachine guns, he told them to proceed with caution. The general still believed the enemy was something as small as a bacterium or molecule of nerve gas.

The two soldiers hurried along the rows of coolers towards the gate that led into the butcher's work area.

Frank said, 'If Jake could open the door, why couldn't he push it *completely* open and let us see him?'

'He probably used up the last of his strength just getting the door unlatched,' Copperfield said. 'You can hear it in his voice, for God's sake. Utter exhaustion.'

Harker and Pascalli went through the gate, behind the coolers.

Bryce's hand tightened on the butt of his holstered revolver.

Tal Whitman said, 'There's too much wrong with this set-up, dammit. If it's really Jake, if he needs help, why did he wait until *now* to open the door?'

'The only way we'll find out is to ask him,' the general said.

'No, I mean, there's an outside entrance to that locker,' Tal said. 'He could've opened the other door earlier and shouted out into the alley. As quiet as this town is, we'd have heard him all the way over at the Hilltop.'

'Maybe he's been unconscious until now,' Copperfield said.

Harker and Pascalli were moving past the work tables and the electric meat saw.

Jake Johnson called out again: *'Is someone . . . coming? Is someone . . . coming now?'*

Jenny began to raise another objection, but Bryce said, 'Save your breath.'

'Doctor,' Copperfield said, 'can you actually expect us to just ignore that man's cries for help?'

'Of course not,' she said. 'But we ought to take time to think of a *safe* way of having a look in there.'

Shaking his head, Copperfield interrupted her: 'We've got to attend to him without delay. *Listen* to him, Doctor. He's hurt bad.'

Jake was moaning in pain again.

Harker moved towards the meat locker door.

Pascalli dropped back a couple of paces and over to one side, covering his sergeant as best he could.

Bryce felt the muscles bunching with tension in his back, across his shoulders, and in his neck.

Harker was at the door.

'No,' Jenny said softly.

The locker door was hinged to swing inward. Harker reached out with the barrel of his submachine gun and shoved the door all the way open. The cold hinges rasped and squealed.

That sound sent a shiver through Bryce.

Jake wasn't sprawled in the doorway. He wasn't anywhere in sight.

Past the sergeant, nothing could be seen except the hanging sides of beef: dark, fat-mottled, bloody.

Harker hesitated—

(*Don't do it!* Bryce thought.)

—and then plunged through the doorway. He crossed the threshold in a crouch, looking left and swinging the gun that way, then almost instantly looking right and bringing the muzzle around.

To his right, Harker saw something. He jerked upright in surprise and fear. Stumbling hastily backwards, he collided with a side of beef. '*Holy shit!*'

Harker punctuated his cry with a short burst of fire from his submachine gun.

Bryce winced. The boom-rattle of the weapon was thunderous.

Something pushed against the far side of the meat locker door and slammed it shut.

Harker was trapped in there with it. *It.*

'Christ!' Bryce said.

Not wasting the time it would have taken to run to the gate, Bryce clambered up onto the waist-high cooler in front of him stepping on packets of Kraft Swiss cheese and wax-encased gouda. He scrambled across and dropped off the other side, into the butcher's area.

Another burst of gunfire. Longer this time. Maybe even long enough to empty the gun's magazine.

Pascalli was at the locker door, struggling frantically with the handle.

Bryce rounded the work tables. 'What's wrong?'

Private Pascalli looked too young to be in the army – and very scared.

'Let's get him the hell out of there!' Bryce said.

'Can't! This fucker won't open!'

Inside the meat locker, the gunfire stopped.

The screaming began.

Pascalli wrenched desperately at the unrelenting handle.

Although the thick, insulated door muffled Harker's screams, they were nevertheless loud, and they swiftly grew even louder. Coming through the walkie-talkie built into Pascalli's suit, the agonized wailing must have been deafening, for the private suddenly put a hand to his helmeted head as if trying to block out the sound.

Bryce pushed the soldier aside. He gripped the long, lever-action door handle with both hands. It wouldn't budge up or down.

In the locker, the piercing screams rose and fell and rose, getting louder and shriller and more horrifying.

What in the hell is it *doing* to Harker? Bryce wondered. Skinning the poor bastard alive?

He looked back towards the coolers. Tal had scrambled over the display case and was coming on the double. The general and another soldier, Private Fodor, were rushing through the gate. Frank had jumped onto one of the coolers but was facing out towards the main part of the store, guarding against the possibility that the commotion at the meat locker was just a diversion. Everyone else was still standing in a group in the aisle beyond the coolers.

Bryce shouted, 'Jenny!'

'Yeah?'

'Does this store have a hardware section?'

253

'Odds and ends.'

'I need a screwdriver.'

'Can do.' She was already running.

Harker screamed.

Jesus, what a terrible cry it was. Out of a nightmare. Out of a lunatic asylum. Out of Hell.

Just listening to it caused Bryce to break out in cold sweat.

Copperfield reached the locker. 'Let me at that handle.'

'It's no use.'

'Let me at it!'

Bryce got out of the way.

The general was a big brawny man – the biggest man there. In fact, he looked strong enough to uproot century-old oaks. Straining, cursing, he moved the door handle no further than Bryce had done.

'The goddamned latch must be broken or bent,' Copperfield said, panting.

Harker screamed and screamed.

Bryce thought of Liebermann's Bakery. The rolling pin on the table. The hands. The severed hands. This was the way a man might scream while he watched his hands being cut off at the wrists.

Copperfield pounded on the door in rage and frustration.

Bryce glanced at Tal. This was a first: Talbert Whitman visibly frightened.

Calling to Bryce, Jenny came through the gate. She had three screwdrivers, each of them sealed in a brightly coloured cardboard and plastic package.

'Didn't know which size you needed,' she said.

'Okay,' Bryce said, reaching for the tools, 'now get out of here fast. Go back with the others.'

Ignoring his command, she gave him two of the screwdrivers, but she held onto the third.

Harker's screams had become so shrill, so awful, that they no longer sounded human.

As Bryce ripped open one package, Jenny tore the third bright yellow container to shreds and extracted the screwdriver from it.

'I'm a doctor. I stay.'

'He's beyond any doctor's help,' Bryce said, frantically tearing open the second package.

'Maybe not. If you thought there wasn't a chance, you wouldn't be trying to get him out of there.'

'Dammit, Jenny!'

He was worried about her, but he knew he wouldn't be able to persuade her to leave if she had already made up her mind to stay.

He took the third screwdriver from her, shouldered past General Copperfield, and returned to the door.

He couldn't remove the door's hinge pins. It swung into the locker, so the hinges were on the inside.

But the lever-action handle fitted through a large cover plate behind which lay the lock mechanism. The plate was fastened to the face of the door by four screws. Bryce squatted down in front of it, selected the most suitable screwdriver, and removed the first screw, letting it drop to the floor.

Harker's screaming stopped.

The ensuing silence was almost worse than the screams.

Bryce removed the second, third, and fourth screws.

There was still no sound from Sergeant Harker.

When the cover plate was loose, Bryce slid it along the handle, pulled it free, and discarded it. He squinted at the guts of the lock, probed at the mechanism with the screwdriver. In response, ragged bits of torn metal popped out of the lock; other pieces rattled down through a hollow space in the interior of the door. The lock had been thoroughly mangled *from within the door*. He found the manual release slot in the shaft of the latch bolt, slid the screwdriver through it, pulled to the right. The spring seemed to have been badly bent or sprung, for there was very little play left in it. Nevertheless, he drew the bolt back far enough to bring it out of the hole in the jamb, then pushed inward. Something clicked; the door started to swing open.

Everyone, including Bryce, backed out of the way.

The door's own weight contributed sufficiently to its momentum, so that it continued to swing, slowly, slowly inward.

Private Pascalli was covering it with his submachine gun, and Bryce drew his own handgun, as did Copperfield, although Sergeant Harker had conclusively proved that such weapons were useless.

The door swung all the way open.

Bryce expected something to rush out at them. Nothing did.

Looking through the doorway and across the locker, he could see that the outer door was open, too, which it definitely hadn't been when Harker had gone inside a couple of minutes ago. Beyond it lay the sun-splashed alleyway.

Copperfield ordered Pascalli and Fodor to secure the locker. They went through the door fast, one turning to the left, the other to the right, out of sight.

In a few seconds, Pascalli returned. 'It's all clear, sir.'

Copperfield went into the locker, and Bryce followed.

Harker's submachine gun was lying on the floor.

Sergeant Harker was hanging from the ceiling meat rack, next to a side of beef – hanging on an enormous, wickedly pointed, two-pronged meat hook that had been driven through his chest.

Bryce's stomach heaved. He started to turn away from the hanging man – and then realized it wasn't really Harker. It was only the sergeant's decontamination suit and helmet, hanging slack, empty. The tough vinyl fabric was slashed. The plexiglass faceplate was broken and torn half out of the rubber gasket into which it had been firmly set. Harker had been pulled from the suit before it had been impaled.

But where was Harker?

Gone.

Another one. Just gone.

Pascalli and Fodor were out on the loading platform, looking up and down the alleyway.

'All that screaming,' Jenny said, stepping up beside Bryce, 'yet there's no blood on the floor or on the suit.'

Tal Whitman scooped up several expended shell casings that had been spat out by the submachine gun; scores of them littered the floor. The brass casings gleamed on his open palm. 'Lots of these, but I don't see many slugs. Looks like the sergeant hit what he was shooting at. Must've scored at least a hundred hits. Maybe two hundred. How many rounds are in one of those big magazines, General?'

Copperfield stared at the shiny casings but didn't answer.

Pascalli and Fodor came back in from the loading platform, and Pascalli said, 'There's no sign of him out there, sir. You want us to search further along the alley?'

Before Copperfield could respond, Bryce said, 'General, you've got to write off Sergeant Harker, painful as that might be. He's dead. Don't hold out any hope for him. Death is what this is all about. *Death.* Not hostage-taking. Not terrorism. Not nerve gas. There's nothing halfway about this. We're playing for all the marbles. I don't know exactly what the hell's out there or where it came from, but I do know that it's Death personified. Death is out there in some form we can't even imagine yet, driven by some purpose we might never understand. The moth that killed Stu Wargle – that wasn't even the true appearance of this thing. I *feel* it. The moth was like the reanimation of Wargle's body, when he went after Lisa in the restroom: it was a bit of misdirection – sleight-of-hand.'

'A phantom,' Tal said, using the word that Copperfield had introduced with a somewhat different meaning.

'A phantom, yes,' Bryce said. 'We haven't yet encountered the real enemy. It's something that just plain likes to kill. It can kill quickly and silently, the way it took Jake Johnson. But it killed

Harker more slowly, hurting him real bad, making him scream. Because it wanted us to hear those screams. Harker's murder was sort of like what you said about T-139: it was a demoralizer. This thing didn't carry Sergeant Harker away. It got him, General. *It* got him. Don't risk the lives of more men searching for a corpse.'

Copperfield was silent for a moment. Then he said, 'But the voice we heard. It was *your* man, Jake Johnson.'

'No,' Bryce said. 'I don't think it really was Jake. It sounded like him, but now I'm beginning to suspect we're up against something that's a terrific mimic.'

'Mimic?' Copperfield said.

Jenny looked at Bryce. 'Those animal sounds on the telephone.'

'Yeah. The cats, dogs, birds, rattlesnakes, the crying child . . . It was almost like a performance. As if it were bragging: "Hey, look what I can do; look how clever I am." Jake Johnson's voice was just one more impersonation in its repertoire.'

'What are you proposing?' Copperfield asked. 'Something supernatural?'

'No. This is real.'

'Then what? Put a name to it,' Copperfield demanded.

'I *can't*, dammit,' Bryce said. 'Maybe it's a natural mutation or even something that came out of a genetic engineering lab somewhere. You know anything about that, General? Maybe the army's got an entire goddamned division of geneticists creating biological fighting machines, man-made monsters designed to slaughter and terrorize, creatures stitched together from the DNA of half a dozen animals. Take some of the genetic structure of the tarantula and combine it with some of the genetic structure of the crocodile, the cobra, the wasp, maybe even the grizzly bear, and then insert the genes for human intelligence just for the hell of it. Put it all in a test tube; incubate it; nurture it. What would you get? What would it look like? Do I sound like a raving lunatic for even proposing such a thing? Frankenstein with a modern twist? Have they actually gone that far with recombinant DNA research? Maybe I shouldn't even have ruled out the supernatural. What I'm trying to say, General, is that it could be *anything*. That's why I can't put a name to it. Let your imagination run wild, General. No matter what hideous thing you conjure up, we can't rule it out. We're dealing with the unknown, and the unknown encompasses all our nightmares.'

Copperfield stared at him, then looked up at Sergeant Harker's suit and helmet which hung from the meat hook. He turned to Pascalli and Fodor. 'We won't search the alley. The sheriff is probably right. Sergeant Harker is lost, and there's nothing we can do for him.'

For the fourth time since Copperfield had arrived in town, Bryce said, 'Do you *still* think it looks as if we're dealing with just a simple incident of CBW?'

'Chemical or biological agents might be involved,' Copperfield said. 'As you observed, we can't rule out anything. But it's not a simple case. You're right about that, Sheriff. I'm sorry for suggesting you were only hallucinating and—'

'Apology accepted,' Bryce said.

'Any theories?' Jenny asked.

'Well,' Copperfield said, 'I want to start the first autopsy and pathology tests right away. Maybe we won't find a disease or a nerve gas, but we still might find something that'll give us a clue.'

'You'd better do that, sir,' Tal said. 'Because I have a hunch that time is running out.'

25

QUESTIONS

CORPORAL BILLY Velazquez, one of General Copperfield's support troops, climbed down through the manhole, into the storm drain. Although he hadn't exerted himself, he was breathing hard. Because he was scared.

What had happened to Sergeant Harker?

The others had come back, looking stunned. Old man Copperfield said Harker was dead. He said they weren't quite sure what had killed Sarge, but they intended to find out. Man, that was bullshit. They must know what killed him. They just didn't want to say. That was typical of the brass, making secrets of everything.

The ladder descended through a short section of vertical pipe, then into the main, horizontal drain. Billy reached the bottom. His booted feet made hard, flat sounds when they struck the concrete floor.

The tunnel wasn't high enough to allow him to stand erect. He crouched slightly and swept his flashlight around.

Grey concrete walls. Telephone and power company pipes. A little moisture. Some fungus here and there. Nothing else.

Billy stepped away from the ladder as Ron Peake, another member of the support squad, came down into the drain.

Why hadn't they at least brought Harker's body back with them when they'd returned from Gilmartin's Market?

Billy kept shining his flashlight around and glancing nervously behind him.

Why had old Iron Ass Copperfield kept stressing the need to be watchful and careful down here?

Sir, what're we supposed to be on the lookout for? Billy had asked.

Copperfield had said, *Anything. Everything. I don't know if there's any danger or not. And even if there is, I don't know exactly what to tell you to look for. Just be damned cautious. And if anything moves down there, no matter how innocent it looks, even if it's just a mouse, get your asses out of there fast.*

Now what the hell kind of answer was that?

Jesus.

It gave him the creeps.

Billy wished he'd had a chance to talk to Pascalli or Fodor. They weren't the damned brass. They would give him the whole story about Harker – if he ever got a chance to ask them about it.

Ron Peake reached the bottom of the ladder. He looked anxiously at Billy.

Velazquez directed the flashlight all the way around them in order to show the other man there was nothing to worry about.

Ron switched on his own flash and smiled self-consciously, embarrassed by his jumpiness.

The men above began to feed a power cable through the open manhole. It led back to the two mobile laboratories, which were parked a few yards from the entrance to the drain.

Ron took the end of the cable, and Billy, shuffling forward in a crouch, led the way east. On the street above, the other men paid more cable into the drain.

This tunnel should intersect an equally large or perhaps larger conduit under the main street, Skyline Road. At that point there ought to be a power company junction box where several strands of the town's electrical web were joined together. As Billy proceeded with all the caution that Copperfield had suggested, he played the beam of his flashlight over the walls of the tunnel, looking for the power company's insignia.

261

The junction box was on the left, five or six feet this side of the intersection of the two conduits. Billy walked past it, to the Skyline Road drain, leaned out into the passageway, and pointed his light to the right and to the left, making sure there was nothing lurking around. The Skyline Road pipe was the same size as the one in which he now stood, but it followed the slope of the street above it, plunging down the mountainside. There was nothing in sight.

Looking downhill, into the dwindling grey bore of the tunnel, Billy Velazquez was reminded of a story he'd read years ago in a horror comic. He'd forgotten the title of it. The tale was about a bank robber who killed two people during a hold-up and then, fleeing police, slipped into the city's storm-drain system. The villain had taken a downward-sloping tunnel, figuring it would lead to the river, but where it had led, instead, was to Hell. That was what the Skyline Road drain looked like as it fell down, down, down; a road to Hell.

Billy turned to peer uphill again, wondering if it would look like a road to Heaven. But it looked the same both ways. Up or down, it looked like a road to Hell.

What had happened to Sergeant Harker?

Would the same thing happen to everyone, sooner or later?

Even to William Luise Velazquez, who had always been so sure (until now) that he would live forever?

His mouth was suddenly dry.

He turned his head inside his helmet and put his parched lips on the nipple of the nutrient tube. He sucked on it, drawing a sweet, cool, carbohydrate-packed, vitamin- and mineral-rich fluid into his mouth. What he wanted was a beer. But until he could get out of this suit, the nutrient solution was the only thing available. He carried about a forty-eight-hour supply – if he didn't take more than two ounces an hour.

Turning away from the road to Hell, he went to the junction box.

Ron Peake was at work already. Moving efficiently despite their bulky decon suits and the cramped quarters, they tapped into the power supply.

The unit had brought its own generator, but it would be used only if the more convenient municipal power were lost.

In a few minutes, Velazquez and Peake were finished. Billy used his suit-to-suit radio to call up to the surface. 'General, we've made the tap. You should have power now, sir.'

The response came at once: 'We do. Now get your asses out of there on the double!'

'Yes, sir,' Billy said.

Then he heard . . . something.

Rustling.

Panting.

And Ron Peake grabbed Billy's shoulder. Pointed. Past him. Back towards the Skyline drain.

Billy whirled around, crouched down even further, and shone his flashlight out into the intersection, where Peake's flash was focused.

Animals were streaming down the Skyline Road tunnel. Dozens upon dozens. Dogs. White and grey and black and brown and rust-red and golden dogs of all sizes and descriptions: mostly mongrels but also beagles, toy poodles, full-size poodles, German shepherds, spaniels, two Great Danes, a couple of Airedales, a schnauzer, a pair of coal-black Dobermans with brown-trimmed muzzles. And there were cats, too. Big and small. Lean cats and fat cats. Black and calico and white and yellow and ring-tailed and brown and spotted and striped and grey cats. None of the dogs barked or growled. None of the cats meowed or hissed. The only sounds were their panting and the soft padding and scraping of their paws on the concrete. The animals poured down through the drain with a curious intensity, all of them looking straight ahead, none of them even glancing into the intersecting drain, where Billy and Ron Peake stood.

'What're they doing down here?' Billy wanted to know. 'How'd they get here?'

From the street above, Copperfield radioed down: 'What's wrong? Velazquez?'

Billy was so amazed by the procession of animals that he didn't immediately respond.

Other animals began to appear, mixed in among the cats and dogs. Squirrels. Rabbits. A grey fox. Racoons. More foxes and more squirrels. Skunks. All of them were staring straight ahead, oblivious to everything except the need to keep moving. Possums and badgers. Mice and chipmunks. Coyotes. All rushing down the road to Hell, swarming over and around and under one another, yet never once stumbling or hesitating or snapping at one another. This strange parade was as swift, continuous, and harmonious as flowing water.

'Velazquez! Peake! Report in!'

'Animals,' Billy told the general. 'Dogs, cats, racoons, all kinds of things. A river of 'em.'

'Sir, they're running down the Skyline tunnel, just beyond the mouth of this pipe,' Ron Peake said.

'Underground,' Billy said, baffled. 'It's crazy.'

'Retreat, goddammit!' Copperfield said urgently. 'Get out of there now. *Now!*'

Billy remembered the general's warning, issued just before they had descended through the manhole: *If anything moves down there . . . even if it's just a mouse, get your asses out of there fast.*

Initially, the subterranean parade of animals had been startling but not particularly frightening. Now, the bizarre procession was suddenly eerie, even threatening.

And now there were snakes among the animals. Scores of them. Long blacksnakes, slithering fast, with their heads raised a foot or two above the floor of the storm drain. And there were rattlers, their flat and evil heads held lower than those of the longer blacksnakes, but moving just as fast and just as sinuously, swarming with mysterious purpose towards a dark and equally mysterious destination.

Although the snakes paid no more attention to Velazquez and Peake than the dogs and cats did, their slithering arrival was enough to snap Billy out of his trance. He hated snakes. He turned back the way he had come, prodded Peake. 'Go. Go on. Get out of here. Run!'

Something shrieked-screamed-roared.

Billy's heart pounded with jackhammer ferocity.

The sound came from the Skyline drain, from back there on the road to Hell. Billy didn't dare look back.

It was neither a human scream nor like any animal sound, yet it was unquestionably the cry of a living thing. There was no mistaking the raw emotions of that alien, blood-freezing bleat. It wasn't a scream of fear or pain. It was a blast of rage, hatred, and feverish blood-hunger.

Fortunately, that malevolent roar didn't come from nearby, but from farther up the mountain, towards the uppermost end of the Skyline conduit. The beast – whatever in God's name it was – was at least not already upon them. But it was coming fast.

Ron Peake hurried back towards the ladder, and Billy followed. Encumbered by their bulky decontamination suits, slowed by the curved floor of the pipe, they ran in a lurching shuffle. Although they hadn't far to go, their progress was maddeningly slow.

The thing in the tunnel cried out again.

Closer.

It was a whine and a snarl and a howl and a roar and a petulant squeal all tangled together, a barbed-wire sound that punctured Billy's ears and raked cold metal spikes across his heart.

Closer.

If Billy Velazquez had been a god-fearing Nazarene or a Bible-thumping, fire-and-brimstone, fundamentalist Christian, he would have known what beast might make such a cry. If he had been taught that the Dark One and His wicked minions stalked the earth in fleshy forms, seeking unwary souls to devour, he would have identified this beast at once. He would have said, 'It's Satan.' The roar echoing through the concrete tunnels was truly *that* terrible.

And closer.

Getting closer.

Coming fast.

But Billy was a Catholic. Modern Catholicism tended to downplay the sulphurous-pits-of-Hell stories in favour of emphasizing God's great mercy and infinite compassion. Extremist Protestant fundamentalists saw the hand of the Devil in everything from television programming to the novels of Judy Blume to the invention of the push-up bra. But Catholicism struck a quieter, more lighthearted note than that. The Church of Rome now gave the world such things as singing nuns, Wednesday Night Bingo, and priests like Andrew Greeley. Therefore, Billy Velazquez, raised a Catholic, did not immediately associate supernatural Satanic forces with the chilling cry of this unknown beast – not even though he so vividly remembered that old road-to-Hell comic book story. Billy just knew that the bellowing creature approaching through the bowels of the earth was a *bad thing*. A *very* bad thing.

And it was getting closer. Much closer.

Ron Peake reached the ladder, started up, dropped his flashlight, didn't bother to return for it.

Peake was too slow, and Billy shouted at him: 'Move your ass!'

The scream of the unknown beast had become an eerie ululation that filled the subterranean warren of storm drains as completely as flood water. Billy couldn't even hear himself shouting.

Peake was halfway up the ladder.

There was almost enough room for Billy to slip in under him and start up. He put one hand on the ladder.

Peake's foot slipped. He dropped down a rung.

Billy cursed and snatched his hand out of the way.

The banshee keening grew louder.

Peake's fallen flashlight was pointing off towards the Skyline drain, but Billy didn't look back that way. He stared only up towards the sunlight. If he glanced behind and saw something hideous, his strength would flee him, and he would be unable to move, and it would get him, by God, it would get him.

Peake scrambled upwards again. His feet stayed on the rungs this time.

The concrete drain was transmitting thunderous vibrations that Billy could feel through the soles of his boots. The vibrations were like heavy, lumbering, yet lightning-quick footsteps.

Don't look, don't look!

Billy grabbed the sides of the ladder and clawed his way up as rapidly as Peake's progress would allow. One rung. Two. Three.

Above, Peake passed through the manhole and into the street.

With Peake out of the way, a fall of autumn sunlight splashed down over Billy Velazquez, and there was something about it that was like light piercing a church window – maybe because it represented hope.

He was halfway up the ladder.

Going to make it, going to make it, definitely going to make it, he told himself breathlessly.

But the shrieking and howling, Jesus, like being in the centre of a cyclone!

Another rung.

And another one.

The decontamination suit felt heavier than it had ever felt before. A ton. A suit of armour. Weighing him down.

He was in the vertical pipe now, moving out of the horizontal drain that ran beneath the street. He looked up longingly at the light and the faces peering down at him, and he kept moving.

Going to make it.

His head rose through the manhole.

Someone reached out, offering a hand. It was Copperfield himself.

Behind Billy, the shrieking stopped.

He climbed another rung, let go of the ladder with one hand, and reached for the general—

—but something seized his legs from below before he could grasp Copperfield's hand.

'*No!*'

Something grabbed him, wrenched his feet off the ladder, and yanked him away. Screaming – strangely, he heard himself screaming for his mother – Billy went down, cracking his helmet against the wall of the pipe and then against a rung of the ladder, stunning himself, smashing his elbows and knees, trying desperately to catch hold of a rung but failing, finally collapsing into the powerful embrace of an unspeakable something that began to drag him backwards towards the Skyline conduit.

He twisted, kicked, struck out with his fists, to no effect. He was held tightly and dragged deeper into the drains.

In the backsplash of light coming through the manhole, then in the rapidly dimming beam of Peake's discarded flashlight, Billy saw a bit of the thing that had him in its grip. Not much. Fragments looking out of the shadows, then vanishing into darkness again. He saw just enough to make his bowels and bladder loosen. It was lizardlike. But not a lizard. Insectlike. But not an insect. It hissed and mewled and snarled. It snapped and tore at his suit as it pulled him along. A double row of razor-edge spikes. It had claws, and it was huge, and its eyes were smoky red with elongated pupils as black as the bottom of a grave. It had scales instead of skin, and two horns, thrusting from its brow above its baleful eyes, curving out and up, as sharply pointed as daggers. A snout rather than a nose, a snout that oozed snot. A forked tongue that flickered in and out and in and out across all those deadly fangs, and something that looked like the stinger on a wasp or maybe a pincer.

It dragged Billy Velazquez into the Skyline conduit. He clawed at the concrete, desperately seeking something to hold onto, but he only succeeding in abrading away the fingers and palms of his gloves. He felt the cool underground air on his hands, and he realized he might now be contaminated, but that was the least of his worries.

It dragged him into the hammering heart of darkness. It stopped, held him tightly. It tore at his suit. It cracked his helmet. It pried at his plexiglass faceplate. It was after him as if he were a delicious morsel of nut meat in a hard shell.

His hold on sanity was tenuous, but he struggled to keep his wits about him, tried to understand. At first, it seemed to him that this was a prehistoric creature, something millions of years old that had somehow dropped through a time warp into the storm drains. But that was crazy. He felt a silvery, high-pitched, lunatic giggle coming over him, and he knew he would be lost if he gave voice to it. The beast tore away most of his decontamination suit. It was on him now, pressing hard, a cold and disgustingly slick thing that seemed to pulse and somehow to *change* when it touched him. Billy, gasping and weeping, suddenly remembered an illustration in an old catechism text. A drawing of a demon. That was what *this* was. Like the drawing. Yes, exactly like it. The horns. The dark, forked tongue. The red eyes. A demon risen from Hell. And then he thought: No, no; that's crazy, too! And all the while that those thoughts raced through his mind, the ravenous creature stripped him and pulled his helmet almost completely apart. In the unrelieved darkness, he sensed its snout pressing through the halves of the broken helmet, towards his face, sniffing. He felt its tongue fluttering against his mouth and nose. He smelled a vague but repellent odour, like nothing he had ever smelled before. The beast gouged at his belly and thighs, and then he felt a strange and brutally painful fire eating into him; acid fire. He writhed, twisted, bucked, strained – all to no avail. Billy heard himself crying out in terror and pain and confusion: 'It's the Devil, it's the Devil!' He realized he had been shouting and screaming things almost continuously, from the moment he had been dragged off the ladder. Now, unable to speak as the flameless fire burned his lungs to ash and churned into his throat, he prayed in a silent singsong chant, warding off fear and death and the terrible feeling of smallness and worthlessness that had come over him: *Mary, Mother of God, Mary, hear my plea . . . hear my plea, Mary, pray for me . . . pray, pray, pray for me, Mary, Mother of God, Mary, intercede for me and—*

His question had been answered.

He knew what had happened to Sergeant Harker.

Galen Copperfield was an outdoorsman, and he knew a great deal about the wildlife of North America. One of the creatures he found most interesting was the trap-door spider. It was a clever engineer, constructing a deep, tubular nest in the ground with a hinged lid at the top. The lid blended so perfectly with the soil in which it was set that other insects wandered across it, unaware of the danger below, and were instantly snatched into the nest, dragged down, and devoured. The suddenness of it was horrifying and fascinating. One instant, the prey was there, standing atop the trap-door, and the next instant it was gone, as if it had never been.

Corporal Velazquez's disappearance was as sudden as if he had stepped upon the lid of a trap-door spider's lair.

Gone.

Copperfield's men were already edgy about Harker's disappearance and were frightened by the nightmarish howling that ceased just before Velazquez was dragged down. When the corporal was taken, they all stumbled back across the street, afraid that something was about to launch itself out of the manhole.

Copperfield, in the act of reaching for Velazquez when he was snatched, jumped back. Then froze. Indecisive. That was not like him. He had never before been indecisive in a crisis.

Velazquez was screaming through the suit-to-suit radio.

Breaking the ice that locked his joints, Copperfield went to the manhole and looked down. Peake's flashlight lay on the floor of the drain. But there was nothing else. No sign of Velazquez.

Copperfield hesitated.

The corporal continued to scream.

Send other men down after the poor bastard?

No. It would be a suicide mission. Remember Harker. Cut the losses here, now.

But, good God, the screaming was terrible. Not as awful as Harker's. Those had been screams born of excruciating pain. These were screams of mortal terror. Not as bad, perhaps, but bad enough. As bad as anything Copperfield had heard on the battlefield.

There were words among the screams, spat out in explosive gasps. The corporal was making a desperate, babbling attempt to explain to those above ground – and maybe to himself – just what he was seeing.

'. . . lizard . . .'

'. . . bug . . .'

'. . . dragon . . .'

'. . . prehistoric . . .'

'. . . demon . . .'

And finally, with both physical pain and anguish of the soul in his voice, the corporal cried out, 'It's the Devil, it's the Devil!'

After that, the screams were every bit as bad as Harker's. At least these didn't last as long.

When there was only silence, Copperfield slid the manhole cover back into place. Because of the power cable, the metal plate didn't fit tightly and was tilted up at one end, but it covered most of the hole.

He stationed two men on the pavement, ten feet from the entrance to the drain, and ordered them to shoot anything that came out.

Because a gun had been of no help to Harker, Copperfield and a few other men collected everything they needed to manufacture Molotov cocktails. They got a couple of dozen bottles of wine from

271

Brookhart's liquor store on Vail Lane, emptied them, put an inch of soap powder in the bottom of each, filled them with gasoline, and twisted rag fuses into the necks of them until they were snugly stoppered.

Would fire succeed where bullets had failed?

What had happened to Harker?

What had happened to Velazquez?

What will happen to me? Copperfield wondered.

The first of the two mobile field laboratories had cost more than three million dollars, and the Defence Department had got its money's worth.

The lab was a marvel of technological microminiaturization. For one thing, its computer – based on a trio of Intel 432 micromainframes; 690,000 transistors squeezed onto only nine silicon chips – took up no more room than a couple of suitcases, yet it was a highly sophisticated system that was capable of complex medical analyzes. In fact, it was a more elaborate system – with greater logic and memory capacities – than could be found in most major university hospitals' pathology labs.

There was a great deal of diagnostic equipment in the mobile home, all of it designed and positioned for maximum utilization of the limited space. In addition to a pair of computer access terminals along one wall, there were a number of devices and machines: a centrifuge that would be used to separate the major components of blood, urine, and other fluid samples; a spectrophotometer; a spectrograph; an electron microscope with an image interpretation-enhancement read-out link to one of the computer screens; a compact appliance that would quick-freeze blood and tissue samples for storage and for use in tests in which element extractions were more easily performed on frozen materials; and much, much more.

Towards the front of the vehicle, behind the driver's compartment, was an autopsy table that collapsed into the wall when not in use. At the moment, the table was down, and the body of Gary Wechlas – male, thirty-seven, Caucasian – lay on the stainless-steel surface. The blue pyjama bottoms had been scissored away from the corpse and set aside for later examination.

Dr Seth Goldstein, one of the three leading forensic medicine specialists on the West Coast, would perform the autopsy. He stood at one side of the table with Dr Daryl Roberts, and General Copperfield stood at the other side, facing them across the dead body.

Goldstein pressed a button on a control panel that was set in the wall to his right. A recording would be made of every word spoken during the autopsy; this was common procedure in even ordinary post-mortems. A visual record was also being made: two ceiling-mounted videotape cameras were focused on the corpse; they, too, were activated when Dr Goldstein pressed the button on the wall panel.

Goldstein began by closely examining and describing the corpse: the unusual facial expression, the universal bruising, the curious swelling. He was especially searching for punctures, abrasions, localized contusions, cuts, lesions, blisters, fractures, and other indications of specific points of injury. He could not find any.

With his gloved hand poised over the instrument tray, Goldstein hesitated, not quite sure where to start. Usually, at the beginning of an autopsy, he already had a pretty good idea of the cause of death. When the deceased had been wasted by a disease, Goldstein usually had seen the hospital report. If death had resulted from an accident, there was visible trauma. If it was death at the hand of another, there were signs of violence. But in this case, the condition of the corpse raised more questions than it answered, strange questions unlike any he had ever faced before.

As if sensing Goldstein's thoughts, Copperfield said, 'You've got to find some answers for us, Doctor. Our lives very probably depend on it.'

*

273

The second mobile home had many of the same diagnostic machines and instruments that were in the lead vehicle – a test tube centrifuge, an electron miscroscope, and so forth – in addition to several pieces of equipment that were not duplicated in the other vehicle. It contained no autopsy table, however, and only one videotape system. There were three computer terminals instead of two.

Dr Enrico Valdez was sitting at one of the programming boards, in a deep-seated chair designed to accommodate a man in a decontamination suit complete with air tank. He was working with Houk and Niven on chemical analyzes of samples of various substances collected from several business places and dwellings along Skyline Road and Vail Lane – such as the flour and dough taken from the table in Leibermann's Bakery. They were seeking traces of nerve gas condensate or other chemical substances. So far, they had found nothing out of the ordinary.

Dr Valdez didn't believe that nerve gas or disease would turn out to be the culprit.

He was beginning to wonder if this whole thing might actually be in Isley's and Arkham's territory. Isley and Arkham, the two men without names on their decontamination suits, were not even members of the Civilian Defence Unit. They were from a different project altogether. Just this morning, before dawn, when Dr Valdez had been introduced to them at the team rendezvous point in Sacramento, when he had heard what kind of research they were doing, he had almost laughed. He had thought their project was a waste of taxpayers' money. Now he wasn't so sure. Now he wondered . . .

He wondered . . . and he worried.

Dr Sara Yamaguchi was also in the second mobile home.

She was preparing bacteria cultures. Using a sample of blood taken from the body of Gary Wechlas, she was methodically contaminating a series of growth media, jellied compounds filled with nutrients on which bacteria generally thrived: horse blood agar, sheep blood agar, simplex, chocolate agar, and many others.

Sara Yamaguchi was a geneticist who had spent eleven years in recombinant DNA research. If it turned out that Snowfield had been stricken by a man-made microorganism, Sara's work would become central to the investigation. She would direct the study of the microbe's morphology, and when that was completed, she would have a major role in attempting to determine the function of the bug.

Like Dr Valdez, Sara Yamaguchi had begun to wonder if Isley and Arkham might become more essential to the investigation than she had thought. This morning, their area of expertise had seemed as exotic as voodoo. But now, in light of what had taken place since the team's arrival in Snowfield, she was forced to admit that Isley's and Arkham's speciality seemed increasingly pertinent.

And, like Dr Valdez, she was worried.

Dr Wilson Bettenby, chief of the civilian scientific arm of the CBW Civilian Defence Unit's East Coast team, sat at a computer terminal, two seats away from Dr Valdez.

Bettenby was running an automated analysis program on several water samples. The samples were inserted into a processor that distilled the water, stored the distillate, and subjected the filtered-out substances to spectrographic analysis and other tests. Bettenby was not searching for micro-organisms; that would require different procedures to these. This machine only identified and quantified all mineral and chemical elements present in the waters, the data was displayed on the cathode ray tube.

All but one of the water samples had been taken from taps in the kitchens and bathrooms of houses and businesses along Vail Lane. They proved to be free of dangerous chemical impurities.

The other water sample was the one that Deputy Autry had collected from the kitchen floor of the apartment of Vail Lane, sometime last night. According to Sheriff Hammond, puddles of water and saturated carpets had been discovered in several buildings. By this morning, however, the water had pretty much evaporated, except for a couple of damp carpets from which Bettenby wouldn't have been able to obtain a clean sample. He put the deputy's sample into the processor.

In a few minutes, the computer flashed up the complete chemical-mineral analysis of the water and of the residue that remained after all the liquid in the sample had been distilled:

	PERCENT OF SOLUTION	PERCENT OF RESIDUE
H	11.188	00.00
LI	00.00	00.00
B	00.00	00.00
N	00.00	00.00
NA	00.00	00.00
AL	00.00	00.00
P	00.00	00.00
CL	00.00	00.00
HE	00.00	00.00
BE	00.00	00.00
C	00.00	00.00
O	88.812	00.00
MG	00.00	00.00
SI	00.00	00.00
S	00.00	00.00
K	00.00	00.00

The computer went on at considerably greater length, flashing up the findings for every substance that might ordinarily be detected. The results were the same. In its undistilled state, the water contained absolutely no traces of any elements other than its two components, hydrogen and oxygen. And complete distillation and filtration had left behind no residue whatsoever, not even any trace elements. Autry's sample couldn't have come from the town's water supply, for it was neither chlorinated nor fluoridated. It wasn't bottled water, either. Bottled water would have had a normal mineral content. Perhaps there was a filtration system underneath the kitchen sink in that apartment – a Culligan unit – but even if there was, the water that passed through it would still possess more mineral content than this. What Autry had collected was the purest laboratory grade of distilled and multiply filtered water.

So . . . what was it doing all over the kitchen floor?

Bettenby stared at the computer screen, frowning.

Was the small lake at Brookhart's liquor store also composed of this ultra-pure water?

Why would anyone go around town, emptying out gallons and gallons of distilled water?

And where would they find it in such a quantity to begin with?

Strange.

Jenny, Bryce and Lisa were at a table in one corner of the dining room at the Hilltop Inn.

Major Isley and Captain Arkham, who wore the decontamination suits that had no names on the helmets, were sitting on two stools, across the table. They had brought the news about Corporal Velazquez. They had also brought a tape recorder, which was now in the centre of the table.

'I still don't see why this can't wait,' Bryce said.

'We won't take long,' Major Isley said.

'I've got a search team ready to go,' Bryce said. 'We've got to go through every building in this town, take a body count, find out how many are dead and how many are missing, and look for some clue as to what the hell killed all these people. There's several days of work ahead of us, especially since we can't continue with the search past sundown. I won't let my men go prowling around at night, when the power might go off at any second. Damned if I will.'

Jenny thought of Wargle's eaten face. The hollow eye sockets.

Major Isley said, 'Just a few questions.'

Arkham switched on the tape recorder.

Lisa was staring hard at the major and at the captain.

Jenny wondered what was on the girl's mind.

'We'll start with you, Sheriff,' Major Isley said. 'In the forty-eight hours prior to these events, did your office receive any reports of power failures or telephone service interruptions?'

'If there were problems of that nature,' Bryce said, 'people would generally call the utility companies, not the sheriff.'

'Yes, but wouldn't the utilities notify you? Aren't power and telephone failures contributory to criminal activity?'

Bryce nodded. 'Of course. And to the best of my knowledge, we didn't receive any such alerts.'

Captain Arkham leaned forward. 'What about difficulties with television and radio reception in this area?'

'Not that I'm aware of,' Bryce said.

'Any reports of unexplainable explosions?'

'Explosions?'

'Yes,' Isley said. 'Explosions or sonic booms or any unusually loud and untraceable noises.'

'No. Nothing like that.'

Jenny wondered what in the devil they were driving at.

Isley hesitated and said, 'Any reports of unusual aircraft in the vicinity?'

'No.'

Lisa said, 'You guys aren't part of General Copperfield's team, are you? That's why you don't have names on your helmets.'

Bryce said, 'And your decontamination suits don't fit as well as everyone else's. Theirs are custom tailored. Yours are strictly off the rack.'

278

'Very observant,' Isley said.

'If you aren't with the CBW project,' Jenny said, 'what *are* you doing here?'

'We didn't want to bring it up at the start,' Isley said. 'We thought we might get straighter answers from you if you weren't immediately aware of what we were looking for.'

Arkham said, 'We're not Army Medical Corps. We're Air Force.'

'Project Skywatch,' Isley said. 'We're not exactly a secret organization, but . . . well . . . let's just say we discourage publicity.'

'Skywatch?' Lisa said, brightening. 'Are you talking about UFOs? Is that it? Flying saucers?'

Jenny saw Isley wince at the words 'flying saucers'.

Isley said, 'We don't go around checking out every crackpot report of little green men from Mars. For one thing, we don't have the funds to do that. Our job is planning for the scientific, social and military aspects of mankind's first encounter with an alien intelligence. We're really more of a think tank than anything else.'

Bryce shook his head. 'No one around here's been reporting flying saucers.'

'But that's just what Major Isley means,' Arkham said. 'You see, our studies indicate the first encounter might start out in such a bizarre way that we wouldn't even recognize it as a first encounter. The popular concept of spaceships descending from the sky . . . well, it might not be like that. If we find ourselves dealing with *truly* alien intelligences, their ships might be so different from our concept of a ship that we wouldn't even be aware they'd landed.

'Which is why we check into strange phenomena that don't seem to be UFO related at first glance,' Arkham said. 'Like last spring, up in Vermont, there was a house in which an extremely active poltergeist was at work. Furniture was levitated. Dishes flew across the kitchen and smashed against the wall. Streams of water burst from walls in which there were no water pipes. Balls of flame erupted out of empty air—'

'Isn't a poltergeist supposed to be a ghost?' Bryce asked. 'What could ghosts have to do with your area of interest?'

'Nothing,' Isley said. 'We don't believe in ghosts. But we wondered if perhaps poltergeist phenomena might result from an attempt at inter-species communication gone awry. If we were to encounter an alien race that communicated only by telepathy, and if we were unable to receive those telepathic thoughts, maybe the unreceived psychic energy would produce destructive phenomena of the sort sometimes attributed to malign spirits.'

'And what did you finally decide about the poltergeist up there in Vermont?' Jenny asked.

'Decide? Nothing,' Isley said.

'Just that it was . . . interesting,' Arkham said.

Jenny glanced at Lisa and saw that the girl's eyes were very wide. *This* was something Lisa would grasp, accept, and cling to. This was a fear she had been thoroughly prepared for, thanks to movies and books and television. Monsters from outer space. Invaders from other worlds. It didn't make the Snowfield killings any less gruesome. But it was a *known* threat, and that made it infinitely preferable to the unknown. Jenny strongly doubted this was mankind's first encounter with creatures from the stars, but Lisa seemed eager to believe.

'And what about Snowfield?' the girl asked. 'Is that what's going on? Has something landed from . . . *out there*?'

Arkham looked uneasily at Major Isley.

Isley cleared his throat: as translated by the squawk box on his chest, it was a racheting, machine-like sound. 'It's much too soon to make any judgment about that. We *do* believe there's a small chance the first contact between man and alien might involve the danger of biological contamination. That's why we've got an information-sharing arrangement with Copperfield's project. An inexplicable outbreak of an unknown disease might indicate an unrecognized contact with an extra-terrestrial presence.'

'But if it *is* an extra-terrestrial creature we're dealing with,' Bryce said, obviously doubtful, 'it seems damned savage for a being of "superior" intelligence.'

'The same thought occurred to me,' Jenny said.

Isley raised his eyebrows. 'There's no guarantee that a creature with a greater intelligence would be a benevolent pacifist.'

'Yeah,' Arkham said. 'That's a common conceit: the notion that aliens would've learned how to live in complete harmony among themselves and with other species. As that old song says . . . it ain't necessarily so. After all, mankind is considerably further along the road of evolution than gorillas, but as a species we're definitely more warlike than gorillas at their most aggressive.'

'Maybe one day we *will* encounter a benevolent alien race that'll teach us how to live in peace,' Isley said. 'Maybe they'll give us the knowledge and technology to solve all our earthly problems and even to reach the stars. Maybe.'

'But we can't rule out the alternative,' Arkham said grimly.

26

LONDON, ENGLAND

ELEVEN O'CLOCK Monday morning in Snowfield was seven o'clock Monday evening in London.

A miserably wet day had flowed into a miserably wet night. Raindrops drummed on the window in the cubbyhole of Timothy Flyte's two-room, attic apartment.

The professor was standing in front of a cutting board, making a sandwich.

After partaking of that magnificent champagne breakfast at Burt Sandler's expense, Timothy hadn't felt up to lunch. He had foregone afternoon tea, as well.

He'd met with two students today. He was tutoring one of them in hieroglyphics analysis and the other in Latin. Surfeited with breakfast, he had nearly fallen asleep during both sessions. Embarrassing. But, as little as his pupils were paying him, they could hardly complain too strenuously if, just once, he dozed off in the middle of a lesson.

As he put a thin slice of boiled ham and a slice of Swiss cheese on mustard-slathered bread, he heard the telephone ringing down in the front hall of the rooming house. He didn't think it was for him. He received few calls.

But, seconds later, there was a knock at the door. It was the young Indian fellow who rented a room on the first floor. In heavily accented English, he told Timothy the call was for him. And urgent.

'Urgent? Who is it?' Timothy asked as he followed the young man down the stairs. 'Did he give his name?'

'Sand-leer,' the Indian said.

Sandler? Burt Sandler?

Over breakfast, they had agreed on terms for a new edition of *The Ancient Enemy*, one that was completely rewritten to appeal to the average reader. Following the original publication of the book, almost seventeen years ago, he had received several offers to popularize his theories about historical mass disappearances, but he had resisted the idea; he had felt that issuing a popularized version of *The Ancient Enemy* would be playing into the hands of all those who had so unfairly accused him of sensationalism, humbug, and money grabbing. Now, however, years of want had made him more amenable to the idea. Sandler's appearance on the scene and his offer of a contract had come at a time when Timothy's ever-worsening poverty had reached a critical stage; it was truly a miracle. This morning, they had settled on an advance (against royalties) of fifteen thousand dollars. At the current rate of exchange, that amounted to a little more than eight thousand pounds sterling. It wasn't a fortune, but it was more money than Timothy had seen in a long, long time, and at the moment it seemed like wealth beyond counting.

As he went down the narrow stairs, towards the front hall, where the telephone stood on a small table beneath a cheap print of a bad painting, Timothy wondered if Sandler was calling to back out of the agreement.

The professor's heart began to pound with almost painful force.

The young Indian gentleman said, 'I hope is no trouble, sir.'

Then he returned to his own room and closed the door.

Flyte picked up the phone. 'Hello?'

'My God, do you get an evening newspaper?' Sandler asked. His voice was shrill, almost hysterical.

Timothy wondered if Sandler was drunk. Was *this* what he considered urgent business?

Before Timothy could respond, Sandler said, 'I think it's happened! By God, Dr Flyte, I think it's actually happened! It's in the newspaper tonight. And on the radio. Not many details yet. But it sure looks as if it's happened.'

The professor's worry about the book contract was now compounded by exasperation. 'Could you please be more specific, Mr Sandler?'

'The ancient enemy, Dr Flyte. One of those creatures has struck again. Just yesterday. A town in California. Some are dead. Most are missing. Hundreds. An entire town. Gone.'

'God help them,' Flyte said.

'I've got a friend in the London office of the Associated Press, and he's read me the latest wire service reports,' Sandler said. 'I know things that aren't in the papers yet. For one thing, the police out there in California have put out an all-points bulletin for you. Apparently, one of the victims had read your book. When the attack came, he locked himself in a bathroom. It got him anyway. But he gained enough time to scrawl your name and the title of your book on the mirror!'

Timothy was speechless. There was a chair beside the telephone. He suddenly needed it.

'The authorities in California don't understand what's happened. They don't even realize *The Ancient Enemy* is the title of a book, and they don't know what part you play in all this. They think it was a nerve gas attack or an act of biological warfare or even extra-terrestrial contact. But the man who wrote your name on that mirror knew better. And so do we. I'll tell you more in the car.'

'Car?' Timothy said.

'My God, I hope you have a passport!'

'Uh . . . yes.'

'I'm coming by with a car to take you to the airport. I want you to go to California, Dr Flyte.'

'But—'

'Tonight. There's an available seat on a flight from Heathrow. I've reserved it in your name.'

'But I can't afford—'

'Your publisher is paying all expenses. Don't worry. You *must* go to Snowfield. You won't be writing just a popularization of *The Ancient Enemy*. Not any more. Now, you're going to write a well-rounded human story about Snowfield, and all of your material on historical mass disappearances and your theories about the ancient enemy support that narrative. Do you see? Won't it be great?'

'But would it be right for me to rush in there now?'

'What do you mean?' Sandler asked.

'Would it be proper?' Timothy asked worriedly. 'Wouldn't it appear as if I was attempting to cash in on a terrible tragedy?'

'Listen, Dr Flyte, there are going to be a hundred hustlers in Snowfield, all with book contracts in their back pockets. They'll rip off your material. If you don't write *the* book on the subject, one of them will write it at your expense.'

'But hundreds are dead,' Timothy said. He felt ill. 'Hundreds. The pain, the tragedy . . .'

Sandler was clearly impatient with the professor's hesitancy. 'Well . . . okay, okay. Maybe you're right. Maybe I haven't really stopped to think about the horror of it. But don't you see – that's why you *must* be the one to write the ultimate book on the subject. No one else can bring your erudition or compassion to the project.'

'Well . . .'

Seizing on Timothy's hesitation, Sandler said, 'Good. Pack a suitcase fast. I'll be there in half an hour.'

Sandler hung up, and Timothy sat for a moment, holding the receiver, listening to the dead line. Stunned.

285

*

In the taxi's headlights, the rain was silvery. It slanted on the wind, like thousands of thin streamers of glittering Christmas tinsel. On the pavement, it puddled in quicksilver pools.

The taxi driver was reckless. The car careened along the slick streets. With one hand, Timothy held tightly to the safety bar on the door. Evidently Burt Sandler had promised a very large tip as a reward for speed.

Sitting next to the professor, Sandler said, 'There'll be a layover in New York, but not too long. One of our people will meet you and shepherd you through. We won't alert the media in New York. We'll save the press conference for San Francisco. So be prepared to face an army of eager reporters when you get off the plane there.'

'Couldn't I just go quietly to Santa Mira and present myself to the authorities there?' Timothy asked unhappily.

'No, no, no!' Sandler said, clearly horrified by the very thought. 'We've got to have a press conference. You're the only one with the *answer*, Dr Flyte. We've got to let everyone know that you're the one. We've got to start beating the drum for your next book before Norman Mailer puts aside his latest study of Marilyn Monroe and jumps into this thing with both feet!'

'I haven't even begun to write that book yet.'

'God, I know. And by the time we publish, the demand will be phenomenal!'

The taxi turned a corner. Tyres squealed. Timothy was thrown against the door.

'A publicist will meet you at the plane in San Francisco. He'll guide you through the press conference,' Sandler said. 'One way or another he'll get you to Santa Mira. It's a fairly long drive, so maybe it can be done by helicopter.'

'Helicopter?' Timothy said, astonished.

The taxi sped through a deep puddle, casting up plumes of silvery water.

The airport was within sight.

Burt Sandler had been talking nonstop since Timothy had got into the car. Now he said, 'One more thing. At your press conference, tell them the stories you told me this morning. About the disappearing Mayans. And three thousand Chinese infantrymen who vanished. And be sure to make any references you possibly can to mass disappearances that took place in the US — even before there *was* a United States, even in previous geological eras. That'll appeal to the American press. Local ties. That always helps. Didn't the first British colony in America vanish without a trace?'

'Yes. The Roanoke Island colony.'

'Be sure to mention it.'

'But I can't say conclusively that the disappearance of the Roanoke colony is connected with the ancient enemy.'

'Is there any chance whatsoever that it might've been?'

Fascinated, as always, by this subject, Timothy was able, for the first time, to wrench his mind away from the suicidal behaviour of the taxi driver. 'When a British expedition, funded by Sir Walter Raleigh, returned to the Roanoke Colony in March of 1590, they found everyone gone. One hundred and twenty people had vanished without trace. Countless theories have been advanced regarding their fate. For example, the most popular theory holds that the people at Roanoke Island fell victim to the Croatoan Indians, who lived nearby. The only message left by the colonists was the name of that tribe, hastily slashed into the bark of a tree. But the Croatoans professed to know nothing about the disappearance. And they were peaceful Indians. Not the least bit warlike. Indeed, they had initially helped the colonists settle in. Furthermore, there were no signs of violence at the settlement. No bodies were ever found. No bones. No graves. So you see, even the most widely accepted theory raises a greater number of questions than it answers.'

The taxi swept around another curve, braked abruptly to avoid colliding with a truck.

But now Timothy was only passingly aware of the driver's dare-devil conduct. He continued:

'It occurred to me that the word the colonists had carved into that tree – *Croatoan* – might not have been intended to point an accusing finger. It might have meant that the Croatoans would know what had happened. I read the journals of several British explorers who later talked with the Croatoans about the colony's disappearance, and there's evidence the Indians did, indeed, have some idea of what had happened. Or *thought* they knew. But they were not taken seriously when they tried to explain to the white man. The Croatoans reported that, simultaneously with the disappearance of the colonists, there was a great depletion of game in the forests and fields in which the tribe hunted. Virtually all species of wildlife had abruptly dwindled drastically in numbers. A couple of the more perceptive explorers noted in their journals that the Indians regarded the subject with superstitious dread. They seemed to have a religious explanation for the disappearance. But, unfortunately, the white men who talked with them about the missing colonists were not interested in Indian superstitions and did not pursue that avenue of enquiry.'

'I gather you've researched Croatoan religious beliefs,' Burt Sandler said.

'Yes,' Timothy said. 'Not an easy subject, for the tribe has been extinct itself for many, many years. What I've found is that the Croatoans were spiritualists. They believed that the spirit endured and walked the earth even after the death of the body, and they believed there were "greater spirits" that manifested themselves in the elements – wind, earth, fire, water and so forth. Most important of all – as far as we're concerned – they also believed in an *evil* spirit, a source of *all* evil, an equivalent to the Christians' Satan. I forget the exact Indian word for it, but it translated roughly as He Who Can Be Anything Yet Is Nothing.'

'My God,' Sandler said, 'that's not a bad description of the ancient enemy.'

'Sometimes there are truths hidden in superstitions. The Croatoans believed that both the wildlife and the colonists had been taken away by He Who Can Be Anything Yet Is Nothing. So . . . while I cannot say conclusively that the ancient enemy had something to do with the disappearance of the Roanoke Islanders, it seems to me sufficient reason to consider the possibility.'

'Fantastic!' Sandler said. 'Tell them all of that at the press conference in San Francisco. Just the way you've told me.'

The taxi squealed to a stop in front of the terminal.

Burt Sandler shoved a few five-pound notes into the driver's hand. He glanced at his watch. 'Dr Flyte, let's get you on that plane.'

From his window seat, Timothy Flyte watched the city lights disappearing beneath the storm clouds. The jet speared upward through the thin rain. Soon, they rose above the overcast; the storm was below them, clear sky overhead. The rays of the moon bounced off the churning tops of the clouds, and the night beyond the plane was filled with soft, eerie light.

The seatbelt sign winked off.

He unbuckled but couldn't relax. His mind was churning just like the storm clouds.

The stewardess came around, offering drinks. He asked for Scotch.

He felt like a coiled spring. Overnight, his life had changed. There had been more excitement in this one day than in the entire past year.

The tension that gripped him was not unpleasant. He was more than happy to slough off his dreary existence; he was putting on a new and better life as quickly as he might have put on a new suit of clothes. He was risking ridicule and all the old familiar accusations by going public with his theories again. But there was also a chance that he would at last be able to prove himself.

The Scotch came, and he drank it. He ordered another. Slowly, he relaxed.

Beyond the plane, the night was vast.

27

ESCAPE

FROM THE barred window of the temporary holding cell, Fletcher Kale had a good view of the street. All morning he watched the reporters congregating. Something really big had happened.

Some of the other inmates were sharing news cell to cell, but none of them would share anything with Kale.

They hated him. Frequently, they taunted him, called him a baby killer. Even in jail, there were social classes, and no one was further down the ladder than child killers.

It was almost funny. Even car thieves, muggers, burglars, holdup men, and embezzlers needed to feel morally superior to someone. So they reviled and persecuted anyone who had harmed a child, and somehow that made them feel like priests and bishops by comparison.

Fools. Kale despised them.

He didn't ask anyone to share information with him. He wouldn't give them the satisfaction of freezing him out.

He stretched out on his bunk and daydreamed about his magnificent destiny: fame, power, wealth . . .

At eleven-thirty, he was still lying on his bunk when they came to take him to the courthouse for arraignment on two counts of murder. The cellblock guard unlocked the door. Another man – a grey-haired, pot-bellied deputy – came in and put handcuffs on Kale.

'We're short-handed today,' he told Kale. 'I'm the only one detailed for this. But don't you get some damn-fool idea that you'd have a chance to make a break for it. You're cuffed, and I've got the gun, and nothing would please me as much as shooting your ass off.'

In both the guard's and the deputy's eyes, there was loathing.

At last, the possibility of spending the rest of his life in prison became real to Kale. To his surprise, he began to cry as they led him out of the cell.

The other prisoners hooted and laughed and called him names.

The pot-bellied man prodded Kale in the ribs. 'Get a move on.'

Kale stumbled along the corridor on weak legs, through a security gate that rolled open for them, out of the cell-block, into another hall. The guard remained behind, but the deputy prodded Kale towards the elevators, prodded him too often and too hard, even when it wasn't necessary. Kale felt his self-pity giving way to anger.

In the small, slowly descending elevator, he realized that the deputy no longer saw any threat in his prisoner. He was disgusted, impatient, embarrassed by Kale's emotional collapse.

By the time the doors opened, a change had occurred in Kale, as well. He was still weeping quietly, but the tears were no longer genuine, and he was shaking with excitement rather than with despair.

They went through another checkpoint. The deputy presented a set of papers to another guard who called him Joe. The guard looked at Kale with unconcealed disdain. Kale averted his face as if he were ashamed of himself. And continued to cry.

Then he and Joe were outside, crossing a large parking lot towards a row of green and white police cruisers that were lined up in front of a cyclone fence. The day was warm and sunny.

Kale continued to cry and to pretend that his legs were rubbery. He kept his shoulders hunched and his head low. He shuffled along listlessly, as if he were a broken, beaten man.

Except for him and the deputy, the parking lot was deserted. Just the two of them. Perfect.

All the way to the car, Kale looked for the right moment in which to make his move. For a while he thought it wouldn't come.

Then Joe shoved him against a car and half turned away to unlock the door – and Kale struck. He threw himself at the deputy as the man bent to insert a key into the lock. The deputy gasped and swung a fist at him. Too late. Kale ducked under the blow and came up fast and slammed him against the car, pinning him. Joe's face went white with pain as the door handle rammed hard against the base of his spine. The ring of keys flew out of his hand, and even as they were falling, he was using the same hand to grab for his holstered revolver.

Kale knew, with his own hands cuffed, he couldn't wrestle the gun away. As soon as the revolver was drawn, the fight was finished.

So Kale went for the other man's throat. Went for it with his teeth. He bit deep, felt blood gushing, bit again, pushed his mouth into the wound, like an attack dog, and bit again, and the deputy screamed, but it was only a yelp-rattle-sigh that no one could have heard, and the gun fell out of the holster and out of the deputy's spasming hand, and both men went down hard, with Kale on top, and the deputy tried to scream again, so Kale rammed a knee into his crotch, and blood was pump-pump-pumping out of the man's throat.

'Bastard,' Kale said.

The deputy's eyes froze. The blood stopped spurting from the wound. It was over.

Kale had never felt so powerful, so *alive*.

He looked around the parking lot. Still no one in sight.

He scrambled over to the ring of keys, tried them one by one until he unlocked his handcuffs. He threw the cuffs under the car.

He rolled the dead deputy under the cruiser, too, out of sight.

He wiped his face on his sleeve. His shirt was spotted and stained with blood. There was nothing he could do about that. Nor could he change the fact that he was wearing baggy, blue, coarsely woven institutional clothing and a pair of canvas and rubber slip-on shoes.

Feeling conspicuous, he hurried along the fence, through the open gate. He crossed the alley and went into another parking lot behind a large, two-storey apartment complex. He glanced up at all the windows and hoped no one was looking.

There were perhaps twenty cars in the lot. A yellow Datsun had keys in the ignition. He got behind the wheel, closed the door, and sighed with relief. He was out of sight, and he had transportation.

A box of Kleenex stood on the console. Using paper tissues and spit he cleaned his face. With the blood removed, he looked at himself in the rearview mirror – and grinned.

28

BODY COUNT

WHILE GENERAL Copperfield's unit was conducting the autopsy and tests in the mobile field lab, Bryce Hammond formed two search teams and began a building-by-building inspection of the town. Frank Autry led the first group, and Major Isley went along as an observer for Project Skywatch. Likewise, Captain Arkham joined Bryce's group. Block by block and street by street, the two teams were never more than one building apart, remaining in close touch with walkie-talkies.

Jenny accompanied Bryce. More than anyone else, she was familiar with Snowfield's residents, and she was the one most likely to identify any bodies that were found. In most cases, she could also tell them who had lived in each house and how many people had been in each family – information they needed to compile a list of the missing.

She was troubled at the thought of exposing Lisa to more grue-some scenes, but she couldn't refuse to assist the search team. She couldn't leave her sister behind at Hilltop Inn, either. Not after what had happened to Harker. And to Velazquez. But the girl coped well with the tension of the house-to-house search. She was still prov-ing herself to Jenny, and Jenny was becoming increasingly proud of her.

They didn't find any bodies for a while. The first businesses and houses they entered were deserted. In several houses, tables were set for Sunday dinner. In others, baths were filled with water that had grown cold. In a number of places, television sets were still on, but there was no one to watch them.

In one kitchen they discovered Sunday dinner on the electric stove. The food in the three pots had cooked for so many hours that all the water content had evaporated. The remains were dry, hard, burnt, blistered, and unidentifiable. The stainless-steel pots were ruined; they had turned bluish-black both inside and out. The plastic handles of the pots had softened and partially melted. The entire house reeked with the most acrid, nauseating stench Jenny had ever encountered.

Bryce switched off the burners. 'It's a miracle the whole place wasn't set on fire.'

'It probably would've been if that were a gas stove,' Jenny said.

Above the three pots, there was a stainless-steel range hood with an exhaust fan. When the food had burned, the hood had contained the short-lived flash of flames and had prevented the fire from spreading to the surrounding cabinetry.

Outside again, everyone (except Major Arkham in his decontamination suit) took deep breaths of the clean mountain air. They needed a couple of minutes to purge their lungs of the vile stuff they had breathed inside that house.

Then, next door, they found the first body of the day. It was John Farley, who owned the Mountain Tavern, which was open only during the ski season. He was in his forties. He had been a striking man, with salt-and-pepper hair, a large nose, and a wide mouth that had frequently curved into an immensely engaging smile. Now he was bloated and bruised, his eyes bulging out of his skull, his clothes bursting at the seams as his body swelled.

Farley was sitting at the breakfast table, at one end of his big kitchen. On a plate before him was a meal of cheese-filled ravioli and meatballs. There was also a glass of red wine. On the table, beside the plate, there was an open magazine. Farley was sitting up straight in his chair. One hand lay palm-up in his lap. His other arm was on the table, and in that hand was clenched a crust of bread. Farley's mouth was partly open, and there was a bite of bread trapped between his teeth. He had perished in the act of chewing; his jaw muscles had never even relaxed.

'Good God,' Tal said, 'he didn't have time to spit the stuff out or swallow it. Death must've been instantaneous.'

'And he didn't see it coming, either,' Bryce said. 'Look at his face. There's no expression of horror or surprise or shock as there is with most of the others.'

Staring at the dead man's clenched jaws, Jenny said. 'What I don't understand is why death doesn't bring any relaxation of the muscles whatsoever. It's weird.'

In Our Lady of the Mountains Church, sunlight streamed through the stained-glass windows, which were composed predominantly of blues and greens. Hundreds of irregularly shaped patches of royal blue, sky blue, turquoise, aquamarine, emerald green, and many other shades dripped across the polished wooden pews, puddled in the aisles, and shimmered on the walls.

It's like being underwater, Gordy Brogan thought as he followed Frank Autry into the strangely and beautifully illuminated nave.

Just beyond the narthex, a stream of crimson light splashed across the white marble font that contained the holy water. It was the crimson of Christ's blood. The sun pierced a stained-glass image of Christ's bleeding heart and sprayed blood-touched rays upon the water that glistened in the pale marble bowl.

Of the five men in the search team, only Gordy was a Catholic. He moistened two fingers in the holy water, crossed himself, and genuflected.

The church was solemn, silent, still.

The air was softened by a pleasant trace of incense.

In the pews, there were no worshippers. At first it appeared as if the church was deserted.

Then Gordy looked more closely at the altar and gasped.

Frank saw it, too. 'Oh, my God.'

The chancel was cloaked in deeper shadows than the rest of the church, which was why the men hadn't immediately noticed the hideous – and sacrilegious – thing above the altar. The altar candles had burned down all the way and gone out.

However, as the men in the search team progressed hesitantly down the centre aisle, they got a clearer and clearer view of the life-size crucifix that rose up from the centre of the altar, along the rear wall of the chancel. It was a wooden cross, with an exquisitely detailed, hand-painted, glazed plaster figure of Christ fixed to it. At the moment, much of the godly image was obscured by another body that hung in front of it. A real body, not another plaster corpse. It was the priest in his robes; he was nailed to the cross.

Two altar boys knelt on the floor in front of the altar. They were dead, bruised, bloated.

The priest's flesh had begun to darken and to show other signs of imminent decomposition. His body was not in the same bizarre condition as all the others that had been found thus far. In his case, the discolouration was what you would expect of a day-old corpse.

Frank Autry, Major Isley, and the other two deputies continued through the gate in the altar railing and stepped up into the chancel.

Gordy wasn't able to go with them. He was too badly shaken and had to sit in the front pew to keep from collapsing.

After inspecting the chancel and glancing through the sacristy door, Frank used his walkie-talkie to call Bryce Hammond in the building next door. 'Sheriff, we've found three here in the church. We need Doc Paige for positive IDs. But it's especially grisly, so better leave Lisa in the vestibule with a couple of guys.'

'We'll be there in two minutes,' the sheriff said.

Frank came down from the chancel, through the gate in the railing, and sat down beside Gordy. He was holding the walkie-talkie in one hand and a gun in the other. 'You're Catholic.'

'Yeah.'

'Sorry you had to see this.'

'I'll be okay,' Gordy said. 'It's no easier for you just because you're not a Catholic.'

'You know the priest?'

'I think his name's Father Callahan. I didn't go to this church, though. I attended St Andrew's, down in Santa Mira.'

Frank put the walkie-talkie down and scratched his chin. 'From all the other indications we've had, it's looked like the attack came yesterday evening, not long before Doc and Lisa came back to town. But now this . . . If these died in the morning, during Mass—'

'It was probably during Benediction,' Gordy said. 'Not Mass.'

'Benediction?'

'The Benediction of the Blessed Sacrament. The Sunday evening service.'

'Ah. Then it fits right in with the timing of the others.' He looked around at the empty pews. 'What happened to the parishioners? Why are only the altar boys and the priests here?'

'Well, not an awful lot of people come to Benediction,' Gordy said. 'There were probably at least two or three others. But *it* took them.'

'Why didn't it just take everyone?'

Gordy didn't answer.

'Why did it have to do something like this?' Frank pressed.

'To ridicule us. To mock us. To steal our hope,' Gordy said miserably.

Frank stared at him.

Gordy said, 'Maybe some of us have been counting on God to get us through this alive. Probably most of us have. I know I've sure been praying a lot since we came here. Probably you have, too. It knew we would do that. It knew we would ask God for help. So this is its way of letting us know that God *can't* help us. Or at least that's what it would like us to believe. Because that's its way. To instill doubt about God. That's always been its way.'

Frank said, 'You sound as if you know exactly what we're up against here.'

'Maybe,' Gordy said. He stared at the crucified priest, then turned to Frank again. 'Don't you know? Don't you really, Frank?'

After they left the church and went around the corner onto the cross street, they found two wrecked cars.

A Cadillac Seville had run across the front lawn of the church rectory, mowing down the shrubbery in its path, and had collided with a porch post at one corner of the house. The post was nearly splintered in two. The porch roof was sagging.

Tal Whitman squinted through the side window of the Caddy. 'There's a woman behind the wheel.'

'Dead?' Bryce asked.

'Yeah. But not from the accident.'

At the other side of the car, Jenny tried to open the driver's door. It was locked. All the doors were locked, and all the windows were rolled up tight.

Nevertheless, the woman behind the wheel – Edna Gower; Jenny knew her – was like the other corpses. Darkly bruised. Swollen. A scream of terror frozen on her twisted face.

'How could it get in there and kill her?' Tal wondered aloud.

'Remember the locked bathroom at the Candleglow Inn,' Bryce said.

'And the barricaded room at the Oxleys',' Jenny said.

Captain Arkham said, 'It's almost an argument for the general's nerve gas theory.'

Then Arkham unclipped a miniaturized geiger counter from his utility belt and carefully examined the car. But it wasn't radiation that had killed the woman inside.

The second car, half a block away, was a pearl-white Lynx. On the pavement behind it were black skid marks. The Lynx was angled across the street, blocking it. The front end was punched into the side of a yellow Chevy van. There wasn't a lot of damage because the Lynx had almost braked to a stop before hitting the parked vehicle.

The driver was a middle-aged man with a bushy moustache. He was wearing cut-off jeans and a Dodgers T-shirt. Jenny knew him, too. Marty Sussman. He had been Snowfield's city manager for the past six years. Affable, earnest Marty Sussman. Dead. Again, the cause of death was dearly not related to the collision.

The doors of the Lynx were locked. The windows were rolled up tight, just as they had been on the Cadillac.

'Looks like they both were trying to escape from something,' Jenny said.

'Maybe,' Tal said. 'Or they might just have been out for a drive or going somewhere on an errand when the attack came. If they were trying to escape, something sure stopped them cold, forced them right off the street.'

'Sunday was a warm day. Warm but not *too* warm,' Bryce said. 'Not hot enough to ride around with the windows closed and the air conditioner on. It was the kind of day when most people keep the windows down, taking advantage of the fresh air. So it looks to me as if, after they were forced to stop, they put up the windows and locked themselves in, trying to keep something out.'

'But it got them anyway,' Jenny said.

It.

Ned and Sue Marie Bischoff owned a lovely Tudor-style home set on a large site, nestled among huge pine trees. They lived there with their two boys. Eight-year-old Lee Bischoff could already play the piano surprisingly well, in spite of the smallness of his hands, and once told Jenny he was going to be the next Stevie Wonder 'only not blind'. Six-year-old Terry looked exactly like a black-skinned Dennis the Menace, but he had a sweet temper.

Ned was a successful artist. His oil paintings sold for as much as six and seven thousand dollars, and his limited-edition prints went for four or five hundred dollars apiece.

He was a patient of Jenny's. Although he was only thirty-two and was already a success in life, she had treated him for an ulcer.

The ulcer wouldn't be bothering him any more. He was in his studio, lying on the floor in front of an easel, dead.

Sue Marie was in the kitchen. Like Hilda Beck, Jenny's house-keeper, and like many other people all over town, Sue Marie had died while preparing dinner. She had been a pretty woman. Not any more.

They found the two boys in one of the bedrooms.

It was a wonderful room for kids, large and airy, with bunk beds. There were built-in bookshelves full of children's books. On the walls were paintings that Ned had done just for his kids, whimsical fantasy scenes quite unlike the pieces for which he was well known: a pig in a tuxedo, dancing with a cow in an evening gown; the interior of a spaceship command chamber, where all the astronauts were toads; an eerie yet charming scene of a school playground at night, bathed in the light of a full moon, no kids around, but with a huge and monstrous-looking werewolf having a grand and giddy time on a set of swings.

The boys were in one corner, beyond an array of overturned Tonka toys. The youngest boy, Terry, was behind Lee, who seemed to have made a valiant effort to protect his smaller brother. The boys were staring out into the room, eyes bulging, their dead gazes still fixed upon whatever had threatened them yesterday. Lee's muscles had locked, so that his thin arms were in the same position now as they had been in the last seconds of his life; raised in front of him, shielding him, palms spread, as if warding off blows.

Bryce knelt in front of the kids. He put one trembling hand against Lee's face, as if unwilling to believe that the child was actually dead.

Jenny knelt beside him.

'Those are the Bischoffs' two boys,' she said, unable to keep her voice from breaking. 'So now the whole family's accounted for.'

Tears were streaming down Bryce's face.

Jenny tried to remember how old his own son was. Seven or eight? About the same age as Lee Bischoff. Little Timmy Hammond was lying in the hospital in Santa Mira this very minute, comatose, just as he had been for the past year. He was pretty much a vegetable. Yes, but even that was better than this. Anything was better than *this*.

Eventually, Bryce's tears dried up. There was rage in him now. 'I'll get them for this,' he said. 'Whoever did this . . . I'll make them pay.'

Jenny had never met a man quite like him. He had considerable masculine strength and purpose, but he was also capable of tenderness.

She wanted to hold him. And be held.

But, as always, she was far too guarded about expressing her own emotional state. If she had possessed his openness, she would never have become estranged from her mother. But she wasn't that way, not yet, although she wanted to be. So, in response to his vow to get the killers of the Bischoffs' children, she said, 'But what if it isn't anything human that killed them? Not all evil is in men. There's evil in nature. The blind maliciousness of earthquakes. The uncaring evil of cancer. This thing here could be like that – remote and unaccountable. There'll be no taking it to court if it isn't even human. What then?'

'Whoever or whatever the hell it is, I'll get it. I'll stop it. I'll make it pay for what's been done here,' he said stubbornly.

*

303

Frank Autry's search team prowled through three deserted houses after leaving the Catholic church. The fourth house wasn't empty. They found Wendell Hulbertson, a high school teacher who worked in Santa Mira but who chose to live here in the mountains, in a house that had once belonged to his mother. Gordy had been in Hulbertson's English class only five years ago. The teacher was not swollen or bruised like the other corpses; he had taken his own life. Backed into a corner of his bedroom, he had put the barrel of a .32 automatic in his mouth and had pulled the trigger. Evidently, death by his own hand had been preferable to whatever *it* had been about to do to him.

After leaving the Bischoff residence, Bryce led his group – through a few houses without finding any bodies. Then, in the fifth house, they discovered an elderly husband and wife locked in a bathroom, where they had tried to hide from their killer. She was sprawled in the tub. He lay in a heap on the floor.

'They were patients of mine,' Jenny said. 'Nick and Melina Papandrakis.'

Tal wrote their names down on a list of the dead.

Like Harold Ordnay and his wife in the Candleglow Inn, Nick Papandrakis had attempted to leave a message that would point a finger at the killer. He had taken some iodine from the medicine cabinet and had used it to paint on the wall. He hadn't had a chance to finish even one word. There were only two letters and part of a third:

'Can anyone figure out what he intended to write?' Bryce asked.

They all took turns squeezing into the bathroom and stepping over Nick Papandrakis's corpse to have a look at the orange-brown letters on the wall, but none of them had any flashes of inspiration.

Bullets.

In the house next to the Papandrakises', the kitchen floor was littered with expended bullets. Not entire cartridges. Just dozens of lead slugs, minus their brass casings.

The fact that there were no ejected casings anywhere in the room indicated that no gunfire had taken place here. There was no odour of gunpowder. No bullet holes in the walls or cabinets.

There were just bullets all over the floor, as if they had rained magically out of thin air.

Frank Autry scooped up a handful of the grey lumps of metal. He wasn't a ballistics expert but, oddly enough, none of the bullets was fragmented or badly deformed, and that enabled him to see that they had come from a variety of weapons. Most of them – *scores* of them – appeared to be the type and calibre of ammunition that was spat out by the submachine guns with which General Copperfield's support troops were armed.

Are these slugs from Sergeant Harker's gun? Frank wondered. Are these the rounds Harker fired at his killer in the meat locker at Gilmartin's Market?

He frowned, perplexed.

He dropped the bullets, and they clattered on the floor. He plucked several other slugs off the tiles. There was a .22 and a .32 and another .22 and a .38. There were even a lot of shotgun pellets.

He picked up a single .45-calibre bullet and examined it with special interest. It was exactly the ammunition that his own revolver handled.

Gordy Brogan squatted down beside him.

Frank didn't look at Gordy. He continued to stare intently at the slug. He was wrestling with an eerie thought.

Gordy scooped a few bullets off the kitchen tiles. 'They aren't deformed at all.'

Frank nodded.

'They had to've hit *something*,' Gordy said. 'So they should be deformed. Some of them should be, anyway.' He paused, then said, 'Hey, you're a million miles away. What're you thinking about?'

'Paul Henderson.' Frank held the .45 slug in front of Gordy's face. 'Paul fired three like this last night, over at the substation.'

'At his killer.'

'Yeah.'

'So?'

'So I have this crazy hunch that if we asked the lab to run ballistics tests on it, they'd find it came from Paul's revolver.'

Gordy blinked at him.

'And,' Frank said, 'I also think that if we searched through all of the slugs on the floor here, we'd find exactly two more like this one. Not just one more, mind you. And not three more. Just two more with precisely the same markings as this one.'

'You mean . . . the same three Paul fired last night.'

'Yeah.'

'But how'd they get from there to here?'

Frank didn't answer. Instead, he stood and thumbed the send button on the walkie-talkie. 'Sheriff?'

Bryce Hammond's voice issued crisply from the small speaker. 'What is it, Frank?'

'We're still here at the Sheffield House. I think you'd better come over. There's something you ought to see.'

'More bodies?'

'No, sir. Uh . . . something sort of weird.'

'We'll be there,' the sheriff said.

Then, to Gordy, Frank said, 'What I think is . . . sometime within the past couple of hours, sometime after Sergeant Harker was taken from Gilmartin's Market, *it* was here, right in this room. It got rid of all the bullets it'd taken last night and this morning.'

'The hits it took?'

'Yes.'

'Got *rid* of them? Just like that?'

'Just like that,' Frank said.

'But how?'

'Looks like it just sort of . . . expelled them. Looks like it shed those bullets the way a dog shakes off loose hairs.'

29

ON THE RUN

Driving through Santa Mira in the stolen Datsun, Fletcher Kale heard about Snowfield on the radio.

Although it had captured the rest of the country's attention, Kale wasn't very interested. He was never particularly concerned about other people's tragedies.

He reached out to switch off the radio, already weary of hearing about Snowfield when he had so many problems of his own – and then he caught a name that *did* mean something to him. Jake Johnson. Johnson was one of the deputies who had gone up to Snowfield last night. Now he was missing and might even be dead.

Jake Johnson . . .

A year ago, Kale had sold Johnson a solidly built log cabin on five acres in the mountains.

Johnson had professed to be an avid hunter and had pretended to want the cabin for that purpose. However, from a number of things the deputy let slip, Kale decided that Johnson was actually a survivalist, one of those doomsayers who believed the world was rushing towards Armageddon and that society was going to collapse either because of runaway inflation or nuclear war or some other catastrophe. Kale became increasingly convinced that Johnson wanted the cabin for a hiding place that could be stocked with food and ammunition – and then easily defended in times of social upheaval.

The cabin was certainly remote enough for that purpose. It was on Snowtop Mountain, all the way around the other side from the town of Snowfield. To get to the place, you had to go up a country fire road, a narrow dirt track that was passable virtually only to a four-wheel-drive vehicle, then switch to another, even tougher track. The final quarter-mile had to be covered on foot.

Two months after Johnson purchased the mountain property, Kale sneaked up there on a warm June morning when he knew the deputy was on duty in Santa Mira. He wanted to see if Johnson was turning the place into a wilderness fortress, as he suspected.

He found the cabin untouched, but he discovered that Johnson was doing extensive work in some of the limestone caves to which there was an entrance on his land. Outside the caves, there were sacks of cement and sand, a wheelbarrow, and a pile of stones.

Just inside the mouth of the first cave, there had been two Coleman gas lanterns standing on the stone floor, by the wall. Kale had picked up one of the lanterns and had gone deeper into the subterranean chambers.

The first cave was long and narrow, little more than a tunnel. At the end of it, he followed a series of doglegs, twisting through irregular limestone antechambers, before he came into the first room-like cave.

Stacked against one wall were cases of five-pound, vacuum-sealed cans of nitrogen-preserved milk powder, freeze-dried fruits and vegetables, freeze-dried soup, powdered eggs, cans of honey, drums of whole grain. An air mattress. And much more. Jake had been busy.

The first underground room led to another. In this one, there was a naturally formed hole in the floor, about ten inches in diameter, and odd noises were rising out of it. Whispering voices.

Menacing laughter. Kale almost turned and ran, but then he realized that he was hearing nothing more sinister than the chuckling of running water. An underground stream. Jake Johnson had lowered one-inch rubber tubing into the natural well and had rigged a hand pump beside it.

All the comforts of home.

Kale decided that Johnson was not merely cautious. The man was *obsessed*.

On another day at the end of that same summer, late in August, Kale returned to the mountain property. To his surprise, the cave mouth – which was about four feet high and five feet wide – was no longer visible. Johnson had created an effective barrier of vegetation to conceal the entrance to his hideaway.

Kale pushed through the brush, careful not to trample it.

He had brought his own flashlight this time. He crawled through the mouth of the cave, stood up once he was inside, followed the tunnel through three doglegs – and suddenly came up against an unexpected dead end. He knew there should be one more short doglegged passageway and then the first of the large caves. Instead, there was only a wall of limestone, a flat face that sealed off the rest of the caverns.

For a moment Kale stared at the barrier, confused. Then he examined it closely, and in a few minutes he found the hidden release. The rock was actually a thin façade that had been bonded with epoxy to a door that Johnson had clearly mounted in the natural frame between the final dogleg and the first of the room-size caves.

That day in August, marvelling over the hidden door, Kale decided that he would take the retreat for his own if the need ever arose. After all, maybe these survivalists were on to something. Maybe they were right. Maybe the fools out there would try to blow up the world some day. If so, Kale would get to this retreat first, and when Johnson came through his cleverly hidden door, Kale would simply blow him away.

That thought pleased him.

It made him feel shrewd. Superior.

Thirteen months later, he had, much to his surprise and horror, seen the end of the world coming. The end of *his* world. Locked up in the county jail, charged with murder, he knew where he could go if he could only manage to escape: into the mountains, to the caves. He could stay up there for several weeks, until the cops finally stopped looking for him in and around Santa Mira County.

Thank you, Jake Johnson.

Jake Johnson . . .

Now, in the stolen yellow Datsun, with the county jail only a few minutes behind him, Kale heard about Johnson on the radio. As he listened, he began to smile. Fate was on his side.

After escaping, his biggest problem was disposing of his jail clothes and getting properly outfitted for the mountains. He hadn't been quite sure how he would do that.

As soon as he heard the radio reporter say that Jake Johnson was dead — or at least out of the way, up there in Snowfield — Kale knew he would go straight to Johnson's house, here in Santa Mira. Johnson wasn't exactly Kale's size, but they were close enough so that Kale could swap his jail uniform for the most suitable items in the deputy's closet.

And guns. Jake Johnson, survivalist that he was, would surely have a gun collection somewhere in the house.

The deputy lived in the same one-storey, three-bedroom house that he had inherited from his father, Big Ralph Johnson. It wasn't what you would call a showplace. Big Ralph hadn't spent his bribe and graft money with reckless abandon; he had known how to keep a low profile when it came to anything that might draw the attention of a passing IRS agent. Not that the Johnson place was a shack. It was in the centre block of Pine Shadow Lane, a well-established neighbourhood of mostly larger homes, oversized plots, and mature trees. The Johnson house, one of the smaller ones, had a large jacuzzi sunk in the tile floor of its rear sun porch, an enormous games room with an antique pool table, and a number of other creature comforts not visible from outside.

Kale had been there twice during the course of selling Johnson the mountain property. He had no difficulty finding the house again.

He pulled the Datsun into the drive, cut the engine, and got out. He hoped no neighbours were watching.

He went around towards the back of the house, broke a kitchen window, and clambered inside.

He went directly to the garage. It was big enough for two cars, but only a four-wheel-drive Jeep station wagon was there. He had known Johnson owned the Jeep, and he had hoped to find it here. He opened the garage door and drove the stolen Datsun inside. When the door was closed again and the Datsun could not be seen from the street, he felt safer.

In the master bedroom, he went through Johnson's closet and found a pair of sturdy hiking boots only half a size larger than he required. Johnson was a couple of inches shorter than Kale, so the trousers weren't the right length, but tucked into the boots, they looked good enough. The waist was too large for Kale, but he cinched it in with a belt. He selected a sports shirt and tried it on. Good enough.

Once dressed, he studied himself in the full-length mirror.

'Looking good,' he told his reflection.

Then he went through the house, looking for guns. He couldn't find any.

All right, then they were hidden somewhere. He'd tear the joint to pieces to find them, if it came to that.

He started in the master bedroom. He emptied out the contents of the bureau and dresser drawers. No guns. He went through both nightstands. No guns. He took everything out of the walk-in wardrobe: clothes, shoes, suitcases, boxes, a steamer trunk. No guns. He pulled up the edges of the carpet and searched under it for a hidden storage area. He found nothing.

Half an hour later, he was sweating but not tired. Indeed, he was exhilarated. He looked around at the destruction he had wrought, and he was strangely pleased. The room appeared to have been bombed.

He went into the next room – probing, ripping, overturning, and smashing everything in his path.

He wanted very much to find those guns.

But he was also having fun.

30

SOME ANSWERS/MORE
QUESTIONS

THE HOUSE was exceptionally neat and clean, but the colour scheme and the unrelenting frilliness made Bryce Hammond nervous. Everything was either green or yellow. *Everything.* The carpets were green, and the walls were pale yellow. In the living room, the sofas were done in a yellow and green floral print that was bright enough to send you running for an ophthalmologist. The two armchairs were emerald green, and the two side chairs were canary yellow. The ceramic lamps were yellow with green swirls, and the shades were chartreuse with tassels. On the walls were two big prints – yellow daisies in a verdant field. The master bedroom was worse: floral wallpaper brighter than the fabric on the living room sofas, searingly yellow curtains with a scalloped valance. A dozen accent pillows were scattered across the upper end of the bed; some of them were green with a yellow lace trim, and some were yellow with a green lace trim.

According to Jenny, the house was occupied by Ed and Theresa Lange, their three teenagers, and Theresa's seventy-year-old mother.

None of the occupants could be found. There were no bodies, and Bryce was thankful for that. Somehow, a bruised and swollen corpse would have looked especially terrible here, in the midst of this almost maniacally cheerful decor.

The kitchen was green and yellow, too.

At the sink, Tal Whitman said, 'Here's something. Better have a look at this, Chief.'

Bryce, Jenny and Captain Arkham went over to Tal, but the other two deputies remained back by the doorway with Lisa behind them. It was hard to tell what might turn up in a kitchen sink in this town, in the middle of this Lovecraftian nightmare. Someone's head, maybe. Or another pair of severed hands. Or worse.

But it wasn't worse. It was merely odd.

'A regular jewellery store,' Tal said.

The double sink was filled with jewellery. Mostly rings and watches. There were both men's and women's watches: Timex, Seiko, Bullova, even a Rolloflex; some of them were attached to flexible bands; some with no bands at all; none of them was attached to a leather or plastic band. Bryce saw scores of wedding and engagement rings; the diamonds glittered brilliantly. Birthstone rings, too: garnet, amethyst, bloodstone, topaz, tourmaline; rings with ruby and emerald chips. High school and college rings. Junk jewellery was all mixed up with the high-priced pieces. Bryce dug his hands into one of the piles of valuables the way a pirate, in the movies, always drenched his hands in the contents of a treasure chest. He stirred up the shining baubles and saw other kinds of jewellery: earrings, charm bracelets, loose pearls from a broken necklace or two, gold chains, a lovely cameo pendant . . .

'This stuff can't all belong to the Langes,' Tal said.

'Wait,' Jenny said. She snatched a watch from the pile and examined it closely.

'Recognize that one?' Bryce asked.

'Yes. Cartier. A tanque watch. Not the classic tanque with Roman numerals. This has no numerals and a black face. Sylvia Kanarsky gave it to her husband, Dan, for their fifth wedding anniversary.'

Bryce frowned. 'Where do I know that name from?'

'They own the Candleglow Inn,' Jenny said.

'Oh, yes. Your friends.'

'Among the missing,' Tal said.

'Dan loved this watch,' Jenny said. 'When Sylvia bought it for him, it was a terrible extravagance. The inn was still on a rather shaky financial footing, and the watch cost three hundred and fifty dollars. Now, of course, it's worth considerably more. Dan used to joke that it was the best investment they'd ever made.'

She held the watch up, so Tal and Bryce could see the back. At the top of the gold case, above the Cartier logo, was engraved: TO MY DAN. At the bottom, under the serial number, was LOVE, SYL.

Bryce looked down at the sink full of jewellery. 'So this stuff probably belongs to people from all over Snowfield.'

'Well, I'd say it belongs to those who're missing, anyway,' Tal said. 'The victims we've found so far were still wearing their jewellery.'

Bryce nodded. 'You're right. So those who're missing were stripped of all their valuables before they were taken to . . . to . . . well, to wherever the hell they were taken.'

'Thieves wouldn't leave the loot lying around like this,' Jenny said. 'They wouldn't collect it and then just dump it in someone's kitchen sink. They'd pack it up and take it with them.'

'Then what's all this stuff doing here?' Bryce asked.

'Beats me,' Jenny said.

Tal shrugged.

In the two sinks, the jewellery gleamed and flashed.

The cries of sea gulls.

Dogs barking.

Galen Copperfield looked up from the computer terminal, where he had been reading data. He was sweaty inside his decon suit, tired and achy. For a moment, he wasn't sure he was really hearing the birds and dogs.

316

Then a cat squealed.

A horse whinnied.

The general glanced around the mobile lab, frowning.

Rattlesnakes. A lot of them. The familiar, deadly sound: *chicka-chicka-chicka-chicka*.

Buzzing bees.

The others heard it too. They looked at one another uneasily.

Roberts said, 'It's coming through the suit-to-suit radio.'

'Affirmative,' Dr Bettenby said from over in the second mobile home. 'We hear it here, too.'

'Okay,' Copperfield said, 'let's give it a chance to perform. If you want to speak to one another, use your external corn systems.'

The bees stopped buzzing.

A child – the sex indeterminate, androgynous – began to sink very softly, far away:

> *'Jesus loves me; this I know.*
> *for the Bible tells me so.*
> *Little ones to him are drawn.*
> *They are weak, but he is strong.'*

The voice was sweet. Melodic.

Yet it was also blood-freezing.

Copperfield had never heard anything quite like it. Although it was a child's voice, tender and fragile, it nevertheless contained . . . something that shouldn't be in a child's voice. A profound lack of innocence. Knowledge, perhaps. Yes. Too much knowledge of too many terrible things. Menace. Hatred. Scorn. It wasn't audible on the surface of the lilting song, but it was there beneath the surface, pulsing and dark and immeasurably disturbing.

> *'Yes, Jesus loves me*
> *Yes, Jesus loves me.*

Yes, Jesus loves me—
the Bible tells me so.'

'They told us about this,' Goldstein said. 'Dr Paige and the sheriff. They heard it on the phone and coming out of the kitchen drains at the inn. We didn't believe them; it sounded so ridiculous.'

'Doesn't sound ridiculous now,' Roberts said.

'No,' Goldstein said. Even inside his bulky suit, his shivering was visible.

'It's broadcasting on the same wavelength as our suit radios,' Roberts said.

'But how?' Copperfield wondered.

'Velazquez,' Goldstein said suddenly.

'Of course,' Roberts said. 'Velazquez's suit had a radio. It's broadcasting through Velazquez's radio.'

The child stopped singing. In a whispery voice, it said, *'Better say your prayers. Everyone say your prayers. Don't forget to say your prayers.'* Then it giggled.

They waited for something more.

There was only silence.

'I think it was threatening us,' Roberts said.

'Dammit, put a lid on that kind of talk right now,' Copperfield said. 'Let's not panic ourselves.'

'Have you noticed we're saying *it* now?' Goldstein asked.

Copperfield and Roberts looked at him and then at each other, but they said nothing.

'We're saying *it* the same way that Dr Paige and the sheriff and the deputies do. So . . . have we come completely around to their way of thinking?'

In his mind, Copperfield could still hear the child's haunting, human-yet-not-human voice.

It.

'Come on,' he said gruffly. 'We've still got a lot of work to get done.'

He turned his attention back to the computer terminal, but he had difficulty concentrating.

It.

By 4.30 Monday afternoon, Bryce called off the house-to-house search. A couple of hours of daylight remained, but everyone was bone weary. Weary from climbing up and down stairs. Weary of grotesque corpses. Weary of nasty surprises. Weary of the extent of the human tragedy, of horror that numbed the senses. Weary of the fear knotted in their chests. Constant tension was as tiring as heavy manual labour.

Besides, it had become apparent to Bryce that the job was simply too big for them. In five and a half hours, they had covered only a small portion of the town. At that rate, confined to a daylight schedule, and with their limited numbers, they would need at least two weeks to give Snowfield a thorough inspection. Furthermore, if the missing people didn't turn up by the time the last building was explored, and if a clue to their whereabouts could not be found, then an even more difficult search of the surrounding forest would have to be undertaken.

Last night, Bryce hadn't wanted the National Guard tramping through town. But now he and his people had had the town to themselves for the better part of a day, and Copperfield's specialists had collected their samples and had begun their work. As soon as Copperfield could certify that the town had not been stricken by a bacteriological agent, the Guard could be brought in to assist Bryce's own men.

Initially, knowing little about the situation here, he had been reluctant to surrender any of his authority over a town in his own jurisdiction. But now, although not willing to surrender authority, he was certainly willing to share it. He needed more men. Hour by hour, the responsibility was becoming a crushing weight, and he was ready to shift some of it to other shoulders.

Therefore, at 4.30 Monday afternoon, he took his two search teams back to the Hilltop Inn, placed a call to the governor's office, and spoke with Jack Retlock. It was agreed that the Guard would be placed on standby for a call-up, pending an all-clear signal from Copperfield.

He had no sooner hung up the phone than Charlie Mercer, the desk-sergeant at HQ in Santa Mira, rang through. He had news. Fletcher Kale had escaped while being taken to the county courthouse for arraignment on two charges of murder in the first degree.

Bryce was furious.

Charlie let him rage on for a while, and when Bryce quieted down, Charlie said, 'There's worse. He killed Joe Freemont.'

'Aw, shit,' Bryce said. 'Has Mary been told?'

'Yeah. I went over there myself.'

'How's she taking it?'

'Bad. They were married twenty-six years.'

More death.

Death everywhere.

Christ.

'What about Kale?' Bryce asked Charlie.

'We think he took a car from the apartment complex across the alley. One's been stolen from that lot. So we put up the roadblocks as soon as we knew Kale had slipped, but I figure he had almost an hour's lead on us.'

'Long gone.'

'Probably. If we don't nab the son of a bitch by seven o'clock, I want to call the blocks off. We're so shorthanded – what with everything that's going on – we can't keep tying men up on roadblocks.'

'Whatever you think's best,' Bryce said wearily. 'What about the San Francisco police? You know – about that message Harold Ordnay left on the mirror up here?'

320

'That was the other thing I called about. They finally got back to us.'

'Anything useful?'

'Well, they talked to the employees at Ordnay's bookstores. You remember, I told you one of the shops deals strictly in out-of-print and rare books. The assistant manager at that store, name of Celia Meddock, recognized the Timothy Flyte monniker.'

'He's a customer?' Bryce asked.

'No. An author.'

'Author? Of what?'

'One book. Guess the title.'

'How the devil could I . . . Oh. Of course. *The Ancient Enemy.*'

'You got it,' Charlie Mercer said.

'What's the book about?'

'That's the best part. Celia Meddock says she thinks it's about mass disappearances throughout history.'

For a moment, Bryce was speechless. Then: 'Are you serious? You mean there've been a lot of others?'

'I guess so. At least a bookful of 'em.'

'Where? When? How come I've never heard about them?'

'Meddock said something about the disappearance of ancient Mayan populations—'

(Something stirred in Bryce's mind. An article he had read in an old science magazine. Mayan civilizations. Abandoned cities.)

'—and the Roanoke Colony, which was the first British settlement in North America,' Charlie finished.

'*That* I've heard about. It's in the school books.'

'I guess maybe a lot of the other disappearances go back to ancient times,' Charlie said.

'Christ!'

'Yeah. Flyte apparently has some theory to account for such things,' Charlie said. 'The books explains it.'

'What's the theory?'

321

'The Meddock woman didn't know. She hasn't read the book.'

'But Harold Ordnay must've read it. And what he saw happening here in Snowfield must've been exactly what Flyte wrote about. So Ordnay printed the title on the bathroom mirror.'

'So it seems.'

With a rush of excitement, Bryce said, 'Did the San Francisco PD get a copy of the book?'

'Nope. Meddock didn't have one. The only reason she knew about it was because Ordnay recently sold a copy – two, three weeks ago.'

'Can *we* get a copy?'

'It's out of print. In fact, it never was in print in this country. The copy they sold was British, which is evidently the only edition there ever was – and a small one. It's a *rare* book.'

'What about the person Ordnay sold it to? The collector. What's his name and address?'

'Meddock doesn't remember. She says the guy's not a heavy customer of theirs. She says Ordnay would probably know.'

'Which doesn't do us one damned bit of good. Listen, Charlie, I've *got* to get a copy of that book.'

'I'm working on it,' Charlie said. 'But maybe you won't need it. You'll be able to get the whole story from the horse's mouth. Flyte's on his way here from London right now.'

Jenny was sitting on the edge of the central operations desk in the middle of the lobby, gaping at Bryce as he leaned back in his chair; she was amazed by what he had told her. 'He's on his way here from London? Now? Already? You mean he *knew* this was going to happen?'

'Probably not,' Bryce said. 'But I guess the minute he heard the news, he knew it was a case that fits his theory.'

'Whatever it is.'

'Whatever.'

Tal was standing in front of the desk. 'When's he due in?'

'He'll be in San Francisco shortly after midnight. His US publisher has arranged a news conference for him at the airport. Then he'll come straight to Santa Mira.'

'US publisher?' Frank Autry said, 'I thought you told us his book was never in print over here.'

'It wasn't,' Bryce said. 'Evidently, he's writing a new one.'

'About Snowfield?' Jenny asked.

'I don't know. Maybe. Probably.'

'He sure works fast,' Jenny said, frowning. 'Less than a day after it happens, he's got a contract to write a book about it.'

'I wish he worked even faster. I wish to God he was here right now.'

Tal said, 'I think what Doc means is that this Flyte character might just be another sharp hustler out to make a fast buck.'

'Exactly,' Jenny said.

'Could be,' Bryce admitted. 'But don't forget Ordnay wrote Flyte's name on that mirror. In a way, Ordnay's the only witness we have. And from his message, we have to deduce that what happened was very much like the thing Timothy Flyte wrote about.'

'Damn,' Frank said. 'If Flyte's really got some information that could help us, he should've called. He shouldn't have made us wait.'

'Yeah,' Tal said. 'We could all be dead by midnight. He should have called to tell us what we can do.'

'There's the rub,' Bryce said.

'What do you mean?' Jenny asked.

Bryce sighed. 'Well, I have a hunch that Flyte *would* have called if he could've told us how to protect ourselves. Yeah, I think maybe he knows exactly what sort of creature or force we're dealing with, but I strongly suspect he doesn't have the faintest idea what to do about it. Regardless of how much he can tell us, I suspect he won't be able to tell us the one thing we need to know the most – *how to save our asses*.'

*

323

Jenny and Bryce were having coffee at the operations desk. They were talking about what they had discovered during today's search, trying to make sense of senseless things: the mocking crucifixion of the priest; the bullets all over the kitchen floor of the Sheffield House; the bodies in the locked cars . . .

Lisa was sitting nearby. She appeared to be totally involved in a crossword puzzle magazine, which she had picked up somewhere along the search route. Suddenly she looked up and said, 'I know why the jewellery was piled in those two sinks.'

Jenny and Bryce looked at her expectantly.

'First,' the girl said, leaning forward on her chair, 'you've got to accept that all the people who're missing are really dead. And they are. Dead. No question about that.'

'But there *is* some question about that, honey,' Jenny said.

'They're dead,' Lisa said softly. 'I know it. So do you.' Her vivid green eyes were almost feverish. 'It took them, and it *ate* them.'

Jenny recalled Lisa's response last night, at the substation, after Bryce had told them about hearing tortured screams on the phone, when *it* had been in control of the line. Lisa had said, *Maybe it spun a web somewhere, down in a dark place, in a cellar or a cave, and maybe it tied all the missing people into its web, sealed them up in cocoons, alive. Maybe it's just saving them until it gets hungry again.*

Last night, everyone had stared at the girl, wanting to laugh, but realizing there could be a crazy sort of truth to what she said. Not necessarily a web or cocoons or a giant spider. But something. None of them had wanted to admit it, but the possibility was there. The unknown. The unknown *thing*. The unknown thing that ate people.

And now Lisa returned to the same theme. 'It *ate* them.'

'But how does that explain the jewellery?' Bryce asked.

'Well,' Lisa said, 'after it ate the people, maybe it . . . maybe it just spat out all that jewellery . . . the same way you would spit out cherry pips.'

*

324

Dr Sara Yamaguchi walked into the Hilltop Inn, paused to answer a question from one of the guards at the front door, and came across the lobby towards Jenny and Bryce. She was still dressed in her decontamination suit, but she was no longer wearing a helmet, the tank of compressed air, or the waste recycling unit. She was carrying some folded clothes and a thick sheaf of pale green papers.

Jenny and Bryce rose to meet her, and Jenny said, 'Doctor, has the quarantine been lifted already?'

'Already? Seems like I've been trapped inside this suit for *years*.' Dr Yamaguchi's voice was different from what it had sounded like through the squawk box. It was fragile and sweet. Her voice was even more diminutive than she was. 'It feels good to breathe air again.'

'You've run bacteria cultures, haven't you?' Jenny asked.

'Started to.'

'Well, then . . . doesn't it take twenty-four to forty-eight hours to get results?'

'Yes. But we've decided it's pointless to wait for the cultures. We're not going to grow any bacteria on them – neither benign bacteria nor otherwise.

Neither benign bacteria nor otherwise. That peculiar statement intrigued Jenny, but before she could ask about it, the geneticist said:

'Besides, Meddy told us it was safe.'

'Meddy?'

'That's shorthand for Medanacomp,' Dr Yamaguchi said. 'Which is itself short for Medical Analysis and Computation Systems. Our computer. After Meddy assimilated all the data from the autopsies and tests, she gave us a probability figure for biological causation. Meddy says there's a zero point zero chance that a biological agent is involved here.'

'And you trust a computer's analysis enough to breathe real air,' Bryce said, clearly surprised.

'In over eight hundred trial runs, Meddy's never been wrong.'

'But this isn't just a trial run,' Jenny said.

'Yes. But after what we found in the autopsies and in all pathology tests . . .' The geneticist shrugged and handed the sheaf of green papers to Jenny. 'Here. It's all in the results. General Copperfield thought you'd like to see them. If you have any questions, I'll explain. Meanwhile, all the men are up at the field lab, changing out of their decon suits, and I'm itching to do the same. And I do mean *itching*.' She smiled and scratched her neck. Her gloved fingers left faint red marks on her porcelain-smooth skin. 'Is there somewhere I could wash?'

Jenny said, 'We've got soap, towels, and a washbasin set up in one corner of the kitchen. It doesn't offer much privacy, but we're willing to sacrifice a little privacy rather than be alone.'

Dr Yamaguchi nodded. 'Understandable. How do I get to this washbasin?'

Lisa jumped up from her chair, casting aside the crossword puzzle. 'I'll show you. And I'll make sure the guys who're working in the kitchen keep their backs turned and their eyes to themselves.'

The pale green papers were computer print-outs that had been cut into eleven-inch pages, numbered, and clipped together along the left-hand margin with plastic pressure binding.

With Bryce looking over her shoulder, Jenny leafed through the first section of the report, which was a computer transcription of Seth Goldstein's autopsy notes. Goldstein noted indications of possible suffocation, as well as even more evident signs of severe allergic reaction to an unidentified substance, but he could not fix a cause of death.

Then her eyes came to rest on one of the first pathology tests. It was a light microscopy examination of unstained bacteria in a long series of hanging-drop preparations that had been contaminated by tissue and fluid samples from Gary Wechlas's body; darkfield illumination had been used to identify even the smallest microorganisms. They had been searching for bacteria that were still thriving in the cadaver. What they found was startling.

```
HANGING-DROP PREPARATIONS
AUTO SCAN — MEDANACOMP
EYE VERIFICATION — BETTENBY
FREQUENCY OF EYE VERIFICATION — 20% OF SAMPLES
PRINT


SAMPLE 1
ESCHERICHIA GENUS      FORMS PRESENT:
     NO FORMS PRESENT
NOTE: ABNORMAL DATA.
NOTE: IMPOSSIBLE VARIANT — NO ANIMATE E. COLI
IN BOWEL — CONTAMINATE SAMPLE.


CLOSTRIDIUM GENUS      FORMS PRESENT:
     NO FORMS PRESENT
NOTE: ABNORMAL DATA.
NOTE: IMPROBABLE VARIANT — NO ANIMATE
C. WELCHII
IN BOWEL — CONTAMINATE SAMPLE.


PROTEUS GENUS      FORMS PRESENT:
     NO FORMS PRESENT
NOTE: ABNORMAL DATA.
NOTE: IMPROBABLE VARIANT — NO ANIMATE P.
VULGARIS
IN BOWEL — CONTAMINATE SAMPLE.
```

The print-out continued to list other bacteria for which the computer and Dr Bettenby had searched, all with the same results.

Jenny remembered what Dr Yamaguchi had said, the statement that she had wondered about and about which she had wanted to question: *neither benign bacteria nor otherwise*. And here was the data, every bit as abnormal as the computer said it was.

'Strange,' Jenny said.

Bryce said, 'It doesn't mean a thing to me. Translation?'

'Well, you see, a cadaver is an excellent breeding ground for all sorts of bacteria – at least in the short run. This many hours after death, Gary Wechlas's corpse ought to be teaming with *Clostridium welchii*, which is associated with gas gangrene.'

'And it isn't?'

'They couldn't find even one lonely, living *C. welchii* in the water droplet that had been contaminated with bowel material. And that is precisely the sample that ought to be swarming with it. It should be teeming with *Proteus vulgaris*, too, which is a saprophytic bacterium.'

'Translation?' he asked patiently.

'Sorry. Saprophytic means it flourishes in dead or decaying matter.'

'And Wechlas is unquestionably dead.'

'Unquestionably. Yet there's no *P. vulgaris*. There should be other bacteria, too. Maybe *Micrococcus albus* and *Bacillus mesentericus*. Anyway, there aren't any of the micro-organisms that're associated with decomposition, not any of the forms you'd expect to find. Even stranger, there's no living *Escherichia coli* in the body. Now, dammit, that would've been there, thriving, even before Wechlas was killed. And it should be there now, still thriving. *E. coli* inhabits the colon. Yours, mine, Gary Wechlas's, everyone's. As long as it's contained within the bowel, it's generally a benign organism.' She paged through the report. 'Now, here. Here, look at this. When they used general and differential stains to search for dead microorganisms, they found plenty of *E. coli*. But all the specimens are dead. There are no living bacteria in Wechlas's body.'

'What's that supposed to tell us?' Bryce asked. That the corpse isn't decomposing as it should be?'

'It isn't decomposing *at all*. Not only that. Something a whole lot stranger. The reason it isn't decomposing is because it's apparently been injected with a massive dose of sterilizing and stabilizing agent. A preservative, Bryce. The corpse seems to have been injected with an extremely effective preservative.'

Lisa brought a tray to the table. There were four mugs of coffee, spoons, napkins. The girl passed coffee to Dr Yamaguchi, Jenny and Bryce; she took the fourth mug for herself.

They were sitting in the dining room at the Hilltop, near the windows. Outside, the street was bathed in the orange-gold sunlight of late afternoon.

In an hour, Jenny thought, it'll be dark again. And then we'll have to wait through another long night.

She shivered. She sure needed hot coffee.

Sara Yamaguchi was now wearing tan corduroy jeans and a yellow blouse. Her long, silky, black hair spilled over her shoulders. 'Well,' she was saying, 'I guess everyone's seen enough of those old Walt Disney wildlife documentaries to know that some spiders and mud wasps – and certain other insects – inject a preservative into their victims and put them aside for consumption later or to feed their unhatched young. The preservative distributed through Mr Wechlas's tissues is vaguely similar to those substances, but far more potent and sophisticated.'

Jenny thought of the impossibly large moth that had attacked and killed Stewart Wargle. But that wasn't the creature that had depopulated Snowfield. Definitely not. Even if there were hundreds of those things lurking somewhere in town, they couldn't have destroyed everyone. No moth that size could have found its way into locked cars, locked houses, and barricaded rooms. Something *else* was out there.

'Are you saying it was an insect that killed these people?' Bryce asked Sara Yamaguchi.

'Actually, the evidence doesn't point that way. An insect would employ a stinger to kill and to inject the preservative. There would be a puncture wound, however minuscule. But Seth Goldstein went over the Wechlas corpse with a magnifying glass. Literally. Over every square inch of skin. Twice. He even used a depilatory cream to remove all the body hair in order the examine the skin more closely. Yet he couldn't find a puncture or any other break in the skin through which an injection might have been administered. We were afraid we had atypical or inaccurate data. So a second post-mortem was performed.'

'On Karen Oxley,' Jenny said.

'Yes.' Sara Yamaguchi leaned towards the windows and peered up the street, looking for General Copperfield and the others. When she turned back to the table, she said, 'However, everything tested out the same. No animate bacteria in the corpse. Decomposition unnaturally arrested. Tissues saturated with preservative. It was bizarre data again. But we were satisfied that it wasn't atypical or inaccurate data.'

Bryce said, 'If the preservative wasn't injected, how was it administered?'

'Our best guess is that it's highly absorbable and enters the body by skin contact, then circulates through the tissues within seconds.'

Jenny said, 'Could it be a nerve gas, after all? Maybe the preservative aspect is only a side-effect.'

'No,' Sara Yamaguchi said. 'There aren't any traces on the victims' clothes, as there would absolutely have to be if we're dealing here with gas saturation. And although the substance has a toxic

330

effect, chemical analysis shows it isn't primarily a toxin, which a nerve gas would be; primarily, it's a preservative.'

'But was it the cause of death?' Bryce asked.

'It contributed. But we can't pinpoint the cause. It was partly the toxicity of the preservative, but other factors lead us to believe death also resulted from oxygen deprivation. The victims suffered either a prolonged constriction or a complete blockage of the trachea.'

Bryce leaned forward. 'Strangulation? Suffocation?'

'Yes. But we don't know precisely which.'

'But how can it be either one?' Lisa asked. 'You're talking about things that took a minute or two to happen. But these people died *fast*. In just a second or two.'

'Besides,' Jenny said, 'as I remember the scene in the Oxleys' den, there weren't any signs of struggle. People being smothered to death will generally thrash like hell, knock things over—'

'Yes,' the geneticist said, nodding. 'It doesn't make sense.'

'Why are all the bodies swollen?' Bryce asked.

'We think it's a toxic reaction to the preservative.'

'The bruising, too?'

'No. That's . . . different.'

'How?'

Sara didn't answer right away. Frowning, she stared down at the coffee in her mug. Finally: 'Skin and subcutaneous tissue from both corpses clearly indicate that the bruising was caused by compression *from an external source*; they were classic contusions. In other words, the bruising wasn't due to the swelling, and it wasn't a separate allergic reaction to the preservative. It seems as if something struck the victims. Hard. Repeatedly. Which is just crazy. Because to cause that much bruising, there would have to be at least a fracture, one fracture, somewhere. Another crazy thing: the degree of bruising is the same all over the body. The tissues are damaged to precisely the same degree on the thighs, on the hands, on the chest, everywhere. Which is impossible.'

'Why?' Bryce asked.

Jenny answered him. 'If you were to beat somebody with a heavy weapon, some areas of the body would be more severely bruised than others. You wouldn't be able to deliver every blow with precisely the same force and precisely the same angle as all the other blows, which is what you would've *had* to've done to create the kind of contusions on these bodies.'

'Besides,' Sara Yamaguchi said, 'they're bruised even in places where a club wouldn't land. In their armpits. Between the cheeks of their buttocks. And on the soles of their feet! Even though, in the case of Mrs Oxley, she had her shoes on.'

'Obviously,' Jenny said, 'the tissue compression that resulted in bruising was caused by something other than blows to the body.'

'Such as?' Bryce asked.

'I've no idea.'

'And they died fast,' Lisa reminded everyone.

Sara leaned back in her chair, tilting it onto its rear legs, and looked out of the window again. Up the hill. Towards the labs.

Bryce said, 'Dr Yamaguchi, what's your opinion? Not your professional opinion. Personally, informally, what do you think's going on here. Any theories?'

She turned to him, shook her head. Her black hair tossed, and the beams of the late-afternoon sunlight played upon it, sending brief ripples of red and green and blue through it the same way that light, shimmering on the black surface of oil, creates short-lived, wriggling rainbows. 'No. No theories, I'm afraid. No coherent thoughts. Just that . . .'

'What?'

'Well . . . now I believe Isley and Arkham were wise to come along.'

Jenny was still sceptical about extra-terrestrial connections, but Lisa continued to be intrigued. The girl said, 'You really think it's from a different world?'

'There may be other possibilities,' Sara said, 'but at the moment, it's difficult to see what they are.' She glanced at her wristwatch and scowled and fidgeted and said, 'What's taking them so long?' She turned her attention to the window again.

Outside, the trees were motionless.

The awnings in front of the stores hung limp.

The town was dead-still.

'You said they were packing away the decon suits.'

Sara said, 'Yes, but that just wouldn't take this long.'

'If there'd been any trouble, we'd have heard gunfire.'

'Or explosions,' Jenny said. 'Those firebombs they made.'

'They should've been here at least five . . . maybe ten minutes ago,' the geneticist insisted. 'And still no sign of them.'

Jenny remembered the incredible stealth with which *it* had taken Jake Johnson.

Bryce hesitated, then pushed his chair back. 'I suppose it won't hurt if I take a few men to have a look.'

Sara Yamaguchi swung away from the window. The front legs of her chair came down hard against the floor, making a sharp, startling sound. She said, 'Something's wrong.'

'No, no. Probably not,' Bryce said.

'You feel it, too,' Sara said. 'I can tell you do. Jesus.'

'Don't worry,' Bryce said calmly.

However, his eyes were not as calm as his voice. During the past twenty-some hours, Jenny had learned to read those hooded eyes quite well. Now they were expressing tension and icy, needle-sharp dread.

'It's much too soon to be worried,' he said.

But they all knew.

They didn't want to believe it, but they *knew*.

The terror had begun again.

Bryce chose Tal, Frank and Gordy to accompany him to the lab.

Jenny said, 'I'm going, too.'

Bryce didn't want her to come. He was more afraid for her than he was for Lisa or for his own men or even for himself.

An unexpected and rare connection had taken place between them. He felt *right* with her, and he believed she felt the same. He didn't want to lose her.

And so he said, 'I'd rather you didn't go.'

'I'm a doctor,' Jenny said, as if that were not only a calling but an armour that would shield her from all harm.

'It's a regular fortress here,' he said, 'It's safer here.'

'It's not safe anywhere.'

'I didn't say safe. I said *safer*.'

'They might need a doctor.'

'If they've been attacked, they're either dead or missing. We haven't found anyone just wounded, have we?'

'There's always a first time.' Jenny turned to Lisa and said, 'Get my medical bag, honey.'

The girl ran towards the makeshift infirmary.

'*She* stays here for sure,' Bryce said.

'No,' Jenny said. 'She stays with me.'

Exasperated, Bryce said, 'Listen, Jenny, this is virtually a martial law situation. I can *order* you to stay here.'

'And enforce the order – how? At gunpoint?' she asked, but with no antagonism.

Lisa returned with the black leather bag.

Standing by the front doors of the inn, Sara Yamaguchi called to Bryce: 'Hurry. Please hurry.'

If *it* had struck at the field lab, there was probably no use hurrying.

Looking at Jenny, Bryce thought: I can't protect you, Doc. Don't you see? Stay here where the windows are locked and the doors are guarded. Don't rely on me to protect you because, sure as hell, I'll fail. Like I failed Ellen . . . and Timmy.

'Let's go,' Jenny said.

Agonizingly aware of his limitations, Bryce led them out of the inn and up the street towards the corner – beyond which *it* might very well be waiting for them. Tal walked at the head of the procession, beside Bryce. Frank and Gordy brought up the rear. Lisa, Sara Yamaguchi, and Jenny were in the middle.

The warm day was beginning to turn cool.

In the valley below Snowfield, a mist had begun to form.

Less than three-quarters of an hour remained before nightfall. The sun spilled a final flood of bloody light through the town. Shadows were extremely long, distorted. Windows blazed with reflected solar fire, reminding Bryce of eyeholes in Halloween jack-o'-lanterns.

The street seemed even more ominously silent than it had been last night. Their footsteps echoed as if they were crossing the floor of a vast, abandoned cathedral.

They rounded the corner cautiously.

Three decontamination suits lay tangled and untenanted in the middle of the street. Another empty suit lay half in the gutter and half on the pavement. Two of the helmets were cracked.

Submachine guns were scattered around, and unused Molotov cocktails were lined up along the kerb.

The back of the truck was open. More empty decontamination suits and submachine guns were piled in there. No people.

Bryce shouted: 'General? General Copperfield?'

Graveyard silence.

Surface-of-the-moon silence.

'Seth!' Sara Yamaguchi cried. 'Will? Will Bettenby? Galen? Somebody, please answer me.'

Nothing. No one.

Jenny said, 'They didn't even manage to fire one shot.'

Tal said, 'Or scream. The guards at the front door of the inn would've heard them even if they'd just screamed.'

Gordy said, 'Oh, shit.'

The rear doors on both labs were ajar.

Bryce had the feeling that something was waiting for them inside.

He wanted to turn and walk away. Couldn't. He was the leader here. If he panicked, they would all panic. Panic was an invitation to death.

Sara started towards the rear of the first lab.

Bryce stopped her.

'They're my friends, dammit,' she said.

'I know. But let me look first,' he said.

For a moment, however, he couldn't move.

He was immobilized by fear.

Couldn't move an inch.

But then, at last, of course, he did.

31

COMPUTER GAMES

BRYCE'S SERVICE revolver was drawn and cocked. He seized the door with his other hand and threw it wide open. At the same time, he jumped back pointing his gun into the lab.

It was deserted. Two crumpled decon suits lay on the floor, and another was draped over a swivel chair in front of a computer terminal.

He went to the rear of the second lab.

Tal said, 'Let me do this one.'

Bryce shook his head. 'You stay back there. Protect the women; they don't have guns. If anything comes out of here when I open the door, run like hell.'

Heart pounding, Bryce hesitated behind the second field lab. Put his hand on the door. Hesitated again. Then pulled it open even more carefully than he had opened the first.

It was deserted, too. Two decontamination suits. Nothing else.

As Bryce peered into the lab, all the ceiling lights winked out, and he jerked in surprise at the sudden darkness. In a second, however, light sprang up once more, although not from the ceiling bulbs; this was an unusual light, a green flash that startled him. Then he saw it was only the three video display terminals, which had all come on at once. Now they went off. And came on. Off, on, off, on, off . . . At first they flashed simultaneously, then in sequence, around and around. Finally they all came on and stayed on, filling the otherwise unlit work area with an eerie glow.

'I'm going in,' Bryce said.

The others protested, but he was already up the step and through the door. He went to the first terminal screen, where six words burned in pale green letters across a dark green background.

JESUS LOVES ME — THIS I KNOW.

Bryce glanced at the other two screens. They bore the same six words.

Blink. Now there were new words:

FOR THE BIBLE TELLS ME SO.

Bryce frowned.

What sort of program was this? These were the words to one of the songs that had come out of the kitchen drain at the inn.

THE BIBLE IS FULL OF SHIT, the computer told him.

Blink.

JESUS FUCKS DOGS.

The last three words remained on the screen for several seconds. It seemed to Bryce as if the green light from the display terminals was cold. Just as a fireplace light carries a dry heat with it, so this radiance carried a chill that pierced him.

This was no ordinary program being run on the displays. This was nothing General Copperfield's people had put into the computer, no form of code, no exercise of logic, no systems test of any kind.

Blink.

JESUS IS DEAD. GOD IS DEAD.

Blink.

I AM ALIVE.

Blink.

DO YOU WANT TO PLAY 20 QUESTIONS?

Gazing at the screen, Bryce felt a primitive, superstitious terror rising within him; terror and awe, twisting his gut and clutching his throat. But he didn't know why. On a deep, almost subconscious level, he sensed that he was in the presence of something evil, ancient, and . . . familiar. But how could it be familiar? He didn't even know what *it* was. And yet . . . And yet perhaps he did know. Deep down. Instinctively. If only he could reach inside himself, down past his civilized veneer which embodied so much scepticism, if he could reach into his racial memory, he might find the truth about the thing that had seized and slaughtered the people of Snowfield.

Blink.

SHERIFF HAMMOND?

Blink.

DO YOU WANT TO PLAY 20 QUESTIONS WITH ME?

The use of his name jolted him. And then a far bigger and more disturbing surprise followed:

ELLEN

The name burned on the screen, the name of his dead wife, and every muscle in his body grew tense, and he waited for something more to flash up, but for long seconds, there was only the precious name, and he could not take his eyes away from it, and then—

ELLEN ROTS.

He couldn't breathe.

How could it know about Ellen?

Blink.

ELLEN FEEDS THE WORMS.

What kind of shit was this? What was the point of this?

TIMMY WILL DIE.

The prophecy glowed, green on green.

He gasped. 'No,' he said softly. For the past year, he had thought it would be better if Timmy succumbed. Better than a slow wasting away. Only yesterday, he would have said that his son's swift death would be a blessing. But not any longer. Snowfield had taught him that nothing is worse than death. In the arms of death, there was no hope. But as long as Timmy lived, there was a possibility of recovery. After all, the doctors said the boy hadn't suffered massive brain damage. Therefore, if Timmy ever woke from his unnatural sleep, he had a good chance of retaining his normal faculties and functions. Chance, promise, hope. So Bryce said, 'No,' to the computer. 'No.'

Blink.

TIMMY WILL ROT. ELLEN ROTS. ELLEN ROTS IN HELL.

'Who *are* you?' Bryce demanded.

The moment he spoke, he felt foolish. He couldn't just talk to a computer as if it were another human being. If he wanted to ask a question, he would have to type it out.

SHALL WE HAVE A LITTLE CHAT?

Bryce turned away from the terminal. He went to the door and leaned outside.

The others looked relieved to see him.

Clearing his throat, trying to conceal the fact that he was badly shaken, he said, 'Dr Yamaguchi, I need your help here.'

Tal, Jenny Lisa, and Sara Yamaguchi stepped into the field lab. Frank and Gordy remained outside, by the door, nervously surveying the street, where the daylight was fading fast.

Bryce showed Sara the computer screens.

SHALL WE HAVE A LITTLE CHAT?

He told them what had flashed onto the video displays, and before he was finished, Sara interrupted him to say, 'But that's not possible. This computer has no program, no vocabulary that would enable it to—'

'Something has control of your computer,' he said.

Sara scowled. 'Control? How?'

'I don't know.'

'Who?'

'Not, *who*,' Jenny said, putting an arm around her sister. 'More like *what*.'

340

'Yeah,' Tal said. 'This thing, this killer, whatever the hell it is, *it* has control of your computer, Dr Yamaguchi.'

Obviously doubtful, the geneticist sat down at one of the display terminals and threw a switch on an automatic typewriter. 'Might as well have a print-out just in case we actually get something from this.' She hesitated with her delicate, almost childlike hands poised above the keyboard. Bryce watched over her shoulder. Tal, Jenny and Lisa turned to the other two screens – just as all the displays went blank. Sara stared at the smooth field of green light in front of her, and then finally keyed in the access code and typed a question.

IS SOMEONE THERE?

The automatic typewriter chattered, beginning the print-out, and the answer came at once: YES.

WHO ARE YOU?

COUNTLESS.

'What's it mean?' Tal asked.

'I don't know,' the geneticist said.

Sara tapped out the question again and received the same obscure response: COUNTLESS.

'Ask it for a name,' Bryce said.

Sara typed, and the words she composed appeared instantly on all three of the display screens: DO YOU HAVE A NAME?

YES.

WHAT IS YOUR NAME?

MANY.

YOU HAVE MANY NAMES?

YES.

WHAT IS ONE OF YOUR NAMES?

CHAOS.

WHAT OTHER NAMES DO YOU HAVE?

YOU ARE A BORING, STUPID CUNT. ASK ANOTHER QUESTION.

341

Visibly shocked, the geneticist glanced up at Bryce. '*That* is definitely not a word you're going to find in any computer language.'

Lisa said, 'Don't ask it who it is. Ask it *what* it is.'

'Yeah,' Tal said. 'See if it'll give you a physical description.'

'It'll think we're asking it to run diagnostic tests on itself,' Sara said. 'It'll start flashing up circuitry diagrams.'

'No, it won't,' Bryce said. 'Remember, it's not the computer you're having a dialogue with. It's something else. The computer is only the means of communication.'

'Oh. Of course,' Sara said. 'In spite of the word it just used, I still want to think of it as good old Meddy.'

After a moment's thought, she typed: PROVIDE A PHYSICAL DESCRIPTION OF YOURSELF.

I AM ALIVE.

BE MORE SPECIFIC, Sara directed.

I AM BY NATURE UNSPECIFIC.

ARE YOU HUMAN?

I ENCOMPASS THAT POSSIBILITY ALSO.

'It's just playing with us,' Jenny said. 'Amusing itself.'

Bryce wiped a hand over his face, 'Ask it what happened to Copperfield.'

WHERE IS GALEN COPPERFIELD?

DEAD.

WHERE IS HIS BODY?

GONE.

WHERE HAS IT GONE?

BORING BITCH.

WHERE ARE THE OTHERS WHO WERE WITH GALEN COPPERFIELD?

DEAD.

DID YOU KILL THEM?

YES.

342

WHY DID YOU KILL THEM?

YOU

Sara tapped the keyboard: CLARIFY.

YOU ARE

CLARIFY.

YOU ARE ALL DEAD.

Bryce saw that the woman's hands were shaking. Yet they moved across the keys with skill and accuracy: WHY DO YOU WANT TO KILL US?

THAT IS WHAT YOU ARE FOR.

ARE YOU SAYING WE EXIST ONLY TO BE KILLED?

YES. YOU ARE CATTLE. YOU ARE PIGS. YOU ARE WORTHLESS.

WHAT IS YOUR NAME?

VOID.

CLARIFY.

NOTHINGNESS.

WHAT IS YOUR NAME?

LEGION.

CLARIFY.

CLARIFY MY COCK, YOU BORING BITCH.

Sara blushed and said, 'This is madness.'

'You can almost feel it in here with us now,' Lisa said.

Jenny squeezed her sister's shoulder encouragingly and said, 'Honey? What do you mean by that?'

The girl's voice was strained, tremulous. 'You can almost feel its presence.' Her gaze roamed over the lab. 'The air seems thicker — don't you think? And colder. It's as if something's going to . . . materialize right here in front of us.'

Bryce knew what she meant.

Tal caught Bryce's eye and nodded. He felt it, too.

However, Bryce was certain that what they felt was entirely a subjective sensation. Nothing was really going to materialize. The air wasn't actually thicker than it had been a minute ago; it just seemed thicker because they were all tense, and when you were rigid with tension, it was just naturally somewhat more difficult to draw your breath. And if the air was colder . . . well, that was only because the night was coming.

The computer screens went blank. Then: WHEN IS HE COMING?

Sara typed, CLARIFY.

WHEN IS THE EXORCIST COMING?

'Christ,' Tal said. 'What *is* this?'

CLARIFY, Sara typed.

TIMOTHY FLYTE.

'I'll be damned,' Jenny said.

'It knows this Flyte character,' Tal said. 'But how? And is it afraid of him – or what?'

ARE YOU AFRAID OF FLYTE?

STUPID BITCH.

ARE YOU AFRAID OF FLYTE? she persisted, undeterred.

I AM AFRAID OF NOTHING.

WHY ARE YOU INTERESTED IN FLYTE?

I HAVE DISCOVERED THAT HE KNOWS.

WHAT DOES HE KNOW?

ABOUT ME.

'Evidently,' Bryce said, 'we can rule out the possibility that Flyte is just another hustler.'

Sara tapped the keys: DOES FLYTE KNOW WHAT YOU ARE?

YES. I WANT HIM HERE.

WHY DO YOU WANT HIM HERE?

HE IS MY MATTHEW.

CLARIFY.

HE IS MY MATTHEW, MARK, LUKE AND JOHN.

Frowning, Sara paused, glanced at Bryce. Then her fingers flew over the keys again: DO YOU MEAN THAT FLYTE IS YOUR APOSTLE?

NO. HE IS MY BIOGRAPHER. HE CHRONICLES MY WORK. I
WANT HIM TO COME HERE.

DO YOU WANT TO KILL HIM TOO?

NO. I WILL GRANT HIM SAFE PASSAGE.

CLARIFY.

YOU WILL ALL DIE. BUT FLYTE WILL BE ALLOWED TO LIVE.
YOU MUST TELL HIM. IF HE DOES NOT KNOW THAT HE HAS
SAFE PASSAGE, HE WILL NOT COME.

Sara's hands were shaking worse than ever. She missed a key, hit
a wrong letter, had to cancel out and start over again. She asked: IF
WE BRING FLYTE TO SNOWFIELD, WILL YOU LET US LIVE?

YOU ARE MINE.

WILL YOU LET US LIVE?

NO.

Thus far, Lisa had been braver than her years. However, seeing
her fate spelled out so bluntly on a computer display was too much
for her. She began to cry softly.

Jenny comforted the girl as best she could.

'Whatever it is,' Tal said, 'it sure is arrogant.'

'Well, we're not dead yet,' Bryce told them. 'There's hope.
There's always hope as long as we're still alive.'

Sara used the keyboard again: WHERE ARE YOU FROM?

TIME IMMEMORIAL.

CLARIFY.

BORING BITCH.

ARE YOU EXTRA-TERRESTRIAL?

NO.

'So much for Isley and Arkham,' Bryce said, before realizing that
Isley and Arkham were already dead and gone.

'Unless it's lying,' Jenny said.

Sara returned to a question she had posed earlier: WHAT
ARE YOU?

YOU BORE ME.

WHAT ARE YOU?

STUPID SLUT.

WHAT ARE YOU?

FUCK OFF.

WHAT ARE YOU? she typed again, pounding at the keys so hard that Bryce thought she might break them. Her anger appeared to have outgrown her fear.

I AM GLASYALABOLAS.

CLARIFY.

THAT IS MY NAME. I AM A WINGED MAN WITH THE TEETH OF A DOG. I FOAM AT THE MOUTH. I HAVE BEEN CONDEMNED TO FOAM AT THE MOUTH FOR ALL ETERNITY.

Bryce stared at the display, uncomprehending. Was it serious? A winged man with the teeth of a dog? Surely not. It must be playing with them, amusing itself again. But what was so amusing about this?

The screens went blank.

A pause.

New words appeared, even though Sara had posed no question.

I AM HABORYM. I AM A MAN WITH THREE HEADS — ONE HUMAN, ONE CAT, ONE SERPENT.

'What's this crap all about?' Tal asked, frustrated.

The air in the room was definitely colder.

Only the wind Bryce told himself. The wind at the door, bringing the coolness of the oncoming night.

I AM RANTAN

Blink.

I AM PALLANTRE

Blink.

I AM AMLUTIAS, ALFINA, EPYN, FUARD, BELIAL, OMGORMA, NEBIROS, BAAL, ELIGOR, AND MANY OTHERS.

The strange names glowed on all three screens for a moment, then winked off.

I AM ALL AND NONE. I AM NOTHING. I AM EVERYTHING.

Blink.

The trio of video displays shone brightly, greenly, blankly for a second, two, three. Then went dark.

The overhead lights came on.

'End of interview,' Jenny said.

Belial. That was one of the names it had given itself.

Bryce was not an ardently religious man, but he was sufficiently well-read to know that Belial was either another name for Satan or the name of one of the other fallen angels. He wasn't sure which it was.

Gordy Brogan was the most religious one among them, a devout Roman Catholic. When Bryce came out of the field lab, the last to leave it, he asked Gordy to look at the names towards the end of the print-out.

They stood on the pavement by the lab, in the dwindling light of day, while Gordy read the pertinent lines. In twenty minutes, perhaps less, it would be dark.

'Here,' Gordy said. 'This name. Baal.' He pointed to it on the accordion-folded length of computer paper. 'I don't know exactly where I've seen it before. Not in church or catechism. Maybe I read it in a book somewhere.'

Bryce detected an odd tone and rhythm in Gordy's speech. It was more than just nervousness. He spoke too slowly for a few words, then much too fast, then slowly again, then almost frenetically.

'A book?' Bryce asked. 'The *Bible*?'

'No, I don't think so. I'm not much of a Bible reader. Should be. Should read it regularly. But where I saw this name was in an ordinary book. A novel. I can't quite remember.'

'So who is this Baal?' Bryce asked.

'I think he's supposed to be a very powerful demon,' Gordy said. And something was definitely wrong with his voice; with *him*.

'What about the other names?' Bryce asked.

'They don't mean anything to me.'

'I thought they might be the names of other demons.'

'Well, you know, the Catholic Church doesn't go in much for fire-and-brimstone preaching,' Gordy said, still speaking oddly. 'Maybe it should. Yeah. Maybe it should. 'Cause I think you're right. I think those are the names of demons.'

Jenny sighed wearily. 'So it was just playing another one of its games with us.'

Gordy shook his head vigorously. 'No. Not a game. Not at all. It was telling the truth.'

Bryce frowned. 'Gordy, you don't actually think it's a demon or Satan himself or anything like that – do you?'

'That's all nonsense,' Sara Yamaguchi said.

'Yes,' Jenny said. 'The entire performance on the computer, this demonic image it wants to project – all of that's only more misdirection. It's never going to tell us the truth about itself because if we knew the truth, then we might be able to think of a way to beat it.'

'How do you explain the priest who was crucified above the altar at Our Lady of the Mountains?' Gordy asked.

'But that was just one more part of the charade,' Tal said.

Gordy's eyes were strange. It wasn't just fear. They were the eyes of a man who was in spiritual distress, even agony.

I should've noticed this coming sooner, Bryce berated himself.

Speaking softly but with spellbinding intensity, Gordy said, 'I think maybe the time has come. The end. The time of the ending. At last. Just like the Bible says. That was something I never believed. I believed in everything else the church taught. But not that. No judgment day. I just sort of thought everything would go on like this forever. But now it's here, isn't it? Yes. The judgment. Not just for the people who live in Snowfield. For all of us. The end. So I've been asking myself how I'll be judged. And I'm scared. I mean, I was given a gift, a very special gift, and I threw it away. I was given the gift of St Francis. I've always had a way with animals. It's true. No dog ever barks at me. Did you know that? No cat has ever scratched me. Animals respond to me. They trust me. Maybe they even love me. Never met one that didn't. I've coaxed some wild squirrels to eat right out of my hand. It's a gift. So my folks wanted me to be a vet. But I turned my back on them and on my gift. Became a cop instead. Picked up a gun. A *gun*. I wasn't meant to pick up a gun. Not me. Not ever. I did it partly 'cause I knew it would bother my folks. I was expressing my independence, see? But I forgot. I forgot about where it tells you in the Bible to honour thy father and thy mother. What I did instead was hurt them. And I turned my back on God's gift to me. More than that. Worse than that. What I did was to spit on the gift. Last night I made up my mind to quit the force, put away the gun, and become a vet. But I think I was too late. Judgment was already underway, and I didn't realize it. I've spat on the gift God gave me, and now . . . I'm afraid.'

Bryce didn't know what to say to Gordy. His imagined sins were so far removed from genuine evil that it was almost laughable. If there was anyone here who was destined for heaven, it was Gordy. Not that Bryce believed judgment day had come. He didn't. But he couldn't think of a thing to say to Gordy, for the big, raw-boned kid was too far gone to be talked out of his delusion.

'Timothy Flyte is a scientist, not a theologian,' Jenny said, firmly. 'If Flyte's got an explanation for what's happening here, it's strictly scientific not religious.'

Gordy wasn't listening to her. Tears were streaming down his face. His eyes looked glazed. When he tilted his head and stared up at the sky, he was not seeing the sunset; he was obviously seeing, instead, some grand celestial highway on which the archangels and hosts of heaven would soon descend in their chariots of fire.

He was in no condition to be entrusted with a loaded gun. Bryce slipped the revolver out of Gordy's holster and took possession of it. The deputy didn't even seem to notice.

Bryce saw that Gordy's bizarre soliloquy had had a serious effect on Lisa. She looked as if she had been hit very hard, stunned.

'It's all right,' Bryce told her. 'It's not really the end of the world. It's not judgment day. Gordy's just . . . disturbed. We're going to come through this just fine. Do you believe me, Lisa? Can you keep that pretty chin of yours lifted? Can you be brave for just a little while longer?'

She didn't immediately respond. Then she reached into herself and found yet another reserve of strength and nerve. She nodded. She even managed a weak, uncertain smile.

'You're a hell of a kid,' he said. 'A lot like your big sister.'

Lisa glanced at Jenny, then brought her eyes back to Bryce again. 'You're a hell of a sheriff,' she said,

He wondered if his own smile was as shaky as hers.

He was embarrassed by her trust, for he wasn't worthy of it.

I lied to you, girl, he thought. Death is still with us. It'll strike again. Maybe not for an hour. Maybe not even for a whole day. But sooner or later, it *will* strike again.

In fact, although he couldn't possibly have known it, one of them would die in the next minute.

32

DESTINY

In Santa Mira, Fletcher Kale spent the greatest part of Monday afternoon tearing apart Jake Johnson's house, room by room. He thoroughly enjoyed himself.

In a walk-in pantry, off the kitchen, he at last located Johnson's cache. It wasn't on the shelves, which were crammed full of at least a year's supply of canned and bottled food, or on the floor with stacks of other supplies. No, the *real* treasure was *under* the pantry floor: under the loose linoleum, under the sub-flooring, in a secret compartment.

A small, carefully slected, formidable collection of guns was hidden there; each of the weapons individually wrapped in water-tight plastic. Feeling as if it were Christmas morning, Kale unwrapped all of them. There were a pair of Smith & Wesson Combat Magnums, perhaps the best and most powerful handgun in the world. Loaded with .357s, it was the deadliest piece a man could carry, with enough punch to stop a grizzly bear; and with light-loaded .38s, it was an equally useful and extremely accurate gun for small game. One shotgun: a Remington 870 Brushmaster 12-gauge with adjustable rifle sights, a folding stock, a pistol grip, magazine extension, and sling. Two rifles. An M-1 semi-automatic. But far better than that, there was a Heckler & Koch HK91, a superb assault rifle, complete with eight thirty-round magazines, already loaded, and a couple of thousand rounds of additional ammunition.

For almost an hour, Kale sat examining and playing with the rifles. Fondling them. If the cops happened to spot him on his way out to the mountains, they would wish they had looked the other way.

The hole beneath the pantry also contained money. A lot of it. The bills were tightly rolled wads, encircled by rubber bands, and then stuffed into five large, well-sealed mason jars; there were anywhere from three to five rolls in each container.

He took the jars out to the kitchen and stood them on the table. He looked in the refrigerator for beer, had to settle for a can of Pepsi, sat down at the table, and began to count his treasure.

$63,440.

One of the most enduring modern legends of Santa Mira County was the one that concerned Big Ralph Johnson's secret fortune, amassed (so it was rumoured) through graft and bribe-taking. Obviously, this was what remained of Big Ralph's ill-gotten stash. Just the kind of grubstake Kale needed to start on a new life.

The ironic thing about finding the stash was that he wouldn't have had to kill Joanna and Danny if only he'd had this money in his hands last week. This was more than he had needed to bail himself out of his difficulties with High Country Investments.

A year and a half ago, when he had become a partner in High Country, he couldn't have foreseen that it would lead to disaster. Back then, it had seemed like the golden opportunity that he knew was destined to come his way sooner or later.

Each of the partners in High Country Investments had put up one-seventh of the necessary funds to acquire, subdivide, and develop a thirty-acre parcel over at the eastern edge of Santa Mira, on top of Highline Ridge. To get in on the ground floor, Kale had been forced to commit every available dollar he could lay his hands on, but the potential return had seemed well worth the risk.

However, the Highline Ridge project turned out to be a money-eating monster with a voracious appetite.

The way the deal was set up, each partner was liable for additional assessments if the initial pool of capital proved inadequate to the task. If Kale (or any other partners) failed to meet an assessment, he was out of High Country Investments, immediately, without any compensation for what he had already paid in, thank you very much and goodbye. Then the remaining partners became liable for equal portions of his assessment – and acquired equal fractions of his share of the project. It was the sort of arrangement that facilitated the financing of the project by enticing (usually) only those investors who had a lot of liquidity – but it also required an iron stomach and steel nerves.

Kale hadn't thought there would be any assessments. The original capital pool had looked more than adequate to him. But he was wrong.

When the first of the special assessments was levied for thirty-five thousand dollars, he had been shocked but not defeated. He figured they could borrow ten thousand from Joanna's parents, and there was sufficient equity in their house to arrange refinancing to free another twenty. The last five thousand could be pieced together.

The only problem was Joanna.

Right from the start, she hadn't wanted him to become involved in High Country Investments. She had said the deal was too rich for him, that he should stop trying to play the big shot wheeler-dealer.

He had gone ahead anyway, and then the assessment had come, and she had revelled in his despair. Not openly, of course. She was too clever for that. She knew she could play the martyr more effectively than she could play the harpy. She never said I-told-you-so, not directly, but that smug accusation was in her eyes, humiliatingly evident in the way she treated him.

Finally, he talked her into refinancing the house and taking a loan from her parents. It had not been easy.

He had smiled and nodded and taken all their smarmy advice and snide criticism, but he had promised himself he would

353

eventually rub their faces in all the crap they'd thrown at him. When he hit it big with High Country, he'd make them crawl, Joanna most of all.

Then, to his consternation, the second special assessment had been levied on the seven partners. It was forty thousand dollars.

He could have met that obligation too, if Joanna had sincerely wanted him to succeed. She could have tapped the trust fund for it. When Joanna's grandmother had died, five months after Danny was born, the old hag had left almost half her estate – fifty thousand dollars – in trust for her only great-grandson. Joanna was appointed the chief administrator of the fund. So when the second assessment came from High Country, she could have taken forty thousand of the trust fund money and paid the bill. But Joanna had refused. She has said, 'What if there's *another* assessment? You lose everything, Fletch, everything, and Danny loses most of his trust fund, too.' He had tried to make her see that there wouldn't be a third assessment. But, of course, she would not listen to him because she didn't really want him to succeed, because she wanted to see him lose everything and be humiliated, because she wanted to ruin him, break him.

He'd had no choice but to kill her and Danny. The way the trust was set up, if Danny were to die before his twenty-first birthday, the fund would be dissolved. The money, after taxes, would become Joanna's property. And if Joanna died, all of her estate went to her husband; that's what her will said. So if he got rid of them both, the proceeds of the trust fund – plus a twenty-thousand-dollar bonus in the form of Joanna's life insurance policy – wound up in his hands.

The bitch had left him no choice.

It wasn't his fault she was dead.

She had done it to herself, really. She had arranged things so that there wasn't any other way out for him.

He smiled, remembering her expression when she had seen the boy's body – and when she'd seen him point the gun at her.

354

Now, sitting at Jake Johnson's kitchen table, Kale looked at all the money, and his smile grew even broader.

$63,440.

A few hours ago, he had been in jail, virtually penniless, facing a trial that could result in a death penalty. Most men would have been immobilized by despair. But Fletcher Kale had not been beaten. He knew he was destined for great things. And here was proof. In an incredibly short time, he had gone from jail to freedom, from penury to $63,440. He now had money, guns, transportation, and a safe hideout in the nearby mountains.

It had begun at last.

His special destiny had begun to unfold.

33

PHANTOMS

BRYCE SAID, 'We'd better get back to the inn.'

Within the next quarter of an hour, night would take possession of the town.

Shadows were growing with cancerous speed, oozing out of hiding places, where they had slept the day away. They spread towards one another, forming pools of darkness.

The sky was painted in carnival colours – orange, red, yellow, purple – but it cast only meagre light upon Snowfield.

They turned away from the field lab, where they'd recently had a conversation with *it*, by way of computer, and they headed towards the corner as the streetlamps came on.

At the same moment, Bryce heard something. A whimper. A mewling. And then a bark.

The whole group turned as one and looked back.

Behind them, a dog was limping along the pavement, past the field lab, trying hard to catch up with them. It was an Airedale. Its left foreleg appeared to be broken. Its tongue was lolling. Its hair was lank and knotted; it looked dishevelled, whipped. It took another lurching step, paused to lick its wounded leg, and whined pitifully.

Bryce was riveted by the sudden appearance of the dog. This was the first survivor they had found, not in very good shape, but *alive*.

But *why* was he alive? What was different about him that had saved him when everything else had perished?

If they could discover the answer, it might help them save themselves.

Gordy was the first to act.

The sight of the injured Airedale affected him more strongly than it affected any of the others. He couldn't bear to see an animal in pain. He would rather suffer himself. His heart started beating faster. This time, the reaction was even stronger than usual, for he knew that this was no ordinary dog needing help and comfort. This Airedale was a sign from God. Yes. A sign that God was giving Gordon Brogan one more chance to accept His gift. He had the same way with animals that St Francis of Assisi had, and he must not spurn it or take it lightly. If he turned his back on God's gift, as he had done before, he would be damned for sure this time. But if he chose to help this dog . . . Tears burned in the corners of Gordy's eyes; they trickled down his cheeks. Tears of relief and happiness. He was overwhelmed by the mercy of God. There was no doubt what he must do. He hurried towards the Airedale, which was about twenty feet away.

At first, Jenny was dumbstruck by the dog. She gaped at it. And then a fierce joy began to swell within her. Life had somehow triumphed over death. *It* hadn't gotten every living thing in Snowfield, after all. This dog (which sat down wearily when Gordy started towards it) had survived, which meant maybe they, themselves, would manage to leave this town alive—

—and then she thought of the moth.

The moth had been a living thing. But it hadn't been friendly.

And Stu Wargle's reanimated corpse.

Back there on the pavement, at the edge of shadows, the dog put its head down and whimpered, begging to be comforted.

Gordy approached it, crouching, speaking in encouraging, loving tones: 'Don't be afraid, boy. Easy, boy. Easy now. What a nice dog you are. Everything'll be okay. Everything'll be all right, boy. Easy . . .'

Horror rose in Jenny. She opened her mouth to scream, but others beat her to it.

'Gordy, *no!*' Lisa cried.

'Get back!' Bryce shouted, as did Frank Autry.

Tal shouted: 'Get away from it, Gordy!'

But Gordy didn't seem to hear them.

As Gordy drew near the Airedale, it lifted its chin off the pavement, raised its square head, and made soft, ingratiating noises. It was a fine specimen. With its leg mended, with its coat washed and brushed and shining, it would be beautiful.

He put a hand out to the dog.

It nuzzled him but didn't lick.

He stroked it. The poor thing was cold, incredibly cold, and slightly damp.

'Poor baby,' Gordy said.

The dog had an odd smell, too. Acrid. Nauseating, really. Gordy had never smelled anything quite like it.

'Where on earth have you been?' he asked the dog. 'What kind of muck have you been rolling around in?'

The pooch whined and shivered.

Behind him, Gordy heard the others shouting, but he was much too involved with the Airedale to listen. He got both hands around the dog, lifted it off the pavement, stood up, and held it close to his chest, with its injured leg dangling.

He had never felt an animal this cold. It wasn't just that its coat was wet, and therefore cold; there didn't seem to be any heat rising up from beneath the coat, either.

It licked his hand.

Its *tongue* was cold.

*

358

Frank stopped shouting. He just stared. Gordy had picked up the mutt, had begun cuddling it and fussing over it, and nothing terrible had happened. So maybe it was just a dog, after all. Maybe it—

Then.

The dog licked Gordy's hand, and a strange expression crossed Gordy's face, and the dog began to . . . change.

Christ.

It was like a lump of putty being reshaped under an invisible sculptor's swiftly working hands. The matted hair appeared to melt and change colour, then the texture changed, too, until it looked more like scales than anything else, greenish scales, and the head began to sink back into the body, which wasn't really a body any more, just a shapeless *thing*, a lump of writhing tissue, and the legs shortened and grew thicker, and all this happened in just five or six seconds, and then—

Gordy stared in shock at the thing in his hands.

A lizard head with wicked yellow eyes began to take form in the amorphous mass into which the dog had degenerated. The lizard's mouth appeared in the pudding-like tissue, and a forked tongue flickered, and there were lots of pointed little teeth.

Gordy tried to throw the thing down, but it clung to him, Jesus, clung tight to him, as if it had reshaped itself around his hands and arms, as if his hands were actually *inside* of it now.

Then it ceased to be cold. Suddenly it was warm. And then hot. Painfully hot.

Before the lizard had completely risen out of the throbbing mass of tissue, it began to dissolve, and a new animal started to take shape, a fox, but the fox quickly degenerated before it was entirely formed, and it became squirrels, a pair of them, their bodies joined like Siamese twins but swiftly separating, and—

Gordy began to scream. He shook his arms up and down, trying to throw the thing off.

359

The heat was like a fire now. The pain was unbearable.

Jesus, *please*.

Pain ate its way up his arms, across his shoulders.

He screamed and sobbed and staggered forward one step, shook his arms again, tried to pull his hands apart, but the thing clung to him.

The half-formed squirrels melted away, and a cat began to appear in the amorphous tissue that he held and that held him, and then the cat swiftly faded, and something else arose – Jesus, no, no, Jesus, no – something insectile, big as an Airedale but with six or eight eyes across the top of its hateful head and a lot of spiky legs and—

Pain roared through him. He stumbled sideways, fell to his knees, then onto his side. He kicked and thrashed in agony, writhed and heaved on the pavement.

Sara Yamaguchi stared in disbelief. The thing attacking Gordy seemed to have total control of its DNA. It could change its shape at will and with astonishing speed.

No such creature could exist. She should know; she was a biologist, a geneticist. Impossible. Yet here it was.

The spider form degenerated and no new phantom shape took its place. In a natural state, the creature seemed to be simply a mass of jellid tissue, mottled grey-maroon-red, a cross between an enlarged amoeba and some disgusting fungus. It oozed up over Gordy's arms—

—and suddenly, one of Gordy's hands poked through the slime that had sheathed it. But it wasn't a hand any more. God, no. It was only bones. Skeletal fingers, stiff and white, picked clean. The flesh had been eaten away.

She gagged, stumbled backwards, turned to the gutter, vomited.

Jenny pulled Lisa two steps back, further away from the thing with which Gordy was grappling.

The girl was screaming.

360

The slime oozed around the bony hand, reclaimed those denuded fingers, enfolded them, sheathed them in a glove of pulsing tissue. In a couple of seconds, the bones were gone as well, dissolved, and the glove folded up into a ball and melted back into the main body of the organism. The thing writhed obscenely, churned within itself, swelled, bulged here, formed a concavity there, now a concavity where the bulge had been, now a swelling nodule where the concavity had been, feverishly changing, as if even a moment's stillness meant death. It pulled itself up Gordy's arms, and he struggled desperately to rid himself of it, and as it progressed towards his shoulders, it left nothing behind it, nothing, no stumps, no bones; it devoured everything. It began to spread across his chest, too, and wherever it went, Gordy simply disappeared into it and did not come out, as if he was sinking into a vat of fiercely corrosive acid.

Lisa looked away from the dying man and clung to Jenny, sobbing.

Gordy's screams were unbearable.

Tal's revolver was already in his hand. He hurried towards Gordy.

Bryce stopped him. 'Are you crazy? Tal, dammit, there's nothing we can do.'

'We can put him out of his misery.'

'Don't get close to that damned thing!'

'We don't have to get *too* dose to get a good shot.'

Gordy's cries became more tortured by the second, and now he began to scream for Jesus's help, and he drummed his heels on the pavement, arched his back, vibrated with the strain, trying to push up from under the growing weight of the nightmarish assailant.

Bryce winced. 'All right. Quickly.'

They both edged nearer to the thrashing, dying deputy and opened fire. Several shots struck him. His screaming stopped.

They quickly backed off.

They didn't try to kill the thing that was feeding on Gordy. They knew bullets had no effect on it, and they were beginning to understand why. Bullets kill by destroying vital organs and essential blood vessels. But from the look of it, this thing had no organs and no conventional circulatory system. No skeleton either. It seemed to be a mass of undifferentiated – yet highly sophisticated – protoplasm. A bullet would pierce it, but the amazingly malleable flesh would flow into the channel carved by the bullet, and the wound would heal in an instant.

The thing fed more frantically than before, in a silent frenzy, and in seconds there was no sign of Gordy at all. He had ceased to exist. There was only the shape-changer, grown larger, much bigger than the dog that it had been, even bigger than Gordy, whose substance it now incorporated.

Tal and Bryce rejoined the others, but they didn't run for the inn. As the twilight was slowly squeezed out of the sky in a vice of darkness, they watched the amoeboid thing on the pavement.

It began to take a new shape. In a matter of seconds, all of the freeform protoplasm had been moulded into a huge, menacing timber wolf, and the creature threw its head back and howled at the sky.

Then its face rippled, and elements of its ferocious countenance shifted, and Tal could see human features trying to rise up through the image of a wolf. Human eyes replaced the animal's eyes, and there was part of a human chin. Gordy's eyes? Gordy's chin? The lycanthropic metamorphosis lasted only seconds, and then the thing's features flowed back into the wolf form.

Werewolf, Tal thought.

But he knew it wasn't anything like that. It wasn't *anything.* The wolf identity, as real and frightening as it looked, was as false as all the other identities.

For a moment it stood there, confronting them, baring its enormous and wickedly sharp teeth, far greater in size than any wolf that had ever stalked the plains or forests of this world. Its eyes blazed with the muddy-bloody colour of the sunset.

It's going to attack, Tal thought.

He fired at it. The bullets penetrated but left no visible wound, drew no blood, caused no apparent pain.

The wolf turned away from Tal, with a sort of cool indifference to the gunfire, and trotted towards the open manhole, into which the field lab's electric power cables disappeared.

Abruptly, something rose out of that hole, came from the storm drain below the street, rose and rose into the twilight, shuddering, smashing up into the air with tremendous power, a dark and pulsating mass, like a flood of sewage, except that it was not a fluid but a jelloid substance that formed itself into a column almost as wide as the hole from which it continued to extrude itself in an almost obscene, rhythmic gush. It grew and grew; four feet high, six feet, eight . . .

Something struck Tal across the back. He jumped, tried to turn, and realized that he had only collided with the wall of the inn. He hadn't been aware he'd been backing away from the towering thing that had soared out of the manhole.

He saw now that the pulsing, rippling column was another body of free-form protoplasm like the Airedale that had become a timber wolf; however, this thing was considerably larger than the first creature. Immense. Tal wondered how much of it was still hidden below the street, and he had a hunch that the storm drain was filled with it, that what they were seeing here was only a small portion of the beast.

When it reached a height of ten feet, it stopped rising and began to change. The upper half of the column broadened into a hood, a mantle, so that the thing now resembled the head of a cobra. Then more of the amorphous flesh flowed out of the oozing, glistening, shifting column and poured into the hood, so that the hood rapidly grew wider, wider, until it was not a hood at all any more; now it was a pair of gigantic wings, dark and membraneous, like a bat's wings, sprouting out of the central (and still shapeless) trunk. And then the body segment between the wings began to acquire a texture – coarse, overlapping scales – and small legs and clawed feet began to form. It was becoming a winged serpent.

The wings flapped.

The sound was like a whip cracking.

Tal pressed back against the wall.

The wings flapped.

Lisa's grip on Jenny tightened.

Jenny held the girl close, but her eyes, mind and imagination were fixed upon the monstrous thing that had risen out of the storm drain. It flexed and throbbed and writhed in the twilight and seemed like nothing so much as a shadow that had come to life.

The wings flapped again.

Jenny felt a cold, wing-stirred breeze.

This new phantom looked as if it would detach itself from whatever additional protoplasm lay within the storm drain. Jenny expected it to leap into the darkening air and soar away – or come straight at them.

Her heart thumped; slammed.

She knew escape was impossible. Any movement she made would only draw unwanted attention from *it*. There was no point wasting energy in flight. There was nowhere to hide from a thing like this.

More streetlamps came on, and shadows slunk in with ghostly stealth.

Jenny watched in awe as a serpent's head took shape at the top of the ten-foot-high column of mottled tissue. A pair of hate-filled green eyes swelled out of the shapeless flesh; it was like viewing time-lapse photography of the growth of two malignant tumours. Cloudy eyes, obviously blind, milky green ovals; they quickly cleared, and the elongated back pupils became visible, and the eyes glared down at Jenny and the others with malevolent intent. A foot-wide, slitted mouth sprang open; a row of sharp white fangs grew from the black gums.

Jenny thought of the demonic names that had glowed on the video display terminals, the Hell-born names the thing had given itself. The mass of amorphous flesh, forming itself into a winged serpent, *was* like a demon summoned from beyond.

The phantom wolf, which incorporated the substance of Gordy Brogan, approached the base of the towering serpent. It brushed against the column of pulsing flesh – and simply melted into it. In less than a blink of an eye, the two creatures became as one.

Evidently, the first shape-changer wasn't a separate individual. It was now, and perhaps always had been, part of the gargantuan creature that moved within the storm drains, under the streets. Apparently, that massive mother-body could detach pieces of itself and despatch them on tasks of their own – such as the attack on Gordy Brogan – and then recall them at will.

The wings flapped, and the whole town reverberated with the sound. Then they began to melt back into the central column, and the column grew thicker as it absorbed that tissue. The serpent's face dissolved, too. *It* had grown tired of this performance. The legs and three-toed feet and vicious talons withdrew into the column, until there was nothing left but a churning, oozing mass of darkly mottled tissue, as before. For several seconds, it posed in the gloomy dusk, a vision of evil, then began to shrink down into the drains under it, down through the manhole.

Soon it was gone.

Lisa had stopped screaming. She was gasping for air and crying.

Some of the others were nearly as shaken as the girl. They looked at one another, but none of them spoke.

Bryce looked as if he had been clubbed.

At last he said, 'Come on. Let's get back to the inn before it gets any darker.'

There was no guard at the front entrance of the inn.

'Trouble,' Tal said.

Bryce nodded. He stepped through the double doors with caution and almost put his foot on a gun. It was lying on the floor.

The lobby was deserted.

'Damn,' Frank Autry said.

They searched the place, room by room. No one in the cafeteria. No one in the makeshift dormitory. The kitchen was deserted too.

Not a shot had been fired.

No one had cried out.

No one had escaped, either.

Ten more deputies were gone.

Outside, night had fallen.

34

SAYING GOODBYE

THE SIX survivors – Bryce, Tal, Frank, Jenny, Lisa and Sara – stood at the windows in the lobby of the Hilltop Inn. Outside, Skyline Road was still and silent, rendered in stark patterns of night-shadow and streetlamp-glow. The night seemed to tick softly, like a bomb clock.

Jenny was remembering the covered passageway beside Leibermann's Bakery. Last night, she had thought something was in the rafters of the service tunnel, and Lisa had believed something was crouching along the wall; very likely, they had both been right. The shape-changer – or at least a part of it – had been there, slithering soundlessly through the rafters and down the wall. Later, when Bryce had caught a glimpse of something in the drain inside that passage, he had surely seen a dark glob of protoplasm creeping through the pipe, either keeping tabs on them or engaged upon some alien and unfathomable task.

Thinking, also, of the Oxleys in their barricaded den, Jenny said, 'The locked-room mysteries suddenly aren't very mysterious any more. That thing could ooze under a door or through a heating duct. The smallest hole or crack would be big enough. As for Harold Ordnay . . . after he locked himself in the bathroom at the Candleglow Inn, the thing probably got at him through the sink and bathtub drains.'

'The same for the locked cars with victims in them,' Frank said.

'It could surround a car, envelope it, and squeeze in through the vents.'

'If it wanted to,' Tal said, 'it could move real quietly. That's why so many people were caught by surprise. It was behind them, oozing under a door or out of a heating vent, getting bigger and bigger, but they didn't *know* it was there until it attacked.'

Outside, a thin fog was coming up the street, rising out of the valley below. Misty auras began to form around the streetlights.

'How big do you think it is?' Lisa asked.

No one responded for a moment. Then Bryce said, 'Big.'

'Maybe the size of a house,' Frank said.

'Or as big as this entire inn,' Sara said.

'Or even bigger,' Tal said. 'After all, it struck in every part of town, apparently simultaneouly. It could be like . . . like an underground lake, a lake of living tissue, beneath most of Snowfield.'

'Like God,' Lisa said.

'Huh?'

'It's everywhere,' Lisa said. 'It sees all and knows all. Just like God.'

'We've got five patrol cars,' Frank said. 'If we split up, take all five cars, and drive out of here at exactly the same time—'

'It would stop us,' Bryce said.

'Maybe it wouldn't be able to stop all of us. Maybe one car would get through.'

'It stopped a whole town.'

'Well . . . yeah,' Frank said reluctantly.

Jenny said, 'Anyway, it's probably listening to us right this minute. It would stop us before we even reached the cars.'

They all looked at the heating ducts near the ceiling. There was nothing to be seen beyond the metal grilles. Nothing but darkness.

*

They gathered around a table in the dining room of the fortress that was no longer a fortress. They pretended to want coffee because, somehow, sharing coffee gave them a sense of community and normality.

Bryce didn't bother putting a guard on the front doors. Guards were useless. If *it* wanted them, it would surely get them.

Beyond the windows, the fog was getting thicker. It pressed against the glass.

They were compelled to talk about what they had seen. They were all aware that death was coming for them, and they needed to understand why and how they were meant to die. Death was terrifying, yes; however, senseless death was the worst of all.

Bryce knew about senseless death. A year ago, a runaway truck had taught him everything he needed to know about that subject.

'The moth,' Lisa said. 'Was that like the Airedale, like the thing that . . . that got Gordy?'

'Yes,' Jenny said. The moth was just a phantom, a small piece of the shape-changer.'

To Lisa, Tal said, 'When Stu Wargle came after you last night, it wasn't actually him. The shape-changer probably absorbed Wargle's body after we left it in the utility room. Then, later, when it wanted to terrorize you, it assumed his appearance.'

'Apparently,' Bryce said, 'the damned thing can impersonate anyone or any animal that it's previously fed upon.'

Lisa frowned. 'But what about the moth? How could it have fed on anything like the moth? Nothing like that *exists*.'

'Well,' Bryce said, 'maybe insects that size thrived a long time ago, tens of millions of years ago, back in the age of dinosaurs. Maybe that's when the shape-changer fed on them.'

Lisa's eyes widened. 'You mean the thing that came out of the manhole might've been millions of years old?'

'Well,' Bryce said, 'it certainly doesn't conform to the rules of biology as we know them – does it, Dr Yamaguchi?'

'No,' the geneticist said.

'So why shouldn't it also be immortal?'

Jenny looked dubious.

Bryce said, 'You have an objection?'

'To the possibility that it's immortal? Or the next thing to immortal? No. I'll accept that. It might be something out of the Mesozoic, all right, something so self-renewing that it's virtually immortal. But how does the winged serpent fit? I find it damned hard to believe that anything like that has ever existed. If the shape-changer becomes only those things it has previously ingested, then how could it become something like the winged serpent?'

'There've been animals like that,' Frank said. 'Pterodactyls were winged reptiles.'

'Reptiles, yes,' Jenny said. 'But not serpents. Pterodactyls were the ancestors of birds. But that thing was clearly a serpent, which is very different. It looked like something out of a fairytale.'

'No,' Tal said. 'It was straight out of voodoo.'

Bryce turned to Tal, surprised. 'Voodoo? What would you know about voodoo?'

Tal didn't seem to be able to look at Bryce, and he spoke with evident reluctance. 'In Harlem, when I was a kid, there was this enormous fat lady, Agatha Peabody, in our apartment building, and she was a *boko*. That's a sort of witch who uses voodoo for immoral or evil purposes. She sold charms and spells, helped people strike back at their enemies, that sort of thing. All nonsense. But to a kid, it seemed exciting and spooky. Mrs Peabody ran an open apartment, with clients and hangers-on going in and out all day and night. For a few months I spent a lot of time there, listening and watching. And there were quite a few books on the black arts. In a couple of them, I saw drawings of Haitian and African versions of Satan, voodoo and juju devils. One of them was a giant, winged serpent. Black, with bat wings. And terrible green eyes. It was *exactly* like the thing we saw tonight.'

370

In the street, beyond the windows, the fog was very thick now. It churned sluggishly through the diffused glow of the streetlamps.

Lisa said, 'Is it *really* the devil? A demon? Something from Hell?'

'No,' Jenny said. 'That's just a . . . pose.'

'But then why does it take the shape of the devil?' Lisa asked. 'And why does it call itself by the names of demons?'

'I figure the satanic mumbo-jumbo is just something that amuses it,' Frank said. 'One more way to tease us and demoralize us.'

Jenny nodded. 'I suspect it isn't limited to the forms of its victims. It can assume the shape of anything it has absorbed *and* anything it can imagine. So if one of the victims was somebody familiar with voodoo, then *that*'s where it got the idea of becoming a winged serpent.'

That thought startled Bryce. 'Do you mean it not only absorbs and incorporates the *flesh* of its victims *but their knowledge and memories as well?*'

'It sure looks that way,' Jenny said.

'Biologically, that's not unheard of,' Sara Yamaguchi said, combing her long black hair with both hands and nervously tucking it behind her delicate ears. 'For instance . . . If you put a certain kind of flatworm through a maze often enough, with food at one end, eventually it'll learn to negotiate the maze more quickly than it did at first. Then, if you grind it up and feed it to another flatworm, the new worm will negotiate the maze quickly, too, even though it's never been put through the test before. Somehow, it ate the knowledge and experience of its cousin when it ate the flesh.'

'Which is how the shape-changer knows about Timothy Flyte,' Jenny said. 'Harold Ordnay knew about Flyte, so now *it* knows about him, too.'

'But how in the name of God did Flyte know about it?' Tal asked.

Bryce shrugged. That's a question only Flyte can answer.'

*

371

'Why didn't it take Lisa last night in the restroom? For that matter, why hasn't it taken all of us?'

'It's just toying with us.'

'Having fun. A sick kind of fun.'

'There's that. But I think it's also kept us alive so we could tell Flyte what we've seen and lure him here.'

'It wants us to pass along the offer of safe conduct to Flyte.'

'We're just bait.'

'Yes.'

'And when we've served our purpose . . .'

'Yes.'

Something thumped solidly against the outside of the inn. The windows rattled, and the building seemed to shake.

Bryce stood so fast that he knocked over his chair.

Another crash. Harder; louder. Then a scraping noise.

Bryce listened intently, trying to get a fix on the sound. It seemed to be coming from the north wall of the building. It started at ground level but swiftly began to move up, away from them.

A clattering-rattling sound. A bony sound. Like the skeletons of long-dead men clawing their way out of a sepulchre.

'Something big,' Frank said. 'Pulling itself up the side of the inn.'

'The shape-changer,' Lisa said.

'But not in its jellied form,' Sara said. 'In its natural state, it would just flow up the wall silently.'

They all stared at the ceiling, listening, waiting.

What phantom form has it assumed this time? Bryce wondered.

Scrape. Tick. Clatter.

The sound of death.

Bryce's hand was colder than the butt of his revolver.

The six of them went to the windows and looked out. The fog swirled everywhere.

Then, down the street, almost a block away, at the penumbra of a sodium-vapour lamp, something moved. Half-seen. A menacing shadow, distorted by the fog. Bryce got an impression of a crab as large as a car. He glimpsed arachnoid legs. A monstrous claw with saw-toothed edges flashed into the light, immediately into darkness again. And there: the febrile, quivering, seeking length of antennae. Then the thing scuttled off into the night again.

'That's what's climbing the building,' Tal said. 'Another damned crab thing like that one. Something straight out of an alky's DTs.'

They heard it reach the roof. Its chitinous limbs tapped and scraped across the slate shingles.

'What's it up to?' Lisa asked worriedly. 'Why's it pretending to be what it isn't?'

'Maybe it just enjoys mimickry,' Bryce said. 'You know . . . the same way some tropical birds like to imitate sounds just for the pleasure of it, just to hear themselves.'

The noises on the roof stopped.

The six waited.

The night seemed to be crouched like a wild thing, studying its prey, timing its attack.

They were too restless to sit down. They continued to stand by the windows.

Outside, only the fog moved.

Sara Yamaguchi said, 'The universal bruising is understandable now. The shape-changer enfolded its victims, squeezed them. So the bruising came from a brutal, sustained, universally applied pressure. That's how they suffocated, too – wrapped up inside the shape-changer, totally encapsulated in it.'

'I wonder,' Jenny said, 'if maybe it produces its preservative while squeezing its victims.'

'Yes, probably,' Sara said. 'That's why there's no visible point of injection in either body we studied. The preservative is most likely applied to every square inch of the body, squeezed into every pore. Sort of an osmotic application.'

Jenny thought of Hilda Beck, her housekeeper, the first victim she and Lisa had found.

She shuddered.

'The water,' Jenny said.

'What?' Bryce said.

'Those pools of distilled water we found. The shape-changer expelled that water.'

'How do you work that out?'

'The human body is mostly water. So after the thing absorbed its victims, after it used every milligram of mineral content, every vitamin, every usable calorie, it expelled what it didn't need: excess amounts of absolutely pure water. Those pools and puddles we found were all the remains we'll ever find of the hundreds who're missing. No bodies. No bones. Just water . . . which has already evaporated.'

The noises on the roof did not resume; silence reigned. The phantom crab was gone.

In the dark, in the fog, in the sodium-yellow light of the streetlamps, nothing moved.

They turned away from the windows at last and went back to the table.

'Can the damned thing be killed?' Frank wondered.

'We know for sure that bullets won't do the job,' Tal said.

'Fire?' Lisa said.

'The soldiers had firebombs they'd made,' Sara reminded them. 'But the shape-changer evidently struck so suddenly, so unexpectedly, that no one had time to grab the bottles and light the fuses.'

'Besides,' Bryce said, 'fire most likely won't do the trick. If the shape-changer caught fire, it could just . . . well . . . *detach* itself from that part of it that was aflame and move the bulk of itself to a safe place.'

'Explosives are probably useless, too,' Jenny said. 'I have a hunch that, if you blew the thing into a thousand pieces, you'd wind up with a thousand smaller shape-changers, and they'd all flow together again, unharmed.'

'So can the thing be killed or not?' Frank asked again.

They were silent, considering.

Then Bryce said, 'No. Not so far as I can see.'

'But then what can we do?'

'I don't know,' Bryce said. 'I just don't know.'

Frank Autry phoned his wife, Ruth, and spoke with her for nearly half an hour. Tal called a few friends on the other telephone. Later, Sara Yamaguchi tied up one of the lines for almost an hour. Jenny called several people, including her aunt in Newport Beach, to whom Lisa talked, as well. Bryce spoke with several men at head-quarters in Santa Mira, deputies with whom he had worked for years and with whom he shared a bond of brotherhood; he spoke with his parents in Glendale and with Ellen's father in Spokane.

All six survivors were optimistic in their conversations. They talked about whipping this thing, about leaving Snowfield soon.

However, Bryce knew that they were all just putting the best possible face on a bad situation. He knew these weren't ordinary phone calls; in spite of their cheerful tone, these calls had only one grim purpose: the six survivors were saying goodbye.

35

PANDEMONIUM

SAL CORELLO, the publicity agent who had been hired to meet Timothy Flyte at San Francisco International Airport, was a small yet hard-muscled man with corn-yellow hair and purple-blue eyes. He looked like a leading man. If he had been six foot two instead of just five foot one, his face might have been as famous as Robert Redford's. However, his intelligence, wit, and aggressive charm compensated for his lack of height. He knew how to get what he wanted for himself and for his clients.

Usually, Corello could even make newsmen behave so well that you might mistake them for civilized people – but not tonight. This story was too big and much too hot. Corello had never seen anything like it: Hundreds of reporters and curious civilians rushed at Flyte the instant they saw him, pulling and tugging at the professor, shoving microphones in his face, blinding him with batteries of camera lights, and frantically shouting questions, 'Dr Flyte . . .' 'Professor Flyte . . .' '. . . Flyte!' *Flyte, Flyte, Flyte-Flyte-Flyte, FlyteFlyteFlyteFlyte* . . . The questions were reduced to meaningless gabble by the roar of competing voices. Sal Corello's ears hurt. The professor looked bewildered, then scared. Corello took the old man's arm and held it tightly and led him through the surging flock, turning himself into a small but highly effective battering ram. By the time they reached the small platform that Corello and airport security officers had set up at one end of the passengers' lounge, Professor Flyte looked as if he might expire of fright.

Corello took the microphone and quickly silenced the throng. He urged them to let Flyte deliver a brief statement, promised that a few questions would be permitted later, introduced the speaker, and stepped out of the way.

When everyone got a good, clear look at Timothy Flyte, they couldn't conceal a sudden attack of scepticism. It swept the crowd; Corello saw it in their faces: a very visible apprehension that Flyte was hoaxing them. Indeed, Flyte appeared to be a maniac. His white hair was frizzed out from his head, as if he had just stuck a finger in an electric socket. His eyes were wide, both with fear and with an effort to stave off fatigue, and his face had the dissipated look of a wino's grizzled visage. He needed a shave. His clothes were rumpled, wrinkled; they hung like shapeless bags. He reminded Corello of one of those street corner fanatics declaring the imminence of Armageddon.

Earlier in the day, on the telephone from London, Burt Sandler, the editor from Wintergreen and Wyle, had prepared Corello for the possibility that Flyte would make a negative impression on the newsmen, but Sandler needn't have worried. The newsmen grew restless as Flyte cleared his throat half a dozen times, loudly, into the microphone, but when he began to speak at last, they were enthralled within a minute. He told them about the Roanoke Island colony, about vanishing Mayan civilizations, about mysterious depletions of marine populations, about an army that disappeared in 1711. The crowd grew hushed. Corello relaxed.

Flyte told them about the Eskimo village of Anjikuni, five hundred miles north-west of the Royal Canadian Mounted Police outpost at Churchill. On a snowy afternoon in November of 1930, a French-Canadian trapper and trader, Joe LaBelle, stopped at Anjikuni – only to discover that everyone who lived there had disappeared. All belongings, including precious hunting rifles, had been left behind. Meals had been left half-eaten. The dog-sleds (but no dogs) were still there, which meant there was no way the entire village could have moved overland to another location. The settlement was, as LaBelle put it later, 'as eerie as a graveyard in the very dead of night'. LaBelle hastened to the Mounted Police Station at Churchill, and a major investigation was launched, but no trace was ever found of the Anjikunians.

As the reporters took notes and aimed tape-recorder microphones at Flyte, he told them about his much-maligned theory: the ancient enemy. There were gasps of surprise, incredulous expressions, but no noisy questioning or blatantly expressed disbelief.

The instant Flyte finished reading his prepared statement, Sal Corello reneged on his promise of a question-and-answer session. He took Flyte by the arm and hustled him through a door behind the makeshift platform on which the microphones stood.

The newsmen howled with indignation at this betrayal. They rushed the platform, trying to follow Flyte.

Corello and the professor entered a service corridor where several airport security men were waiting. One of the guards slammed and locked the door behind them, cutting off the reporters, who howled even louder than before.

'This way,' a security man said.

'The chopper's here,' another added.

They hurried along a maze of hallways, down a flight of concrete stairs, through a metal fire door, and outside, onto a wind-swept expanse of tarmac, where a sleek, blue helicopter waited. It was a plush, well-appointed, executive craft, a Bell JetRanger II.

'It's the governor's chopper,' Corello told Flyte.

'The governor?' Flyte said. 'He's here?'

'No. But he's put his helicopter at your disposal.'

As they climbed through the door, into the comfortable passengers' compartment, the rotars began to churn overhead.

*

Forehead pressed to the cool window, Timothy Flyte watched San Francisco fall away into the night.

He was excited. Before the plane had landed, he had felt dopey and bedraggled; not any more. He was alert and eager to learn more about what was happening in Snowfield.

The JetRanger had a high cruising speed for a helicopter, and the trip to Santa Mira took less than two hours. Corello – a clever, fast-talking, amusing man – helped Timothy prepare another statement for the media people who were waiting for them. The journey passed quickly.

They touched down with a thump in the middle of the fenced parking lot behind the county sheriff's headquarters. Corello opened the door of the passengers' compartment even before the chopper's rotars had stopped whirling; he plunged out of the craft, turned to the door again, buffeted by the wind from the blades, and lent a hand to Timothy.

An aggressive contingent of newsmen – even more of them than in San Francisco – filled the alleyway. They were pressed against the chainlink fence, shouting questions, aiming microphones and cameras.

'We'll give them a statement later, at *our* convenience,' Corello told him, shouting in order to be heard above the din. 'Right now, the police here are waiting to put you on the phone to the sheriff up in Snowfield.'

A couple of deputies hustled Timothy and Corello into the building, along the hallway, and into an office where another uniformed man was waiting for them. His name was Charlie Mercer. He was husky, with the bushiest eyebrows that Timothy had ever seen – and the briskly efficient manner of a first-rate executive secretary.

Timothy was escorted to the chair behind the desk.

Mercer dialled a number in Snowfield, making the connection with Sheriff Hammond. The call was put on a conference speaker, so that Timothy didn't have to hold a receiver, and so that everyone in the room could hear both sides of the conversation.

Hammond delivered the first shocker as soon as he and Timothy had exchanged greetings: 'Dr Flyte, we've seen the ancient enemy. Or at least I guess it's the thing you had in mind. A massive . . . amoeboid thing. A shape-changer that can mimic anything.'

Timothy's hands were shaking; he gripped the arms of his chair. 'My God.'

'Is that your ancient enemy?' Hammond asked.

'Yes. A survivor from another era. Millions of years old.'

'You can tell us more when you get here,' Hammond said. 'If I can persuade you to come.'

Timothy only heard half of what the sheriff was saying. He was thinking of the ancient enemy. He had written about it; he had truly believed in it; yet, somehow, he had not been prepared to actually have his theory confirmed. It rocked him.

Hammond told him about the hideous death of a deputy named Gordy Brogan.

Besides Timothy himself, only Sal Corello looked stunned and horrified by Hammond's story. Mercer and the others had evidently heard all about it hours ago.

'You've seen it *and lived*?' Timothy said, amazed.

'It had to leave some of us alive,' Hammond said, 'so that we'd try to convince you to come. It has guaranteed your safe conduct.'

Timothy chewed thoughtfully on his lower lip.

Hammond said, 'Dr Flyte? Are you still there?'

'What? Oh . . . yes. Yes, I'm still here. What do you mean by saying it *guaranteed* my safe passage?'

Hammond told him an astonishing story about communication with the ancient enemy by way of a computer.

As the sheriff talked, Timothy broke into a sweat. He saw a box of Kleenex on one corner of the desk in front of him; he grabbed a handful of tissues and mopped his face.

When the sheriff finished, the professor drew a deep breath and spoke in a strained voice. 'I never anticipated . . . I mean . . . well, it never occurred to me that . . .'

'What's wrong?' Hammond asked.

Timothy cleared his throat. 'It never occurred to me that the ancient enemy would possess *human-level* intelligence.'

'I suspect it may even be a *superior* intelligence,' Hammond said.

'But I always thought of it as just a dumb animal, of distinctly limited self-awareness.'

'It's not.'

'That makes it a lot more dangerous. My God. A *lot* more dangerous.'

'Will you come up here?' Hammond asked.

'I hadn't intended to come any closer than I am now,' Timothy said. 'But if it's *intelligent* . . . and if it's offering me safe passage . . .'

On the telephone, a child's voice piped up, the sweet voice of a young boy, perhaps five or six years old: 'Please, please, please come play with me, Dr Flyte. Please. We'll have lots of fun. Please?'

And then, before Timothy could respond, there came a woman's soft and musical voice: 'Yes, dear Dr Flyte, by all means, do come pay us a visit. You're more than welcome. No one will harm you.'

Finally, the voice of an old man came over the line, warm and tender: 'You have so much to learn about me, Dr Flyte. So much wisdom to acquire. Please come and begin your studies. The offer of safe passage is sincere.'

Silence.

Confused, Timothy said, 'Hello? Hello? Who's this?'

'I'm still here,' Hammond answered.

The other voices did not return.

'Just me now,' Hammond said.

Timothy said, 'But who were those people?'

'They're not actually people. They're just phantoms. Mimicry.

381

Don't you get it? In three different voices, *it* just offered you safe passage again. The ancient enemy, Doctor.'

Timothy looked at the other four men in the room. They were all staring intently at the black conference box from which Hammond's voice – and the voices of the creature – had issued.

Clutching a wad of already sodden tissues in one hand, Timothy wiped his sweat-slick face again. 'I'll come.'

Now, everyone in the room looked at him.

On the telephone, Sheriff Hammond said, 'Doctor, there's no good reason to believe that it'll keep its promise. Once you're here, you may very well be a dead man, too.'

'But if it's intelligent—'

'That doesn't mean it plays fair,' Hammond said. 'In fact, all of us up here are certain of one thing: this creature is the very essence of evil. Evil, Dr Flyte. Would you trust in the devil's promise?'

The child's voice came on the line again, still lilting and sweet: 'If you come, Dr Flyte, I'll not only spare you but these six people who're trapped here. I'll let them go if you come play with me. But if you don't come, I'll take these pigs. I'll crush them. I'll squeeze the blood and shit out of them, squeeze them into pulp, and use them up.'

Those words were spoken in light, innocent, childlike tones – which somehow made them far more frightening than if they had been shouted in a basso profundo rage.

Timothy's heart was pounding.

'That settles it,' he said. 'I'll come. I have no choice.'

'Don't come on our account,' Hammond said. 'It might spare you because it calls you its Saint Matthew, its Mark, its Luke and John. But it sure as hell won't spare us, no matter what it says.'

'I'll come,' Timothy insisted.

Hammond hesitated. Then: 'Very well. I'll have one of my men drive you to the Snowfield roadblock. From there, you'll have to come alone. I can't risk another man. Do you drive?'

'Yes, sir,' Timothy said. 'You provide the car, and I'll get there by myself.'

The line went dead.

'Hello?' Timothy said. 'Sheriff?'

No answer.

'Are you there? Sheriff Hammond?'

Nothing.

It had cut them off.

Timothy looked up at Sal Corello, Charlie Mercer, and the two men whose names he didn't know.

They were all staring at him as if he were already dead and lying in a casket.

But if I die in Snowfield, if the shape-changer takes me, he thought, there'll be no casket. No grave. No everlasting peace.

'I'll drive you as far as the roadblock,' Charlie Mercer said. 'I'll drive you myself.'

Timothy nodded.

It was time to go.

36

FACE TO FACE

AT 3.12 AM, Snowfield's church bells began to clang.

In the lobby of the Hilltop Inn, Bryce got up from his chair. The others rose, too.

The firehouse siren wailed.

Jenny said, 'Flyte must be here.'

The six of them went outside.

The streetlights were flashing off and on, casting leaping marionette shadows through the shifting banks of fog.

At the foot of Skyline Road, a car turned the corner. Its headlights speared upward, imparting a silvery sheen to the mist.

The streetlamps stopped blinking, and Bryce stepped into the soft cascade of yellow light beneath one of them, hoping that Flyte would be able to see him through the veils of fog.

The bells continued to peal, and the siren shrieked, and the car crawled slowly up the long hill. It was a green and white sheriff's department cruiser. It pulled to the kerb and stopped ten feet from where Bryce stood; the driver extinguished the headlights.

The driver's door opened, and Flyte got out. He wasn't what Bryce had expected. He was wearing thick glasses that made his eyes appear abnormally large. His fine, white, tangled hair bristled in a halo around his head. Someone at headquarters had lent him an insulated jacket with the Santa Mira County Sheriff's Department seal on the left breast.

The bells stopped ringing.

The siren groaned to a throaty finish.

The subsequent silence was profound.

Flyte gazed around the fog-shrouded street, listening and waiting.

At last Bryce said, 'Apparently, it's not ready to show itself.'

Flyte turned to him. 'Sheriff Hammond?'

'Yes. Let's go inside and be comfortable while we wait.'

The inn's dining room. Hot coffee.

Shaky hands clattered china mugs against the table top. Nervous hands curled and clamped around the warm mugs in order to make themselves be still.

The six survivors leaned forward, hunched over the table, the better to listen to Timothy Flyte.

Lisa was clearly enthralled by the British scientist, but at first Jenny had serious doubts. He seemed to be an outright caricature of the absent-minded professor. But when he began to speak about his theories, Jenny was forced to discard her initial, unfavourable opinion, and soon she was as fascinated as Lisa.

He told them about vanishing armies in Spain and China, about abandoned Mayan cities, the Roanoke Island colony.

And he told them of Joya Verde, a South American jungle settlement that had met a fate similar to Snowfield's. Joya Verde, which means Green Jewel, was a trading post on the Amazon River, far from civilisation. In 1923, six hundred and five people – every man, woman and child who lived there – vanished from Joya Verde in a single afternoon, some time between the morning and evening visits of regularly scheduled riverboats. At first it was thought that nearby Indians, who were normally peaceful, had become inexplicably hostile and had launched a surprise attack. However, there were no bodies found, no indications of fighting, and no evidence of looting. A message was discovered on the blackboard at the mission school: *It has no shape, yet it has every shape.* Many who investigated the Joya

385

Verde mystery were quick to dismiss those nine chalk-scrawled words as having no connection to the disappearances. Flyte believed otherwise, and after listening to him, so did Jenny.

'A message of sorts was also left in one of those ancient Mayan cities,' Flyte said. 'Archaeologists have unearthed a portion of a prayer, written in hieroglyphics, dating from the time of the great disappearance.' He quoted from memory: ' "Evil gods live in the earth, their power asleep in rock. When they awake, they rise up as lava rises, but cold lava, flowing, and they assume many shapes. Then proud men know that we are only voices in the thunder, faces on the wind, to be dispersed as if we never lived." ' Flyte's glasses had slid down his nose. He pushed them back into place. 'Now, some say that particular part of the prayer refers to the power of earthquakes and volcanoes. I think it's about the ancient enemy.'

'We found a message here, too,' Bryce said. 'Part of a word.'

'We can't make anything of it,' Sara Yamaguchi said.

Jenny told Flyte about the two letters – P and R – that Nick Papandrakis had painted on his bathroom wall, using a bottle of iodine. 'There was a portion of a third letter, too. It might have been the beginning of a U or an O.'

'Papandrakis,' Flyte said, nodding vigorously. 'Greek. Yes, yes, yes – here's confirmation of what I'm telling you. Was this fellow Papandrakis proud of his heritage?'

'Yes,' Jenny said. 'Extremely proud of it. Why?'

'Well, if he was proud of being Greek,' Flyte said, 'he might well have known Greek mythology. You see, in ancient Greek myth, there was a god named Proteus. I suspect that was the word your Mr Papandrakis was trying to write on the wall. Proteus. A god who lived in the earth, crawled through its bowels. A god who was without any shape of his own. A god who could take any form he wished – and who fed upon everything and everyone that he desired.'

386

With frustration in his voice, Tal Whitman said, 'What is all this supernatural stuff? When we communicated with it through the computer, it insisted on giving itself the names of demons.'

Flyte said, 'The amorphous demon, the shapeless and usually evil god that can assume any form it wishes – those are relatively common figures in most ancient myth systems and in most if not all of the world's religions. Such a mythologial creature appears under scores of names, in all of the world's cultures. Consider the Old Testament of the Bible, for example. Satan first appears as a serpent, later as a goat, a ram, a stag, a beetle, a spider, a child, a beggar, and many other things. He is called, among other names: Master of Chaos and Formlessness, Master of Deceit, the Beast of Many Faces. The Bible tells us that Satan is "as changeable as shadows" and "as clever as water, for as water can become steam or ice, so Satan can become that which he wishes to become."'

Lisa said, 'Are you saying the shape-changer here in Snowfield *is* Satan?'

'Well . . . in a way, yes.'

Frank Autry shook his head. 'No. I'm not a man who believes in spooks, Dr Flyte.'

'Nor am I,' Flyte assured him. 'I'm not arguing that this thing is a supernatural being. It isn't. It's real, a creature of flesh – although not flesh like ours. It's not a spirit or a devil. Yet . . . in a way . . . I believe it *is* Satan. Because, you see, I believe it was this creature – or another like it, another monstrous survivor from the Mesozoic Era – that inspired the myth of Satan. In prehistoric times, men must have encountered one of these things, and some of them must have lived to tell the tale. They naturally described their experiences in the terminology of myth and superstition. I suspect most of the demonic figures in the world's various religions are actually reports of these shape-changers, reports passed down through countless generations before they were at last committed to hieroglyphics, scrolls, and then print. They were reports of a very rare, very real, very dangerous beast . . . but described in the language of religious myth.'

Jenny found this part of Flyte's thesis both crazy and brilliant, unlikely yet convincing. 'The thing somehow absorbs the knowledge and memories of those on whom it feeds,' she said, 'so it knows that many of its victims see it as the devil, and it gets some sort of perverse pleasure out of playing that role.'

Bryce said, 'It seems to enjoy mocking us.'

Sara Yamaguchi tucked her long hair behind her ears and said, 'Dr Flyte, how about explaining this in scientific terms. How can such a creature exist? How can it function biologically? What's your scientific rationalisation, your theory?'

Before Flyte could answer her, *it* came.

High on one wall, near the ceiling, a metal grille covering a heating duct suddenly popped from its screws. It flew into the room, crashed onto an empty table, slid off the table, clattered-rattled-banged onto the floor.

Jenny and the others leapt up from their chairs.

Lisa screamed, pointed.

The shape-changer bulged out of the duct. It hung there on the wall. Dark. Wet. Pulsing. Like a mass of glistening, bloody snot suspended from the edge of a nostril.

Bryce and Tal reached for their revolvers, then hesitated. There was nothing whatsoever that they could do.

The thing continued to surge out of the duct, swelling, rippling, growing into an obscene, gnarled, shifting lump the size of a man. Then, still flowing out of the wall, it began to slide down. It formed into a mound on the floor. Much bigger than a man now, still oozing out of the duct. Growing, growing.

Jenny looked at Flyte.

The professor's face could not settle on a single expression. It tried wonder, then terror, then awe, then disgust, then awe and terror and wonder again.

The viscous, ever-churning mass of dark protoplasm was now as large as three or four men, and still more of the vile stuff gushed from the heating duct in a revolting, vomitous flow.

Lisa gagged and averted her face.

But Jenny couldn't take her eyes from the thing. There was a grotesque fascination that couldn't be denied.

In the already enormous agglomeration of shapeless tissue that had extruded itself into the room, limbs began to form, although none of them maintained its shape for more than a few seconds. Human arms, both male and female, reached out as if seeking help. The thin, flailing arms of children were formed from the jellid tissue, some of them with their small hands open in a silent, pathetic plea. It was difficult to keep in mind that these were not the arms of children trapped within the shape-changer; they were imitation, phantom arms, a part of *it*, not a part of any child. And claws. A startling, frightening variety of claws and animal limbs appeared out of the protoplasmic soup. There were insect parts, too, enormous, hugely exaggerated, terrifyingly frenetic and grasping. But all of these swiftly melted back into the formless protoplasm almost as soon as they took shape.

The shape-changer bulged across the width of the room. It was now larger than an elephant.

As the thing engaged upon a continuous, relentless, mysterious pattern of apparently purposeless change, Jenny and the others edged back towards the windows.

Outside, in the street, the fog roiled in its own formless dance, as if it were a ghostly reflection of the shape-changer.

Flyte spoke with a sudden urgency, answering the questions that Sara Yamaguchi had posed, as if he felt he didn't have much time left to explain. 'About twenty years ago, it occurred to me that there might be a connection between mass disappearances and the unexplained extinction of certain species in pre-human geological eras. Like the dinosaurs, for instance.'

The shape-changer pulsed and throbbed, towering almost to the ceiling, filling the entire far end of the room.

Lisa dung to Jenny.

A vague but repellent odour laced the air. Slightly sulphurous. Like a draught from Hell.

'There are a host of theories purporting to explain the demise of the dinosaurs,' Flyte said. 'But no single theory answers all the questions. So I wondered . . . what if the dinosaurs were exterminated by another creature, a natural enemy, that was a superior hunter and fighter? It would have to have been something large. And it would have been something with a very frail skeleton or perhaps with no skeleton whatsoever, for we've never found a fossil record of any species that would have given those great saurians a real battle.'

A shudder passed through the entire bulk of tenebrous, churning slime. Across the oozing mass, dozens of faces began to appear.

'And what if,' Flyte said, 'several of those amoeboid creatures had survived through millions of years . . .'

Human and animal faces arose from the amorphous flesh, shimmered in it.

'. . . living in subterranean rivers or lakes . . .'

There were faces that had no eyes. Others had no mouths. But then the eyes appeared, blinked open. They were achingly real, penetrating eyes, filled with pain and fear and misery.

'. . . or in deep ocean trenches . . .'

And mouths cracked into existence on their previously seamless countenances.

'. . . thousands of feet below the surface of the sea . . .'

Lips formed around the gaping mouths.

'. . . preying on marine life . . .'

The phantom faces were screaming, yet they made no sound.

'. . . infrequently rising to feed . . .'

Cat faces. Dog faces. Prehistoric reptile visages. Ballooning up from the slime.

'. . . and even less frequently feeding on human beings . . .'

To Jenny, the human faces looked as if they were peering out the far side of a smoky mirror. None of them ever quite finished taking shape. They *had* to melt away, for there were countless new faces surging and coalescing beneath them. It was an endlessly flickering shadow show of the lost and the damned.

Then the faces stopped forming.

The huge mass was quiescent for a moment, slowly and almost imperceptibly pulsing, but otherwise still.

Sara Yamaguchi was groaning softly.

Jenny held Lisa close.

No one spoke. For several seconds, no one even dared breathe.

Then in a new demonstration of its plasticity, the ancient enemy abruptly spouted a score of tentacles. Some of them were thick, with the suction pads of a squid or an octopus. Others were thin and ropy; some of these were smooth, and some were segmented; they were even more obscene than the fat, moist-looking tentacles. Some of the appendages slid back and forth across the floor, knocking over chairs and pushing tables aside, while others wriggled in the air, like cobras swaying to the music of a snake charmer.

Then it struck. It moved fast, gushed forward.

Jenny stumbled back one step. She was at the end of the room.

The many tentacles snapped towards them, whiplike, cutting the air with a hiss.

Lisa could no longer keep from looking. She gasped at what she saw.

In just a fraction of a second, the tentacles grew dramatically.

A rope of cold, slick, utterly alien flesh fell across the back of Jenny's hand. It curled around her wrist.

No!

With a shudder of relief, she pulled loose. It hadn't taken much effort to free herself. Evidently, the thing really wasn't interested in her; not now; not yet.

She crouched as tentacles lashed the air above her head, and Lisa huddled with her.

In his haste to get out of the creature's way, Flyte tripped and fell.

A tentacle moved towards him.

Flyte scooted backwards across the floor, came to the wall.

The tentacle followed, hovered over him, as if it would smash him. Then it moved away. It wasn't interested in Flyte, either.

Although the gesture was pointless, Bryce fired his revolver.

Tal shouted something Jenny couldn't understand. He moved in front of her and Lisa, between them and the shape-changer.

After passing over Sara, the thing seized Frank Autry. *That* was who it wanted. Two thick tentacles snapped around Frank's torso and dragged him away from the others.

Kicking, flailing with his fists, clawing at the thing that held him, Frank cried out wordlessly, face contorted with horror.

Everyone was screaming now – even Bryce, even Tal.

Bryce went after Frank. Clutched his right arm. Tried to pull him away from the beast, which was relentlessly reeling him in.

'Get it off me! Get it off me!' Frank shouted.

Bryce tried peeling one of the tentacles away from the deputy.

Another of the thick, slimy appendages swept up from the floor, whirled, whipped, struck Bryce with tremendous force, sent him sprawling.

Frank was lifted off the floor and held in mid-air. His eyes bulged as he looked down at the dark, oozing, changing bulk of the ancient enemy. He kicked and fought to no avail.

Yet another pseudopod erupted from the central mass of the shape-changer and rose into the air, trembling with savage eagerness. Along part of the tentacle's repulsive length, the mottled grey-maroon-red-brown skin seemed to dissolve. Raw, weeping tissue appeared.

Lisa gagged.

It wasn't just the sight of the suppurating flesh that was loathsome and sickening. The foul odour had become stronger, too.

A yellowish fluid began to drip from the open wound in the tentacle. Where the drops struck the floor, they sizzled and foamed and ate into the tile.

Jenny heard someone say, 'Add!'

Frank's screaming became a desperate, piercing shriek of terror and despair.

The acid-dripping tentacle slipped sinuously around the deputy's neck and drew as tight as a garrote.

'Oh, Jesus, no!'

'Don't look,' Jenny told Lisa.

The shape-changer was showing them how it had beheaded Jakob and Aida Liebermann. Like a child showing off.

Frank Autry's scream died in a bubbling, mucous-thick, blood-choked gurgle. The flesh-eating tentacle cut through his neck with startling speed. Only a second or two later Frank was silenced. His head popped loose and fell to the floor, smashed into the tiles.

Jenny tasted bile in the back of her throat, choked it down.

Sara Yamaguchi was sobbing.

The thing still held Frank's headless body in mid-air. Now, in the mass of shapeless tissue from which the tentacles sprouted, a huge toothless maw opened hungrily. It was more than large enough to swallow a man whole. The tentacles drew the deputy's decapitated corpse into the gaping, ragged mouth. The dark flesh oozed around the body. Then the mouth closed up tight and ceased to exist.

Frank Autry had ceased to exist, too.

Bryce stared in shock at Frank's severed head. The sightless eyes gazed at him, through him.

Frank was gone. Frank, who had survived several wars, who had survived a life of dangerous work, had not survived this.

Bryce thought of Ruth Autry. His heart, already jack-hammering, twisted with grief as he pictured Ruth alone. She and Frank had been exceptionally close. Breaking the news to her would be painful.

The tentacles shrank back into the pulsing glob of shapeless tissue; in a second or two, they were gone.

The formless, rippling hulk filled a third of the room.

Bryce could imagine it oozing swiftly through prehistoric swamps, blending with the muck, creeping up on its prey. Yes, it would have been more than a match for the dinosaurs.

Earlier, he had believed that the shape-changer had spared him and a few of the others so that they could entice Flyte to Snowfield. Now he realized that wasn't the case. It could have consumed them and then imitated their voices on the telephone, and Flyte would have been coaxed to Snowfield just as easily. It had saved them for some other reason. Perhaps it had spared them only in order to kill them, one at a time, in front of Flyte, so that Flyte would be able to see precisely how it functioned.

Christ.

The shape-changer towered over them, quivering gelatinously, its entire, grotesque bulk pulsating as if with the unsynchronized beats of a dozen hearts.

In a voice even shakier than Bryce felt, Sara Yamaguchi said, 'I wish there was some way we could get a tissue sample. I'd give anything to be able to study it under a microscope . . . get some idea of the cell structure. Maybe we could find a weakness . . . a way to deal with it, maybe even a way to defeat it.'

Flyte said, 'I'd like to study it . . . just to be able to understand . . . just to *know*.'

An extrusion of tissue oozed out from the centre of the shapeless mass. It began to acquire a human form. Bryce was shocked to see Gordy Brogan coalescing in front of him. Before the phantom was entirely realized, while the body was still lumpy and half detailed, and although the face wasn't finished, the mouth nevertheless opened and the replica of Gordy spoke, though not with Gordy's voice. It was Stu Wargle's voice, instead, a supremely disconcerting touch.

'Go to the lab,' it said, its mouth only half formed, yet speaking with perfect clarity. 'I will show you everything you want to see, Dr Flyte. You are my Matthew. My Luke. Go to the lab. Go to the lab.'

The unfinished image of Gordy Brogan dissolved almost as if it had been composed of smoke.

The extruded man-size lump of gnarled tissue flowed back into the larger bulk behind it.

The entire pulsating, heaving mass began to surge back through the umbilical that led up the wall and into the heating duct.

How much more of it lies there within the walls of the inn? Bryce wondered uneasily. How much more of it waits down in the storm drains? How large *is* the god Proteus?

As the thing oozed away from them, oddly shaped orifices opened all over it, none bigger than a human mouth, a dozen of them, two dozen, and noises issued forth: the chirruping of birds, the cries of sea gulls, the buzzing of bees, snarling, hissing, child-sweet laughter, distant singing, the hooting of an owl, the maraca-like warning of a rattlesnake. Those noises, all ringing out simultaneously, blended into an unpleasant, irritating, decidedly ominous chorus.

Then the shape-changer was gone back through the wall vent. Only Frank's severed head and the bent grille from the heating duct remained as proof that something Hell-born had been here.

According to the electric wall clock, the time was 3.44.

The night was nearly gone.

How long until dawn? Bryce wondered. An hour and a half? An hour and forty minutes or more?

He supposed it didn't matter.

He didn't expect to live to see the sunrise, anyway.

37

EGO

THE DOOR of the second lab stood wide open. The lights were on.
The computer screens glowed. Everything was ready for them.

Jenny had been trying to hold to the belief that they could still
somehow resist, that they still had a chance, however small, of
influencing the course of events. Now that fragile, cherished belief
had been blown away. They were powerless. They would do only
what *it* wanted, go only where *it* allowed.

The six of them crowded inside the lab.

'Now what?' Lisa asked.

'We wait.' Jenny said.

Flyte, Sara, and Lisa sat down at the three bright video display
terminals. Jenny and Bryce leaned against a counter, and Tal stood
by the open door, looking out.

Fog foamed past the door.

We *wait*, Jenny had told Lisa. But waiting wasn't easy. Each
second was an ordeal of tense and morbid expectations.

Where would death come from next?

And in what fantastic form?

And to whom would it come this time?

At last Bryce said, 'Dr Flyte, if these prehistoric creatures have
survived for millions of years in underground lakes and rivers, in
the deepest sea trenches . . . or wherever . . . and if they surface to
feed . . . then why aren't mass disappearances more common?'

Flyte pulled at his chin with one thin, long-fingered hand and said, 'Because it seldom encounters human beings.'

'But why seldom?'

'I doubt that more than a handful of them have survived. There may have been a climatic change that killed off most and drove the few remaining into a subterranean and suboceanic existence.'

'Nevertheless, even a few of them—'

'A rare few,' Flyte stressed, 'scattered over the earth. And perhaps they feed only infrequently. Consider the boa constrictor, for example. That snake takes nourishment only once every few weeks. So perhaps this thing feeds irregularly, as seldom as once every several months or even once every couple of years. Its metabolism is so utterly different from ours that almost anything may be possible.'

'Could its life cycle include periods of hibernation?' Sara asked. 'Lasting not just a season or two, but years at a time.'

'Yes, yes,' Flyte said, nodding. 'Very good. Very good, indeed. That would also help explain why the thing only infrequently encounters men. And let me remind you that mankind inhabits less than one per cent of the planet's surface. Even if the ancient enemy did feed with some frequency, it would hardly ever run up against us.'

'And when it *did*,' Bryce said, 'it would very likely encounter us at sea because the largest part of the earth is covered with water.'

'Exactly,' Flyte said. 'And if it seized everyone aboard a ship, there wouldn't be witnesses; we'd never know about *those* contacts. The history of the sea *is* replete with stories of vanished ships and ghost ships from which the crews disappeared.'

'The *Mary Celeste*,' Lisa said, glancing at Jenny.

Jenny remembered when her sister had first mentioned the *Mary Celeste*. It had been early Sunday evening, when they had gone next door to the Santinis' house and had found the table set for dinner.

'The *Mary Celeste* is a famous case,' Flyte agreed. 'But it's not unique. Literally hundreds upon hundreds of ships have vanished under mysterious circumstances ever since reliable nautical records have been kept. In good weather, in peacetime, with no "logical" explanation. In aggregate, the missing crews must surely number in the tens of thousands.'

From his post by the open door of the lab, Tal said, 'That area of the Caribbean where so many ships have disappeared . . .'

'The Bermuda Triangle,' Lisa said quickly.

'Yeah,' Tal said. 'Could that be . . . ?'

'The work of a shape-changer?' Flyte said. 'Yes. Possibly. Over the years, there have been a few mysterious depletions of fish populations in that area, too, so the ancient enemy theory is applicable.'

Data flashed up on the video displays: I SEND YOU A SPIDER.

'What's that supposed to mean?' Flyte asked.

Sara tapped the keys: CLARIFY.

The same message repeated: I SEND YOU A SPIDER.

CLARIFY

LOOK AROUND YOU.

Jenny saw it first. It was poised on the work surface to the left of the VDT that Sara was using. A black spider. Not as big as a tarantula, but much bigger than an ordinary spider.

It curled into a lump, retracting its long legs. It changed. First, it shimmered dully. The black colouration was replaced by the familiar grey-maroon-red of the shape-changer. The spider form melted away. The lump of amorphous flesh assumed another, longer shape: it became a cockroach, a hideously ugly, unrealistically large cockroach. And then a small mouse, with twitching whiskers.

New words appeared on the video displays.

HERE IS THE TISSUE SAMPLE THAT YOU REQUESTED, DR FLYTE.

'It's so damned cooperative all of a sudden,' Tal said.

'Because it knows that nothing we find out about it will help us destroy it,' Bryce said morosely.

'There must be a way,' Lisa insisted. 'We can't lose hope. We just can't.'

Jenny stared in wonder as the mouse dissolved into a wad of shapeless tissue.

THIS IS MY SACRED BODY, WHICH I GIVE UNTO THEE, it told them, continuing to mock them with religious references.

The lump rippled and churned within itself, formed minute concavities and convexities, nodules and holes. It was unable to remain entirely still, just as the larger mass, which had killed Frank Autry, had seemed unable or unwilling to remain motionless for even a second.

BEHOLD THE MIRACLE OF MY FLESH, FOR IT IS ONLY IN ME THAT THOU CANST ACHIEVE IMMORTALITY. NOT IN GOD. NOT IN CHRIST. ONLY IN ME.

'I see what you mean about it taking pleasure in mockery and ridicule,' Flyte said.

The screen blinked. A new message flashed up: YOU MAY TOUCH IT.

Blink.

YOU WILL NOT BE HARMED IF YOU TOUCH IT.

No one moved towards the quivering wad of strange flesh.

TAKE SAMPLES FOR YOUR TESTS. DO WITH IT WHAT YOU WISH.

Blink.

I WANT YOU TO UNDERSTAND ME.

Blink.

I WANT YOU TO KNOW THE WONDERS OF ME.

'It isn't only self-aware; it appears to possess a well-developed ego, too,' Flyte said.

Finally, hesitantly, Sara Yamaguchi reached out, put the tip of one finger against the small glob of protoplasm.

'It's not warm like our flesh. Cool. Cool and a little . . . greasy.'

The small piece of the shape-changer quivered agitatedly.

Sara quickly pulled her hand away. 'I'll need to section it.'

'Yeah,' Jenny said, 'we'll need one or two thin cross-sections for light microscopy.'

'And another one for the electron miscroscope,' Sara said. 'And a larger piece for analysis of the chemical and mineral composition.'

Through the computer, the ancient enemy encouraged them.

PROCEED, PROCEED, PROCEED,

PROCEED, PROCEED, PROCEED, PROCEED

38

A FIGHTING CHANCE

Tendrils of fog slipped through the open door, into the lab.

Sara was seated at a work counter, hunched over a microscope. 'Incredible,' she said softly.

Jenny was seated at another microscope, beside Sara, examining another slide of the shape-changer's tissue. 'I've never seen cellular structure like this.'

'It's impossible . . . yet here it is,' Sara said.

Bryce stood behind Jenny. He was eager for her to let him have a look at the slide. It wouldn't mean much to him, of course. He wouldn't know the difference between normal and abnormal cellular structure. Nevertheless, he *had* to have a look at it.

Although Dr Flyte was a scientist, he wasn't a biologist; cell structure would mean little more to him than it would to Bryce. Yet he, too, was eager to take a peek. He hung over Sara's shoulder, waiting. Tal and Lisa remained nearby, equally anxious to get a look at the devil on a glass slide.

Still peering intently into the microscope, Sara said, 'Most of the tissue is *without* cell structure.'

'The same with this sample,' Jenny said.

'But all organic matter must have cell structure,' Sara said. 'Cell structure is virtually a definition of organic matter, a requisite of all living tissue, plant or animal.'

'Most of this stuff looks inorganic to me,' Jenny said, 'but of course it can't be.'

Bryce said, 'Yeah. We know all too well how alive it is.'

'I do see cells here and there,' Jenny said. 'Not many; a few.'

'A few in this sample, too,' Sara said. 'But each cell appears to exist independently of the others.'

'They're widely separated, all right,' Jenny said. 'They're just sort of swimming in a sea of undifferentiated matter.'

'Very flexible cell walls,' Sara said. 'A trifurcated nucleus. That's odd. And it occupies about half the interior cell space.'

'What's that mean?' Bryce asked. 'Is it important?'

'I don't know if it's important or not,' Sara said, leaning away from the microscope and scowling. 'I just don't know what to make of it.'

On all three computer screens, a question flashed up: DID YOU NOT EXPECT THE FLESH OF SATAN TO BE MYSTERIOUS?

The shape-changer had sent them a mouse-size sample of its flesh, but thus far not all of it had been needed for the various tests. Half remained in a petri dish on the counter.

It quivered gelatinously.

It became a spider again and circled the dish restlessly.

It became a cockroach and darted back and forth for a while.

It became a slug.

A cricket.

A green beetle with a lacy red pattern on its shell.

Bryce and Dr Flyte were seated in front of the microscopes now, while Lisa and Tal waited their turn.

Jenny and Sara stood in front of a VDT, where a computer-enhanced representation of an electron microscope autoscan was underway. Sara had directed the system to zero in and fix upon the nucleus in one of the shape-changer's widely scattered cells.

'Any ideas?' Jenny asked.

Sara nodded but didn't look away from the screen. 'At this point, I can only make an educated guess. But I'd say the undifferentiated matter, which is clearly the bulk of the creature, is the stuff that can imprint any cell structure it wants; it's the tissue that mimics. It can form itself into dog cells, rabbit cells, human cells . . . But when the creature is at rest, that tissue has no cellular structure of its own. As for the few scattered cells we see . . . well, they must somehow control the amorphous tissue. The cells give the orders; they produce enzymes or chemical signals which tell the unstructured tissue what it should become.'

'So those scattered cells would remain unchanged at all times, regardless of what form the creature took.'

'Yes. So it would seem. If the shape-changer became a dog, for instance, and if we took a sample of the dog's tissue, we'd see dog cells. But here and there, spread through the sample, we'd come across these flexible cells with their trifurcated nuclei, and we'd have proof that it wasn't really a dog at all.'

'So does this tell us anything that'll help us save ourselves?' Jenny asked.

'Not that I can see.'

In the petri dish, the scrap of amorphous flesh had assumed the identity of a spider once again. Then the spider dissolved, and there were dozens of tiny ants, swarming across the floor of the dish and across one another. The ants rejoined to form a single creature – a worm. The worm wriggled for a moment and became a very large sow bug. The sow bug became a beetle. The pace of the changes seemed to be speeding up.

'What about a brain?' Jenny wondered aloud.

Sara said, 'What do you mean?'

'The thing must have a centre of intellect. Surely, its memory, knowledge, reasoning abilities aren't stored in those scattered cells.'

'You're probably right,' Sara said. 'Somewhere in the creature, there's most likely an organ that's analogous to the human brain. Not the same as our brain, of course. Very, very different. But with some similar functions. It probably controls the cells we've seen, and they in turn control the formless protoplasm.'

With growing excitement, Jenny said, 'The brain cells would have at least one important thing in common with the scattered cells in the amorphous tissue: they would *never* change form themselves.'

'That's most likely true. It's hard to imagine how memory, logical function, and intelligence could be stored in any tissue that didn't have a relatively rigid, permanent cell structure.'

'So the brain would be vulnerable,' Jenny said.

Hope crept into Sara's eyes.

Jenny said, 'If the brain's not amorphous tissue, then it can't repair itself when it's damaged. Punch a hole in it, and the hole will *stay* there. The brain will be permanently damaged. If it's damaged extensively enough, it won't be able to control the amorphous tissue that forms its body, and the body will die, too.'

Sara stared at her. 'Jenny, I think maybe you've got something.'

Bryce said, 'If we could locate the brain and fire a few shots into it, we'd stop the thing. But how do we locate it? Something tells me the shape-changer keeps its brain well protected, hidden far away from us, underground.'

Jenny's excitement faded. Bryce was right. The brain might be its weak spot, but they'd have no opportunity to test that theory.

Sara pored over the results of the mineral and chemical analyzes of the tissue sample.

'An extremely varied list of hydrocarbons,' she said. 'And some of them are more than trace elements. A very high hydrocarbon content.'

404

'Carbons are a basic element of living tissue,' Jenny said. 'What's different about this?'

'Degree,' Sara said. 'There's such an abundance of carbon in such various forms . . .'

'Does that help us somehow?'

'I don't know,' Sara said thoughtfully. She riffled through the print-out, looking at the rest of the data.

Sow bug.

Grasshopper.

Caterpillar.

Beetle. Ants. Caterpillar. Sow bug.

Spider, earwig, cockroach, centipede, spider.

Beetle-worm-spider-snail-earwig.

Lisa stared at the lump of tissue in the petri dish. It was going through a rapid series of changes, much faster than before, faster and faster by the minute.

Something was wrong.

'Petrolatum,' Sara said.

Bryce said, 'What's that?'

'Petroleum jelly,' Jenny said.

Tal said, 'You mean . . . like Vaseline?'

And Flyte said to Sara. 'But surely you're not saying the amorphous tissue is anything as simple as petrolatum.'

'No, no, no,' Sara said quickly. 'Of course not. This is living tissue. But there are similarities in the ratio of hydrocarbons. The composition of the tissue is far more complex than the composition of petrolatum, of course. An even longer list of minerals and chemicals than you'd find in the human body. An array of acids and alka-lines . . . I can't begin to figure out how it makes use of nourishment, how it respires, how it functions without a circulatory system, without any apparent nervous system, or how it builds new tissue without using a cellular format. But these extremely high hydrocarbon values . . .'

Her voice trailed away. Her eyes appeared to swim out of focus, so that she was no longer actually looking at the test results.

Watching the geneticist, Tal had the feeling that she was suddenly excited about something. It didn't show in her face or in any aspect of her body or posture. Nevertheless, there was definitely a new air about her that told him she was onto something important.

Tal glanced at Bryce. Their eyes met. He saw that Bryce, too, was aware of the change in Sara.

Almost unconsciously, Tal crossed his fingers.

'Better come look at this,' Lisa said urgently.

She was standing by the petri dish that contained the portion of the tissue sample they hadn't yet used.

'Hurry, come here!' Lisa said when they didn't immediately respond.

Jenny and the others gathered around and stared at the thing in the petri dish.

Grasshopper-worm-centipede-snail-earwig.

'It just goes faster and faster and faster,' Lisa said.

Spider-worm-centipede-spider-snail-spider-worm-spider-worm . . .

And then even faster.

. . .spiderwormspiderwormspiderwormspider . . .

'It's only half-changed into a worm before it starts changing back into a spider again,' Lisa said. 'Frantic-like. See? Something's happening to it.'

'Looks as if it's lost control, gone crazy,' Tal said.

'Having some sort of breakdown,' Flyte said.

Abruptly, the small wad of amorphous tissue lost its jellid consistency. A milky fluid seeped from it; the wad collapsed into a runny pile of lifeless mush.

It didn't move.

It didn't take on another form.

Jenny wanted to touch it; didn't dare.

Sara picked up a small lab spoon, poked at the stuff in the dish.

It still didn't move.

She stirred it.

The tissue liquefied even further, but otherwise did not respond.

'It's dead,' Flyte said softly.

Bryce seemed electrified by this development. He turned to Sara. 'What was in the petri dish before you put the tissue sample there?'

'Nothing.'

'There must've been a residue.'

'No.'

'Think, dammit. Our lives depend on this.'

'There was nothing in the dish. I took it from the sterilizer.'

'A trace of some chemical . . .'

'It was perfectly clean.'

'Wait, wait, wait. Something in the dish must've reacted with the shape-changer's tissue,' Bryce said. 'Right? Isn't that dear?'

'And whatever was in the dish,' Tal, said, *that's* our weapon.'

'It's the stuff that'll kill the shape-changer,' Lisa said.

'Not necessarily,' Jenny said, hating to shatter the girl's hopes.

'Sounds too easy,' Flyte agreed, combing his wild white hair with a trembling hand. 'Let's not leap to conclusions.'

'Especially when there're other possibilities,' Jenny said.

'Such as?' Bryce asked.

'Well . . . we know that the main mass of the creature can shed pieces of itself in about any form it chooses, can direct the activities of those detached parts, and can summon them back the way it summoned the part of itself that it sent to kill Gordy. But now suppose that a detached portion of the shape-changer can only survive for a relatively short period of time on its own, away from the mother-body. Suppose the amorphous tissue needs a steady supply

407

of a particular enzyme in order to maintain its cohesiveness, an enzyme that *isn't* manufactured in those independently situated control cells that're scattered throughout the tissue—'

'—an enzyme that's produced only by the shape-changer's brain,' Sara said, picking up on Jenny's chain of thought.

'Exactly,' Jenny said. 'So . . . any detached portion would have to reintegrate itself with the main mass in order to replenish its supply of that vital enzyme, or whatever the substance may be.'

'That's not unlikely,' Sara said. 'After all, the human brain produces enzymes and hormones without which our own bodies wouldn't be able to survive. Why shouldn't the shape-changer's brain fulfil a similar function?'

'All right,' Bryce said. 'What does this discovery mean to us?'

'If it *is* a discovery and not just a wrong-headed guess,' Jenny said, 'then it means we could definitely destroy the entire shape-changer if we could destroy the brain. The creature wouldn't be able to separate into several parts and crawl away and go on living in other incarnations. Without the essential brain-manufactured enzymes – or hormones or whatever – the separate parts would all eventually dissolve into lifeless mush, the way the thing in the petri dish has just done.'

Bryce sagged with disappointment. 'We're back at square one. We have to locate its brain before we have any chance of striking a death blow, but the thing's never going to let us do that.'

'We're *not* back to square one,' Sara said, pointing to the lifeless slime in the petri dish. 'This tells us something else that's important.'

'What?' Bryce asked, his voice heavy with frustration. 'Is it something useful, something that could save us – or is it just another item of bizarre information?'

Sara said, 'We now know the amorphous tissue exists in a delicate chemical balance *that can be disrupted.*'

She let that sink in.

The deep worry lines in Bryce's face softened a bit.

Sara said, 'The flesh of the shape-changer can be damaged. It can be killed. Here's proof in the petri dish.'

'How do we use that knowledge?' Tal asked. 'How do we disrupt the chemical balance?'

'That's what we've got to find out,' Sara said.

'Do you have any ideas?' Lisa asked the geneticist.

'No,' Sara said. 'None.'

But Jenny suddenly had the feeling that Sara Yamaguchi was lying.

Sara wanted to tell them about the plan that had occurred to her, but she couldn't say a word. For one thing, her strategy offered only a fragile thread of hope. She didn't want to raise their hopes unrealistically and then see them dashed again. More importantly, if she told them what was on her mind, and if by some miracle she actually had found a way to destroy the shape-changer, *it* would hear what she said, and it would know her plans, and it would stop her. There was no place where she could safely discuss her thoughts with Jenny and Bryce and the others. Their best hope was to keep the ancient enemy smug and complacent.

But she had to buy some time, several hours, in which to set her plan in motion. The shape-changer was millions and millions of years old, virtually immortal. What were a few hours to this creature? Surely, it would comply with her request. Surely.

She sat down at one of the computer terminals, her eyes burning with weariness. She needed sleep. They all needed sleep. The night was nearly gone. She wiped one hand across her face, as if she could slough off her weariness. Then she typed: ARE YOU THERE?

YES.

WE HAVE COMPLETED A NUMBER OF TESTS, she typed as the other crowded around her.

I KNOW, it replied.

WE ARE FASCINATED. THERE IS MORE WE WISH TO KNOW.

OF COURSE.

THERE ARE OTHER TESTS WE WANT TO CONDUCT.

WHY?

IN ORDER THAT WE CAN KNOW MORE ABOUT YOU.

CLARIFY, it answered teasingly.

Sara thought for a moment, then typed: DR FLYTE NEEDS ADDITIONAL DATA IF HE IS TO WRITE ABOUT YOU WITH AUTHORITY.

HE IS MY MATTHEW.

HE NEEDS MORE DATA TO TELL YOUR STORY AS IT SHOULD BE TOLD.

It flashed back a three-line response in the centre of the video display:

A FLOURISH OF TRUMPETS

THE GREATEST STORY EVER TOLD

A FLOURISH OF TRUMPETS

Sara couldn't be sure if it was merely mocking them or whether its ego was actually so large that it could seriously equate its own story with the story of Christ.

The screen blinked. New words appeared: PROCEED WITH YOUR TESTS.

WE WILL NEED TO SEND FOR MORE LAB EQUIPMENT.

WHY? YOU HAVE A FULLY EQUIPPED LAB.

Sara's hands were moist. She blotted them on her jeans before tapping out her answer.

THIS LAB IS FULLY EQUIPPED ONLY FOR A NARROW AREA OF SCIENTIFIC ENQUIRY: THE ANALYSIS OF CHEMICAL AND BIOLOGICAL WARFARE AGENTS. WE DID NOT ANTICIPATE ENCOUNTERING A BEING OF YOUR NATURE. WE MUST HAVE OTHER EQUIPMENT IN ORDER TO DO A PROPER JOB.

PROCEED.

IT WILL TAKE SEVERAL HOURS TO HAVE THE EQUIPMENT SENT HERE, she told it.

PROCEED.

She stared at the word, green on green, hardly daring to believe that gaining more time would be this easy.

She tapped the keys: WE WILL NEED TO RETURN TO THE INN AND USE THE TELEPHONE THERE.

PROCEED, YOU BORING BITCH. PROCEED, PROCEED, PRO-CEED, PROCEED.

Her hands were damp again. She wiped them on her jeans and stood up.

From the way the others were looking at her, she realized that they knew she was hiding something, and they understood why she was remaining silent about it.

But how did they know? Was she that obvious? And if they knew, did *it* know, too?

She cleared her throat. 'Let's go,' she said shakily.

'Let's go,' Sara Yamaguchi said shakily, but Timothy said, 'Wait. Just a minute or two, please. There's something I've got to try.'

He sat down at a computer terminal. Although he had snatched some sleep on the plane, his mind was not as sharp as it ought to be. He shook his head and took several deep breaths, then typed: THIS IS TIMOTHY FLYTE.

I KNOW.

WE MUST HAVE A DIALOGUE.

PROCEED.

MUST WE DO IT THROUGH THE COMPUTER?

IT IS BETTER THAN A BURNING BUSH.

For a second or two, Timothy didn't understand what it meant. When he got the joke, he almost laughed aloud. The damned thing had its own perverse sense of humour. He typed: YOUR SPECIES AND MINE SHOULD LIVE IN PEACE.

411

WHY?

BECAUSE WE SHARE THE EARTH.

AS THE FARMER SHARES THE FARM WITH HIS CATTLE. YOU ARE MY CATTLE.

WE ARE THE ONLY TWO INTELLIGENT SPECIES ON EARTH.

YOU THINK YOU KNOW SO MUCH. IN FACT YOU KNOW SO LITTLE.

WE SHOULD COOPERATE, Flyte persisted doggedly.

YOU ARE INFERIOR TO ME.

WE HAVE MUCH TO LEARN FROM EACH OTHER.

I HAVE NOTHING TO LEARN FROM YOUR KIND.

WE MAY BE MORE CLEVER THAN YOU BELIEVE.

YOU ARE MORTAL. IS THAT NOT TRUE?

YES.

TO ME, YOUR LIVES ARE AS BRIEF AND UNIMPORTANT AS THE LIVES OF MAYFLIES SEEM TO YOU.

IF THAT IS THE WAY YOU FEEL, WHY DO YOU CARE WHETHER OR NOT I WRITE ABOUT YOU?

IT AMUSES ME THAT ONE OF YOUR SPECIES HAS THEORIZED MY EXISTENCE. IT IS LIKE A PET MONKEY LEARNING A DIFFICULT TRICK.

I DO NOT BELIEVE WE ARE YOUR INFERIORS, Flyte typed gamely.

CATTLE.

I BELIEVE YOU WANT TO BE WRITTEN ABOUT BECAUSE YOU HAVE ACQUIRED A VERY HUMAN EGO.

YOU ARE WRONG.

I BELIEVE THAT YOU WERE NOT AN INTELLIGENT CREATURE UNTIL YOU BEGAN FEEDING UPON INTELLIGENT CREATURES, UPON MEN.

YOUR IGNORANCE DISAPPOINTS ME.

Timothy continued to challenge it: I BELIEVE THAT ALONG WITH KNOWLEDGE AND MEMORY THAT WAS ABSORBED FROM

YOUR HUMAN VICTIMS, YOU ALSO ACQUIRED INTELLIGENCE.
YOU OWE US FOR YOUR OWN EVOLUTION.

It did not reply.

Timothy cleared the screen and typed more: YOUR MIND SEEMS
TO HAVE A VERY HUMAN STRUCTURE — EGO, SUPEREGO, AND
SO FORTH.

CATTLE, it replied.

Blink.

PIGS, it said.

Blink.

GROVELLING ANIMALS, it said.

Blink.

YOU BORE ME, it said.

And then all the screens went dark.

Timothy leaned back in his chair and sighed.

Sheriff Hammond said, 'Nice try, Dr Flyte.'

'Such arrogance,' Timothy said.

'Befitting a god,' Dr Paige said. 'And that's more or less how it
thinks of itself.'

'In a way,' Lisa Paige said, 'that's what it really *is*.'

'Yeah,' Tal Whitman said, 'to all intents and purposes, it might
as well *be* a god. It has all the powers of a god, doesn't it?'

'Or a devil,' Lisa said.

Beyond the streetlamps and above the fog, the night was grey now.
The first vague glow of dawn had sparked the far end of the sky.

Sara wished Dr Flyte hadn't challenged the shape-changer so
boldly. She was worried that he had antagonized it, and that now it
would renege on its promise to give them more time.

During the short walk from the field lab to the Hilltop Inn, she
kept expecting a grotesque phantom to lope or scuttle at them from
out of the fog. It must not take them now. Not now. Not when there
was, at long last, a glimmer of hope.

413

Elsewhere in town, off in the fog and shadows, there were strange animal sounds, eerie ululating cries like nothing that Sara had ever heard before. *It* was still engaged upon its ceaseless mimicry. A hellish shriek, uncomfortably close at hand, caused the survivors to bunch together.

But they were not attacked.

The streets, although not silent, were still. There was not even a breeze; the mist hung motionless in the air.

Nothing waited for them inside the inn, either.

At the central operations desk, Sara sat down and dialled the number of the CBW Civilian Defence Unit's home base in Dugway, Utah.

Jenny, Bryce and the others gathered around to listen.

Because of the ongoing crisis in Snowfield, there was not just the usual night-duty sergeant at the Dugway headquarters. Captain Daniel Tersch, a physician in the Army Medical Corps, a specialist in containing contagious disease, third in charge of the unit, was standing by to direct any support operations, that might become necessary.

Sara told him about their latest discoveries – the microscopic examinations of the shape-changer's tissue, the results of the various mineral and chemical analyzes – and Tersch was fascinated, though this was well beyond his field of expertise.

'Petrolatum?' he asked at one point, surprised by what she had told him.

'The amorphous tissue resembles petrolatum only in that it has a somewhat similar mix of hydrocarbons that register very high values. But of course it's much more complex, much more sophisticated.'

She stressed this particular discovery, for she wanted to be certain that Tersch passed it along to other scientists on the CBW team at Dugway. If another geneticist or a biochemist were to consider this data and then look at the list of materials she was going to ask for, he would almost certainly know what her plan was. If someone in the CBW unit *did* get her message, he would assemble the weapon for her before it was sent into Snowfield, sparing her the time-consuming and dangerous job of assembling it with the shape-changer looking over her shoulder.

She couldn't just tell Tersch what she had in mind, for she was certain the ancient enemy was listening in. There was an odd, faint hissing on the line . . .

Finally she spoke of her need for additional laboratory equipment. 'Most of this stuff can be borrowed from university and industry labs right here in Northern California,' she told Tersch. 'I just need you to use the army's manpower, transportation, and authority to put together the package and get it to me as quickly as possible.'

'What do you need?' Tersch asked. 'Just tell me, and you'll have it in five or six hours.'

She recited a list of equipment in which she actually had no real interest, and then she finished by saying, 'I will also need as much of the fourth generation of Dr Chakrabarty's little miracle as it's feasible to send. And I'll need two or three compressed-air dispersal units, too.'

'Who's Chakrabarty?' Tersch asked, puzzled.

'You wouldn't know him.'

'What's his little miracle? What do you mean?'

'Just write down Chakrabarty, fourth generation.' She spelled the name for him.

'I haven't the vaguest idea what this is,' he said.

Good, Sara thought with considerable relief. Perfect.

If Tersch had known what Dr Ananda Chakrabarty's little miracle was, he might have blurted out something before she could stop him. And the ancient enemy would have been forewarned.

'It's outside your area of specialization,' she said. 'There's no

415

reason you should recognize the name or know the device.' She spoke hurriedly now, trying to move away from the subject as smoothly and as rapidly as possible. 'I don't have time to explain it, Dr Tersch. Other people in the CBW programme will definitely know what it is I need. Let's get moving on this. Dr Flyte very much wants to continue his studies of the creature, and he needs all the items on my list just as soon as he can get them. Five or six hours, you said?'

'That should do it,' Tersch said. 'How should we deliver?'

Sara glanced at Bryce. He wouldn't want to risk yet another one of his men in order to have the cargo driven into town. To Captain Tersch, she said, 'Can it be brought in by army helicopter?'

'Will do.'

'Better tell the pilot not to try landing. The shape-changer might think we were trying to escape. It would almost certainly attack the crew and kill all of us the moment the chopper touched down. Just have them hover and lower the package on a cable.'

'This could be quite a large bundle,' Tersch said.

'I'm sure they can lower it,' she said.

'Well . . . all right. I'll get on it right away. And good luck to you.'

'Thanks,' Sara said. 'We'll need it.'

She hung up.

'All of a sudden, five or six hours seems like a long time,' Jenny said.

'An eternity,' Sara said.

They were all clearly eager to hear about her scheme but knew it couldn't be discussed. However, even in their silence, Sara detected a new note of optimism.

Don't get your hopes too high, she thought anxiously.

There was a chance that her plan had no merit. In fact, the odds were stacked against them. And if the plan failed, the shape-changer would know what they had intended to do, and it would wipe them out in some particularly brutal fashion.

Outside, dawn had come.

The fog had lost its pale glow. Now the mist was dazzling, white-white, shining with refractions of the morning sunlight.

39

THE APPARITION

FLETCHER KALE woke in time to see the first light of dawn.

The forest was still mostly dark. Milky daylight speared down in shafts, through scattered holes in the green canopy that was formed by the densely interlaced branches of the mammoth trees. The sunshine was diffused by the fog, muted, revealing little.

He had passed the night in the Jeep station wagon that belonged to Jake Johnson. Now he got out and stood beside the Jeep, listening to the woods, alert for the sounds of pursuit.

Last night, a few minutes after eleven o'clock, heading for Jake Johnson's secret retreat, Kale had driven up the Mount Larson Road, had swung the Jeep onto the unpaved fire lane that led up the wild north slopes of Snow-top – and had run smack into trouble. Within twenty feet, his headlights picked up signs posted on both sides of the roadway – large red letters on a white background read QUARANTINE. Going too fast, he swung around a bend, and directly ahead of him was a police blockade, one county cruiser angled across the road. Two deputies started getting out of the car.

He remembered hearing about a quarantine zone encircling Snowfield, but he'd thought it was in effect only on the other side of the mountain. He hit the brakes, wishing that, for once, he'd paid more attention to the news.

There was an APB circulating with his photograph. These men would recognize him, and within an hour he'd be back in jail.

Surprise was his only hope. They wouldn't be expecting trouble. Maintaining a quarantine checkpoint would be easy, lulling duty.

The HK91 assault rifle was on the seat beside Kale, covered with a blanket. He grabbed the gun, got out of the Jeep, and opened fire on the cops. The semi-automatic weapon chattered, and the deputies did a brief, erratic dance of death, spectral figures in the fog.

He rolled the bodies into a ditch, pulled the patrol car out of the way, and drove the Jeep past the checkpoint. Then he went back and repositioned the car, so that it would appear that the deputies' killer hadn't continued up the mountain.

He drove three miles up the rugged fire lane, until he came to an even more rugged, overgrown track. A mile later, at the end of that trail, he parked the Jeep in a tunnel of brush and climbed out.

In addition to the HK91, he had a sackful of other guns from Johnson's closet, plus the $63,440, which was distributed through the seven zippered pockets in the hunting jacket he wore. The only other thing he carried was a flashlight, and that was really all he needed because the limestone caves would be well stocked with supplies.

The last quarter of a mile had to be covered on foot, and he had intended to finish the journey right away, but he had quickly found that even with the flashlight the forest was confusing at night, in the fog. Getting lost was almost a certainty. Once lost in this wilderness, you could wander in circles, within yards of your destination, never discovering how close you were to salvation. After only a few paces, Kale had turned back to the Jeep to wait for daylight.

Even if the two dead deputies at the blockade were discovered before morning, and even if the cops figured the killer had come onto the mountain, they wouldn't launch a manhunt until first light. By the time the posse reached here tomorrow, Kale would be snug in the caves.

He had slept on the front seat of the Jeep. It wasn't the Plaza Hotel, but it was more comfortable than jail.

Now, standing beside the Jeep in the wan light of early morning, he listened for the sounds of a search party. He heard nothing. He hadn't really expected to hear anything. It wasn't his destiny to rot in prison. His future was golden. He was sure of that.

He yawned, stretched, then pissed against the trunk of a big pine.

Thirty minutes later, when there was more light, he followed the footpath he hadn't been able to find last night. And he saw something that hadn't been obvious in the dark; the brush was extensively trampled. People had been through here recently.

He proceeded with caution, cradling the HK91 in his right arm, ready to blow away anyone who might try to rush him.

In less than half an hour, he came out of the trees, into the clearing around the log cabin – and saw why the footpath had been trampled. Eight motorcycles were lined up alongside the cabin, big Harleys, all emblazoned with the name DEMON CHROME.

Gene Terr's bunch of misfits. Not all of them. About half the gang, by the looks of it.

Kale crouched against an outcropping of limestone and studied the mist-wrapped cabin. No one in sight. He quietly fished in the laundry bag, located a fresh magazine for the HK91, rammed it in place.

How had Terr and his vicious playmates got here? A two-wheel trip up the mountain would have been difficult, wildly dangerous, a nerve-twisting bit of motor-cross. Of course, those crazy bastards thrived on danger.

But what the devil were they *doing* here? How had they found the cabin, and why had they come?

As he listened for a voice, for some indication of where the

420

cyclists were and what they were up to, Kale realized there weren't even any animal or insect sounds. No birds. Absolutely nothing. Spooky.

Then, behind him, a rustle in the brush. A soft sound. In the preternatural silence, it might as well have been a cannon shot.

Kale had been kneeling on the ground. With catlike speed he fell on his side, rolled onto his back, brought up the HK91.

He was prepared to kill, but he wasn't prepared for what he saw. It was Jake Johnson, about twenty-five feet away, coming out of the trees and fog, grinning. Naked. Utterly bare-assed.

Other movement. To the left of Johnson. Further along the treeline.

Kale caught it from the corner of his eye and whipped his head around, swung the rifle in that direction.

Another man came out of the woods, through the mist, with the tall grass fluttering around his bare legs. He was also naked. And grinning broadly.

But that wasn't the worst of it. The worst part was that the second man was also Jake Johnson.

Kale looked from one to the other, startled and baffled. They were as perfectly alike as a set of identical twins.

But Jake was an only child – wasn't he? Kale had never heard anything about a twin.

A third figure advanced from the shadows beneath the spreading boughs of a huge spruce. This one, too, was Jake Johnson.

Kale couldn't breathe.

Maybe there was an outside chance that Johnson had a twin, but he damned well wasn't one of triplets.

Something was horribly wrong. Suddenly, it wasn't just the impossible triplets that frightened Kale. Suddenly, everything seemed menacing: the forest, the mist, the stony contours of the mountainside . . .

The three look-alikes walked slowly up the slope on which Kale was sprawled, closing in from different angles. Their eyes were strange, and their mouths were cruel.

Kale scrambled to his feet, heart lurching. 'Stop right there!'

But they didn't stop, even though he brandished the assault rifle.

'Who are you? What are you? What *is* this?' Kale demanded.

They didn't answer. Kept coming. Like zombies.

He grabbed the bag that was filled with guns, and he backed rapidly and clumsily away from the nightmarish trio.

No. Not a trio any more. A quartet. Downslope, a fourth Jake Johnson came out of the threes, stark naked like the rest.

Kale's fear trembled on the edge of panic.

The four moved towards Kale with hardly a sound; dried leaves underfoot; nothing else. They made no complaint about the stones and sharp weeds and prickly burrs that must have hurt their feet. One of them began to lick his lips hungrily. The others immediately began to lick their lips, too.

A quiver of icy dread went through Kale's bowels, and he wondered if he had lost his mind. But that thought was short-lived. Unfamiliar with self-doubt, he didn't know how to entertain it for long.

He dropped the laundry bag, clutched the HK91 in both hands, and opened fire, describing an arc with the spurting muzzle of the gun. The bullets hit. He saw them tear into the four men, saw the wounds burst open. But there was no blood. And as soon as the wounds blossomed, they withered; they healed, vanished within seconds.

The men kept coming.

No. Not men. Something else.

Hallucinations? Years ago, in high school, Kale had dropped a lot of acid. Now he remembered that flashbacks could plague you months – even years – after you stopped using LSD. He'd never had acid flashbacks before, but he'd heard about them. Was that what was happening here? Hallucinations?

Perhaps.

On the other hand . . . all four of the men were glistening, as if the morning mists were condensing on their bare skin, and that wasn't the sort of detail you usually noticed in a hallucination. And this entire situation was *very* different from any drug experience he'd ever known.

Still grinning, the nearest doppeigänger raised one arm, pointed at Kale. Incredibly, the flesh of that hand split and peeled away from the fingers, from the palm. The flesh actually appeared to *ooze* bloodlessly back into the arm, as if it were wax melting and running from a flame; the wrist became thicker with this tissue, and then the hand was nothing but bones, white bones. One skeletal finger pointed at Kale.

Pointed with anger, scorn and accusation.

Kale's mind reeled.

The other three look-alikes had undergone even more macabre changes. One had lost the flesh from part of his face: a cheekbone shone through, a row of teeth; the right eye, deprived of a lid and of all surrounding tissue, gleaming wetly in the calcimine socket. The third man was missing a chunk of flesh from his torso; you could see his sharp ribs and slick wet organs pulsing darkly inside. The fourth walked on one normal leg and on one leg that was only bones and tendons.

As they dosed on Kale, one of them spoke: 'Baby killer.'

Kale screamed, dropped the HK91, and ran. Stopped short when he saw two more Johnson look-alikes approaching from behind, from the cabin. Nowhere to run. Except up towards the high limestone outcroppings above the cabin. He bolted that way, gasping and wheezing, reached the brush, whimpering, waded through it to the mouth of the cave, glanced behind, saw that the six were still coming after him, and he plunged into the cave, into darkness, wishing he'd held onto his flashlight, and he put one hand against the wall, shuffled along, feeling his way, trying to recall the layout, remembering it was more or less a long tunnel ending in a series of doglegs – and suddenly he realized this might not be a safe place; it might be a trap, instead; yes, he was sure of it; they *wanted* him to come here – and he looked back, saw two decomposing men at the entrance, heard himself wail, and hurried faster, faster, into the deep blackness because there was nowhere else to go, even if it was a trap, and he scraped his hand on a sharp projection of rock, stumbled, flailed, charged on, reached the doglegs, one after the other, and then the door, and he went through, slammed it behind him, but he knew it wouldn't keep them out, and then he was aware of light, in the next chamber, towards which he now began to move in a dreamlike haze of terror, passing stacks of supplies and equipment.

The light came from a Coleman lantern.

Kale stepped into the third chamber.

In the frost-pale glow, he saw something that made him freeze. It had risen from the subterranean river, up through the cave floor, out of the hole in which Jake Johnson had rigged a water pump. It writhed. It churned, pulsated, rippled. Dark, blood-mottled flesh. Shapeless.

Wings began to form. Then melted away.

A sulphurous odour, not strong yet nauseating.

Eyes opened all over the seven-foot column of slime. They focused on Kale.

He shrank from them, backed into a wall, held onto the stone as if it were reality, a last place to grip on the precipice of madness.

Some of the eyes were human. Some were not. They fixed on him – then closed and disappeared.

Mouths opened where no mouths had been. Teeth. Fangs. Forked tongues lolled over black lips. From other mouths, worm-like tentacles erupted, wriggled in the air, withdrew. Like the wings and eyes, the mouths eventually vanished into the formless flesh.

A man sat on the floor. He was a few feet from the pulsing thing that had come up from beneath the cave, and he was seated in the penumbra of the lantern's glow, his face in shadow.

Aware that Kale had noticed him, the man leaned forward slightly, putting his face in the light. He was six feet four or taller, with long curly hair and a beard. He wore a rolled bandanna around his head. One gold earring dangled. He smiled the most peculiar smile Kale had ever seen, and he raised one hand in greeting, and on the palm of the hand was a red and yellow tattoo of an eyeball.

It was Gene Terr.

40

BIOLOGICAL WARFARE

THE ARMY helicopter arrived three and a half hours after Sara spoke to Daniel Tersch in Dugway, two hours earlier than promised. Evidently, it had been despatched from a base in California, and evidently her colleagues in the CBW programme had worked out her war plan. They had realized she didn't actually need most of the equipment she had asked for, and they had collected only what she required for the attack on the shape-changer. Otherwise, they wouldn't have been so quick.

Please, God, let it be true. Sara thought. They must have brought the right stuff. They *must* have.

It was a large, camouflage-painted chopper with two full sets of whirling blades. Hovering sixty to seventy feet above Skyline Road, it stirred the morning air, created a turbulent downdraught, and sliced up what little mist remained. It sent waves of hard sound crashing through the town.

A door slid open on the side of the helicopter, and a man leaned out of the cargo hold, looked down. He made no attempt to call to them, for the chattering blades and roaring engines would have scattered his words. Instead, he used a series of incomprehensible hand signals.

Finally Sara realized that the crew was waiting for some indication that this was the drop spot. With hand signals of her own, she urged everyone to form a circle with her, in the middle of the street.

They didn't join hands, but stood with a couple of yards between each of them. The circle had a diameter of twelve to fifteen feet.

A canvas-wrapped bundle, somewhat larger than a man, was pushed out of the chopper. It was attached to a cable, which was reeled out by an electric winch. Initially, the bundle descended slowly, then slower still, at last settling to the pavement in the centre of the circle, so gently that it seemed the chopper crewman thought they were delivering raw eggs.

Bryce broke out of the formation before the package touched down and was the first to reach it. He located the snaplink and released the cable by the time Sara and the others joined him.

As the chopper reeled in the line, it swung towards the valley below, moved off, out of the danger zone, gaining altitude as it went.

Sara crouched beside the bundle and started loosening the nylon rope that was threaded through the eyelets in the canvas. She worked feverishly and, in a few seconds, had unpacked the contents.

There were two blue cannisters bearing white stencilled words and numbers. She sighed with relief when she saw them. Her message had been properly interpreted. There were also three aerosol tank sprayers similar in size and appearance to those used to spread weed killer and insecticide on a lawn, except that these were not powered by a hand pump but by cylinders of compressed air. Each tank was equipped with a harness that made it easy to carry on the back. A flexible rubber hose, ending in a four-foot metal extension with a high-pressure nozzle, made it possible to stand twelve to fourteen feet from the target that you wished to spray.

Sara lifted one of the pressurised tanks. It was heavy, already filled with the same fluid that was in the two spare, blue cannisters.

The helicopter dwindled into the Western sky, and Lisa said, 'Sara, this isn't everything you asked for – is it?'

'This is everything we need,' Sara said evasively.

She looked around nervously, expecting to see the shape-changer rushing towards them. But there was no sign of it.

She said, 'Bryce, Tal, if you would take two of these tanks . . .'

The sheriff and his deputy grabbed two of the units, slipped their arms through the harness loops, buckled the chest straps, shrugged their shoulders to settle the tanks as comfortably as possible.

Without having been told, both men clearly realized the tanks contained a weapon that might destroy the shape-changer. Sara knew they must be eaten by curiosity, and she was impressed that they asked no questions.

She had intended to handle the third sprayer herself, but it was considerably heavier than she'd expected. Straining, she would be able to carry it, but she wouldn't be able to manoeuvre quickly. And during the next hour or so, survival would depend on speed and agility.

Someone else would have to use the third unit. Not Lisa; she was no bigger than Sara. Not Flyte; he had some arthritis in his hand, of which he'd complained last night, and he seemed frail. That left Jenny. She was only three or four inches taller than Sara, only fifteen or twenty pounds heavier, but she appeared to be in excellent physical condition. She almost certainly would be able to handle the sprayer.

Flyte protested but then relented after trying to heft the tank. 'I must be older than I think,' he said wearily.

Jenny agreed that she was the one best suited, and Sara helped her get into the harness, and they were ready for battle.

Still no sign of the shape-changer.

Sara wiped sweat from her brow. 'All right. The instant it shows itself, spray it. Don't waste a second. Spray it, saturate it, keep backing away if possible, try to draw more of it out of hiding, and spray, spray, spray.'

'Is this some sort of add – or what?' Bryce asked.

'Not add,' Sara said. 'Although the effect will be something very like acid – if it works at all.'

'So if it's not an acid,' Tal said, 'what is it?'

'A unique, highly specialized micro-organism,' Sara said.

'Germs?' Jenny asked, eyes widening in surprise.

'Yes. They're suspended in a liquid growth culture.'

'We're gonna made the shape-changer *sick*?' Lisa asked, frowning.

'I sure to God hope so,' Sara said.

Nothing moved. Nothing. But something was out there, and it was probably listening. With the ears of the cat. With the ears of the fox. With highly sensitive ears of its own special design.

'Very, very sick, if we're lucky,' Sara said. 'Because disease would seem to be the only way to kill it.'

Now their lives were at risk because *it* knew they had tricked it.

Flyte shook his head. 'But the ancient enemy's so utterly alien, so different from man and animals . . . diseases dangerous to other species would have no effect whatsoever on it.'

'Right,' Sara said. 'But this microbe isn't an ordinary disease. In fact, it isn't a disease-causing organism at all.'

Snowfield shelved down the mountain, still as a postcard painting.

Looking around uneasily, alert for movement in and around the buildings, Sara told them about Ananda Chakrabarty and his discovery.

In 1972, on behalf of Dr Chakrabarty, his employer – the General Electric Corporation – applied for the first-ever patent on a man-made bacterium. Using sophisticated cell fusion techniques, Chakrabarty had created a micro-organism that could feed upon, digest, and thereby transform the hydrocarbon compounds of crude oil.

Chakrabarty's bug had at least one obvious commercial application: it could be used to clean up oil spills at sea. The bacteria literally *ate* an oil slick, rendering it harmless to the environment.

After a series of vigorous legal challenges from many sources,

General Electric won the right to patent Chakrabarty's discovery. In June, 1980, the Supreme Court handed down a landmark decision, ruling that Chakrabarty's discovery was 'not nature's handiwork, but his own; accordingly, it's patentable subject matter'.

'Of course,' Jenny said, 'I read about the case. It was a big story that June – man competing with God and all that.'

Sara said, 'Originally, GE didn't intend to market the bug. It was a fragile organism that couldn't survive outside strictly controlled lab conditions. They applied for a patent to test the legal question, to settle the matter before other experiments in genetic engineering produced more usable and more valuable discoveries. But after the court's decision, other scientists spent a few years working with the organism, and now they have a hardier strain that'll stand up outside the lab for twelve to eighteen hours. In fact it's been on the market under the trade name Biosan-4, and it's been used successfully to clean up oil slicks all over the world.'

'And that's what's in these tanks?' Bryce asked.

'Yes. Biosan-4. In a sprayable solution.'

The town was funereal. The sun beat down from an azure sky, but the air remained chilly. In spite of the uncanny silence, Sara had the unshakable feeling that *it* was coming, that it had heard and was coming and was very, very near, indeed.

The others felt it, too. They looked around uneasily.

Sara said, 'Do you remember what we discovered when we studied the shape-changer's tissue?'

'You mean the high hydrocarbon values,' Jenny said.

'Yes. But not just hydrocarbons. All forms of carbon. Very high values all across the board.'

Tal said, 'You told us something about it being like petrolatum.'

'Not the same. But reminiscent of petrolatum in some respects,' Sara said. 'What we have here is living tissue, very alien but complex and alive. And with such extraordinarily high carbon

430

content . . . Well, what I mean is, this thing's tissue seems like an organic, metabolically active cousin of petrolatum. So I'm hoping Chakrabarty's bug will . . .'

Something is coming.

Jenny said, 'You're hoping it will eat into the shape-changer the same way it would eat into an oil slick.'

Something . . . something . . .

'Yes,' Sara said nervously. 'I'm hoping it'll attack the carbon and break down the tissue. Or at least interfere with the delicate chemical balance enough to—'

Coming, coming . .

'—uh, enough to destabilise the entire organism,' Sara finished, weighed down by a sense of impending doom.

Flyte said, 'Is that really the best chance we have?'

'I think it is.'

Where is it? Where's it coming from? Sara wondered, looking at the deserted buildings, the empty street, the motionless trees.

'Sounds awfully thin to me,' Flyte said doubtfully.

'It *is* awfully thin,' Sara said. 'It's not much of a chance, but it's the only one we've got.'

A noise. A chittering, hissing, hair-raising sound.

They froze. Waited.

But, again, the town pulled a cloak of silence around itself.

The morning sun cast its fiery reflection in some windows and glinted off the curved glass of the streetlamps. The black slate roofs looked as if they had been polished during the night; the last of the mist had condensed on those smooth surfaces, leaving a moist sheen.

Nothing moved. Nothing happened. The noise did not resume.

Bryce Hammond's face clouded with worry. 'This Biosan . . . I gather it isn't harmful to us.'

'Utterly harmless,' Sara assured him.

The noise again. A short burst. Then silence.

'Something's coming,' Lisa said softly.

God help us, Sara thought.

'Something's coming,' Lisa said softly, and Bryce felt it, too. A sense of onrushing horror. A thickening and cooling of the air. A new predatory quality to the stillness. Reality? Imagination? He could not be certain. He only knew that he *felt* it.

The noise burst forth again, a sustained squeal, not just a short blast. Bryce winced. It was piercingly shrill. Buzzing. Whining. Like a power drill. But he knew it wasn't anything as harmless and ordinary as that.

Insects. The coldness of the sound, the metallic quality made him think of insects. Bees. Yes. It was the greatly amplified buzzing-screeching of hornets.

He said, 'The three of you who aren't armed with sprayers, get in the middle here.'

'Yeah,' Tal said. 'We'll circle around, give you a little protection.'

Very damned little if this Biosan doesn't work, Bryce thought.

The strange noise grew louder.

Sara, Lisa, and Dr Flyte stood together, while Bryce and Jenny and Tal ringed them, facing outward.

Then, down the street, near the bakery, something monstrous appeared in the sky, skimming over the tops of the buildings, hovering for a few seconds above Skyline Road. A wasp. A phantom the size of a German shepherd. Nothing remotely like this insect had ever existed during the tens of millions of years that the shape-changer had been alive. This was surely something that had sprung from its vicious imagination, a horrible invention. Six-foot, opalescent wings beat furiously upon the air, glimmered with rainbow colour. The multifaceted black eyes were slant-set in the narrow, pointed, wicked head. There were four twitching legs with pincered feet. The curled, segmented, mould-white body terminated in a foot-long stinger with a needle-sharp point.

Bryce felt as if his intestines were turning to ice water.

The wasp stopped hovering. It struck.

Jenny screamed as the wasp streaked towards them, but she didn't run. She aimed the nozzle of the sprayer and squeezed the pressure-release lever. A cone-shaped, milky mist erupted for a distance of about six feet.

The wasp was twenty feet away and closing fast.

Jenny squeezed the lever all the way down. The mist became a stream, arcing fifteen or sixteen feet out from the nozzle.

Bryce loosed a stream from his sprayer. The two trails of Biosan played across each other, steadied, took the same aim, flowed together in mid-air.

The wasp came within range. The high-pressure streams struck it, dulled the rainbow colour of the wings, soaked the segmented body.

The insect stopped abruptly, hesitated, dipped lower, as if unable to maintain altitude. Hovered. Its attack had been arrested, although it still regarded them with hate-filled eyes.

Jenny felt a surge of relief and hope.

'It works!' Lisa cried.

Then the wasp came at them again.

Just when Tal thought they were safe, the wasp came at them again, through the mist of Biosan-4, flying slow but still flying.

'Down!' Bryce shouted.

They crouched, and the wasp swept over them, dripping milky fluid from its grotesque legs and from the tip of its stinger.

Tal stood again, so that he could give the thing a long squirt now that it was within range.

It swung towards him, but before he could give it a shot, the wasp faltered, fluttered wildly, then plummeted to the pavement. It flopped and buzzed angrily. It tried to rise up. Couldn't. Then it changed.

*

It changed.

With the others, Timothy Flyte edged closer to the wasp and watched as it melted into a shapeless mass of protoplasm. The hind legs of a dog began to form. And the snout. It was going to be a Dobermann, judging by that snout. One eye began to open. But the shape-changer couldn't complete the transformation; the dog's features vanished. The amorphous tissue shuddered and pulsed in a manner unlike anything that Timothy had seen it do before.

'It's dying,' Lisa said.

Timothy stared in awe as the strange flesh convulsed. This heretofore immortal being now knew the meaning and the fear of death.

The unformed mass broke out in pustule-like sores, leaking a thin yellow fluid. The thing spasmed violently. Additional sores opened in hideous profusion, lesions of all shapes and sizes that split and cracked and popped across the pulsating surface. Then, just as the tiny wad of tissue in the petri dish had done, this phantom degenerated into a lifeless pile of stinking, watery mush.

'By God, you've done it!' Timothy said, turning towards Sara.

Tentacles. Three of them. Behind her.

They rose out of a drain grating in the gutter, fifteen feet away. Each was as big in circumference as Timothy's wrist. Already, their questing tips had slithered across the pavement, within a yard of Sara.

Timothy shouted a warning, but he was too late.

Flyte shouted, and Jenny whirled. *It* was among them.

Three tentacles whipped up from the pavement with shocking speed, surged forward with sinuous malevolence, and dropped onto Sara. In an instant, one lashed around the geneticist's legs, one around her waist, and the third around her slender neck.

Christ, it's too fast, too fast for us! Jenny thought.

She pointed the nozzle of her sprayer even as she turned,

cursing, squeezing the lever, spewing Biosan-4 over Sara and the tentacles.

Bryce and Tal stepped in, using their sprayers, but they were all too slow, too late.

Sara's eyes widened; her mouth opened in a silent scream. She was lifted into the air and—

No! Jenny prayed.

—flung back and forth as if she were a doll—

No!

—and then her head fell from her shoulders and struck the street with a hard, sickening crack.

Gagging, Jenny stumbled back.

The tentacles rose twelve feet into the air. They writhed and twisted and foamed, broke open in sores as the bacteria destroyed the binding structure of the amorphous tissue. As Sara had hoped, Biosan affected the shape-changer almost the way sulphuric acid affected human tissue.

Tal darted past Jenny, heading straight towards the three tentacles, and she screamed at him to stop.

What in God's name was he doing?

Tal ran through the weaving shadows cast by the moving tentacles and prayed that none of them would fall on him. When he reached the drain from which the things were extruded, he could see that the three appendages were separating from the main body of dark, throbbing protoplasm in the drain pipe below. The shape-changer was shedding the infected tissue before the bacteria could reach into the main body mass. Tal poked the nozzle of the sprayer through the gate and released Biosan-4 into the drain below.

The tentacles tore loose from the rest of the creature. They flopped and wriggled in the street. Down in the drain, the oozing slime retreated from the spray, shedding another piece of itself, which began to foam and spasm and die.

435

Even the devil could be wounded. Even Satan was vulnerable.

Exhilarated, Tal shot more of the fluid into the drain.

The amorphous tissue withdrew, out of sight, creeping deeper into the subterranean passageways, no doubt shedding more pieces of itself.

Tal turned away from the drain and saw the severed tentacles had lost their definition; they were now just long, tangled ropes of suppurating tissue. They lashed themselves and one another in apparent agony and rapidly degenerated into stinking, lifeless slop.

He looked at another gutter drain, at the silent buildings, at the sky, wondering where the next attack would come from.

Suddenly the pavement rumbled and heaved under his feet. In front of him, Flyte was thrown to the ground, his glasses shattered. Tal staggered sideways, nearly trampling Flyte.

The street leapt and shuddered again, harder than before, as if earthquake shockwaves had passed beneath it. But this was not a quake. *It* was coming – not just a fragment, not just another phantom, but the largest part of it, perhaps the entire great bulk, surging towards the surface with unimaginable destructive power, rising like a god betrayed, bringing its unholy wrath and vengeance to the men and women who had dared to strike at it, forming itself into an enormous mass of muscle fibre and pushing, pushing, until the macadam bulged and cracked.

Tal was thrown to the ground. His chin snapped hard against the street; he was dazed. He tried to get up, so that he could use the sprayer when the creature appeared. He got as far as his hands and knees. The street was still rocking too much. He lay down again to wait it out.

We're going to die, he thought.

Bryce was flat on his face, hugging the pavement.

Lisa was beside him. She might have been crying or screaming. He couldn't hear her; there was too much other noise.

Along this entire block of Skyline Road, an atonal symphony of destruction reached an ear-shattering crescendo: squealing, grinding, cracking, splitting sounds; the world itself coming asunder. The air was filled with dust that spurted up from widening fissures in the pavement.

The roadbed tilted with tremendous force. Chunks of it spewed into the air. Most were the size of gravel, but some were as large as a fist. A few were even larger than that, fifty- and hundred- and two-hundred-pound blocks of concrete, leaping five or ten feet into the air as the protean creature below rammed relentlessly towards the surface.

Bryce pulled Lisa against him and tried to shield her. He could feel the violent tremors passing through her.

The earth under them lifted. Fell with a crash. Lifted and fell again. Gravel-size debris rained down, clanked off the tank sprayer strapped to Bryce's back, thumped off his legs, snapped against his head, making him wince.

Where was Jenny?

He looked around in sudden desperation.

The street had hoved up; a ridge had formed down the middle of Skyline. Apparently, Jenny was on the other side of the hump, clinging to the street over there.

She's alive, he thought. She's alive. Dammit, she *has* to be!

A huge slab of concrete erupted from the roadbed to their left and was flung eight or ten feet into the air. He was sure it was going to crash down on them, and he hugged Lisa as tight as he could, although nothing he could do would save them if the slab struck. But it hit Timothy Flyte instead. It slammed across the scientist's legs, breaking them, pinning Flyte, who howled in pain, howled so loudly that Bryce could hear him above the roar of the disintegrating pavement.

Still, the shaking continued. The street heaved up farther. Ragged teeth of macadam-coated concrete bit at the morning air.

In seconds, *it* would break through and be upon them before they had a chance to stand and fight back.

A baseball-sized missile of concrete, spat into the air by the shape-changer's volcanic emergence from the storm drain, now slammed back to the pavement, impacting two or three inches from Jenny's head. A splinter of concrete pierced her cheek, drew a trickle of blood.

Then the ridge-forming pressure from below was suddenly withdrawn. The street ceased shaking. Ceased rising.

The sounds of destruction faded. Jenny could hear her own raspy, harried breathing.

A few feet away, Tal Whitman started getting to his feet.

On the far side of the hoved-up pavement, someone wailed in agony. Jenny couldn't see who it was.

She tried to stand, but the street shuddered once more, and she was pitched flat on her face again.

Tal went down again, too, cursing loudly.

Abruptly, the street began caving in. It made a tortured sound, and pieces broke loose along the fracture lines. Slabs tumbled into the emptiness below. Too much emptiness: it sounded as if things were falling into a chasm, not just a drain. Then the entire hoved-up section collapsed with a thunderous roar, and Jenny found herself at the brink.

She lay belly-down, head lifted, waiting for something to rise up from the depths, dreading to see what form the shape-changer would assume this time.

But it didn't come. Nothing rose out of the hole.

The pit was ten feet across, at least fifty feet long. On the far side, Bryce and Lisa were trying to get to their feet. Jenny almost cried out in happiness at the sight of them. They were alive!

Then she saw Timothy. His legs were pinned under a massive hunk of concrete. Worse than that – he was trapped on a precarious piece of roadbed that thrust over the rim of the hole, with no support beneath it. At any moment, it might crack and fall into the pit, taking him with it.

Jenny edged forward a few inches and stared into the hole. It was at least thirty feet deep, probably a lot deeper in places; she couldn't gauge it accurately because there were many shadows along its fifty-foot length. Apparently, the ancient enemy hadn't merely surged up from the storm drains; it had risen from some previously stable, limestone caves far below the solid ground on which the street was built.

But what degree of phenomenal strength, what an unthinkably huge *size* must it possess in order to shift not only the street but the natural rock formations before! And where had it gone?

The pit appeared untenanted, but Jenny knew *it* must be down there somewhere, in the deeper regions, in the subterranean warrens, hiding from the Biosan spray, waiting, listening.

She looked up and saw Bryce making his way towards Flyte.

A crisp, cracking noise split the air. Flyte's concrete perch shifted. It was going to break loose and tumble into the chasm.

Bryce saw the danger, He clambered over a tilted slab of pavement, trying to reach Flyte in time.

Jenny didn't think he'd make it.

Then the pavement under her groaned, trembled, and she realized that she, too, was on treacherous territory. She started to get up. Beneath her, the concrete snapped with a bomb blast of sound.

41

LUCIFER

THE SHADOWS on the cave walls were ever-changing; so was the shadowmaker. In the moon-strange glow of the gas lantern, the creature was like a column of dense smoke, writhing, formless, blood-dark.

Although Kale wanted to believe it *was* only smoke, he knew better. Ectoplasm. That's what it must be. The other-worldly stuff of which demons, ghosts, and spirits were said to be composed.

Kale had never believed in ghosts. The concept of life after death was a crutch for weaker men, not for Fletcher Kale. But now . . .

Gene Terr sat on the floor, staring at the apparition. His one gold earring glittered.

Kale stood with his back pressed to a cool limestone wall. He felt as if he were fused to the rock.

The repellent, sulphurous odour still hung on the dank air.

To Kale's left, a man came through the opening from the first room of the underground retreat. No; not a man. It was one of the Jake Johnson look-alikes. The one that had called him a baby killer.

Kale made a small, desperate sound.

This was the demonic version of Johnson whose skull was half-stripped of flesh. One wet, lidless eye peered out of a bony socket, glaring malevolently at Kale. Then the demon turned towards the oozing monstrosity in the centre of the chamber. It walked to the column of roiling slime, spread its arms, embraced the gelatinous flesh – and simply melted into it.

Kale stared uncomprehendingly.

Another Jake Johnson entered. The one that lacked flesh along his flank. Beyond the exposed rib cage, the bloody heart throbbed; the lungs expanded; yet, somehow, the organs didn't spill through the gaps between the ribs. Such a thing was impossible. Except that this was an apparition, a Hell-born presence that had swarmed up from the Pit – just smell the sulphur, the scent of Satan! – and therefore *anything* was possible.

Kale *believed* now.

The only alternative to belief was madness.

One by one, the remaining four Johnson look-alikes entered, glanced at Kale, then were absorbed by the oozing, rippling slime.

The Coleman lantern made a soft, continuous hissing.

The jelloid flesh of the nether-world visitor began to sprout black, terrible wings.

The hissing of the lantern echoed sibilantly off the stone walls.

The half-formed wings degenerated into the column of slime from which they had sprung. Insectile limbs started to take shape.

Finally, Gene Terr spoke. He might have been in a trance – except that there was a lively sparkle in his eyes. 'We come up here, me and some of my guys, two or maybe three times a year. You know? What it is . . . this here's a perfect place for a fuck an' waste party. Nobody to hear nothin'. Nobody to see. You know?'

At last Jeeter looked away from the creature and met Kale's eyes.

Kale said, 'What the hell's a . . . a fuck and waste party?'

'Oh, every couple months, sometimes more often, a chick shows up and wants to join the Chrome, wants to be somebody's old lady, you know, doesn't care whose, or maybe she'll settle for bein' an all-purpose bitch that all the guys can hack at when they want a little variety in their pussy. You know?' Jeeter sat with his legs crossed in a yoga position. His hands lay unmoving in his lap. He looked like an evil Buddha. 'Sometimes, one of us happens to be lookin' for a new main squeeze, or maybe the chick is really foxy, so we make room for her. But it don't happen like that very often. Most of the time we tell them to beat it.'

In the centre of the cave, the insectile legs melted back into the oozing column of muck. Dozens of hands began to form, the fingers opening like petals of strange blossoms.

Jeeter said, 'But then once in a while, a chick shows us, and she's damned good lookin', but we don't happen to need or want her with us, and what we want instead is to have fun with her. Or maybe we see a kid who's run away from home, you know, sweet sixteen, some hitchhiker, and we pick her up, no matter whether she wants to come along or not. We give her some nose candy or hash, get her feelin' good, then we bring her up here where it's real remote, and what we do is we fuck her brains out for a couple of days, turn her inside out, and then when none of us can get it up any more, we waste her in really interestin' ways.'

The demonic presence in the centre of the room changed yet again. The multitude of hands melted away. A score of mouths opened along the dark length of it, every one filled with razor-edged fangs.

Gene Terr glanced at this latest manifestation but didn't seem frightened. In fact, Jeeter smiled at it.

'Waste them?' Kale said. 'You kill them?'

'Yeah,' Jetter said. 'In interestin' ways. We bury 'em around here, too. Who's ever gonna find the bodies in the middle of nowhere like this? It's always a kick. Thrills. Until Sunday. Sunday afternoon late, we was out there in the grass by the cabin, drinkin' and gangin' a chick, and all of a sudden Jake Johnson comes out of the woods, bare-assed, like he figured on fuckin' the bitch too. At first I thought we'd have some fun with him. I figured, well, we'll waste him when we waste the girl, get rid of the witness, you know, but before we can grab him, another Jake comes out of the woods, then a third—'

'Just like what happened to me,' Kale said.

'—and another one and another. We shot 'em, hit 'em square in the chest, in the face, but they didn't go down, didn't even pause, just kept comin'. So Little Willie, one of my main men, rushes the nearest one and uses a knife, but it doesn't do no good. Instead, *that* Johnson grabs Willie, and he can't break loose, and then all of a sudden like ... well ... Johnson isn't Johnson any more. He's just this *thing*, this bloody-lookin' thing without no shape at all. The thing eats Willie ... eats into him like ... well, hell, it just sort of *dissolves* Willie, man. And the thing gets bigger, and then it turns into the craziest damn big wolf—'

'Jesus,' Kale said.

'—biggest wolf you ever saw, and then the other Jakes turn into other things, like big lizards with the nastiest jaws, but one of them wasn't a lizard or a wolf but somethin' I just can't describe, and they all come after us. We can't get to our bikes, man, cause these things are between us and them, and so they kill a couple more of my guys, and then they start to herd us up the hill.'

'Towards the caves,' Kale said. 'That's what they did to me.'

'We never even knew about these caves,' Terr said. 'So we get in here, way in here in the dark, and the things start killin' more of us, man, killin' us in the dark—'

The fang-filled mouths vanished.

'—and there's all this screamin', you know, and I couldn't see where I was, so I crawled into a corner to hide, hoped they wouldn't smell me out, though I figured for sure they would.'

The blood-streaked, jelloid tissue pulsed, rippled.

'—and after a while the screamin' stops. Everyone's dead. It's real quiet ... and then I hear somethin' movin' around.'

Kale was listening to Terr but staring at the column of slime. A different kind of mouth appeared, a sucker, like you might see on an exotic fish. It sucked greedily at the air, as if seeking flesh.

Kale shuddered. Terr smiled.

Other sucker-mouths began to form all over the creature.

Still smiling, Jeeter said, 'So I'm there in the dark, and I hear movement, but nothin' comes at me. Instead a light comes on. Faint at first, then brighter. It's one of the Jakes, lightin' a Coleman. He tells me to come with him. I don't want to go. He grabs my arm, and his hand's cold, man. *Strong*. He won't let go, makes me come here, where that thing's pushing up out of the floor, and I never seen anythin' like *that* before; never, nowhere. I almost shit. He makes me sit down, leaves the lantern with me, then just walks into the oozin' crud over there, melts into it, and I'm left alone with the thing, which starts right away goin' though all kinds of changes.'

It was still going through changes, Kale saw. The suckerlike mouths vanished. Viciously pointed horns formed along the churning flanks of the creature; dozens of horns, barbed and unbarbed, in a variety of textures and colours, rising from the gelatinous mass.

'So for about a day and a half now,' Terr said, 'I've been sittin' here, watchin' it, except when I doze off or go into the other room for somethin' to eat. Now and then it talks to me, you know. It seems to know almost everythin' there is to know about me, things that only my closest brother bikers ever knew. It knows all about the bodies buried up here, and it knows about the Mex bastards we wasted when we took the drug business away from them, and it knows about the cop we chopped to pieces two years ago, and like, see, not even the other cops suspect we had anythin' to do with *that* one. This thing here, this beautiful strange thing, it knows all my little secrets, man. And what it doesn't know about, it asks to hear, and it listens real good. It approves of me, man. I never thought I'd really meet up with it. I always hoped, but I never thought I would. I've been worship-pin' it for years, man, and the whole gang used to hold these black masses once a week, but I never thought it would ever really appear to me. We've given it sacrifices, even human sacrifices, and chanted all the right chants, but we never were able to conjure up anythin'. So this here's a miracle.' Jeeter laughed. 'I've been doin' its work all my life, man. Praying to it all my life, prayin' to the Beast. Now here it is. It's a fuckin' miracle.'

Kale didn't want to understand. 'You've lost me.'

Terr stared at him. 'No, I haven't. You know what I'm talkin' about, man. You *know*.'

Kale said nothing.

'You've been thinkin' this must be a demon, somethin' from Hell. And it *is* from Hell, man. But it's no demon. It's *Him*. *Him*. Lucifer.'

Among the dozen of sharply pointed horns, small red eyes opened in the tenebrous flesh. A multitude of piercing little eyes glowed crimson with hatred and evil knowledge.

Terr motioned for Kale to come closer. 'He's allowing me to go on living because He knows I'm His true disciple.'

Kale didn't move. His heart boomed. It wasn't fear that loosed the adrenalin in him. Not fear alone. There was another emotion that shook him, overwhelmed him, an emotion he couldn't quite identify . . .

'He let me live,' Jeeter repeated, 'because He knows I always do His work. Some of the others . . . maybe they weren't as purely devoted to His work as I am, so He destroyed them. But me . . . I'm different. He's lettin' me live to do His work. Maybe He'll let me live forever, man.'

Kale blinked.

'And he's lettin' you live for the same reason, you know,' Jeeter said. 'Sure. Must be. Sure. Because you do *His* work.'

Kale shook his head. 'I've never been a . . . a devil worshipper. I never believed.'

'Don't matter. You still do His work, and you enjoy it.'

The red eyes watched Kale.

'You killed your wife,' Jeeter said.

Kale nodded dumbly.

'Man, you even killed your own little baby boy. If that isn't *His* work, then what is?'

None of the shining eyes blinked, and Kale began to identify the emotion surging within him. Elation, awe . . . religious rapture.

'Who knows what *else* you've done over the years,' Jeeter said. 'Must've done lots of stuff that was His work. Maybe almost everythin' you ever done was His work. You're like me, man. You were born to follow Lucifer. You and me . . . it's in our genes. In our *genes*, man.'

At last Kale moved away from the wall.

'That's it,' Jeeter said. 'Come here. Come close to Him.'

Kale was overwhelmed with emotion. He had always known he was different from other men. Better. Special. He had always *known*, but he had never expected *this*. Yet here it was, undeniable proof that he was chosen. A fierce, heart-swelling joy suffused him.

He knelt beside Jeeter, near the miraculous presence.

He had arrived at last.

His moment had come.

Here, Kale thought, is my destiny.

42

THE OTHER SIDE OF HELL

BENEATH JENNY, the concrete roadbed snapped with a sound like a cannon shot.

Wham!

She scrambled back but wasn't fast enough. The pavement shifted and began to drop out from under her.

She was going into the pit, *Christ*, no, if she wasn't killed by the fall then *it* would come out of hiding and get her, drag her down, out of sight; it would devour her before anyone could attempt to save her—

Tal Whitman grabbed her ankles and held on. She was dangling in the pit, head down. The concrete tumbled into the hole and landed with a crash. The pavement under Tal's feet shook, started to give way, and he almost lost his grip on Jenny. Then he moved back, hauling her with him, away from the crumbling brink. When she was on solid ground once more, he helped her stand.

Even though she knew it wasn't biologically possible for her heart to rise into her throat, she swallowed it anyway.

'My God,' she said breathlessly, 'thank you! Tal, if you hadn't—'

'All in a day's work,' he said, although he had nearly followed her into the spider's trap.

Just a cakewalk, Jenny thought, remembering the story about Tal that she had heard from Bryce.

She saw that Timothy Flyte, on the far side of the pit, wasn't going to be as fortunate as she had been. Bryce wasn't going to reach him in time.

The pavement beneath Flyte gave way. An eight-foot-long, four-foot-wide slab descended into the pit, carrying the archaeologist with it. It didn't crash to the bottom as the concrete had done on Jenny's side. Over there, the pit had a sloped wall, and the slab scooted down, slid thirty feet to the base, and came to rest against other rubble.

Flyte was still alive. He was screaming in pain.

'We've got to get him out of there fast,' Jenny said.

'No use even trying,' Tal said.

'But—'

'Look!'

It came for Flyte. It exploded out of one of the tunnels that pocked the floor of the pit and apparently led down into deep caverns. A massive pseudopod of amorphous protoplasm rose ten feet into the air, quivered, dropped to the ground, broke free of the mother-body hiding below, and formed itself into an obscenely fat black spider the size of a pony. It was only ten or twelve feet from Timothy Flyte, and it clambered through the shattered blocks of pavement, heading towards him with murderous intent.

Sprawled helplessly on the concrete sled that had brought him into the pit, Timothy saw the spider coming. His pain was washed away by a wave of terror.

The black spindly legs found easy purchase in the angled ruins, and the thing progressed far more swiftly than a man would have done. There were thousands of bristling, wirelike black hairs on those brittle legs. The bulbous belly was smooth, glossy, pale.

Ten feet away. Eight feet.

It was making a blood-freezing sound, half-squeal, half-hiss.

Six feet. Four.

It stopped in front of Timothy. He found himself looking up into a pair of nightmarishly huge mandibles, sharp-edged chitinous jaws.

The door between madness and sanity began to open in his mind.

Suddenly, a milky rain fell across Timothy. For an instant he though the spider was squirting venom at him. Then he realized it was Biosan-4. They were standing above, on the rim of the pit, pointing their sprayers down.

The fluid spattered over the spider, too. White spots began to speckle its black body.

Bryce's sprayer had been damaged by a chunk of debris. He couldn't get a drop of fluid from it.

Cursing, he unbuckled the harness and shrugged out of it, dropping the tank on the street. While Tal and Jenny shot Biosan down from the other side of the pit, Bryce hurried to the gutter and collected the two spare cannisters of bacteria-rich solution. They had rolled across the pavement, away from the erupting concrete, and had come to rest against the kerb. Each cannister had a handle, and Bryce clutched them both. They were heavy. He rushed back to the brink of the pit, hesitated, then plunged over the side, down the slope, all the way to the bottom. Somehow, he managed to stay on his feet, and he kept a firm grip on both cannisters.

He didn't go to Flyte. Jenny and Tal were doing all that could be done to destroy the spider. Instead, Bryce wound through and clambered over the rubble, heading towards the hole out of which the shape-changer had despatched this latest phantom.

Timothy Flyte watched in horror as the spider, looming over him, metamorphosed into an enormous hound. It wasn't merely a dog; it was a Hellhound with a face that was partly canine and partly human. Its coat (where it wasn't spattered with Biosan) was far blacker than the spider, and its big paws had barbed claws, and its teeth were as large as Timothy's fingers. Its breath sank of sulphur and of something worse.

Lesions began to appear on the hound as the bacteria ate into the amorphous flesh, and hope sparked in Timothy.

Looking down at him, the hound spoke in a voice like gravel rolling on a tin chute: 'I thought you were my Matthew, but you were my Judas.'

The mammoth jaws opened.

Timothy screamed.

Even as the thing succumbed to the degenerative effects of the bacteria, it snapped its teeth together and savagely bit his face.

As he stood at the edge of the pit, looking down, Tal Whitman's attention was torn between the gruesome spectacle of Flyte's murder and Bryce's suicidal mission with the cannisters.

Flyte. Although the phantom dog was dissolving as the bacteria had its acid-like effect, it was not dying fast enough. It bit Flyte in the face, then in the neck.

Bryce. Twenty feet from the Hellhound, Bryce had reached the hole out of which the protoplasm had erupted a couple of minutes ago. He started unscrewing the lid of one of the cannisters.

Flyte. The hound tore viciously at Flyte's head. The hindquarters of the beast had lost their shape and were foaming as they decomposed, but the phantom struggled hard to retain its shape, so that it could slash and chew at Flyte as long as possible.

Bryce. He prised the lid off the first cannister. Tal heard it ring off a piece of concrete as Bryce tossed it aside. Tal was sure something was going to leap out of the hole, up from the caverns below, and seize Bryce in a deadly embrace.

Flyte. He had stopped screaming.

Bryce. He tipped the cannister and poured the bacterial solution into the subterranean warren under the floor of the pit.

Flyte was dead.

The only thing that remained of the hound was its large head. Although it was disembodied, although it was blistering and suppurating, it continued to snap at the dead archaeologist.

Below, Timothy Flyte lay in bloody ruins.

He had seemed like a nice old man.

Shuddering with revulsion, Lisa, who was alone on her side of the pit, backed away from the edge. She reached the gutter, sidled along it, finally stopped, stood there, shaking—

—until she realized she was standing on a drain grate. She remembered the tentacles that had slithered out of the drain, snaring and killing Sara Yamaguchi. She quickly hopped up onto the pavement.

She glanced at the building behind her. She was near one of the covered serviceways between two stores. She stared at the closed gate with apprehension.

Was something lurking in this passageway? Watching her?

Lisa started to step into the street again, saw the drain grate, and stayed on the pavement.

She took a tentative step to the left, hesitated, moved to the right, hesitated again. Doorways and serviceway gates lay in both directions. There was no sense in moving. No other place was any safer.

Just as he began to pour the Biosan-4 out of the blue cannister, into the hole in the floor of the pit, Bryce thought he saw movement in the gloom below. He expected a phantom to launch itself up and drag him down into its subterranean lair. But he emptied the entire contents of the cylinder into the hole, and nothing came after him.

Lugging the second cannister, pouring sweat, he made his way through the angled slabs and spires of concrete and broken pipe. He stepped gingerly around a torn and sputtering electric power line, leapt across a small puddle that had formed beside a leaking water

451

main. He passed Flyte's mangled body and the stinking remains of the decomposed phantom that had killed him.

When Bryce reached the next hole in the pit floor, he crouched, unscrewed the lid from the second cannister, and dumped the contents into the chamber below. Empty. He discarded it, turned away from the hole, and ran. He was anxious to get out of the pit before the phantom came after him the way one had gone after Flyte.

He was a third of the way up the sloped wall of the pit, finding the climb considerably more difficult than he had anticipated, when he heard something terrible behind him.

Jenny was watching Bryce claw his way up towards the street. She held her breath, afraid that he wasn't going to make it.

Suddenly her eyes were drawn to the first hole into which he had dumped Biosan. The shape-changer surged up from underground, gushed out onto the floor of the pit. It looked like a tide of thick, congealed sewage; except for where it was stained by the bacterial solution, it was now darker than it had been before. It rippled, writhed, and churned more agitatedly than ever, which was perhaps a sign of degeneration. The milky stain of infection was spreading visibly through the creature. Blisters formed, swelled, popped; ugly sores broke open and wept a watery yellow fluid. Within only a few seconds, at least a ton of the amorphous flesh had spewed out of the hole. All of it was apparently afflicted with disease, and still it came, ever faster, a lava-like outpouring, a wild spouting of living, gelatinous tissue. Even more of the beast began to issue from another hole. The great oozing mass lapped across the rubble, formed pseudo-pods – shapeless, flailing arms – that rose into the air but quickly fell back in foaming, spasming seizures. And then, from still other holes, there came a ghastly sound: the voices of a thousand men, women, children, and animals, all crying out in pain, horror, and bleak despair. It was an agonized wail of such heartbreak that Jenny could not bear it – especially when a few voices sounded

452

uncannily familiar, like old friends and good neighbours. She put her hands to her ears, but to no avail; the roar of the suffering multitude still penetrated. It was, of course, the death-cry of only one creature, the shape-changer, but since *it* had no voice of its own, it was forced to employ the voices of its victims, expressing its inhuman emotions and inhuman terror in intensely human terms.

It surged across the rubble. Towards Bryce.

Halfway up the slope, Bryce heard the noise behind him change from the wailing of a thousand lonely voices to a roar of rage.

He dared to look back. He saw that three or four tons of amorphous tissue had fountained into the pit, and more was still gushing forth, as if the bowels of the earth were emptying. The ancient enemy's flesh was shuddering, leaping, bursting with leprous lesions. It tried to create winged phantoms, but it was too weak or unstable to competently mimic anything; the half-realized birds and enormous insects either decomposed into a sludge that resembled pus or collapsed back into the pool of tissue beneath them. The ancient enemy was coming towards Bryce nonetheless, coming in a quivering-churning frenzy; it had flowed almost to the base of the slope, and now it was sending degenerating yet still powerful tentacles towards his heels.

He turned away from it and redoubled his efforts to reach the rim of the pit.

The two big windows of the Towne Bar and Grille, in front of which Lisa was standing, exploded out onto the sidewalk. A shard nicked her forehead, but she was otherwise unhurt, for most of the fragments landed on the pavement between her and the building.

An obscene, shadowy mass bulged through the broken windows.

Lisa stumbled backwards and nearly fell off the kerb.

The foul, oozing flesh appeared to fill the entire building out of which it extruded itself.

*

Something snaked around Lisa's ankle.

Tendrils of amorphous flesh had slithered out of the drain grate in the gutter behind her. They had taken hold of her.

Screaming, she tried to pull free of them – and found that it was surprisingly easy to do so. The thin, wormlike tentacles fell away. Lesions broke out along their length; they split open, and in seconds they were reduced to inanimate slime.

The disgusting mass that burgeoned out of the barroom was also succumbing to the bacteria. Gobs of foaming tissue fell away and splattered the pavement. Still, it continued to gush forth, forming tentacles, and the tentacles weaved through the air, seeking Lisa, but with the tentative groping of something sick and blind.

Tal saw the Towne Bar and Grille's windows explode on the other side of the street, but before he could take one step to help Lisa, windows shattered behind him, too, in the lobby and dining room of the Hilltop Inn, and he turned in surprise, and the front doors of the inn flew open, and from both the doors and the windows came tons of jelloid protoplasm that pulsated (Oh, Jesus, how big *was* the goddamned thing? As big as the whole town? As big as the mountain out of which it had come? Infinite?) and roiled, sprouting a score of lashing tentacles as it surged forth, marked by disease but noticeably more active than the extention of itself that it had sent after Bryce in the pit. Before Tal could raise the nozzle of his sprayer and depress the pressure-release lever, the cold tentacle found him, gripped him with dismaying strength, and then he was being dragged across the pavement, towards the inn, towards the oozing wall of slime that was still rupturing through the shattered windows, and the tentacles began to burn through his clothing, he felt his skin burning, blistering, he howled, the digestive acids were eating into his flesh, he felt brands of fire across his chest and arms, he felt one fiery line along his left thigh, he remembered how a tentacle

454

had beheaded Frank Autry by eating swiftly through the man's neck, he thought of his Aunt Becky, he—

Jenny dodged a tentacle that took a swipe at her.

She sprayed Tal and all the snaky appendages – three of them – that had hold of him.

Decomposing tissue sloughed off the tentacles, but they didn't degenerate entirely.

Even where she hadn't sprayed, the creature's flesh broke out in new sores. The entire beast was contaminated, it was being eaten up from within. It couldn't last much longer. Maybe just long enough to kill Tal Whitman.

He was screaming, thrashing.

Frantic, Jenny let go of the sprayer's hose and moved in closer to Tal. She grabbed one of the tentacles that gripped him, and she tried to pry it loose.

Another tentacle clutched at her.

She twisted out of its fumbling grip and realized that, if she could evade it so easily, it must be swiftly losing its battle with the bacteria.

In her hands, pieces of the tentacle came away, chunks of dead tissue that stank horribly.

Gagging, she clawed harder than ever, and the tentacle finally dropped away from Tal, and then so did the other two, and he collapsed in a heap on the pavement, gasping and bleeding.

The blind, groping tentacles never touched Lisa. They receded into the vomitous mass that had poured out of the front of the Towne Bar and Grille. Now, that heaving monstrosity spasmed and flung off foaming, infected gobbets of itself.

'It's dying,' Lisa said aloud, although no one was close enough to hear her. 'The devil is dying.'

*

Bryce crawled on his belly for the last few, almost vertical feet of the pit wall. He reached the rim at last and pulled himself out.

He looked down the way he had come. The shape-changer hadn't come close to him. An incredibly large, gelatinous lake of amorphous tissue lay at the bottom of the pit, pooling over and around the debris, but it was virtually inactive. A few human and animal forms still tried to rise up, but the ancient enemy was losing its talent for mimicry. The phantoms were imperfect and sluggish. The shape-changer was slowly disappearing under a layer of its own dead and decomposing tissue.

Jenny knelt beside Tal.

His arms and chest were marked by livid wounds. A raw, weeping wound extended the length of his left thigh, as well.

'Pain?' she asked.

'When it had me, yeah, a lot. Not so much now,' he said, although his expression left no doubt that he was still suffering.

The enormous bulk of slime that had erupted from the Hilltop Inn now began to withdraw, retreating into the plumbing from which it had risen, leaving behind the steaming residue of its decomposing flesh.

A Mephistophelian retreat. Back to the nether world. Back to the other side of Hell.

Satisfied that they weren't in any immediate danger, Jenny looked more closely at Tal's wounds.

'Bad?' he asked.

'Not as bad as I would've thought.' She forced him to lie back. 'The skin's eaten away in places. And some of the fatty tissue underneath.'

'Veins? Arteries?'

'No. It was weak when it took hold of you, too weak to burn that deep. A lot of ruined capillaries in the surface tissue. That's the cause of the bleeding. But there's not even as much blood as you'd

456

expect. I'll get my bag as soon as it seems safe to go outside, and I'll treat you for infection. I think maybe you ought to be in the hospital for a couple of days, for observation, just to be sure there's no delayed allergic reaction to the acid or any toxins. But I really think you'll be just fine.'

'You know what?' he said.

'What?'

'You're talking like it's all over.'

Jenny blinked.

She looked up at the inn. She could see through the smashed windows, into the dining room. There was no sign of the ancient enemy.

She turned and looked across the street. Lisa and Bryce were making their way around to this side of the pit.

'I think it is,' she said to Tal. 'I think it's all over.'

43

APOSTLES

FLETCHER KALE was no longer afraid. He sat beside Jeeter and watched the satanic flesh metamorphose into ever more bizarre forms.

Gradually, he became aware that the calf of his right leg itched. He scratched continuously, absentmindedly, while he watched the truly miraculous transformation of the demonic visitor.

Restricted to the caves since Sunday, Jeeter knew nothing about what had happened in Snowfield. Kale recounted what little he knew, and Jeeter was thrilled. 'You know, what it is, it's a *sign*. What He did in Snowfield is like a sign tellin' the world His time is comin'. His reign is gonna begin soon. He'll rule the earth for a thousand years. That's what the Bible itself says, man – a thousand years of Hell on earth. Everyone'll suffer – except you and me and others like us. 'Cause we're the chosen ones, man. We're His apostles. We'll rule the world with Lucifer, and it'll belong to us, and we'll be able to do any fuckin' outrageous thing to anybody we happen to want to do it to. *Anybody*. And no one'll touch us, no one, ever. You understand?' Terr demanded, gripping Kale's arm, voice rising with excitement, trembling with evangelical passion, a passion that was easily communicated to Kale and stirred in him a dizzying, unholy rapture.

With Jeeter's hand on his arm, Kale imagined he could feel the hot gaze of the red and yellow eye tattoo. It was a magical eye that peered into his soul and recognized a certain dark kinship.

Kale cleared his throat, scratched his ankle, scratched his calf. He said, 'Yeah. Yeah. I understand. I really do.'

The column of slime in the centre of the room began to form a whiplike tail. Wings emerged, spread, flapped once. Arms grew, large and sinewy. The hands were enormous, with powerful fingers that tapered into talons. At the top of the column, a face took shape in the oozing mass: chin and jaws like chiselled granite; a gash of a mouth with thin lips, crooked yellow teeth, viperous fangs; a nose like the snout of a pig; mad, crimson eyes, not remotely human, like the prismed eyes of a fly. Horns sprouted on the forehead, a concession to Christian myth-conceptions. The hair appeared to be worms; they glistened, fat and green-black, writhing continuously in tangled knots.

The cruel mouth opened. The devil said, 'Do you believe?'

'Yes,' Terr said in adoration. 'You are my lord.'

'Yes,' Kale said shakily. 'I believe.' He scratched at his right calf. 'I do believe.'

'Are you mine?' the apparition asked.

'Yes, always,' Terr said, and Kale agreed.

'Will you ever forsake me?' it asked.

'No.'

'Never.'

'Do you wish to please me.'

'Yes,' Terr said, and Kale said, 'Whatever you want.'

'I will be leaving soon,' the manifestation said. 'It is not yet my time to rule. That day is coming. Soon. But there are conditions that must be met, prophecies to be fulfilled. Then I will come again, not merely to deliver a sign to all mankind, but to stay for a thousand years. Until then, I will leave you with the protection of my power, which is vast; no one will be able to harm or thwart you. I grant you life everlasting. I promise that, for you, Hell will be a place of great pleasure and immense rewards. In return, you must complete five tasks.'

He told them what He would have them do to prove themselves and please Him. As He spoke, He broke out in pustules, hives, and lesions that wept a thin yellow fluid.

Kale wondered what significance these sores might have, then realized Lucifer was the father of all disease. Perhaps this was a not-so-subtle reminder of the terrible plagues He could visit upon them if they were unwilling to undertake the five tasks.

The jelloid flesh foamed, dissolved. Gobs of it dropped to the floor; a few were flung against the walls as the figure heaved and writhed. The devil's tail dropped from the main body and wriggled on the floor; in seconds, it was reduced to inanimate muck that stank of death.

When he finished telling them what He wanted of them, He said, 'Do we have a bargain?'

'Yes,' Terr said, and Kale said, 'Yes, a bargain.'

The face of Lucifer, covered with running sores, melted away. The horns and wings melted, too. Churning, seeping a puslike paste, the thing sank down into the floor, disappeared into the river below.

Strangely, the odourous dead tissue did not vanish. Ectoplasm was supposed to disappear when the supernatural presence had departed, but this stuff remained; foul, nauseating, glistening in the gaslight.

Gradually, Kale's rapture faded. He began to feel the cold radiating from the limestone, through the seat of his pants.

Gene Terr coughed. 'Well ... well now ... wasn't that somethin'?'

Kale scratched his itchy calf. Beneath the itchiness, there was now a dull little spot of pain, throbbing.

It had reached the end of its feeding period. In fact, it had over-fed. It had intended to move towards the sea later today, through a series of caverns, subterranean channels and underground watercourses. It had wanted to travel out beyond the edge of the continent, into the ocean

460

trenches. Countless times before, it had passed its lethargic periods – sometimes lasting many years – in the cool, dark depths of the sea. Down there where the pressure was so enormous that few forms of life could survive, down there where absolute lightlessness and silence provided little stimulation, the ancient enemy was able to slow down its metabolic processes; down there, it could enter a much-desired dreamlike state, in which it could ruminate in perfect solitude.

But it would never reach the sea. Never again. It was dying.

The concept of its own death was so new that it had not yet adjusted to the grim reality. In the geological substructure of Snowtop Mountain, the shape-changer continued to slough off diseased portions of itself. It crept deeper, deeper, across the underworld river that flowed in Stygian darkness, deeper still, farther down into the infernal regions of the earth, into the chambers of Orcus, Hades, Osiris, Erebus, Minos, Loki, Satan. Each time that it believed itself free of the devouring microorganism, a peculiar tingling sensation arose at some point in the amorphous tissue, a wrongness, and then there came a pain quite unlike human pain, and it was forced to rid itself of even more infected flesh. It went deeper, down into jahanna, into Gehenna, into Sheol, Abbadon, into the Pit. Over the centuries, it had eagerly assumed the role of Satan and other evil figures, which men had attributed to it, had amused itself by catering to their superstitions. Now, it was condemned to a fate consistent with the mythology it had helped create. It was bitterly aware of the irony. It had been cast down. It had been damned. It would dwell in darkness and despair for the rest of its life – which could be measured in hours.

At least it had left behind two apostles. Kale and Terr. They would do its work even after it had ceased to exist. They would spread terror and take revenge. They were perfectly suited to the job.

Now, reduced to only a brain and minimal supporting tissue, the shape-changer cowered in a chthonian niche of densely packed rock and waited for the end. It spent its last minutes seething with hatred, raging at all mankind.

*

461

Kale rolled up his trousers and looked at the calf of his right leg. In the lantern light, he saw two small red spots; they were swollen, itchy, and very tender.

'Insect bites,' he said.

Gene Terr looked. 'Ticks. They burrow under the skin. The itchin' won't stop until you get 'em out. Burn 'em out with a cigarette.'

'Got any?'

Kale grinned. 'Couple joints of grass. They'll work just as well, man. And the ticks'll die happy.'

They smoked the joints, and Kale used the glowing tip of his to burn out the ticks. It didn't hurt much.

'In the woods,' Terr said, 'keep your pants tucked in your boots.'

'They *were* tucked into my boots.'

'Yeah? Then how'd them ticks get underneath?'

'I don't know.'

After they had smoked more grass, Kale frowned and said, 'He promised us no one could hurt or stop us. He said we'd be under His protection.'

'That's right, man. Invincible.'

'So how come I've got to put up with tick bites?' Kale asked.

'Hey man, it's no big thing.'

'But if we're really protected—'

'Listen, maybe the tick bites are sort of like His way of sealing the bargain you made with Him. With a little blood. Get it?'

'Then why don't you have tick bites?'

Jeeter shrugged. 'Ain't important, man. Besides, the fuckin' ticks bit you *before* you struck your bargain – didn't they?'

'Oh.' Kale nodded, fuzzy-headed from dope. 'Yeah. That's right.'

They were silent for a while.

Then Kale said. 'When do you think we can leave here?'

'They're probably still lookin' for you pretty hard.'

'But if they can't hurt me—'

462

'No sense makin' the job harder for ourselves,' Terr said.

'I guess so.'

'We'll lay low for like a few days. Worst of the heat will be off by them.'

'Then we do the five like he wants. And after that?'

'Head on out, man. Move on. Make tracks.'

'Where?'

'Somewhere. He'll show us the way.' Terr was silent for a while. Then he said, 'Tell me about it. About killin' your wife and kid.'

'What do you want to know?'

'Everythin' there is to know, man. Tell me what it felt like. What was it like to off your old lady. Mostly, tell me about the kid. What'd it feel like, wastin' a kid? Huh? I never did one that young, man. You kill him fast or drag it out? Did it feel different than killin' her? What exactly did you do to the kid?'

'Only what I had to do. They were in my way.'

'Draggin' you down, huh?'

'Both of them.'

'Sure. I see how it was. But what did you *do*?'

'Shot her.'

'Shoot the kid, too?'

'No. I chopped him. With a meat cleaver.'

'No shit?'

They smoked more joints, and the lantern hissed, and the whisper-chuckle of the underground river came up through the hole in the floor, and Kale talked about killing Joanna, Danny and the county deputies.

Every once in a while, punctuating his words with a little marijuana giggle, Jeeter said, 'Hey, man, are we gonna have some fun? Are we gonna have some fun together, you and me? Tell me more. Tell me. Man, are we gonna have some fun?'

44

VICTORY?

BRYCE STOOD on the pavement studying the town. Listening. Waiting. There was no sign of the shape-changer, but he was reluctant to believe it was dead. He was afraid it would spring at him the moment he relaxed his guard.

Tal Whitman was stretched out on the pavement. Jenny and Lisa cleaned the acid burns, dusted them with antibiotic powder, and applied temporary bandages.

And Snowfield remained as silent as if it were at the bottom of the sea.

Finished ministering to Tal, Jenny said, 'We should get him to the hospital right away. The wounds aren't deep, but there might be a delayed allergic reaction to one of the shape-changer's toxins. He might suddenly start having respiratory difficulties or blood pressure problems. The hospital is equipped for the worst possibilities; I'm not.'

Sweeping the length of the street with his eyes, Bryce said, 'What if we get in the car, trap ourselves in a moving car, and then *it* comes back?'

'We'll take a couple of sprayers with us.'

'There might not be time to use them. It could come up out of a manhole, overturn the car, and kills us that way, without ever touching us, without giving us a chance to use the sprayers.'

They listened to the town. Nothing. Just the breeze.

Lisa finally said, 'It's dead.'

'We can't be sure,' Bryce said.

'Don't you feel it?' Lisa insisted. 'Feel the difference. It's gone! It's dead. You can *feel* the change in the air.'

Bryce realized the girl was right. The shape-changer had not been merely a physical presence, but a spiritual one as well; he had been able to sense the evil of it, an almost tangible malevolence. Apparently, the ancient enemy had emitted subtle emanations – Vibrations? Psychic waves? – that couldn't be seen or heard but which were registered on an instinctual level. They left a stain on the soul. And now those vibrations were gone. There was no menace in the air.

Bryce took a deep breath. The air was clean, fresh, sweet.

Tal said, 'If you don't want to get in a car just yet, don't worry about it. We can wait a while, I'm okay. I'll be fine.'

'I've changed my mind,' Bryce said. 'We can go. Nothing's going to stop us. Lisa's right. It's dead.'

In the patrol car, as Bryce started the engine, Jenny said, 'You remember what Flyte said about the creature's intelligence? When he was speaking to it, through the computer, he told it that it had probably acquired its intelligence and self-awareness only after it had begun consuming intelligent creatures.'

'I remember,' Tal said from the back seat, where he sat with Lisa. 'It didn't like hearing that.'

'And so?' Bryce asked. 'What's your point, Doc?'

'Well, if it acquired its intelligence by absorbing our knowledge and cognitive mechanisms . . . then did it also acquire its cruelty and viciousness from us, from mankind?' She saw that the question made Bryce uneasy, but she plunged on. 'When you come right down to it, maybe the only real devils are human beings; not all of us; not the species as a whole; just the ones who're twisted, the ones who somehow never acquire empathy or compassion. If the

465

shape-changer *was* the Satan of mythology, perhaps the evil in human beings isn't a reflection of the devil; perhaps the devil is only a reflection of the savagery and brutality of our own kind. Maybe what we've done is . . . create the devil in our own image.'

Bryce was silent. Then: 'You may be right. I suspect you are. There's no use wasting energy being afraid of devils, demons, and things that go bump in the night . . . because ultimately, we'll never encounter anything more terrifying than the monsters among us. Hell is where we make it.'

They drove down Skyline Road.

Snowfield looked serene and beautiful.

Nothing tried to stop them.

45

GOOD AND EVIL

ON SUNDAY evening, one week after Jenny and Lisa found Snow-field in its graveyard silence, five days after the death of the shape-changer, they were at the hospital in Santa Mira, visiting Tal Whitman. He had, after all, suffered a toxin reaction to some fluid secreted by the shape-changer and had also developed a mild infection, but he had never been in serious danger. Now he was almost as good as new – and eager to go home.

When Lisa and Jenny stepped into Tal's room, he was seated in a chair by the window, reading a magazine. He was dressed in his uniform. His gun and holster were lying on a small table beside the chair.

Lisa hugged him before he could get up, and Tal hugged her back.

'Lookin' good,' she told him.

'Lookin' fine,' he told her.

'Like a million bucks.'

'Like two million.'

'You'll turn the ladies' heads.'

'And you'll make the boys do back-flips.'

It was a ritual they went through every day, a small ceremony of affection that always elicited a smile from Lisa. Jenny loved to see it; Lisa didn't smile often these days. In the past week, she hadn't laughed at all, not once.

Tal stood up, and Jenny hugged him too. She said, 'Bryce is with Timmy. He'll be up in a little while.'

'You know,' Tal said, 'he seems to be handling that situation a whole lot better. All this past year, you could see how Timmy's condition was killing him. Now he seems able to cope with it.'

Jenny nodded. 'He'd got it in his head that Timmy would be better off dead. But up in Snowfield, he had a change of heart. I think he decided that, after all, there *wasn't* a fate worse than death. Where there's life, there's hope.'

'That's what they say.'

'In another year, if Timmy's still in a coma, Bryce might change his mind again. But for the moment, he seems grateful just to be able to sit down there for a while each day, holding his little boy's warm hand.' She looked Tal over and demanded: 'What's with the street clothes?'

'I'm being discharged.'

'Fantastic!' Lisa said.

Timmy's roommate these days was an 82-year-old man who was hooked up to an IV, a beeping cardiac monitor, and a wheezing respirator.

Although Timmy was attached only to an IV, he was in the embrace of an oblivion as complete as the octogenarian's coma. Once or twice an hour, never more often, never for longer than a minute at a time, the boy's eyelids fluttered or his lips twitched or a muscle ticked in his cheek. That was all.

Bryce sat beside the bed, his hand through the railing, gently gripping his son's hand. Since Snowfield, just this meagre contact was enough to satisfy him. Each day he left the room feeling better.

There wasn't much light now that evening had come. On the wall at the head of the bed, there was a dim lamp that cast a soft glow only as far as Timmy's shoulders, leaving his sheet-covered body in shadow. In that wan illumination, Bryce could see how his boy had withered, losing weight in spite of the IV solution. The cheekbones were too prominent. There were dark circles around his eyes. The chin and jawline looked pathetically fragile. His son had always been small for his age. But now the hand Bryce held seemed to belong to a much younger child than Timmy; it seemed like the hand of an infant.

But it was warm. It was warm.

After a while, Bryce reluctantly let go. He smoothed the boy's hair, straightened the sheet, fluffed the pillow.

It was time to leave, but he couldn't go; not yet. He was crying. He didn't want to step into the hall with tears on his face.

He pulled a few Kleenex from the box on the nightstand, got up, went to the window, and looked out at Santa Mira.

Although he wept every day when he came here, these were different tears from those he had cried before. These scalded, washed away the misery, and healed. Bit by bit, slowly, they healed him.

'Discharged?' Jenny said, scowling. 'Says who?'

Tal grinned. 'Says me.'

'Since when have you become your own doctor?'

'I just thought a second opinion seemed called for, so I asked myself in for consultation, and I recommended to me that I go home.'

'Tal—'

'Really, Doc, I feel great. The swelling's gone. Haven't run a temperature in two days. I'm a prime candidate for release. If you try to make me stay here any longer, my death will be on your hands.'

'Death?'

'The hospital food is sure to kill me.'

'He looks ready to go dancing,' Lisa said.

'And when'd you get *your* medical degree?' Jenny asked. To Tal she said. 'Well . . . let me have a look. Take off your shirt.'

He slipped out of it quickly and easily, not nearly as stiff as he'd been yesterday. Jenny carefully untaped the bandages and found that he was right: no swelling, no breaks in the scabs.

'We've beaten it,' he assured her.

'Usually, we don't discharge a patient in the evening. Orders are written in the morning; release comes between ten o'clock and noon.'

'Rules are made to be broken.'

'What an awful thing for a policeman to say,' she teased. 'Look, Tal, I'd prefer you stayed here one more night, just in case—'

'And I'd prefer I *didn't,* just in case I go *stir* crazy.'

'You're really determined?'

'He's really determined,' Lisa said.

Tal said, 'Doc, they had my gun in a safe, along with their drug supply. I had to wheedle, beg, plead, and tease a sweet nurse named Paula, so she'd get it for me this afternoon. I told her you'd let me out tonight for sure. Now, see, Paula's a soul sister, a very attractive lady, single, eligible, delicious—'

'Don't get too steamy,' Lisa said. 'There's a minor present.'

'I'd like to have a date with Paula,' Tal said. 'I'd like to spend eternity with Paula. But now, Doc, if you say I can't go home, then I'll have to put my revolver back in the safe, and maybe Paula's supervisor'll find out she let me have it before my discharge was final, and then Paula might lose her job, and if she loses it because of me, I'll never get a date with her. If I don't get a date with her, I'm not going to be able to marry her, and if I don't marry her, there won't be any little Tal Whitmans running around, not ever, because I'll go away to a monastery and become celibate, seeing as how I've made up my mind that Paula's the *only* woman for me. So if you won't discharge me, then you'll not only be ruining my life but depriving the world of a little black Einstein or maybe a little black Beethoven.'

Jenny laughed and shook her head. 'Okay, okay. I'll write a discharge order, and you can leave tonight.'

He hugged her and quickly began putting on his shirt.

'Paula better watch out,' Lisa said. 'You're too smooth to be left loose among women without a bell around your neck.'

'Me? Smooth?' He buckled his holster around his waist. 'I'm just good old Tal Whitman, sort of bashful. Been shy all my life.'

'Oh, sure,' Lisa said.

Jenny said, 'If you—'

And suddenly Tal went berserk. He shoved Jenny aside, knocked her down. She struck the footboard of the bed with her shoulder and hit the floor hard. She heard gunfire and saw Lisa falling and didn't know if the girl had been hit or was just diving for cover; and for an instant she thought Tal was shooting at them. Then she saw he was still pulling his revolver out of his holster.

Even as the sound of the shot slammed through the room, glass shattered. It was the window behind Tal.

'*Drop it!*' Tal shouted.

Jenny turned her head, saw Gene Terr standing in the doorway, silhouetted by the brighter light in the hospital corridor behind him.

Standing in the deep shadows by the window, Bryce finished drying his tears and wadded up the damp Kleenex. He heard a soft noise in the room behind him, thought it was a nurse, turned – and saw Fletcher Kale. For a moment Bryce was frozen by disbelief.

Kale was standing at the foot of Timmy's bed, barely identifiable in the weak light. He hadn't seen Bryce. He was watching the boy – and grinning. Madness knotted his face. He was holding a gun.

Bryce stepped away from the window, reaching for his own revolver. Too late, he realized he wasn't in uniform, wasn't wearing a sidearm. He had an off-duty snubnose .38 in an ankle holster; he stooped to get it.

But Kale had seen him. The gun in Kale's hand snapped up, barked once, twice, three times in rapid succession.

Bryce felt a sledgehammer hit him high and on the left side, and pain flashed across his entire chest. As he crumpled to the floor, he heard the killer's gun roar three more times.

'*Drop it!*' Tal shouted, and Jenny saw Jeeter, and another shot ricocheted off the bed rail and must have gone through the ceiling because a couple of squares of acoustic tile fell down.

Crouching, Tal fired two rounds. The first shot took Jester in the left thigh. The second struck him in the gut, lifted him, and threw him backwards, into the corner, where he landed in a spray of blood. He didn't move.

Tal said, 'What the *hell*?'

Jenny cried for Lisa and scrambled on all fours around the bed, wondering if her sister was alive.

Kale had been sick for a couple of hours. He was running a fever. His eyes burned and felt grainy. It had come on him suddenly. He had a headache, too, and standing there at the foot of the boy's bed, he began to feel nauseous. His legs became weak. He didn't understand; he was supposed to be protected, invincible. Of course, maybe Lucifer was impatient with him for waiting five days before leaving the caves. Maybe this illness was a warning to get on with His work. The symptoms would probably vanish the moment the boy was dead. Yeah. That was probably what would happen. Kale grinned at the comatose child, began to raise his revolver, and winced as a cramp twisted his guts.

Then he saw movement in the shadows. Swung away from the bed. A man. Coming at him. Hammond. Kale opened fire, squeezing off six rounds, taking no chances. He was dizzy, and his vision was blurry, and his arm felt weak, and he could hardly keep a grip on the gun; even in those close quarters, he couldn't trust his aim.

Hammond went down hard and lay very still.

Although the light was dim, and although Kale's eyes wouldn't focus properly, he could see spots of blood on the wall and floor.

Laughing happily, wondering when the illness would leave him now that he'd completed one of the tasks Lucifer had given him, Kale weaved towards the body, intending to deliver the *coup de grâce*. Even if Hammond was stone-cold dead, Kale wanted to put a bullet in that snide, smug face, wanted to mess it up real good.

Then he would deal with the boy.

That was what Lucifer wanted. Five deaths. Hammond, the boy, Whitman, Dr Paige and the girl.

He reached Hammond, started to bend down to him—

—and the sheriff moved. His hand was lightning quick. He snatched a gun from an ankle holster, and before Kale could respond, there was a muzzle flash.

Kale was hit. He stumbled, fell. His revolver flew out of his hand. He heard it clang against the leg of one of the beds.

This can't be happening, he told himself. I'm protected. No one can harm me.

Lisa was alive. When she'd fallen behind the bed, she hadn't been shot; she'd just been diving for cover. Jenny held her tightly.

Tal was crouched over Gene Terr. The gang leader was dead, a gaping hole in his chest.

A crowd had gathered: nurses, nurses' aides, a couple of doctors, a patient or two in bathrobe and slippers.

A red-haired orderly hurried up. He looked shellshocked. 'There's been a shooting on the second floor, too!'

'Bryce,' Jenny said, and a cold blade of fear pierced her.

'What's going on here?' Tal said.

Jenny ran for the exit door at the end of hall, slammed through it, went down the stairs two at a time. Tal caught up with her by the time she reached the bottom of the second flight. He pulled open the door, and they rushed out into the second-floor corridor.

Another crowd had gathered outside Timmy's room. Her heart beating twenty to the dozen, Jenny rammed through the onlookers.

A body was on the floor. A nurse stooped beside it.

Jenny thought it was Bryce. Then she saw him in a chair. Another nurse was cutting the shirt away from his shoulder. He was just wounded.

Bryce forced a smile. 'Better be careful, Doc. If you always arrive on the scene this soon, they'll start calling you an ambulance chaser.'

She wept. She couldn't help it. She had never been as glad to hear anything as she was to hear his voice.

'Just a scratch,' he said.

'Now you sound like Tal,' she said, laughing through her tears. 'Is Timmy okay?'

'Kale was going to kill him. If I hadn't been here . . .'

'This is Kale?'

'Yeah.'

Jenny wiped her eyes with her sleeves and examined Bryce's shoulder. The bullet had passed through, in the front and out the back. There was no reason to think it had fragmented, but she intended to order X-rays anyway. The wound was bleeding freely, although it wasn't spurting, and she directed the nurse to staunch the flow with gauze pads soaked in boric acid.

He was going to be all right.

Sure of Bryce's condition, Jenny turned to the man on the floor. He was in a more serious condition. The nurse had torn open his jacket and shirt: he'd been shot in the chest. He coughed, and bright blood sputtered over his lips.

Jenny sent the nurse for a stretcher and put in an emergency call for a surgeon. Then she noticed Kale was running a fever. His forehead was hot, face flushed. When she took his wrist to check his pulse, she saw it was covered with fiery red spots. She pushed up his sleeve and found the spots extended halfway up his arm. They were on his other wrist, too. None on his face or neck. She had noticed pale red marks on his chest but had mistaken them for blood. Looking again, more closely than before, she saw they were like the spots on his wrists.

Measles? No. Something else. Something worse than measles.

The nurse returned with two orderlies and a wheeled stretcher, and Jenny said, 'We'll have to quarantine this floor. And the one above. We've got some disease here, and I'm not entirely sure what it is.'

After X-rays and after his wound had been dressed, Bryce was put in a room down the hall from Timmy. The ache in his shoulder got worse, not better, as the shocked nerves began to regain their function. He refused painkillers, intending to keep a clear head until he knew what had happened and why.

Jenny came to see him half an hour after he was put to bed. She looked exhausted, yet her weariness didn't diminish her beauty. The sight of her was all the medicine he needed.

'How's Kale?' he asked.

'The bullet didn't damage his heart. It collapsed one lung, nicked an artery. Ordinarily, the prognosis would be fair. But he's not only got surgery to recuperate from; he's also got to deal with a case of Rocky Mountain Spotted Fever.'

Bryce blinked. 'Spotted fever?'

'There're two cigarette burns on his right calf, or rather the scars of two burns, where he got rid of the ticks. Wood ticks transmit the disease. Judging from the look of the scars, I'd say he was bitten five or six days ago, which is just about the incubation period for spotted fever. The symptoms must've hit him within the past several hours. He must've been dizzy, chilled, weak in the joints . . .'

'That's why his aim was so bad!' Bryce said. 'He fired three times at close range and only winged me once.'

'You'd better thank God for sending that tick up his pants leg.'

He thought about that and said, 'It almost *does* seem like an act of God, doesn't it? But what were he and Terr up to? Why'd they risk coming here with guns? I can understand Kale might want to kill me and even Timmy. But why Tal and you and Lisa?'

'You're not going to believe this,' she said. 'Since last Tuesday morning, Kale's been keeping a written record of what he calls "The Events After the Epiphany". It seems that Kale and Terr made a bargain with the devil.'

Four o'clock Monday morning, only six days after the epiphany of which Kale had written, he died in the county hospital. Before he passed out of this life, he opened his eyes, stared wildly at a nurse, then looked past her, saw something that terrified him, something the nurse couldn't see. He somehow found the strength to raise his hands, as if trying to protect himself, and he cried out; it was a thin, death-rattle scream. When the nurse tried to calm him, he said, 'But *this* isn't my destiny.' And then he was gone.

On 31 October, more than six weeks after the events in Snowfield, Tal Whitman and Paula Thorne (the nurse he'd been dating) held a Halloween costume party at Tal's house in Santa Mira. Bryce went as a cowboy, Jenny as a cowgirl. Lisa was dressed as a witch, with a tall pointed hat and lots of black mascara.

Tal opened the door and said, 'Cluck, cluck.' He was wearing a chicken suit.

Jenny had never seen a more ridiculous costume. She laughed so hard that, for a while, she didn't realize Lisa was laughing, too.

It was the first laugh the girl had given voice to in the past six weeks. Previously, she'd managed only a smile. Now she laughed until tears ran down her face.

'Well, hey, just a minute here,' Tal said, pretending to be offended. 'You make a pretty silly-looking witch, too.'

He winked at Jenny, and she knew he'd chosen the chicken suit for the effect it would have on Lisa.

'For God's sake,' Bryce said, 'get out of the doorway and let us inside, Tal. If the public sees you in that getup, they'll lose what little respect they have left for the sheriff's department.'

That night, Lisa joined in the conversation and the games, and she laughed a great deal. It was a new beginning.

In August of the following year, on the first day of their honeymoon, Jenny found Bryce on the balcony of their hotel room, overlooking Wakiki Beach. He was frowning.

'You aren't worried about being so far away from Timmy, are you?' she asked.

'No. But it's Timmy I'm thinking about. Lately . . . I've had this feeling everything's going to be all right, after all. It's strange. Like a premonition. I had a dream last night. Timmy woke up from his coma, said hello to me, and asked for a Big Mac. Only . . . it wasn't like any dream I've ever had before. It was so *real*.'

'Well, you've never lost hope.'

'Yes. For a while I lost it. But I've got it back again.'

They stood in silence for a while, letting the warm sea wind wash over them, listening to the waves breaking on the beach.

Then they made love again.

That night they had dinner at a good Chinese restaurant in Honolulu. They drank champagne all evening, even though the waiter politely suggested they switch to tea with their meal, so their palates would not be 'stained'.

Over dessert, Bryce said. 'There was something else Timmy said in that dream. When I was surprised he'd awakened from his coma, he said, "But Daddy, if there's a devil, then there's got to be a god, too. Didn't you already figure that out when you met the devil? God wouldn't let me sleep my whole life away." '

Jenny stared at him uncertainly.

He smiled. 'Don't worry. I'm not flaking out on you. I'm not going to start sending money to those charlatan preachers on TV, asking them to pray for Timmy. Hell, I'm not even going to start attending church. Sunday's the only day I can sleep in! What I'm talking about isn't your standard, garden variety religion . . .'

'Yes, but it wasn't *really* the devil,' she said.

'Wasn't it?'

'It was a prehistoric creature that—'

'Couldn't it be *both*?'

'What're we getting into here?'

'A philosophical discussion.'

'On our honeymoon?'

'I married you partly for your mind.'

Later, in bed, just before sleep took them, he said, 'Well, all I know is that the shape-changer made me realize there's a lot more mystery in this world than I once thought. I just won't rule anything out. And looking back on it, considering what we survived in Snowfield, considering how Tal had just strapped on his gun when Jeeter walked in, considering how the spotted fever screwed up Kale's aim . . . well, it seems to me like we were *meant* to survive.'

They slept, woke towards dawn, made love, slept again.

In the morning, she said, 'I know one thing for *sure*.'

'What's that?'

'We were *meant* to be married.'

'Definitely.'

'No matter what, fate would've run us headlong into each other sooner or later.'

That afternoon, as they strolled along the beach, Jenny thought the waves sounded like huge, rumbling wheels. The sound called to mind an old saying about the mill wheels of heaven grinding slowly.

The rumble of the waves enforced that image, and in her mind she could see immense stone mill wheels turning against each other.

She said, 'You think it has a meaning, then? A purpose?'

He didn't have to ask what she meant. 'Yes. Everything, every twist and turn of life. A meaning, a purpose.'

The sea foamed on the sand.

Jenny listened to the mill wheels and wondered what mysteries and miracles, what horrors and joys, were being ground out at this very moment, to be served up in times to come.

A NOTE TO THE READER

Like all the characters in this novel, Timothy Flyte is a fictional person, but many of the mass disappearances to which he refers are not merely figments of the author's imagination. They really happened. The disappearance of the Roanoke Island colony, the mysteriously deserted Eskimo village of Anjikuni, the vanished Mayan populations, the unexplained loss of thousands of Spanish soldiers in 1711, the equally mystifying loss of the Chinese battalions in 1939, and certain other cases mentioned in *Phantoms* are actually well-documented, historical events.

Likewise, there is a *real* Dr Ananda Chakrabarty. In *Phantoms*, the details of his development of the first patented micro-organism are drawn from public record. Dr Chakrabarty's bacterium was, as stated in this book, too fragile to survive outside of the laboratory. Biosan-4, the trade name of a supposedly hardier strain of Chakrabarty's bug, is a fictional device; to the best of my knowledge, no effort has been made to refine and improve Dr Chakrabarty's discovery, and it remains a laboratory oddity of note, primarily because of its role in the precedent-setting Supreme Court decision.

And of course the ancient enemy is a product of the author's imagination. But what if . . .

We all make mistakes. Maybe you've been at a dinner party, where you've eaten your entire salad before realizing you've used the wrong fork. Faux pas. Maybe you've been a worker in a nuclear power plant, where you've pushed the wrong button, contaminating dozens of fellow workers with plutonium. Oops. In a drunken haze, high on cheap red wine spiked with Listerine, perhaps you have mistaken the neighbor's golden retriever for an attractive blonde and eloped with it to a wedding chapel in Vegas, only to be told by the minister – who is dressed in a sequined jumpsuit and pomaded like Elvis – that the state of Nevada will not permit you to marry a canine without the written consent of its trainer plus a six-figure line of credit in a major casino. Woof. Perhaps you have tried to kill a spider with a nail gun, only to spike your foot to the floor. Ouch. It is possible, I suppose, that on a cold, rainy day in Manhattan, you have stepped out of an open window on the thirty-sixth floor of a high-rise, thinking you were passing through a door into a stairwell, that you plummeted like a wingless ox toward the street below, that you were spared death only because you fell onto a fruit vendor's cart of mush melons, that you then stepped out of the cart into the path of a bus, were knocked aside like a mere rag doll, rolled in a tangle of broken limbs into an open manhole, fell into a storm drain, were swept by surging torrents from one end of the city to the other, and were flushed into the sea, where in your desperation you mistook a shark for a marker buoy, resulting in the loss of two pinkie fingers, an ear, and half a knee-cap. Get insurance. Maybe, in an argument with a Hell's Angel, you've used the words 'kissy-lipped girly man'. Maybe you've eaten live fire ants. Maybe you've left a waffle iron plugged in, on the floor beside your bed, and then awakened in the middle of the night and mistook it for a slipper. Maybe, in spite of the printed warning, you tore the manufacturer's tag off a sofa cushion; and now you are serving twenty years in a federal prison, making crocheted license-plate cozies for three cents an hour. Maybe one of you reading this has made *all* these mistakes, in which case you are not merely exhibiting the fundamental human tendency to err: you are as dumb as a sump pump.

Writing *Phantoms* was one of the ten biggest mistakes of my life, ranking directly above that incident with the angry porcupine and the clown, about which I intend to say nothing more. *Phantoms* has been published in thirty-one languages and has been in print continuously for fifteen years, as I write this. Worldwide, it has sold almost six million copies in all editions. It has been well reviewed, and more than a few critics have called it a modern classic of its genre. Readers write to me by the hundreds every year, even this long after first publication, to tell me how much they like *Phantoms*. I enjoyed writing the book, and when I had to reread it to create a screenplay for the film version, I found it to be just the thrill ride that I had originally hoped to produce. Yet it is this novel, more than any other that earned for me the label of 'horror writer', which I never wanted, never embraced, and have ever since sought to shed.

As I have written in another of these afterwords, I enjoy reading horror novels, have considerable respect for the form, and admire the finest writers who have worked in the genre. I believe, however, that 95 per cent of my work is anything *but* horror. I am a suspense writer. I am a novelist. I write love stories now and then, sometimes humorous fiction, sometimes tales of adventure, sometimes all those things between the covers of a single volume. But *Phantoms* fixed me with a spooky-guy label as surely as if it had been stitched to my forehead by a highly skilled and diligent member of the United Garment Workers Union – making a far better wage than that poor bastard crocheting license-plate cozies.

So why did I write it?

In 1981, after *Whispers* had become a bestseller in paperback, I wanted to follow it with an equally strange novel of psychological suspense, an edgy and chilling tale in which the only monsters were the human kind. My publisher believed the other book had succeeded because readers had thought – solely because of packaging – that *Whispers* was a horror novel. Horror was then a hot genre. Prior to *Whispers*, I had never earned a great deal of money from a book, and the *Whispers* royalties then due were slowly, slowly, slowly moving through a long pipeline. Meanwhile, I needed to pay the bills, and my agent and publisher made it clear that I could not get a substantial advance for another book like *Whispers*, only for a horror novel. I was also told that a horror novel would be backed with major advertising, but that a mere suspense novel would not get much support. If I wanted to build upon the success of *Whispers*, I had no choice but to write a highly promotable horror novel. Against my better judgment, I wrote *Phantoms*.

I thought I would cleverly evade their horror-or-starve ultimatum by making *Phantoms* something of a tour de force, rolling virtually all the monsters of the genre into one beast, and also by providing a credible, scientific explanation for the creature's existence. Instead of fearless vampire hunters armed with wooden stakes, instead of werewolf trackers packing revolvers loaded with silver bullets, my protagonists would save themselves by using logic and reason to determine the nature of their mysterious enemy and to find a way to defeat it. *Phantoms* would be a horror story, yes, but it would also be science fiction, an adventure tale, a wild mystery story, and an exploration of the nature and source of myth.

When I delivered the book, there was little enthusiasm for it. Only five thousand hardcovers were printed and, prior to publication, I was told by most people in my professional life that this was *too much* of a horror story and, therefore, could be of no interest to the broader audience that had made *Whispers* a paperback bestseller. I was flummoxed. I felt I had delivered precisely what had been asked of me, only to be crushed like that Hell's Angel crushed the guy who called him a 'kissy-lipped girly man'. The reviews began to come in, and they were largely excellent, although this praise did not result in a bigger first printing or any promotion, which led to festivals of self-pity and wild storms of depression in the Koontz household. Fortunately, enthusiasm for my work remained strong at the paperback house, and one year after the hardcover bombed, *Phantoms* followed *Whispers* onto the paperback bestseller list, ensuring that my career would not lose momentum. Thereafter, it sold and sold and sold; and as I write this, it is nearing its sixtieth printing in paperback in the United States.

Do I like *Phantoms*? Yes. Do I wish I'd never written it? Yes. Am I happy to have written it? Yes. Am I a little schizo on this issue? Yes. Although as a matter of career planning, *Phantoms* was a major strategic blunder, the writing of it brought me considerable pleasure, and readers' outspoken delight in the book has provided a gratification that has sustained me through some bad days.

The lesson, I suppose, is that beneficial developments can flow even from a mistake. If you work in a nuclear power plant, however, triple check yourself before you push that button.

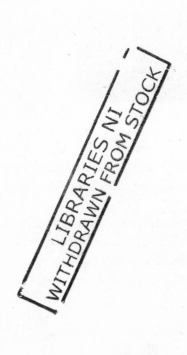

CHASE

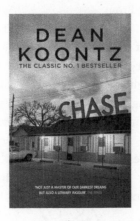

Ben Chase is a war hero with bitter memories.
Vietnam left him with a hard drinking habit, a mental
breakdown – and massive guilt.

So who will believe him when he swears a psychopath is out
to get him? When society is sick, the mad are sane – and
persecution is a killer's game . . .

HEADLINE

You can buy any of these bestselling
books by **Dean Koontz** from your bookshop or direct
from his publisher.

TO ORDER SIMPLY CALL THIS NUMBER
01235 400 414
Or visit our website: www.headline.co.uk
Prices and availability subject to change without notice.